DAUGHTER OF THE PRIDE

BOOK SIX OF
THE GUILD WARS

Jason Cordova

Seventh Seal Press
Virginia Beach, VA

Chris Kennedy/Seventh Seal Press
2052 Bierce Dr.
Virginia Beach, VA 23454
http://chriskennedypublishing.com/

Publisher's Note: This is a work of fiction. Names, characters, places, and incidents are a product of the author's imagination. Locales and public names are sometimes used for atmospheric purposes. Any resemblance to actual people, living or dead, or to businesses, companies, events, institutions, or locales is completely coincidental.

Cover Design by Brenda Mihalko
Original Art by Ricky Ryan

Ordering Information:
Quantity sales. Special discounts are available on quantity purchases by corporations, associations, and others. For details, contact the "Special Sales Department" at the address above.

Daughter of the Pride/Jason Cordova -- 1st ed.
ISBN: 978-1648550485

Acknowledgements

As always, a huge thanks goes out to Mark Wandrey and Chris Kennedy for creating such an awesome galaxy for me to play in. Plus, they also deserve your support (and sympathy) because they have to put up with my random "so...can I do this?" questions at all hours of the day (and oftentimes, night). They're pretty good-natured about it, usually.

Shout out to the members of the Four Horsemen Facebook group as well, since I tend to bounce a lot of ideas and questions off the 1000+ members there. I'm fairly knowledgeable about the events which occur in the 4HU, but when I don't remember what book something occurred in, I go there and they almost always have an answer for me. If you're a fan of the series, then I'd highly recommend you join the group. Plus, they're just awesome people.

Lastly, to my girlfriend, for putting up with me getting lost in this book and pestering her with stupid questions and random scenarios when she least expects it. She deserves a medal for her patience and constant support.

Prologue

Weqq, Fourth Planet of Gharra-4, Cimarron Region

It had only been a few weeks since the Mercenary Guild had taken over Earth. Many not in the immediate area were slow on the uptake as old allegiances remained strong, and all turned their backs on the upstart Humans. Armies and allies regrouped to their respective banners, and rebellious factions within every guild saw opportunities. The status quo had changed, and for the first time in millennia there was a different feel inside the Galactic Union. It was as though a long-festering boil had been lanced and the poison was being drained, albeit slowly.

Blame was laid upon the feet of humanity, but this was an error. Appearances were deceiving. The rot could not be blamed on Earth. After all, the Humans had only been part of the Galactic Union for a mere hundred years or so.

Information was exchanged, and plans were formulated as everyone responded differently to the unprecedented actions of the Mercenary Guild.

This far away, though, information passed at a slower rate than rumor and fear. Not everyone knew of the Mercenary Guild's takeover of Earth, and those who did simply didn't care. What was one planet in the midst of the millions upon millions throughout the galaxy, especially when it was a species whose membership into the Mercenary Guild wasn't yet official?

All this went through the Buma's head as he watched the pilot skillfully handle the control of his personal atmospheric shuttle. They came in slowly and at a shallow angle before landing just outside the rebuilt MinSha research facility on Weqq. He patted the Sidar piloting his shuttle on a narrow shoulder.

"This will be accomplished in less than two hours," the Xeno Guild representative told the pilot. "Keep the pumps primed and ready for liftoff."

"I understand," the Sidar pilot chittered. The guild representative had worked with this individual in the past and knew his capability for efficiency and timeliness. Plus, since the pilot had been paid a hefty sum beforehand, he wanted to be done with the job as quickly as possible.

"When we arrive, if you join me on the platform, stand behind me and to my left," the representative instructed. "Let me go first."

"But if they start firing...?"

"They won't," he replied.

The rear doors opened, and the bright light of Weqq's sun poured into the shuttle. The representative squinted as his eyes tried to adjust to the change. It wasn't difficult to make out the tall MinSha shapes against the bright backdrop. Slightly shorter but thicker figures were also there, intermingled with the insect-like aliens. *Those are definitely TriRusk,* he thought with a satisfied nod of his head. Once more he was blessed with good fortune. *The SooSha's information had been correct.*

Behind him, he could hear his Sidar pilot fall into place. The Buma clicked appreciatively. He hadn't been sure if the Sidar would join him or not. The pilot was unusually skittish for his kind and seemed overly cautious. *Not that caution is necessarily a bad thing,* he observed silently as he began to recite the proper greetings.

"Hullo brave and noble peoples. This is my pilot, Pa'ed," he said from within his billowing cloak. "I am a representative of the Xeno Guild. I am Boileau. On behalf of the Xeno Guild, I would like to extend greetings and welcome."

The lead MinSha administrator stepped forward. His arm was in an immobilizing cast and the MinSha equivalent of a sling, though both appeared old and ready to come off. His ruby red eyes glittered under the light of Weqq's sun. He showed other signs of recent injuries. Upon closer inspection he could see there were signs of recent battle around the area. The Xeno Guild representative felt a shiver run up his spine.

Someone else knows about the planet, he realized. The SooSha really had sold the information to just about everyone, it seems. Time was not an ally.

"I am Tirr," the MinSha said, looking at the representative curiously. "I was under the impression the Peacemaker Guild would be heading their reintroduction to the Galactic Union."

"There have been more pressing matters which have arisen in the weeks since," the representative answered smoothly. "They are currently en route and will not arrive for another two weeks. We are a neutral party in everything involved and were tasked with this assignment. The Administrator spoke with Hak-Chet personally, a rare honor indeed. The Administrator is very busy and can spare no time for idle chitchat. All the details and confirmations are here on this slate."

The representative handed the slate over to Tirr, who accepted it with his good arm. After a few moments of reading he gave the MinSha equivalent of a grunt as he passed it back.

"I see," Tirr muttered. He straightened his back. "Very well. The TriRusk have determined not to send their leader to Capital Planet. They have chosen instead to send the leader's niece, along with a small retinue of guards."

"While I was looking forward to seeing the Peacemakers again, I know my duties," a smaller, female TriRusk stated as she stepped forward. "I am Caarn."

"An honor, Caarn, daughter of the TriRusk." The representative bowed his upper body ever so slightly in her direction. His feathers ruffled slightly in the mild breeze while his large eyes stared out from beneath the cowl, unblinking. "Have you made preparations to depart?"

"We have, but we will need one hour," Caarn replied. "It will take time to load everything we will need for the journey."

"Understood," the representative agreed. "I will be waiting."

An hour later, the TriRusk had said their goodbyes to their families and friends before boarding the shuttle. The Xeno Guild representative turned to Tirr and bowed respectfully.

"You have done well here," the rep stated as his large eyes took everything in. He'd removed his cowl but kept the cloak on for appearances' sake. "The Xeno Guild will undoubtedly place a small relay substation in the system for your use in the future. This will increase your data transmission rate and not leave you at the mercy of the gatekeepers or the Information Guild. It would also be more efficient this way."

"We don't need—" Tirr began but was quickly cut off by the representative.

"We insist."

The Xeno Guild representative watched, bemused. The MinSha squirmed uneasily. It was clear the local MinSha had few dealings with the Xeno Guild in the past. They were undoubtedly one of the quieter guilds in the Galactic Union, often overlooked by others and considered to be one of the weakest. However, the Buma knew Tirr was no fool. He would know the value of information and communication. It was why the MinSha were on Weqq in the first place. The value of the planet was immeasurable, and it was clear they weren't quite ready to let the galaxy know what medicinal research they were accomplishing here.

He is well aware their secret won't remain one for much longer, especially after the Peacemakers become involved, the Buma thought as he watched the dizzying array of emotions pass over the MinSha's insectoid features. Unreadable by most lifeforms, the Buma had great experience dealing with the aliens and knew every one of their subtle facial expressions. It was clear the MinSha Tirr was a warrior and not a politician. His negotiating face told the Xeno Guild representative more than words ever could. *Someone already made a grab for the planet. That much is obvious from the newly arrived battlecruisers in orbit. Someone really determined could dislodge them, but after everything that had happened in the past, who wants to get into an all-out war against the MinSha? Would the ensuing death toll be worth it to the attackers?*

Of course, there was also the unspoken desire for red diamonds. Between the planet and its inhabitants, it might very well be worth it in the end.

"Bahütcagi," Tirr finally responded to the representative in rustic but passable Bumani, catching the Xeno Guild representative slightly off guard. He hadn't known the MinSha were even able to pronounce his people's language with their insectile mouths. "I will inform my superiors so they do not destroy the station builders when they arrive."

"Your people's restraint is much appreciated," the Buma stated as he pulled his cowl back over his head; the sun on Weqq was most unpleasant. His oversized eyes continued to stare unerringly at the MinSha. "I thank you, Tirr, for your assistance."

The MinSha dipped his head a final time as he boarded the shuttle. The doors sealed with a hiss, and the MinSha and TriRusk backed away, giving the shuttle's engines a wide berth as they flared to life. Trees and fauna waved in the stiff winds caused by the powerful engines.

The small shuttle lifted off, leaving behind the MinSha and remaining TriRusk. Within an hour, it rejoined the *Paya Ouvurlar* high above in orbit. MinSha scientists on Weqq would track the ship for an additional three hours before it disappeared through the stargate to its supposed destination of Capital Planet.

Weeks passed, then months. No news returned to either the MinSha administrator on Weqq, Peacemaker Guild Master Rsach, or for the TriRusk involved. The ship never arrived at its final destination. The *Paya Ouvurlar* would be considered lost in hyperspace by everyone involved, though no one ever figured out who chartered the ship when it came time to pay the insurance claim. The loss of all onboard was mourned, especially by the TriRusk who had viewed Caarn as a future leader and their first tentative link to the Galactic Union. The mysterious disappearance of the *Paya Ouvurlar* would go down in history as a minor footnote and nothing more, soon forgotten as more pressing matters arose on Weqq and throughout the galaxy.

* * * * *

Chapter One

L ieutenant Sunshine, late of the Kakata Korps, was going to kill someone in very short order.

It had been many weeks since she left Earth in search of someone, anyone, who could rebuild her CASPer and find the message she was supposed to deliver to the intergalactic police known as the Peacemakers. That was her mission, given to her by her late commander, Mulbah Luo. In a manner of speaking, at least. Nonspecific mission parameters were a tricky thing, and his parting message only offered confusion later as she sought to find help.

Time spent with the terrifying Depik killer named Tsan had given Sunshine a fresh perspective on life in general. Her old *bass* had believed in protecting humanity by assisting the alien occupiers to lessen the damage caused. It was meant to keep the death toll of the occupation down, to assist those in need and prevent further atrocities. Only in his final hours had he realized he'd been wrong and sent Sunshine away. This led to the eventual death of her beloved mercenary company and the man she had come to view as a father. Mulbah was a visionary and had dreamt of a world, a galaxy, where his people would have a chance to not screw everything up the first opportunity they got.

He almost did it, too, Sunshine silently mourned as she recalled the Fall of Liberia and Peepo's betrayal of the Korps.

Sunshine had found Tsan in the middle of the Sahara after trekking for what seemed like forever across the forbidding sands. Or rather, the vengeful little Depik had discovered her. The tiny killer believed Sunshine to be both amusing and mysterious, a lost kit surviving when she should not have. A child inside a fully armed CAS-Per added spice to the mystery. With all these factors combined, it made for one curious Depik. The only thing more dangerous than a curious Depik was a murderous one, and as it turned out, Tsan was both.

Sunshine smiled fondly at those frantic days. Their crazy journey to Sao Paolo, Brazil to assist with the fall of the Mercenary Guild had helped heal her heart a little after the brutal fall of the Kakata Korps. There was still a large scar upon her soul where the loss of her friends and country hurt the most, but thanks to Tsan, Sunshine knew time would help her forget the pain and live with the good memories. She might not fully heal, but sometimes the best way to remember past misdeeds by others was through the very scars they left behind. Sunshine knew she would never forget how the Mercenary Guild had taken everything from her. Everything except the good memories. Nothing they could do now would take those cherished moments away.

There was one recurring issue, though; her sleep was constantly plagued by nightmares. She could never quite remember what they were about, only the sense of looming danger and her own conflicted feelings of guilt which came after. The nightmares woke her up almost every night, but each time she opened her eyes, they quickly faded, leaving only a strong sense of loss and terror. The nightmares threatened to drown out the only good memories she had, but the dreams left nothing but shadowy impressions upon her waking mind.

It was both irritating and chilling. The logical part of her brain suggested this was her subconscious being a jerk, tormenting her with the knowledge that she had left the rest of the Korps to their deaths when she fled the battle because of a message she'd been ordered to deliver. It helped some, knowing she'd been *ordered* to leave.

The illogical part called her a disgusting coward.

Her mind snapped back to her current state of affairs. The merc pit was a dump, though it did offer a room for rent if she needed one. Exhaustion kept her emotionally on edge while also causing her mind to wander.

Sunshine looked up as the merc pit's proprietor, a burly K'kng, came bustling over to her table. The small, gorilla-like alien was nervous around her, which would have been amusing in any other situation. However, alone and on her own, it was disconcerting. She was no threat to anyone. At least, as far as she knew.

"Sorry, so sorry," the K'kng dipped his furred head a few times, trying to apologize. "We don't get many Humans out here and finding things you can drink is difficult. My father owned a Human once who made this undrinkable bile called 'mulled wine' before he went off with two—well, that's another story, and you're probably not interested at all. Many years ago. This was sitting on the shelf, all bottled up. Half a credit for it all."

Sunshine felt an angry shiver race up her spine at the mention of a Human slave but ruthlessly clamped down on it. It was to her detriment to show any emotion whatsoever. Instead, she smiled politely and shook her head.

"Quarter, no more," Sunshine retorted. She wasn't born last night and had learned the subtle art of negotiating in the Duala Market, which hadn't been too far from the Kakata Korps headquarters.

Before it had been destroyed by Peepo, of course. "It's taking up space you need. I'm doing you a favor by buying it."

"I thought Humans were horrible negotiators," the K'kng mumbled. He paused for a moment to consider her counteroffer before nodding his gorilla-like head in a jerking motion. "Fine, a quarter."

Using her pinplants Sunshine slipped a quarter credit to the K'kng from her meager personal account. She had a little bit left, courtesy of the monthly salaried payments received upon joining the Korps, but travel across the Galactic Union was expensive, and she was quickly running low on funds. She really couldn't afford to spend any more, but experience had taught her an important lesson: business owners were more prone to allow a paying customer to linger. Hence, the lack of further argument.

Truth be told, Sunshine was running low on options. Every single mechanic she took to her CASPer told her the same thing: there was no message hidden in her suit. Many tried to purchase the "derelict and destroyed CASPer" from her, but she refused. It wasn't derelict and definitely wasn't destroyed, merely disassembled. Only one other merc race used power armor the way Humans did, that she knew of, and she was not about to encourage more. As limited as her knowledge of galactic politics was, even she knew letting someone like the Zuparti access to a fully functional CASPer was a bad idea.

News from Earth was scattered and disjointed, but after parsing through the data passed along through the gates by the Information Guild, she was able to determine a few things. From what she could gather, the rebuilding of her home planet was ongoing, though she could find no mention whatsoever of anything regarding Monrovia. To be fair, the fall of Liberia was barely covered by the Earth news agencies in the immediate aftermath, so for anyone to expect aliens to care was silly. It still hurt, though, knowing everything the Korps had tried to save was probably going to be forgotten in short order. There was no mention of Peepo or any arrests of Mercenary Guild council members, which irritated her to no end. Once more the Veetanho and her cronies managed to avoid punishment for their crimes. Sunshine could only hope the little rat got what she deserved soon enough.

With no news on the Peepo front, rumor about someone who could find the hidden message within the CASPer had taken her to a place called Troubadour Station. The *bass* and the Korps had once run an op through the location. It was strange being there, though nobody seemed to have heard of the Korps. There she met with a twitchy Zuparti which seemed to have a nose for trouble. In turn, he put her in contact with a representative of an individual named "Mister Z." After paying off the Zuparti with some of her emergency funds, she hopped aboard a transport freighter to come to this forsaken hole in the wall, where she was to meet with a representative of this Mister Z. Supposedly, the contact would help Sunshine find what she was looking for. While she wasn't certain the organization the mysterious representative represented was what one would call "legal," it was her last hope for finding the ghost message her *bass* had left in the worn-out, beaten up, old CASPer.

She'd only been given a codename for the young entrepreneur and the time, day, and location for the meet. In spite of it all, Sunshine found her situation to be darkly humorous. Six months ago, she had been nothing more than a tiny fearful girl who was owned and controlled by a drug lord, pimped out to whoever wanted what she had for the right price. Now? Now she was *free*, and carried a weapon which ensured her freedom. She was in charge of her life now, and would remain so until she ran out of ammunition.

Sunshine was still frustrated, though. Freedom didn't cure this, only exacerbated it. Checking her pinplants for the time, she growled softly. Her contact was over an hour late. She had learned much under the tutelage of Mulbah, but the most important thing was a lesson learned while working with Captain Zion Jacobs, the Third Company's commander.

"If you want to be a true professional, punctuality is key," he had told her what seemed like forever ago. "Leaders who seek to keep people waiting to feed their own egos are not fit to lead."

It was just one of the many lessons she had taken to heart the moment the company had rescued her.

The door to the pit slid open and a silhouette filled the brightly lit doorway. A short, slender woman entered the mercenary pit, catching Sunshine's eye almost immediately. Given the decided lack of Humans this far out in the galaxy, it was almost certain this woman was her contact. Sunshine inspected her from afar, both visually and using her pinplants through the pit's network to run a heat signature scan.

The woman's dark brown hair was pulled back into a tight braid and hung over her right shoulder. A bright pink streak ran through the middle of the braid, offsetting the otherwise professional image the woman maintained about her. The business suit was clearly expensive, more so than anything Sunshine had ever wore in her life. Except for her CASPer, at least. Sunshine suddenly felt very underdressed in her utility coveralls, which were stained from months of abuse and wear. While clean, she felt they were entirely inappropriate for this meeting, and she wished she had picked up something dressier.

The woman approached Sunshine's table and offered a smile. She stuck her hand out.

"Ms. Sunshine? I'm Cubby or, now that we're in person and not on monitored comms, Taryn Lupo."

"Just Sunshine, no miss," Sunshine said as she shook the woman's hand. "Or lieutenant if you have to. Please, sit?"

"Thank you." Taryn slid easily into the chair across from her. Sunshine noticed immediately the woman somehow managed to keep her back toward the entrance without making it painfully obvious. There was an edge about her which fascinated Sunshine.

This is a dangerous woman, Sunshine thought.

Taryn continued, still smiling. "My apologies for running late. Moving unimpeded through certain areas of this sector sometimes requires payment and negotiations. Some need to be negotiated a little more forcefully than others."

"I see," Sunshine said, though she did not. *Just how corrupt is the Galactic Union?* she wondered.

"Yes, well, things happen," Taryn said as she folded her hands on the table. "I was a little surprised to hear about your situation and need, to be frank. If the Fae—excuse me, the *Dusman*—couldn't find what you were looking for, I'm afraid our organization has little more it can offer. But you intrigued my boss, so here I am."

"My *boss* said there was a message for the Peacemakers in my suit," Sunshine answered as her old stubborn streak threatened to boil over into the conversation. She ran her fingers over her close-cropped hair, took a deep breath, and counted to five before continuing in a calmer tone. "Colonel Luo, I mean. The *boss* never lied to me, so there has to be a message somewhere. Even if no one's found it yet."

Taryn tapped her lips with a well-manicured nail, a thoughtful expression upon her face. "And this is a Mk 7 CASPer, but features a fully-integrated pinplant system?"

Sunshine nodded. "Yes, it was designed by...a friend of mine. It used to be a command CASPer but...I never got to use it for command. The *bass* got it from an old merc company on Earth, I think."

"I see," Taryn murmured, her expression vacant. Sunshine recognized the look of someone deep in their pinplants and remained quiet for a moment. Taryn blinked and shook her head. "You know, a fully-integrated Mk 7, while not impossible, is very unusual."

"Why?"

"Well, the design of a Mk 7 is what you can generously call sturdy, not nearly as lumbering as previous versions," Taryn explained. "The circuitry and hardware are usually not up to fully integrate pinplants, which means someone with a lot of money wanted this suit to be able to work on full integration. How many people in your company were fully pinned?"

Sunshine blinked, startled. This was not the direction she had expected the conversation to go. "Three, maybe four? I know everyone had the minimum, but fully? I think it was only the officers who had full pinplants."

"Okay, that could explain it, too," Taryn replied. "Designed for you specifically. Nice. This Mk 7 seems a little odd but...meh. Mechanical stuff isn't really my forte. I'm more of an independent urban chemist and retired street pharmacologist."

"Do I even want to know what that means?"

"No, probably not, given your history." Taryn shrugged. "In any case, I do know someone who can help us get to the bottom of this mystery, but we also need to talk price."

"I'm…not wealthy," Sunshine paused. She wrestled for a moment before deciding upon honesty. "I spent almost all of my money getting here."

"Galactic transport isn't very expensive, especially for a solitary merc," Taryn frowned. "Don't you have funds through a business means?"

"I don't understand." Sunshine rubbed the back of her hand across her sweaty forehead. "Business means?"

"According to the TOE the Kakata Korps filed with the Mercenary Guild before the events in Monrovia—which I'm sorry about, by the way; something like that is what I thought the Peacemakers were created to prevent—you were listed as being in an officer slot. Mercenary Guild rules state that any registered mercenary officer can claim contracts and payouts so long as the mission has been completed," Taryn recited from memory. "As far as my boss can tell, the Korps completed its final mission despite the fallout with the guild afterward. Their earnings have not been confiscated by the guild, nor have their accounts been frozen. The Korps should have millions of credits in their account, if not more."

"How—"

Taryn offered a small smile. "We do our homework on prospective clients. Especially ones who could be potential problems."

"Potential…problems?"

"Yes, Lieutenant. Problems." Taryn chuckled and gently patted Sunshine's arm. "You were listed as presumed dead after the Fall of Monrovia, then miraculously turn up in the company of a *Depik* months later and assist another merc company with a takedown of Peepo's hired thugs and participate somewhat in the ensuing battle, though we lost track of you for a brief time before you turned up with the Fae. Considering the mysterious fate of almost all the Depik, the fact you were assisting one back on Earth was enough to raise more than a few red flags. Then you disappeared again, before suddenly turning up on our radar a week ago when you arrived at Troubadour Station seeking help from a *Zuparti* of all things. You're the walking definition of a mysterious and potential problem. My boss agreed to send someone to meet with you because, according to records, the Korps should be flush with cash. Also, you're not boring and, truth be told, the old man has a soft spot for lost and broken things."

"Lost and broken…"

"Yes, Sunshine, you are lost," Taryn said levelly, staring into Sunshine's dark eyes. "You are not broken, though. I can see that fire in you. Plus, nobody could survive traveling with a Depik unless their heart and mind were solid and powerful. But lost? Yes, you are lost, seeking a way, a new truth since yours was so brutally and viciously taken from you. Until you find your way and your purpose, you will remain so. However, my boss also understands this is not your fault, so instead of being his curmudgeonly old self he sent me. I have a gentler disposition, apparently. He's a weird old man."

Sunshine was quiet. In a manner of speaking, Taryn was spot on with her assessment. Sunshine *was* lost, on a mission which seemed to be all but impossible. Nobody had been able to find anything, and the thought of Mulbah being wrong, potentially lying to her, had begun to chip away at the mental armor she'd built up within her mind. Self-doubt and exhaustion were beginning to creep in, and she had no one else to turn to. Plus, finding a Peacemaker was a lot harder than she had been led to believe.

She'd always believed the whole idea of her escaping during the fighting was to inform the Peacemakers about what the Mercenary Guild was doing right under their noses. The massacre in Liberia was just the tip of the iceberg. She knew Thorpi, who had never returned from his meeting with General Peepo before the assault on Monrovia had begun, had urged Mulbah to prepare for the assault and make contingency plans. She hadn't been to many staff meetings within the Korps, but she had made this particular one.

"You know what?" Taryn abruptly jolted Sunshine out of her memories with a tug on her arm. "Let's discuss us helping you someplace else. I have a ship available. Where is your suit stored? We can transport it and discuss terms there."

"What? Why—" Sunshine stopped as a creature which haunted many mercenary nightmares slipped in through the front door of the pit. Well over two meters tall and covered in fur, the Besquith was an imposing sight. The alien wore a set of crossed harnesses upon its chest, filled with what appeared to be loaded rifle magazines. The yellow eyes of the Besquith scanned the room briefly before it met Sunshine's gaze. A long tongue lolled out of its mouth as it gave her a predatory smile, fangs flashing in the light. They were *very* large indeed. Sunshine swallowed nervously but felt mildly reassured when Taryn reached across the table and patted her arm.

"Don't worry about her," Taryn said. "She's an old acquaintance."

"She's your friend?" Sunshine asked, still anxious.

Taryn chuckled quietly. "I wouldn't say friend, precisely. Let's just say we have a little bit of history together, and she respects my boss."

"Is there going to be a fight?" Sunshine asked, sliding her hand down to thumb the clasp off her thigh holster. Carrying a loaded weapon was something she was still getting used to, but it was better than being unarmed and helpless. Merc pits were not typically known for wild shootouts, but then everything had turned upside down lately. "I'm better in my CASPer than without it."

"Against a Besquith? Aren't we all?" Taryn's voice was filled with dark humor. "No, I don't think there will be a fight. If anything, this will probably be phase one of some odd negotiating. Besides, I'm kinda expecting her. Just play it cool and try not to freak out."

"I don't…" Sunshine's voice trailed off as the massive Besquith approached the two women. Golden eyes sized up both of them before the Besquith let out the equivalent of a chuckle.

"Taryn Lupo, it is a pleasure to speak to you again in person," the Besquith growled humorously. The alien looked over Sunshine a second time and sniffed the air. "Your little friend seems…delectable."

"Quit trying to scare the merc, Dref-na," Taryn said in an easy voice, leaning back in her seat ever so slightly. Neither Sunshine nor the Besquith missed Taryn's hand sliding down to her hip, where her own weapon was obviously stashed. The Besquith's humor became even more evident than before. Taryn continued. "You were supposed to meet us later. *Much* later, in fact."

"Humans usually have a hard time telling us apart, yet you don't seem to have this issue, Taryn Lupo," Dref-na said with a snap of her jaws. "You never cease to amaze me."

"It's simply paying attention to your friends, closer attention to the unknowns, and closest to your enemies," Taryn pointed out. "Besides, how many other Besquith do you think I actually know? One? Two?"

Sunshine's eyes widened as the duo argued a bit more. She had been under the impression Taryn was a friend of Dref-na, but now she was no longer certain. Taryn jerked her chin toward Sunshine. "This is the girl I messaged you about."

"You?" The Besquith looked at her, amazed. "So tiny! You wouldn't even be a snack worth eating! You fought against my kind and lived?"

"And Zuul and Tortantulas." Sunshine nodded, trying not to show the fear which hammered her heart. In a CASPer, she was a goddess of the battlefield, completely in her element. Without the armored suit, she was exposed, but she would not let the alien see a single iota of fear. "It's my job. Kill aliens, get paid."

"Very fierce as well," Dref-na acknowledged, evidently pleased by her response. "Yes, Taryn Lupo, this youngling is one who is born of battle. A true alpha in every sense of the word, and both a worthy adversary and staunch ally. Now I see why you called for this meet. I approve of this one. Tell me, young child, is your mercenary company hiring?"

"Are we—what?" Sunshine looked at her, confused. The conversation had taken a very unexpected turn. She gave herself a mental shake. Unexpected was the theme of her life now, ever since she had been caught stealing from the Korps with the Lakko brothers long before. "What do you mean?"

"You are obviously a leader of mercenaries, and your yack states you are a mercenary officer," Dref-na explained as she casually picked a large chunk of *something* out from between her teeth. She briefly inspected it before popping it back into her mouth and swallowing. "Ah, lunch was better fresh. Just my luck. Such is life, I suppose. As I was saying, you are Lieutenant Sunshine of the Kakata Korps mercenary company, yes?"

"I was," Sunshine answered, her tone carefully neutral. "The Korps was destroyed."

"Not all of it." Dref-na pointed with a razor-sharp claw directly at Sunshine's chest. "An officer still lives; one who has seen battle. One who has the power and authority to hire mercenaries to work for them. Your charter remains as well, and in good standing no less. The Korps has never failed a mission, either. Word spreads among all mercenaries who are the good, who are the bad, and those who would be considered bait by the rest of us. Yours has a very good record, something my old company couldn't even claim. Would you hire me?"

"I'm so confused right now," Sunshine muttered and looked at Taryn for help. There would be none forthcoming, however, because the other woman looked as gob smacked as Sunshine felt. "I wouldn't even know where to begin…Why do you want to work for me?"

"Well, truth be told, I've recently had a bit of a run-in with one of the companies my fellow Besquith operates," Dref-na admitted in a sullen tone. "Their alphas are stupid bitches who simply want to charge blindly in for the kill. To satiate their thirst. Drink the blood of their enemies and so on. They have no concept of flanking, or even how to perform a pincer movement with two squads. I pointed this out and was…spoken to. Harshly."

"Oh, the truth comes out at last!" Taryn laughed. She shifted slightly in her seat and leaned forward, placing her elbows upon the table. "I was wondering why you were so eager to catch up with an old friend, considering the last time I saw you I put a gun to your head."

Dref-na sniffed, her pride and arrogance on full display for all to see. "I would have gutted you before you applied enough pressure to pull the trigger."

"Maybe." Taryn's smile was infectious and, unless Sunshine was sorely mistaken, the Besquith was smiling now as well. One could never be sure with aliens. "We'll never know, will we?"

"I suppose not."

"I don't understand what's going on here," Sunshine murmured as she delved into her pinplants. She needed a task to focus on, since the interplay between Taryn and the Besquith was confusing at best. She began to look into the prospect of her being in charge of the Korps. Was it legal for a Liberian mercenary company to hire an alien? She wasn't sure, though she had seen evidence that other companies like the Winged Hussars did. Well, there was Thorpi, but he was different. How could she afford it, though? Perhaps Taryn was right, and the Korps *was* flush with money, but Sunshine hadn't even thought to look for it. Which would be on par with how things had been happening over the past six months. Searching for Mercenary Guild contracts, she was surprised to see the Korps' number and license was still intact and operational.

So that much is true, she thought and quickly investigated further. She saw, much to her amazement, there were indeed multiple payouts made to the company account just before the Fall of Monrovia. Nobody had shut it down, and the accounts were still active.

On a whim, Sunshine tried to log in to see the account. Predictably, it was password locked. She thought about it for a moment before trying the first thing which came to mind:

PAINTTHESKY

Access denied, the computer told her. She frowned. It would have been so simple, but she knew the *bass* was not stupid. She thought about him some more, his love for both Liberia and the Korps. Sunshine tried to remember things both he and Zion had talked about in her short time with the company and came up with another possibility. *What was his name though,* she asked herself, *and how many tries do I get before it locks me out?*

KHEANWARING

The first casualty of the Korps, and one which had left a lasting impact on Mulbah. On a wet ball of mud protecting a species which was being harvested by pirates for their young, Khean Waring had died ensuring the mission succeeded. He had been a CASPer mechanic, as had the others, before being recruited by Mulbah to become a pilot and founding member of the Kakata Korps. Khean, from everything Sunshine had been told by Samson and Antonious both, had been the diplomat of the original trio, as well as a skilled mechanic. Antonious had been particularly devastated when his friend died. Mulbah and Zion, she recalled, had only met him later when the *bass* had purchased the company.

Access granted, the program replied, and Sunshine saw the account balance. She audibly gasped as she realized just how rich the Korps was, courtesy of the successful contracts paid out by the Mercenary Guild. There was a lot of money, as well as continued payments well after the Fall of Monrovia. Which was odd. Perhaps it had been payments from the varying governments of Africa as a "thank you" to the Korps? She almost laughed out loud at this idea. It was simply too absurd.

On the spot she decided to change the password for security purposes just in case Taryn Lupo and her mysterious associates could do more than simply "confirm" the credits in the account. Sunshine might be ignorant in the ways of the Galactic Union, but the criminal underworld? That was something she was all too familiar with. When credits were involved, trust no one.

"Is this…is this blood money?" she whispered and pulled herself out of the pinplants. She sighed. "The *bass* was paid with blood money. I don't know if I should use it."

"Well, either you use it, or you starve and get abandoned here on this horrid little hellhole," Taryn suggested. She held up an open palm to forestall the expected argument. "I know you're tough and independent, and you have an edge of the street about you which I am *very* familiar with. This is more than a matter of pride, though. This is survival, and you getting your vengeance on. You want to honor your boss and his memory? Use the money to get your message—whatever it is—to the Peacemakers."

Taryn had a point. Sunshine's entire existence since the death of the Korps was to pass along the message to the Peacemaker Guild. While the Fae/Dusman had been unable to find anything, it could have been hardwired so only a Peacemaker could access it. In order to find it, though, it would take a mechanical genius who could put even the irritating little Splunk to shame. But who in the Galactic Union was better at machinery than those who created the Raknar in the first place?

She posed the question to Taryn.

"I know of one, and my boss had it on retainer a long time ago," Taryn replied after giving it some thought. She shrugged. "Helped customize his CASPer, actually. It was who I was going to take you to anyway. She's a Jeha by the name of Kl'nk'nnk. If she can't find your message, she'll at least be able to reassemble your CASPer, and maybe even add a few upgrades to it. Last I heard she was hired by a mining company called B'Hono. She should be relatively easy to track down, all things considered."

"Upgrades to a CASPer?" Sunshine asked, intrigued.

Taryn nodded. "That's right, upgrades," the other woman reiterated. The Besquith laughed, a horrible sound to Sunshine's ears.

"As if the little fierceness needs a more powerful suit," Dref-na pointed out. "Humans are both frustrating and amusing at the same time. Oh, a Human only killed *ten* Tortantulas on the battlefield in their powered armor suit? They make a newer suit so they can kill *twenty* the next time."

"It's a good way of thinking," Sunshine defended. Dref-na chuckled at the comment. "You go step-by-step over your path before you figure out where things went wrong, then fix it for the next time."

"I never claimed to disagree with it," the Besquith pointed out.

"Well, let's get to the *Velut Luna* so we can head out to our rendezvous point with the Jeha," Taryn said as she offered her hand to Sunshine. The young girl accepted it, albeit with some reluctance. She did not know precisely what Taryn's game was, but Sunshine knew this woman was pretty much her last option. It was either go with her or concede defeat and admit the sacrifice of the Korps was all for naught.

"Fine," Sunshine said. She turned and looked at the Besquith. "I don't know about restarting the Korps yet, but I can hire you on as a bodyguard to begin with. Not many will mess with a Besquith, *ken?*" Dref-na's mouth split open wider as her smile grew. "Not many indeed."

* * *

Xeno Guild Relay Substation Jeyla-5, Jeyla System

J unior Administrator Vah Gorna looked nervously around the small, nondescript station one final time before activating the timer for the bombs.

Vah was a CozSha and not particularly prone to violence. Nobody in her race was. The CozSha abhorred it, considering their timid nature, though they were perfect for the boring administrative duties performed within the Galactic Union. Mostly because they were efficient when it came to orderly filing. It was almost borderline obsessive, their instinctual need to categorize and file information away in the proper manner and order. There was a place for everything in the galaxy, and it was up to the CozSha to ensure it was categorized, stamped, and filed away in its proper place, in triplicate no less. She, like the rest of the CozSha who eventually found their way into employment within the various guilds of the union, was content with living in the shadows and performing her task flawlessly, week in and week out.

Which was why when the Administrator, Guild Master of the Xeno Guild, ordered Vah to blow up the relay station which had been her home for years, she had nearly gone catatonic from the shock at his instructions.

Destruction was chaos, not order. Her files, uploaded and forwarded to the next relay station, would remain safe. This was orderly and efficient, true. Destruction was the anathema of order, however. The memory banks and crypto gear used for transmitting data would be lost in the explosion, since it was all too much to be moved off the relay station in the short amount of time she'd been given. Dazed and confused, Vah had consulted a mercenary acquaintance on explosives placement to destroy sensitive equipment. Once the Zuul had quit laughing and realized Vah was deadly serious, he had given some instruction on bomb placement for maximum efficiency, as well as ensuring that electromagnetic pulses from the explosions were strong enough to wipe out any of the equipment which might survive the initial blasts. It had been free advice, which was unexpected but welcomed.

This had pleased Vah somewhat. Chaos and destruction were things she did not understand. Efficiency? This was her bailiwick. It was a word she lived by, one which made her soul sing and her heart beat with excitement. Vah could be efficient, even if she did not truly comprehend violence. Her CozSha brethren would understand this reasoning, the logic behind her efficient usage of the bombs. It was merely a mental block, she had repeatedly told herself as each shaped charge was pressed against the small memory banks within the relay station. There were forty in all, each with a small amount of explosive material powerful enough to take down a quarter of the station. It was overkill. It was necessary, said the Administrator, whose word was law within the Xeno Guild. It was bringing order to chaos in a roundabout manner.

Overkill is efficient, she repeated over and over again as the counter slowly ticked down, *and efficiency is my purpose.* It became a reassuring mantra, one she used to cling to her own sanity. Taking a final breath of the recycled air from her home of three years, she stepped into the shuttle and sealed the doors behind her. The shuttle thrusted away from the access tube and accelerated quickly away from the doomed relay station, the pilot putting as much distance as it could between them. Vah stared out into the blackness, believing she could see her former home in the dark but knowing this was impossible. Daydreaming was not orderly. She rubbed her furred arms and watched the inky blackness of space. *Any moment now...*

The muted explosions were anticlimactic, really. The small shuttle was too far away to see the true carnage wrought by the junior administrator's bombs. In her mind, however, she could see it all. The ruined berthing spaces, her own quarters, destroyed. The precious hardware, gone. It was too much. This was her life's work, and now it was all rendered moot by the Administrator's word. There was nothing left for her now. Her purpose in life had gone up in flames with the destruction of the Jeyla-5 substation.

The shuttle crew found her in the same position an hour later, her vacant expression staring into the void of space. There was little they could do for her except drop her off at their pre-determined destination. She was small, even for a CozSha, and the two larger Maki managed to place her in one of the spare compartments without too much difficulty. They were seasoned pilots and had been hired to transport the junior administrator off-site. However, they were not without heart and understood the tumultuous shock the CozSha was going through, even though they could not relate to it. What was a little violence in order to complete a task? It boggled their minds to see the CozSha in such a state over a little destruction.

Vah began to rock back and forth in her bunk. The safety straps kept her in the bed, though they weren't as tight as they could be. She was upset. The hurt inside was growing with each triple-beat of her multi-chambered heart, a darkness spreading like a poison within. Pain and sadness threatened to break her spirit, and she hated herself for it. Sadness was not efficient. She couldn't help herself from feeling this way. Something wasn't right. Why had the Administrator asked her to embrace chaos, to destroy order? She was methodical, efficient, hardworking, and good at her job. She had run the Jeyla-5 substation perfectly for years. Why now? What had changed? A low moan escaped her lips as no answer was forthcoming.

"I broke it," she whispered and closed her eyes. She dry-heaved and sobbed, her body twisting in the straps as she curled up against the bulkhead. "I ruined order with chaos. It's all my fault."

The shuttle joined with its parent ship, translated through the stargate and disappeared into hyperspace, leaving the destroyed relay substation behind.

* * *

Xeno Guild Outpost, North American District, Earth, Sol System

A senior commissioner of the Xeno Guild was used to having all the information available at hand. Frustrated, Boileau sat back in his seat and frowned after the fifth and final attempt caused his terminal to be locked out of the system. What was supposed to have been a quiet side hustle had turned into something messy and potentially devastating if he did not get a handle on it soon enough. He crooned softly and snapped his beak shut. He tried to think about what had gone wrong and—more importantly—how it could have happened.

Getting the location of the last known TriRusk world from his contact was a boon to him and his bank account. The Mercenary Guild leader—the *true* leader, not the puppets who sat idly on the council and spoke only when told to by Peepo—had given it up almost too easily from all reports, and for such a low price to boot. He chalked it up to her mind simply being on other, more pressing matters. Inattentiveness to detail was always a mercenary's downfall. Earth had been engulfed in the flames of revolution during Peepo's negotiations with the SooSha and the infamous Four Horsemen of Earth were planning to return with a vengeance. The only thing he could imagine was that Peepo, in desperation, had made a mistake while dealing with the treacherous Information Guild member.

Information was more valuable than credits, platinum, or even F11. Without information, the entire Galactic Union would grind to a halt. The Mercenary Guild might carry the biggest guns, and the Trade Guild had the most money, but without the Xeno Guild to allow them to communicate with one another they were all just idle observers reacting to things instead of planning. Even the Information Guild found itself at the mercy of proper communications. Power lay in the weaponization of words.

Using the information sold to him by his SooSha contact, he had immediately made his plans to ensure he got the biggest slice of the pie imaginable. Let his own buyers squabble over who earned the grand prize: the planet itself. The winner did not matter, only the number of contestants. It would keep the Peacemakers busy and out of his feathers. The information he had turned around and sold as well had attracted many interested parties. There had been only one problem, though. If he transferred it through his regular accounts, the Administrator would know immediately and begin asking questions. Questions he did not feel like answering.

Hacking into the Kakata Korps' accounts had originally been childishly easy, given everything he knew about the mercenary company. Mulbah Luo had been a soft-hearted and sentimental individual, which had led to his eventual downfall and death. He had figured this out early on and, once the destruction of Liberia occurred, he checked the accounts to ensure they were still active and valid. He didn't touch the regular credits in the account, as much as he was tempted to. The Mercenary Guild paid very well, and the Korps had benefited from subjugating their fellow Humans. However, Boileau was no fool and left them alone lest they draw attention from any banking authority. Earth still fell under Galactic law, even while pinned beneath Peepo's thumb. Besides, the open account allowed him to funnel funds out into the wilds without alerting the Administrator to what he was doing. Nobody ever checked for money going into an account, merely the outgoing. If the Kakata Korps had been around still, they would be disgustingly wealthy.

For months, he had built up quite a stash of credits within the account, letting it sit there, idle. He was patient, and something this big, which would set him up for life anywhere within the Galactic Union he chose, was well worth the wait. He couldn't just buy a planet, but an entire system. It was a perfectly executed plan. His mentor would have been proud.

Until it had all come crashing down.

He hissed through his beak, trying to figure out where it all went wrong. It took him almost a full hour to determine not only was one of the signees of the account he had been laundering credits through alive, but this person had managed to inadvertently lock him out of the account by the simple measure of changing the password. His anger boiled but deep breaths helped keep him from losing his temper completely. It was temporary, a minor setback. An unexpected turn of events, but one he should have foreseen.

Peepo might believe herself to be infallible, but all of his kind knew from their own history the importance of anticipating something going wrong. Buma were explorers, and to do so in a tumultuous galaxy required planning and having contingencies by the dozens. He had grown careless and complacent, dreaming of how he would live out the rest of his life in grandiose luxury. Planning should have taken precedence over daydreaming, and he cursed his own inattentiveness.

A quick search on his slate brought up the information he needed. After flipping through a few of the security checkpoints designed to keep anyone from doing precisely what he was currently doing, he found just the individual he was looking for.

He never thought he would need this particular assassin's services again. He fired off the message along with the retainer fee and added everything he knew about the officers of the Kakata Korps. They were the only ones who could have accessed the account besides himself, and one of them had screwed him out of a lot of credits. The easiest part? The target hadn't masked their address, so he already knew where the first step of the hunt would begin. He added a quick note to take the target alive for questioning. A corpse couldn't share a secret, after all.

He paused. For the life of him, he couldn't figure out why anyone would want to go to Valyn. The place was a cesspit of scum, only fit for thieves and down-on-their-luck mercenaries. It was the last place any reputable individual would want to be found.

Perhaps this is why they chose this location to run to?

* * * * *

Chapter Two

Having safely emerged from hyperspace a day earlier, the *Velut Luna* began a slow, steady approach to the Jivool-controlled world below. It was a tedious process, especially when the crew onboard the ship couldn't figure out who, precisely, to ask for permission to land.

Three kilometers away, to either side, were four large patrol vessels of XenSha design, evidently under contract with the B'Hono Corporation to protect the area against pirates and saboteurs. Judging by the lack of comms, however, Sunshine wasn't sure what mercenary race, if any, was piloting the vessels. The *Velut Luna*'s databanks could not identify the owners, and neither Dref-na or Taryn could guess precisely who these mysterious aliens were. Taryn was able to joke about the odds being one in thirty-seven but Sunshine didn't get it.

"Let me pass along our request to land and see what happens," Taryn offered as Sunshine began to grow more impatient by the minute. "We're just here to pick up a Jeha. It's not like we're going to rob the place."

"With you? One never knows," Sunshine muttered under her breath. Over the seven-day journey she had gotten to know the temperamental young woman very well.

39

Taryn's head whipped around, and she shot the young teenager a feigned dirty look. "Slander and lies," Taryn replied easily, doing her best to sound insulted. "I have never committed a crime off Earth."

"You mean 'been charged with a crime,' don't you?"

"You say potato, I say corned beef hash. They're all slanderous lies—"

"Why are they so interested in your ship?" Sunshine pressed as she stared at the Tri-V display inside the pilot's cabin. It was clear the nearby vessels were taking a long, hard look at the *Velut Luna*, and the silence from them was unnerving. Usually manned by a crew of five, the ship was running with just Taryn at the controls. The majority of engineering was automated, which saved on manpower, but without a copilot, she was doing extra duty as pilot and comms officer. She needed all of her attention to be on the task at hand. "Did you do something illegal *here*, and they know about it?"

"Look, I don't know why they like us so much. Maybe they think my hair is nice? Maybe Mr. Z was here once, a long time ago. Ships like mine aren't exactly common, you know. Hold a sec, I need to focus." Sunshine scowled. *Piloting a ship couldn't be as hard as driving a CASPer,* she silently argued. However, since this wasn't her ship, she remained still…for the time being.

"*Velut Luna*, this is command ship *Dark Infinity*," a voice suddenly crackled over the comms. "You have been cleared to land on Zav'ax, Subsector 10, Korvar District, Landing Pad 2. Coordinates will follow. Please register all foreign elements with customs control upon arrival."

"Thank you, *Dark Infinity*," Taryn said in a smooth tone before killing the comms. She turned and looked over her shoulder past Sunshine. "Dref-na! I need you!"

"This ship has excellent onboard comms, Taryn Lupo," the Besquith muttered as she made her way forward. "You don't need to shout."

"I take it you heard about the foreign elements?"

"Very well, actually." Dref-na nodded her shaggy head. Her tongue lolled out of her mouth as she offered Taryn the Besquith rendition of a smile. "'Foreign elements' is a pretty loose term for weapons, maybe? I take it this is your first time dealing with the B'Hono Corporation?"

"I can't find anything in the databanks about them," Taryn admitted. "Just their license being filed with the Merchant Guild about twenty years ago just after establishing this mining operation. And those ships…they shouldn't have taken such an interest to us. Those ships are XenSha, but they didn't talk like 'em. Who buys a XenSha ship anyways? They're outdated by at least three generations. This is weird."

"Is there a problem with the company or the alien ships?" Sunshine interjected as she looked at the duo.

"Yes?" Taryn shrugged her shoulders. Dref-na, however, seemed to know more than the captain of the *Velut Luna*.

"Ah, I see your confusion, Taryn Lupo, regarding the B'Hono Corporation. It is the successor company to the ISMC," the Besquith said. Taryn's eyes widened in recognition, but Sunshine was lost.

"ISMC?" the young girl asked.

"Iron Sky Mining Company," Taryn explained. "Entropy, this is bad. What in the hell is Kl'nk'nnk doing working for those crooks?"

"I really don't understand," Sunshine said. It was becoming a theme. Frustrated, she delved into her pinplants and accessed the ship's open source database. After a few seconds of reading she killed the connection. She could see the issue but not why either of her companions was worried. "So, they're crooks. Big deal. Compared to what Peepo did to Earth, these guys are nothing."

"That is not the problem here, my tiny fierceness," Dref-na stated as she looked at the diminutive girl. "What Peepo did was technically legal, even if it was amoral. What ISMC did on Godonnii 2 and to the GenSha, *as well as* the Peacemakers who were sent to deal with the issue, was illegal on a level they shouldn't have ever been able to dig themselves out of. Punitive damages alone should have bankrupted them into oblivion. The majority of their leadership was executed on the spot by..." The Besquith's voice trailed off as she shuddered. Dref-na and Taryn shared a look.

"Do you know what an Enforcer is, Sunshine?" Taryn asked in a quiet voice. Sunshine shook her head. Taryn offered her a weak smile. "Be glad, then. Be very glad."

"How do we handle any potential issues with B'Hono, Taryn Lupo?" Dref-na asked, posing the question nobody else dared. Taryn looked away, uncertain. Sunshine, though, had an idea. It was absurd but they could potentially pull it off. If Dref-na was willing, at least.

"I'm a mercenary company commander," Sunshine reminded the duo. "We just stroll in there and act like we're under contract. Arrest...Kl'nk'nnk? Klink? Klinks. Yeah, that's much easier. We act like we're there to arrest her, hire her instead, then she can fix my suit and find the message once we're off world. We then drop her off back here if she wants or we can take her somewhere else."

"Assuming she has an independent contractor clause in her deal with ISMC," Taryn corrected.

"Yeah, and that," Sunshine allowed. "If she can't fix it here, perhaps she can be hired to come work for us on your ship while she's finding the message in my suit?"

"Well, either way, we're about to find out," Taryn said as the ship shook mildly as winds from the upper atmosphere began to buffet it. "Get your body armor on and grab a weapon. We'll be on the ground in ten minutes and things might get bumpy, and I don't mean from the turbulence."

* * *

Once off the ship, Sunshine and the others were greeted by the dim red star of the It'iek system. The hazy afternoon sky was a deep maroon thanks to the M-class dwarf, and gave the entire scene a very surreal appearance. For the first time since she left Earth, it truly felt as if she were in an alien environment and far from home. It was mildly overwhelming.

Instead of dwelling on where she was, she focused on the why. As soon as they descended the loading ramp of the *Velut Luna*, the trio were greeted by a Jivool representative of the B'Hono Corporation. Things did not get off to a smooth start for the representative.

"We have all the mineral rights to this colony as well as the world," the representative began in lieu of a pleasant greeting. The company rep waved one of his long extendable claws at the towering Besquith as he stared hard at Taryn. "Bringing one of those... *creatures* here to intimidate us will not work, mercenary. If you wish to try and evict us, you need to bring more than a single transport ship and a Besquith. Our charter is legally binding."

Taryn offered a wintry smile in return. She jerked a thumb at Sunshine, who was far younger in appearance and not dressed how anyone would expect the boss to be. "Sorry, I'm just the captain of the ship and her pilot. She's in charge here, not me. I answer to her."

The Jivool was taken aback. Sensing an opportunity, Sunshine struck while the alien was still confused.

"I'm only here because I am seeking a Jeha by the name of Kl'nk'nnk," she said, her posture straightening. She tried to give herself an air of confidence and authority. Considering she had never seen one of the aliens before, it was harder than expected. But instead of dwelling on the odd alien's expression, she focused on maintaining the façade. "My business and contracts have nothing to do with the B'Hono Corporation at this time, or this planet for that matter. Unless you want me to make it my business, *ken?*"

"The Jeha? Is that all?" The representative for the B'Hono Corporation was visibly relieved. Even Sunshine could tell, and this was her first Jivool she had ever come across. *Whatever is going on here,* Sunshine thought as the Jivool continued, *might be something worth looking into later.* "The Jeha is currently at Subsector 14, Satuur District. We would be most pleased to escort you there."

"My pilot is more than capable, thank you," Sunshine told him. She gave him a small wave of her hand. "Just pass her the coordinates and we'll be on our way."

"But—"

"Thank you but my pilot is very skilled," Sunshine said in a forceful tone, effectively dismissing the Jivool. The representative gave her one final look before motioning to Taryn, who looked rather amused by the turn of events. Sunshine looked at Dref-na as Taryn received the coordinates necessary to find the Jeha.

"That name of the district bothers me, tiny fierceness," the Besquith growled softly. "I don't know why."

"It was the name of one of the administrators executed for their crimes against the GenSha and the Peacemakers," Sunshine answered. Dref-na's eyes widened in surprise. Sunshine smiled. "I read the information downloaded from the *Velut Luna* earlier when we were dealing with those ships."

"And you remembered it all, or did you download it for later?"

"Yes."

"Very clever, tiny fierceness."

"Thank you."

"Well, that went swimmingly," Taryn said a few moments later when she rejoined them. The Jivool had moved far enough away to not overhear their conversation yet close enough to remind them to be on their way. She looked disgusted. "It's all the way on the far side of the planet, which means more fuel use. I was hoping we could stay in the upper atmosphere and not go for a hard burn until we leave; so much for that idea. Once we're out of here, we're going to have to make a pit stop at the nearest station *not* controlled by the B'Hono Corp."

"Why not refuel here?" Sunshine asked, confused.

"Because the fuel could be dirty, which would cause engine failure and an 'accident' to occur," Taryn said as she held her fingers and began ticking off reasons. "Their prices are probably worthy of corporate-level extortion. Could be any number of factors. I trust these Jivool less than I trust a MinSha in New Persia not getting killed, and, quite frankly, that slimy little *kopile* makes me sick. He's a low-level corporate stooge with delusions of grandeur, and he's rude to boot."

"My translator didn't get the *kopile* part," Dref-na said but smiled nonetheless and turned to face Sunshine. Her teeth seemed enormous up close and personal. "Do you want me to eat him, tiny fierceness?"

"Uh…no?" Sunshine answered hesitantly. *Is Dref-na serious? Probably,* she decided.

"Entropy," Dref-na complained, but let the matter drop. Sunshine and Taryn both grinned.

"The sooner we find Kl'nk'nnk, the sooner we can get off this world and find your message," Taryn said as the trio quickly walked back to the ship.

Feeling an itch between her shoulder blades, Sunshine turned and glanced back at the Jivool. She could see him speaking quietly into a communicator device of some sort, though his eyes were locked on her. Sunshine frowned. She had seen looks like that before, back in Liberia, from many who roamed the streets of Monrovia and Chocolate City after dark. It was the look of a predator sizing up potential prey.

This prey has teeth, craw-craw boy, she thought as she followed Taryn and Dref-na back onto their ship.

* * *

Three hours later they were safely at Subsector 14 with no incidents, though none of them had missed the four drones following behind them the entire way. It was eerie to watch the propeller driven craft dance just off the wingtips of the *Velut Luna.* In space their craft was fast; in the atmosphere of Zav'ax they were at a huge disadvantage. The *Velut Luna* was aerodynamic, true, but much like a pig in water, it did so with no speed, little agility, and zero grace.

What it lacked in subtlety and nuance, though, it more than made up for it in weaponry. Specifically, the four railguns cleverly hidden inside the hull on the underside of the ship. The desire to shoot down the drones was strong but Taryn's explanation to Sunshine why this was a horrible idea rang true to the young woman.

"If we shoot them down, then B'Hono can say we attacked their worker drones unprovoked," Taryn said as she guided the ship to a landing pad located within the heart of Subsector 14's sprawling industrial complex. To the south they could see a massive open-air mine and thousands of workers moving materials via transport sleds. There was no way to determine the species working in the mine, but Sunshine could tell none of them were Humans. Taryn continued: "Imagine if B'Hono claimed we destroyed four top-of-the-line drones, which are valued in the millions. They could come after us for punitive damages. Given their apparent pull within the Merchants Guild, I wouldn't be surprised if the final tab came out to a little over a billion credits."

"Oh," Sunshine responded meekly. She hadn't considered that. Taryn nodded.

"As pleasing as it would be, we leave them alone for now," she said. Taryn offered the mercenary a wan smile before continuing. "Now, if they 'accidentally' get caught in our blast radius when we do a hard burn to exit the atmosphere? Well, that's on them, and we'll have proof since they already operated inside our safety zone previously. It's a delicate game of cat and mouse. Biggest problem? I'm not yet sure who is the cat and who is the mouse."

"There would be protests in courts," Dref-na said, smirking in a manner only a Besquith could. "I would enjoy seeing their hand wringing and wails of anguish when their claims are found to be wanting. I vote for a hard burn, Taryn Lupo."

"Okay, put on your game faces," Taryn said as the ship at last eased onto the platform with a gentle bump. "Sunshine? Oh, good, you're still in your armor. I want you to grab a different weapon, though. I have a few in the portside storage cabinet near my berthing space. Get something big that looks intimidating but can fit in a thigh holster. Shiny, too. Jivool respond to shiny things, kind of like goldfish but way smarter. Once you're ready, we'll go find Kl'nk'nnk so we can get out of here."

"My game face is best described as murderous or terrifying, Taryn Lupo," Dref-na pointed out as Sunshine went to the left side of the ship and found the compartment Taryn had spoken about. She quickly found the weapons and it took her a scant amount of time to get properly situated. She still felt naked outside of her CAS-Per, but body armor was better than nothing. She rejoined the duo as they made their way to the ship's rear cargo exit. The ramp descended. Blinking at the dim morning light, the trio stepped out and onto the small landing pad.

"It was late afternoon three hours ago," Sunshine complained as she looked east. The system's red star was rising slowly from beneath the horizon. It was eerie to see. Around them, the jungle seemed dark and menacing. "I hate time zones."

"Could be worse," Taryn stated. "Could be on a planet that only gets a few hours of daylight, or we could be far north in the middle of an icy continent. At least here the settlements are in temperate zones. Can you imagine if we were in the middle of the northern hemisphere's winter?"

"Yay," Sunshine grumbled, but quietly. She looked around but with the exception of a few worker drones, the landing pad appeared to be empty. There was no B'Hono representative to greet them this time. It was not as noisy as she had expected, either. The area beneath their ship's gear showed no signs of being used recently, and there was an abundance of old and new growth of plant-life on the edge of the platform to the right. It was clear this landing pad had not seen a ship in a very long time. Sunshine wondered why. "Where is everyone?"

"It's really early still," Taryn pointed out. She pulled a slate out of her pocket and allowed it to connect to the district's GalNet. She frowned. "You know, you'd think finding a Jeha on a planet full of Jivool—well, that's weird."

"What?" Sunshine asked.

"I have a lot of weird readings on the power usage for the planet," Taryn said as she slipped the slate into an unobtrusive pocket. "According to GalNet, it's just the Jivool and a lone Jeha registered as inhabitants on the planet. But the data usage doesn't match the number of registered inhabitants, unless the miners don't have access to the GalNet. It's possible."

"I know we saw robots in the mines to the south, Taryn Lupo," Dref-na said with a snap of her jaws. "Those were not Jivool miners, and they did not resemble Jeha."

"Something to worry about another time," Taryn replied. "We need to find Kl'nk'nnk and get out of here. This doesn't feel right."

"It's a setup," Sunshine hissed as she realized where she had seen something similar before. "I wish I had my CASPer on. I'd know what to look for."

"Dref-na? Hear anybody?" Taryn asked, and the Besquith stretched to her full height. Smaller than the average Besquith, the alien mercenary was still an imposing sight. Her claws fully extended, she looked around the area for any signs an immediate threat.

"No," Dref-na answered a few moments later. "Only the worker drones in the jungle around us and the pesky gnats in the sky which you wouldn't let me use for target practice."

"Objection noted," Taryn grunted. "Still a bad idea; very pricey."

"Something's out there," Sunshine stated firmly. It was there, tickling the edges of her mind. They were being watched. She did not know how, but it was clear as day to her. Electronic eyes were watching them. "Other than the drones, I mean. Something is watching us."

"What would you look for, tiny fierceness?" Dref-na asked.

"If I had my suit? Explosive residue," Sunshine responded, thinking quickly. "A bomb, maybe? Or a wireless transmission or relay. But…I don't understand. If it was a bomb, then why didn't it go off when we landed? Why did they even let us in their air space if they want to kill us? Nothing here makes any sense."

"We're all being a little paranoid here," Taryn interjected. She raised an open hand to forestall Sunshine's coming argument. "I'm not saying it's a bad thing, but we're jumping at shadows which might not be there. They're just as suspicious of us as we are of them. It's obvious they're watching us. Just assume we're under surveillance all of the time. Let's play it cool and see where it goes. Worst case scenario? Dref-na gets to eat a bunch of Jivool."

"I don't like their taste," Dref-na complained. "Too gamey. Don't get me wrong, I *would* if you said to, but I won't enjoy it…too much."

"Okay, so we find the Jeha, and if anyone attacks us, we kill them all, *ken?*" Sunshine asked Taryn, who smiled.

"Yes, exactly. We only kill when attacked."

"I hate waiting for them to come kill us." Sunshine glowered as Taryn secured the ramp to the *Velut Luna*. "We shouldn't give them the chance to attack us at all. I like being proactive."

"I would have thought hunting with a Depik would teach you otherwise," Taryn chuckled. Sunshine shot her a look.

"Tsan was *different*," Sunshine pointed out. "Most Depik strike from the shadows or lie in wait for their prey to come to them, ensnaring them in a trap. They *play* with their prey. Tsan declared war and *hunted* and did not use her best ability. She wanted to be seen and heard. To cause fear and panic, for her victims to dread her coming. Big difference."

"I would have liked to fight a Depik one time," Dref-na said as they found a small path through the thick, overgrown vegetation. The steel walkway eventually led them to a quiet street. There were a few Jivool out and about, but traffic was minimal. Taryn consulted her slate and looked around, confused.

"Where is—ah, there it is," Taryn grunted. "The corporate masters here don't know anything about urban development. You can't have six different streets with the same name and expect people to not get confused or lost. It's like Atlanta all over again. Gods, I hated Atlanta. Peachtree this, Peachtree that…"

As they walked across the street, the Besquith shook her head. She seemed amused with herself. "No, I take that back. I wouldn't want to fight one, just eat it. Depik don't fight fair."

"It'd probably let you swallow it whole just to be able to say it gutted you from the inside," Sunshine commented. Dref-na laughed harshly.

"Indeed, it would, tiny fierceness," Dref-na managed to choke out through her laughter. "They are truly the masters of ingenious kills."

"You have no idea."

"With this level of idiocy, I'd expect them to be an actual government bureaucracy," Taryn continued to complain, seemingly oblivious to the duo's conversation. "This is such a huge waste of time."

"Taryn?" Sunshine interrupted her.

"Hm?"

"Which way are we going?" Sunshine asked.

"Oh," Taryn paused, her lips pursed together thoughtfully. Absentmindedly she pushed a strand of her dyed hair from her face before pointing at a building further up the block. "See the one that looks like a jail? That one."

"Why do you say it looks like a jail?" Sunshine asked as she looked around at the other buildings on the block. While not attractive when compared to the shimmering skyscrapers she'd seen in Brazil, they were still comparatively pretty when standing next to the ugly, squat place their Jeha was apparently located. "It's alien."

"Probably because it's listed as a jail," Taryn observed as she handed over her slate. Sunshine fumbled it before managing to grasp it with both hands. She looked at what was on Taryn's screen and gasped.

"Arrested for corporate espionage?" Sunshine looked up at Taryn, shocked. "And you want to let this *thief* touch my suit?"

"Alleged thief," Taryn corrected mildly as she took her slate back. "Curious. Maybe they think we're here for prisoner transport? Oh, this is good. Sunshine, this is where your idea of being the big bad merc commander will come in handy even more than before."

"How?"

"You stroll in there and demand they release the prisoner to your custody," Taryn suggested as they approached the ugly little building. Standing on either side of the entrance were a duo of armed Jivool guards, both of whom looked very comfortable holding their weapons. It was clear they were the very definition of hired corporate thugs. It made Sunshine wonder why there weren't any mercenaries on the ground. Her instincts were screaming at her that there was more going on than she knew. "They ask why, you say she has an outstanding warrant or something. They won't check, especially once they see your yack and the backing credentials. If they want this settled quickly and quietly, which looks like they do, then they'll tell you to take her and leave. Probably ask us not to come back either, which is fine."

"But what if she really did commit corporate espionage?" Sunshine asked.

"Then she's got some secrets which could come in handy someday," Taryn admitted as they approached the door. She dropped her voice. "But I seriously doubt Kl'nk'nnk even understands espionage. She's more of a *savant* when it comes to engineering. Her social game or even lying? Yeah, neither of those exist in her world. She is honest to a fault and not very graceful with it."

The two Jivool guards gave them the once-over but did not impede their passage, though there were a few nervous glances exchanged as it quickly became apparent to all Dref-na was following the two Human females inside the jail. Their digging claws tightened on their weapons and they were obviously concerned, but they made no effort to halt the trio.

Once inside, Sunshine leaned over and whispered in Taryn's ear. "I thought they were going to stop Dref-na for sure."

"That would have been interesting to see," Taryn chuckled softly. "Jivool dictating terms to a Besquith. I'd have paid good money to see that go down."

"Everyone always assumes we're violent psychopaths," Dref-na complained. Taryn opened her mouth to say something but closed it quickly, shaking her head in obvious amusement. Sunshine looked around the small open area, quickly taking in the layout while her mind automatically planned an exfiltration scenario. The way the few desks were arranged told her this was not an often-used precinct, designed more for the Jivool workers than any other race. Given this was a corporate-run planet, Sunshine couldn't imagine the police here were used to a lot of trouble.

Though the majority of the desks were empty, there were three Jivool officers working diligently on their slates. None looked up at their entrance, though, suggesting to the young mercenary they would be of little help if she bothered to ask them. She continued to scan the room and spotted what she was looking for.

Seated behind a raised desk, a bored looking Jivool was watching them without apparent interest. He would have been right at home on a television show back on Earth. His bland features were studiously schooled, though Sunshine was able to recognize a gleam of interest and intelligence in his eyes. While he sported no sign of rank on his sleeve, a gut feeling told her this was the Jivool they needed to speak to. She nudged Taryn with her elbow and the other woman quickly recognized what Sunshine saw.

"Good eye," Taryn whispered. "Okay, boss, time for you to go to work. Back straight, staring ten centimeters directly above the Jivool's head, and for the love of all that is holy, look *pissed*."

"Be fierce, tiny one," Dref-na encouraged her as they quickly walked over to the Jivool behind the desk.

"I am…Captain Sunshine, commanding officer of the Kakata Korps Mercenary Company," Sunshine announced after rapping on the desk once with a closed fist, only giving herself a brief pause to figure out what rank she needed to be. It made sense for her to be at least a captain now, though it did pain her a bit to do so. Giving herself a violent mental shake, she continued. "You have a Jeha that I want."

The Jivool smirked. At least, Sunshine assumed it was a smirk. She couldn't be certain, since the unusual features of the Jivool were throwing her off a bit. It felt strange. The more she thought about the feeling she had about the behavior patterns of the alien, the less certain she became. Her gut had never steered her wrong before, though. *Very weird,* she thought.

"The Jeha is being held on charges of corporate espionage by order of—" the Jivool began to recite from memory but Sunshine cut him off.

"I want the Jeha, and I want her now," Sunshine said harshly. Behind her Dref-na added a dangerously gentle growl. *This* caused the other Jivool in the room to lift their heads simultaneously. What had started off as a boring shift was quickly turning into something else for them.

"Does, ah, the Jeha have an outstanding warrant which supersedes the jurisdiction of a corporate entity licensed with the Merchant Guild?" the Jivool asked, a nervous edge to his tone. Behind them Sunshine could almost feel the others slowly begin to stand. She pictured their hands straying to their duty belts and guessed each held the Human equivalent of an ancient handgun loaded with chemically propelled rounds. She nearly scoffed at their arrogance. They might slow down the Besquith for a moment, but they wouldn't be able to raise the alarm before their entrails and body parts decorated the otherwise unoccupied desks.

"She does," Sunshine bluffed and passed over her yack. The Jivool gently accepted it and held it to his slate for a moment before passing it back. His eyes never left the Besquith looming behind her. Sunshine could hear her flexing her claws repeatedly.

"Everything...looks in order," he stammered before touching a few commands on his slate. It was clear to Sunshine he had not seen anything on the UAAC and was far more interested in making them go away, just as Taryn predicted. "The Jeha is being brought out now."

"Thank you." Sunshine rewarded the jailer with a bright smile. The Jivool flinched ever so slightly. She kicked herself mentally. Bared teeth to more than a few alien species was considered a threat, she remembered Tsan telling her not too long ago. She quickly closed her smile. The Jivool visibly relaxed, which confirmed what Tsan had said.

Within a minute the Jeha appeared, escorted by an irritated Jivool whose expression changed the moment it saw Dref-na. While it was hard to tell precisely what the Jeha was thinking, she could feel surprise emanating from the alien as it paused and looked at them. Sunshine wondered just how Taryn knew this particular alien, since the impression she was getting was one of fear and terror. Of course, it could have been the towering Besquith.

"Kl'nk'nnk," Sunshine said in a firm voice. She searched her memory for names and recalled one from her brief time while running through sims back on Earth. "You are remanded into custody to be brought before Colonel Alexis Cromwell of the Winged Hussars on criminal charges of aiding the Mercenary Guild during their illegal occupation of Earth."

Sunshine was taking a huge risk. She knew the war for Earth was over, and news of Peepo's defeat at the hands of the Four Horsemen had reached even this far outpost. However, Alexis Cromwell's name was the only one she could think of in a pinch. While she had never really met any of the commanding officers, save for a passing group introduction with Jim Cartwright when Splunk the Fae/Dusman was looking over her CASPer, she doubted any of the Jivool would know this. Plus, it was painfully obvious the Jivool wanted the group gone as quickly as possible and giving up Kl'nk'nnk would make this happen.

The Jivool declined to call her bluff. Kl'nk'nnk shifted her head back and forth in disbelief but wisely kept her mouth shut. Everyone in Sunshine's group knew she was bluffing, and the Jeha had quickly picked up on it, but there was no way the Jivool knew how thoroughly they were being conned. Sunshine bit down on a smile which threatened to appear.

"Take her. This Jeha must be off-world within the hour and it is forbidden from ever returning," the lead jailer declared from behind the raised desk. He motioned toward the door. "Please leave."

Sunshine dipped her head slightly and turned around. She stopped as she saw more Jivool had arrived, though they were not trying to block the exit. Instead they had moved to where the jailers had brought Kl'nk'nnk from. While a bit surprising, she didn't dwell on it for too long. She just wanted the Jeha to fix her suit and find the message Mulbah had left for the Peacemakers. After that…

She paused. What *was* the plan for after? She really hadn't given it much thought. Sure, there was the temptation to return to Earth and live out her days there, though there wasn't really anything left for her. Or of her homeland, which had been destroyed by Peepo.

"Captain?" Taryn derailed her mental train with a cough. Blushing, Sunshine looked over her shoulder and nodded. Taryn beamed a smile and touched the Jeha just behind the head. It appeared threatening but the Jeha didn't so much as twitch. "Let's go, and nothing funny or you'll anger the Besquith."

"I didn't know the Winged Hussars were employing Besquith now," Kl'nk'nnk complained but followed Taryn out of the station, leaving Sunshine and Dref-na alone with eleven Jivool officers. The mercenary turned and motioned toward the door. Dref-na chuffed and went first, with Sunshine right behind her.

She stopped at the door and accessed her pinplants. She had transferred over a million credits from the Korps' account to her slate before they had arrived on planet and she was still within range of the *Velut Luna*'s pinplant system. She quickly pulled 10,000 credits out of the account and slipped it to the general fund of the police station. Though it was corporate-run, she figured they were about as well-paid as police were back in Liberia, and they always appreciated a generous "gift." In truth it was a bribe, but this definition mattered only to the bean counters and morally upstanding individuals. She was certain these Jivool wouldn't mind.

"A token of the Korps' appreciation for your discretion," she added a recorded note with the bribe. She remembered every single lesson Mulbah Luo had ever drilled into her head. Bribes were both good and bad, depending on the circumstances.

Not giving the Jivool time to respond, she followed Dref-na out the door.

The dim morning light was near blinding compared to their arrival, and there were more Jivool wandering the streets as the workday was beginning. Sunshine stopped and leaned up against the Besquith for support as all her nervous energy suddenly drained from her. "Oh boy, that was so *kroo kroo jii*. I thought we were done!"

"Very impressive, tiny fierceness," Dref-na rumbled, pleased. "Now let's leave this planet. The air here is not to my liking."

"Whatever you say," Sunshine agreed as they crossed the road once more and followed Taryn and Kl'nk'nnk through the dark, overgrown path. Within minutes they were back at the ship, where a solitary Jivool stood waiting. His burly arms were crossed over his chest and his features were twisted into a perpetual scowl.

"Caution," the Besquith growled as she surreptitiously sniffed the air. "There's more going on here than we can see."

Sunshine didn't slow her pace as adrenaline poured into her system. It felt as if everything around her buzzed with electricity. She suspected the sensations coursing through her were due to nerves, which was strange. She hadn't felt like this since the Battle for Monrovia. The sensation was eerily similar to her time in the sims, when everything was perfectly clear and time seemed to slow around her.

From his dress and mannerisms, Sunshine immediately pegged the new Jivool as a company stooge, possibly a high-level corporate officer. He obviously believed himself to be important. However, she couldn't think of a reason why he might be there. It had already been made clear to all of them they needed to leave the planet. The arrival of the corporate stooge made her nervous, but not the scared kind. It was a *good* nervous, excitement building up inside her as she mentally readied for battle. This was what she was born to do.

"Despite what the security forces told you, I can't allow you to take that Jeha off world, warrant or not," the Jivool said and waved one of his large extendable claws at them. Sunshine guessed it was supposed to be intimidating. She found it anything but. "Crimes committed on Jivool-held worlds must be punished, and the Mercenary Guild cannot supersede our laws."

"I'm under contract," Sunshine countered.

"So you say," the Jivool sniffed. "However, the ship registry is not with any licensed merc company, which could mean many things. The most likely scenario involved is that you are here under guise of guild work when more than likely you have other, more nefarious purposes in mind."

"Not really," Sunshine shrugged and tried to remain calm. "I just want the Jeha."

"As do I," the Jivool countered. "Leave the spy, and then this planet, and no harm shall come to you."

"Let us go peacefully, and I won't have the Besquith eat you," Sunshine threatened. The Jivool let out a wheezing little laugh.

"You have one Besquith," the Jivool said as he made a funny motion with his digging claw. Immediately a large group of Jivool security forces emerged from the thick, overgrown underbrush of the jungle surrounding the landing platform. Each was armed with the same variation of laser rifle Sunshine had seen the Zuul with during the Fall of Monrovia. She swallowed and felt her own hand drift down to her thigh to check her holstered pistol. The Jivool leader offered up his species version of a smug smile. "I have fifteen armed guards. You might get a few of them, but even a Besquith can't eat enough before we kill you all."

"She doesn't need a Besquith," Taryn interjected, a small smile upon her lips. Her dark eyes twinkled. "She has me—and the *Velut Luna*."

Noise erupted from their ship as panels opened and the four large railguns appeared. They swiveled around and soon all were targeting the company stooge. The Jivool collectively looked nervously at the ship, only relaxing microscopically upon realizing it was their boss and not they who was looking down the barrel of four pintle-mounted railguns. It was apparent their boss was not a popular individual. Taryn's smile grew wider as she explained.

"Those, my friend, are four Izlian-designed, Human-built, Barracuda Mark Three fully automatic railguns," she began. Sunshine recognized just how much Taryn was enjoying herself, though she couldn't say the same for herself. Even with the *Velut Luna*'s guns, they were still vastly outnumbered. "I have complete control over them via pinplants and can activate them faster than you can finish saying 'attack.' They are capable of firing one round every half second at a speed of over seven thousand kilometers per hour. The round is fast enough that you probably wouldn't even hear the shot before you exploded. Notice I did not say die. No, I said exploded. I used the word exploded because the kinetic energy which would follow the teaspoon-sized round as it penetrated your thick skull would create something called hydrostatic shock and cause it to pop like a bubble. Hmm...that's an interesting science question, now that I think about it. Can your brain process the sound of your skull blowing apart before you die? You know what? I'm willing to try it out if you are. Put up or shut up, as my friend would say."

The Jivool nodded slowly. "I see," he murmured. "As much as I would like to let you go, I cannot. I'm far more afraid of my bosses than I am of you, *Human*."

The Jivool surrounding them opened fire without warning. Sunshine yelped and tried to grab her weapon from its holster but was suddenly thrown to the ground. A heavy weight fell on top of her a split second later. It was easy to figure out who was covering her, though she could not figure out why the Besquith was protecting her instead of killing all the Jivool on the landing platform.

"Dref-na!" Sunshine screamed. "Get off me! You're squishing me!"

"Had to make certain you were safe first," Dref-na replied as Taryn targeted different Jivool and, using her pinplants, fired the railguns. Where four Jivool security guards had been moments before there were now large bloody stains on the tarmac. The railguns pivoted as Taryn locked onto new targets. "It's why you pay me, remember?"

"Go!" Sunshine shouted and Dref-na bounded off. She heard a painful squeal of a wounded Jivool just before she saw it explode into a fine red mist.

"That one was *mine*, Taryn Lupo!" Dref-na yelled out.

The Jivool began shooting at the Jeha instead of Taryn or Dref-na, which Sunshine found a little odd. The centipede-like alien squealed in pain as two holes appeared near her midsection. They tried to shoot her again but suddenly a brown blur appeared in their midst. Their arms were removed before they knew what was going on and they were dead before the pain actually sank in. The Besquith had joined the fight, and the odds were suddenly against the Jivool security forces.

Sunshine managed to get her weapon out of the holster and looked it over for a brief moment. She recognized the safety near the slide but wasn't sure about the make or model of the firearm. Mentally cursing herself for not checking to see if the weapon was loaded before they left the ship, it only took her a few moments to ensure there was a fresh magazine of laser charges loaded. It was long enough to expose her to enemy fire.

Three shots spattered against the tarmac near her face, causing sparks to fly up into her eyes. Yowling in pain and surprise, she covered her eyes with her left hand. Though her vision was hazy due to the sparks, she could see a vaguely Jivool-shaped target nearby. Giving her vision two more seconds to adjust, she pulled the trigger multiple times. Two small holes appeared in the Jivool just above the neck of his body armor.

Eyes still burning from the sparks, Sunshine coughed as acrid smoke filled her lungs. She looked around in confusion until she found the source of the smoke. Someone had set fire to the thick underbrush adjacent to the landing pad. The fires weren't much to look at, but the green vegetation made the smoke dark and smoldering. Wracked with pain from not being able to breathe correctly, Sunshine tried to mask her face with her sleeve. It was slightly better than breathing the foul smoke, but only just.

Eyes watering, she desperately sought out someone, anyone, who wasn't trying to kill her. Crawling along the tarmac she found the wounded Jeha. She gingerly touched the alien, who recoiled in pain.

"Sorry, sorry," Sunshine apologized before another coughing fit wracked her entire body. Managing to find a small breath of clean air, she continued. "Are you badly hurt?"

"I am severely injured," the Jeha said in a strange, wheezing voice. Even through the translator Sunshine could hear the pain and anguish. "I require assistance, or I will die soon."

"Dref-na!" Sunshine screamed as loudly as she could over the repeated blasts of *Velut Luna*'s railguns. She looked around but all she could see was smoke. The fires were growing worse. *"Dref-na!"*

The Besquith materialized out of the thick black smoke, tossing a severed Jivool head aside as casually as Sunshine might throw away a bad fig. Dref-na practically swaggered up to them, looking immensely pleased with herself as she spotted Sunshine and the Jeha on the sticky tarmac. Her expression immediately changed as she saw just how badly wounded Kl'nk'nnk was.

"I am here, tiny fierceness," Dref-na said as she knelt next to the two. There was concern etched upon the terrifying visage of the Besquith. "You are not injured?"

"No, but Klinks is," Sunshine panted as she struggled to breathe.

"Who is…Klinks?" the Jeha asked.

"You are," Sunshine explained before gagging on another mouthful of thick black smoke, which stuck to her tongue like oil. She spat angrily before continuing, "Your real name makes my mouth hurt."

"Oh," the Jeha replied as her breathing slowed. "Humans are…very strange."

"Can you carry her back to the *Velut Luna?*" Sunshine asked Dref-na.

"Easily."

Next, Sunshine activated her pinplants and sought out the *Velut Luna*. After achieving a solid link, she began to take stock of the chaos around them. Using the ship as a conduit, Sunshine pinged Taryn. The older woman acknowledged her.

"We're heading toward the ship," she sent via her pinplants as she looked at the ship's sensors. They were remarkable. "I see eight dead and four wounded according to the sensors, not counting us."

"Confirm," Taryn responded immediately. "Four more are jack rabbiting out of here. Remote pre-flight check ongoing."

"You can do that?"

"My boss has this ship tricked out," Taryn explained. "We'll be airborne and hard burning atmo as soon as we get everyone on board. By the way, we need to talk about something."

"What about the fire?"

"Screw it. Accidents happen. Plus, they kinda brought this on themselves."

"Yeah. We're inbound. Ten seconds."

"Hurry," Taryn urged. "The sooner we're off this hellhole, the easier we can avoid the eventual pursuit."

"On our way." Sunshine looked around. Her visibility was greatly limited due to the roiling flames, but she was almost certain the ship lay only a few dozen meters ahead and to her right. She coughed again and squinted. Sure enough, though the smoke was blanketing the tarmac, she could see the faint outline of the *Velut Luna*. She nudged the Besquith's arm and pointed. "Dref-na, over there!"

The Besquith scooped up Kl'nk'nnk in her arms and hurried to the ship with Sunshine right behind her. The ramp was still down but Taryn was nowhere to be found. Sunshine tried to look around, but the smoke was simply too thick to see anything outside a one-meter radius. Coughing again, she covered her face and hurried aboard.

"Taryn?"

"Everyone's on board," came a quick reply from the command deck via the comms. "Sealing the ramp now. Pressurizing...now. Okay, we're good. Lifting off."

The powerful engines of the *Velut Luna* thrummed throughout the ship. Sunshine hurried to the command deck and found Taryn seated in the pilot's chair. Outside the fire raged and was spreading rapidly. Smoke seemed to be everywhere.

"The pressure waves from the engines are causing the fires to spread, like high winds," Taryn explained as they climbed upwards into the sky, breaking through the layer of smoke in moments.

Sunshine shot her a look. "How did you—"

"You don't have a good poker face." Taryn chuckled humorlessly. "I figured you were either concerned about Kl'nk'nnk or the fires."

"Are we safe yet?" Sunshine asked.

"I don't know," Taryn replied with a slight shrug. Her eyes remained locked on the Tri-V display before her. "I'll know more once we're out of the atmosphere."

* * *

Garnon District Building 11, B'Hono Mining Colony-B, Zav'ax, It'iek System

Karvan Di Mobiar looked at the slate he had been given by his secretary. It contained an encoded message which only he could decipher, courtesy of the throwaway encryption key now lying in the waste receptacle. A "clean" slate, so to speak, it would never be traced back to the individual who gave it to him years before. It was just one of the many perks he enjoyed while working for his benefactor within the Xeno Guild.

Had enjoyed, that is. Until the arrival of the mysterious ship identified as the *Velut Luna*, job security with the B'Hono Corporation had been ensured, and the wealth he was accruing while working with his benefactor in the Xeno Guild was a perk which he had hoped would allow him to one day retire to his own private planet. His grandfather had given his life for the Iron Sky Mining Company long before, while his own father had scratched and clawed his way up the corporate ladder to have ISMC rebranded. It fell upon Karvan's rather broad shoulders to finish the job and bring B'Hono back to prominence while clearing away the stench associated with ISMC.

That was why he had accepted his benefactor's offer in the first place. The Xeno Guild held power beyond what even the Mercenary Guild could muster: changing facts and control of information through communication. Information which, given time, could help make people forget just what had occurred at the hands of the Peacemaker Guild long years before and bring closure to the young Jivool.

He kicked over the trash receptacle and scowled. But what was supposed to be a quiet and lucrative job was turning into anything but. A tall stack of carefully balanced *savards* was tumbling, one by one, threatening to bury him in the process. First, the insufferable Jeha had gotten nosy and stuck its antennae into something it had no reason to. His security forces had immediately arrested the alien but somehow Kl'nk'nnk must have gotten a coded message off world, because, in less than two weeks after her arrest, the damnable Human mercenary commander and her ship arrived looking for the Jeha.

Karvan didn't believe for one moment they were simply there to arrest the Jeha on any charges. First off, a bounty hunter would have been used, since the Mercenary Guild wasn't currently allowing anyone to accept new contracts as it struggled to sort out the mess it was in. Secondly, he was a cynical Jivool and did not believe in coincidences.

"Stupid overpaid security forces," he grumbled aloud and picked up the trash receptacle. While irritated at them, he was angrier at himself for not anticipating the Humans bringing some sort of hired muscle and warning the security forces. He was also upset the idiotic subordinate who told the Humans where to find the Jeha was dead, and his lieutenant who had tried to stop them at their secondary site was still missing. Karvan really wanted to kill both of the imbeciles himself. Throw in the fact that someone had been able to bribe the security forces with a paltry amount of credits, and it was clear he needed a new chief of site security.

"Good help is so hard to find."

Finishing up the final part of his message, he pressed "Send" and waited. Three seconds later he received confirmation the encrypted message was passed through the in-system substation and through the gate, eventually ending up in the hands of his benefactor. Turnaround time was usually fairly quick since the Cartography Guild worked with the Xeno Guild quite regularly.

For a moment, Karvan wondered if his message was succinct enough. His beady eyes darted back down to look at the slate's screen.

Jeha escaped with Humans. Human mercs know about Project. No PM Guild yet. Purge the subject matter?

"It's understandable," Karvan decided as the slate eradicated all of the backup memory files and automatically returned to the preset factory mode. It would not activate again until the response arrived, and he used a new encryption key to open it. He sighed and sat in his plush executive chair. He pulled out a different, company-unique slate to go over the false books once more. He was skilled at multi-tasking, but right now, as much as it irritated him, the fiscal quarter numbers were a far more pressing matter. "Running multiple cons at once is a pain in the…" his voice trailed off as he began to make minor adjustments.

The mining colony needed to appear it had more employees than it truly did so the parent company would continue to meet payroll. After all, early retirement wasn't cheap.

* * *

K'tamyl's Merc Pit, Valyn, Entilles System

DexKarr wasn't surprised by the reception he received when he entered the run-down mercenary pit. It wasn't every day a Torokar showed up, after all.

K'tamyl's was the sort of place only the desperate and destitute found themselves. It was perfectly out-of-the-way, a minor hole in the wall in the midst of the sleazy night clubs and entertainment surrounding it. The merc pit was near the starport, though, which made it popular for those who needed a contract in a hurry. In more recent history, it had been a common meeting ground for Pushtal and other fringe merc races.

He scratched his scales and shifted slightly. His armor's lumbar support was digging into his upper spine once more, a result of slight weight gain. He made a mental note to cut back on the fattier meats when he wasn't exercising as often.

His body armor wasn't the typical combat armor the average Torokar mercenary wore. It was lighter, more flexible, and worked better for the assassin when he was stalking a prey. His line of work dictated a long hunt and a swift kill, not a prolonged firefight with the target. An ambush predator historically, the Torokar had evolved into what Humans would have immediately identified as a velociraptor with long, muscular arms and claws which could rend steel. In other words, a walking nightmare.

He let his eyes examine the interior of the merc pit as he looked at the proprietor. He sniffed in disgust at the cowardly alien practically hiding behind the bar. The K'kng stared fearfully at him—or more accurately, the railgun attached to his combat armor's lumbar support system. It would have been amusing had he not been in a hurry.

"You," he pointed one of his diamond-hard claws at the K'kng. "You own this business, yes?"

The K'kng hooted fearfully and nodded with some reluctance. "Yes?"

"There were certain aliens here two weeks ago," DexKarr said, motioning around the room. "Human mercenaries. You know what a Human is, I assume? Yes? Good. Check your security footage and tell me where they were sitting."

"My system isn't working," the K'kng apologized. DexKarr stared at the creature, incredulous. The K'kng continued after a momentary pause, clearly flustered. "I've been meaning to get it fixed…"

"You run a mercenary pit which has *zero* security measures to ensure you are not placed before an arbitrator as a defendant in a civil lawsuit?" DexKarr asked in a shocked tone. "Are you *mad?*"

The K'kng didn't answer, instead vacating the bar and taking refuge in one of his back rooms. The sound of the door being locked could easily be heard.

DexKarr sighed. Well, it wasn't as though he was paid large amounts of credits for quick and easy work. He *wished* it were easy sometimes. If it were, he could go on a real vacation and not one of his so-called "working" vacations. Somewhere warm, with stupid frilly drinks which both poisoned his innards and provided the pleasant buzz of intoxication.

"Stupid *ch'ktarr.*" He muttered the curse as his combat suit's sensors went to work. DexKarr slowly began to make his way through the nearly empty pit, sidestepping around tables as he searched for clues. He knew from experience that Humans did not often come this far from their home planet, though some of the newer colonists might be tempted.

He snapped his jaws in frustration. A Torokar was one of the deadliest stalkers in the galaxy, using methodical planning to initiate a strategic ambush when the time was right. To DexKarr, only a Depik was a better hunter, and this was arguable. After all, everyone knew about the lethality of a Depik. Their exploits were legendary. A Torokar? Nobody knew precisely what they were capable of, which made DexKarr and his kin all the more terrifying.

Here in this merc pit, he saw nothing which would help his pursuit. Well, this was incorrect. The problem was that he saw too much, courtesy of his sensors. His suit began to pick its way through the DNA and RNA compounds on every surface he passed. It ran a chemical analysis and he immediately blanched as the results started to scroll past on his eye reticle. The scanner identified molting from a Goltar, fecal matter from six different species, hair residue of some Zuul, scales from a species which had actually died out almost a century before, and countless others, at the first two tables alone. His scan would be pointless. Too many mercs had contaminated the area for a proper scan.

"By *J'chuu*, man! Have you not heard of disinfectant, you disgusting creature! Clean this place once in a while!"

Eventually he found the correct table. Two Human females had recently sat together at one of the tables near the back of the merc pit, though his sensors put the time at anywhere from six months to a single week. Considering the rest of the merc pit was devoid of leftover Human DNA, save for a peculiar spot near the bar, he felt it highly likely that one of his targets had met someone else.

DexKarr growled, frustrated. He hadn't known any of his targets could be female. It wasn't really a problem but more a sign his current employer had no idea what he was dealing with. Four names had been highlighted among a list of members of the Kakata Korps, three Humans and one Veetanho, the latter of which gave him pause. He had heard of Humans collaborating with the race who pretty much ran the Mercenary Guild, but never saw definitive proof until the list arrived.

"Antonious Karnga, Samson Tolbert, Zion Jacobs, and Thorpi," he muttered the names aloud. None of them *sounded* female, but then, what did he know about Human names? The final name on his list was obviously Veetanho, but the others? All of them could have been female, and he wouldn't have known the difference.

Irritated, he pulled out his slate and dug into the GalNet to find everything he could regarding Humans. Even with the variety of naming functions within the Galactic Union, humanity seemed to have a knack for the bizarre and unusual. Names, foods, battle tactics, mating behavior, irregularities of their archaic personality matrix...it was enough to drive any sensible Torokar insane. In the back of his mind, a nagging voice reminded him this was something he should have done when he first accepted the job.

His annoyance grew the longer he read. Not only were the Kakata Korps not from one of the primary nationalities which produced the infamous Human merc companies, they were a hodgepodge collective of Liberians, Nigerians, and Americans all crammed into one semi-cohesive unit masquerading as a mercenary company. He was almost glad they had been wiped out by the guild. There was a problem with the list, though. None of the nationalities meant anything to him. Perhaps they were different tribes? His tail began to twitch, showing his agitation.

"I really should have researched Humans more," he groused aloud as his gaze swept through the empty merc pit.

"I know Humans," a meek voice offered from near the bar. The K'kng had come out from his room, though his posture suggested he was ready to flee the moment DexKarr showed any signs of hostility. "I know them. My father owned one, once. Many years past. Human females were here, two weeks ago. A duo but not mated. Strangers.

One dark, one not as dark. I didn't know who the dark one was, but I know of the other. I have seen her here before. I can help…for a price?"

DexKarr breathed slowly as he contemplated the deal. While it was true he could probably intimidate everything he needed out of the cowardly K'kng, there was always the possibility the K'kng could become a potentially valuable information source if handled correctly. Violence could get one far in this galaxy, but credits could ensure they lived long enough to enjoy it. Inhibitions were freer when payouts were involved.

"Ten credits, but maybe we can work something out for more at a later date," DexKarr nodded, trying to sound generous. Truth be told, the amount he was being paid by his employer made anything less than one hundred thousand credits seem like pocket change. He sent a ten-credit chit via his slate to the pit's proprietor. This seemed to relax the K'kng, who smiled.

"Yes, the Human female I recognized is well-known in these parts. Her name is Taryn Lupo. You may also know her boss?"

DexKarr nodded. It was definitely a name he was intimately familiar with. He had a full dossier on her, as well as everyone else who worked for her enigmatic boss, Zorgama. A shiver caused his tail to twitch and his claws to flex. Zorgama's official status was as a trader of some sort. He used his contacts to connect seemingly random buyers with mysterious sellers. More than once had he been investigated for moving antiques from long-dead civilizations against the current occupier's wishes. The MinSha in particular wanted his head on a pole, though they refused to explain *why*, precisely. Unfortunately for them, Zorgama was off-limits to the insectoid aliens for the time being since he had not done anything recently to warrant a certified military operation. Bounty hunters had taken contracts placed on him, but all had failed or been subsequently canceled after Zorgama had a "talk" with the contract's issuer. He had political clout and was an extremely dangerous individual to boot.

Taryn Lupo was implicated in dozens of mysterious incidents but never charged with any crimes. It was widely accepted the young woman was either Zorgama's daughter or a trusted confidante, though they were not necessarily mutually exclusive. She had a reputation among the Besquith as a Human female not to cross, though the precise source of this information was somewhat disreputable, considering the low opinion DexKarr had of Besquith. It was rumored she pulled the trigger that set off the entire Kinndee Incident on Sh'laa IV, but he was dismissive of that. She was not the boogeyman, sent to haunt criminal elements in their sleep. No, that title was for him alone.

If it truly were Taryn Lupo the K'kng had seen, then the records would show that one of Zorgama's ships had docked at the starport. His file on the Human female showed she always used a Zorgama-owned ship, though she rotated through them with random frequency. DexKarr nodded as he dug into the records of the starport remotely. His slate was customized and highly illegal, courtesy of a friend he had done a favor for long ago, and the firewalls of the station database were defeated in short order.

"There you are," DexKarr grunted as he found the *Velut Luna*. No flight plan had been filed with the local traffic control, naturally. Locations like Valyn were oftentimes frequented by all sorts of disreputable individuals who liked to keep their comings and goings a secret. It disgusted him on a visceral level. It was too easy to slip in and out of places such as this, where security could only be described as non-existent. He'd once slipped past every single security ship and drone on Capital Planet to make a kill while his ship openly declared who he was and where he was headed, both ways. *Kids these days,* he mentally grumbled. *No respect for the old ways.* "Well, it's a lead, I guess."

The K'kng hooted again. "They left with a female Besquith, the Humans did. I think the dark one hired her. I wasn't listening too closely."

"I understand," DexKarr said, knowing the K'kng had listened in as closely as he could. Instead of pushing the issue, he pocketed the slate and gave the pit owner a toothy grin. The K'kng cowered. There was a Besquith involved now. Things were beginning to look up for him. In battle, Humans were to be respected, but a Besquith? They were something else entirely.

He looked forward to killing the Besquith almost as much as completing the job.

* * * * *

Chapter Three

Velut Luna, **85 Km Above Zav'ax, It'iek System**

"I knew this was going to burn a lot of fuel," Taryn complained as they cleared the atmosphere. She quickly mapped out a new flight plan to the gate for optimal fuel conservation. It was close, but she somehow managed it. Sunshine, despite the massive amount of adrenaline in her system, saw and was impressed. Taryn had figured out the flight path while tweaking the program in less time than it took a Besquith to eat a Jivool. Granted, her current measurement was based on what she had seen Dref-na do on the landing pad not too long ago.

"Are they going to try and stop us?" Sunshine asked as she watched the Tri-V display for any sign of pursuit. She couldn't see any but there was no way to tell how quickly an armed response would occur. The stargate was rather closer to the planet than Earth's due to It'iek's smaller primary star, but thanks to their detour to collect Kl'nk'nnk, the *Velut Luna* was also on the wrong side of the planet.

"Probably going to try," Taryn confirmed. "I'll know more when we get to the gate side of the planet."

"What happens then?"

"We run, more than likely," came the terse response. Taryn sighed and shook her head. "Sorry. I don't know what happened down there. I'm just glad this old tub was retrofitted and everything actually worked. I've never done a hard burn in atmo before."

"I'm going to go check on the Jeha and Dref-na," Sunshine decided as she gently rested her hand on Taryn's shoulder. She really didn't know what else to do for her. "Hey, you did good. You got us out of there alive. Thank you."

"Don't thank me just yet," Taryn pointed out. "Wait until we get to the next refueling point in one piece."

Sunshine nodded and moved to the center of the ship. Thanks to the constant acceleration, the *Velut Luna* still had some gravity. It allowed her to move quickly through the narrow corridor to the infirmary, where she knew Dref-na would be patching up her wounds from the impromptu firefight. Beneath her feet she could feel the constant hum of the powerful engines the *Velut Luna* sported. Eventually, the steady thrust from the engines would disappear once they were lined up for their shot at the stargate, but until then she would enjoy the freedom of movement within the ship's confines.

Inside the dedicated infirmary she found Dref-na applying a nanite aerosol spray to the wound on her upper arm. It was the only area which she seemed concerned with, ignoring the various scrapes and minor cuts across her throat and chest. Sunshine watched in silence as the Besquith checked to see how well the nanites were healing the large hole in her arm before setting the dispenser back on the wall. The magnetic wall mount held it firmly in place so when the *Velut Luna* reached zero-G, it wouldn't float around and become a danger.

"You have questions, tiny fierceness," Dref-na commented as she turned her golden eyes upon the diminutive Sunshine. Dref-na brought herself lower so Sunshine could look her in the face. "Ask."

"Are you injured?" Sunshine began, her eyes drifting to the bloody, matted fur near the wound.

Dref-na snorted, amused, and shook her head. "I was wounded, but I am not injured."

"There's a difference?"

"Indeed," Dref-na stated. "Wounded means you can fight. Injured means you are bait."

"Oh," Sunshine paused for a moment, considering. "Did you need to kill them all?" she finally asked.

"Yes," Dref-na answered. There was no anger or regret in her voice; it was simply a statement of fact. "They were trying to prevent you from leaving the planet. I don't know why, but they were prepared to capture you at any cost, even if it meant harming you."

"Any idea why?" Sunshine asked. She had her own theories but wanted to see if the Besquith was thinking along the same lines.

"Ransom," Dref-na replied almost instantly.

"Ransom?" Not expecting this, Sunshine motioned for the Besquith to continue.

"Yes, tiny fierceness," Dref-na nodded slowly. "You don't understand how tempting a mercenary company commander is as a target for ransom, especially when one only has a few bodyguards around. Some of the biggest companies out there—not Humans, because your species is insane—have at least a company of mercs around the chief commanders of a company at all times. Hostages are just one of the many ways corporations will use to try and exert influence over a mercenary company."

"I didn't think of that," Sunshine admitted, silently kicking herself. Kidnapping was almost a national sport in Liberia. *Had been, at least.* She should have expected something like this. "Back in Monrovia this was always an issue. Stupid of me. The *bass* would be disappointed."

"I found some thin rope in here," Dref-na said suddenly. "It was fun to play with. Do you think Taryn Lupo would mind if I kept it?"

"What?" Sunshine asked. The Besquith pulled out a thin rope over three meters long. It appeared to be a reinforced textile wrapped around a narrow, flexible band of rope. The teenaged mercenary recognized it immediately and grinned. "Oh, paracord. Cheap stuff. I used to tie knots with it to pass the time when I was bored back—anyway, I don't think Taryn would care. Just ask her."

"I shall," Dref-na said and returned the paracord to her pouch. "It was wrapped around a magnetized infrared light and didn't appear necessary, merely cosmetic. Playing with it was…soothing."

Sunshine nodded. "I understand completely."

"We've got company," Taryn interrupted them over the comms. "Dref-na, I need a copilot. Sunshine, make sure Kl'nk'nnk is secure in the medical bay in case we have to do another hard burn to the gate."

"What? Is Taryn planning on sneaking out of here unnoticed?" Sunshine wondered.

The Besquith chuckled. "She's done crazier things in her young life," Dref-na answered as she hurried forward to join Taryn. Sunshine watched her go for a moment before remembering to check on the wounded Jeha. She moved to the attached sterile surgical suite where the Jeha was lying on one of the secured, enclosed beds in the room. A steady hissing sound told her Kl'nk'nnk was still alive and that the nanites being pumped into the enclosed bed were doing their job of keeping her that way. They were very similar to what Dref-na had used on her arm, only multiplied by ten in their effectiveness and potency. Sunshine was amazed. Whoever this Mr. Z was, he was definitely well funded. She hoped to meet him one day, given all Taryn had done for her since K'tamyl's Merc Pit on Valyn, and thank him.

Once she was certain the Jeha was situated, she moved back to the command deck where Taryn and Dref-na were both staring at the Tri-V display with fierce intensity. Sunshine waited patiently for a few moments until Taryn finally grunted.

"Those are cruisers all right." Taryn sounded frustrated to Sunshine. "We saw them when we were coming in, remember?"

"Are those XenSha cruisers?" Dref-na asked her.

"Yep," Taryn nodded. "I don't think those are XenSha piloting them, though."

"They're moving toward the gate," Sunshine realized as she watched the display. She pointed at the ships, which were spread out perfectly to cover one another. "Their sensors are going to pick us before we get to the gate. We have to find a different way."

"This ship only has one way to travel through hyperspace, Sunshine," Taryn informed her in a quiet voice.

Sunshine scratched her chin thoughtfully, her dark eyes locked on the Tri-V before them. "Those are *Kona*-class cruisers…why is this sticking in my mind?"

"I have no idea," Dref-na replied, her mouth open in a Besquith grimace. "Taryn? You need to figure out what we're going to do next."

"Wait," Sunshine said. She closed her eyes as she used her pinplants to dig into the memory banks onboard the *Velut Luna*. She had seen something before while searching for information. It had flitted through her mind at such a speed she wasn't entirely certain she had actually seen it. She pushed deeper into her own search history and tried to rediscover the rabbit trail from before. She suddenly grinned. "We can get away, if your ship is sneaky."

"Mr. Z has this ship retrofitted with non-reactive material on the hull," Taryn answered cautiously. "It's stealthy, but with them between us and the gate, they'll pick us up even with the non-reactive coating. There's nothing we can do except hope we get lucky."

"A long time ago on Earth, there were submarines in the oceans," Sunshine stated as she pointed toward the rear of the cruiser battle group displayed on the Tri-V. "They couldn't see behind them very well because of the cov—no, *cavitation* of the water caused by the propellers passing through the water. So, American submarines created something called a towed array, where the sensors were set to drift far behind the ship to be, uh, towed. If the enemy tried to sneak up on them, they would find them."

"So?" Taryn asked.

"It was a *passive* system," Sunshine stated. She jabbed at the Tri-V display. "Your memory banks say the *Kona*-class cruisers were built by the XenSha, right? Those are the rabbit-looking mercs?"

"Tasty little snacks," Dref-na added. "You can never eat just one."

"Ye-e-es," Taryn let the word draw out as she waited for Sunshine to continue. "And?"

"The engines create a large heat signature and electromagnetic bloom behind the ship, blocking their sensors," Sunshine said excitedly as she found more information. "It was a design flaw of the *Kona*. To fix the issue, the XenSha added the Human equivalent of a towed array system: remote disposable satellites to keep pace with the ship to watch their rear. They cover four areas behind the plume of the engines. It gives them complete overlap, but there's a flaw in this as well. These don't have the power to run active sensors for long. They're passive, to conserve on power."

"How do you know all this stuff?" Taryn asked, irritated at last. "I only let you into the first layer of my system."

"I...don't know," Sunshine reluctantly answered. Everything within the systems of the *Velut Luna* seemed to be laid out for her. There were no barriers within the system she could see. "I didn't see any blocked areas in your data banks. I'm sorry. I didn't know I wasn't supposed to dig."

Taryn sighed. "This was part of what I wanted to talk to you about, you have one hell of a pinplant if you can defeat *my* security.

Argh, you frustrate me a little. We'll discuss my security protocols—and your *violations* of them—later. Okay, so they *do* have a blind spot, though a small one. We're going to have to reduce the signature of our engine, which means we'll be coasting for most of the journey to the gate. Plus, we can't emit any electronic emissions. Zero gravity."

"Kl'nk'nnk is sedated in the med bay," Dref-na stated. She jabbed a long claw at her arm. "I'm healing, and tiny fierceness is uninjured. Zero gravity shouldn't hurt anybody."

"The moment they turn away from the gate and direct their active sensors toward the planet, we're toast," Taryn pointed out.

"How far behind them are we?" Sunshine asked, curious.

"Fifteen thousand kilometers, but we're gaining at one hundred kilometers per minute," Taryn responded as she checked her data. "We're twenty-two minutes out from the gate at current acceleration."

"Increase speed by two-thirds for exactly six minutes," Sunshine instructed without hesitation. Somehow, she knew precisely how to avoid detection of the cruisers hunting them, and if it wasn't such an exhilarating experience, she would have worried. There would be time for concern later. "Then kill the engines. The initial thrust will increase our speed enough so when they make their turn from the gate—probably one thousand kilometers out—and their active sensors are blasting the planet, we'll be two hundred kilometers from the nearest satellite array but otherwise unpowered, according to their sensors. Close, but still safe since we'll be running dark. We power up once we're even with them while they're turning away, and we accelerate for the gate again. By the time they realize what just happened we will be thirty seconds from the gate, and they'll be too far committed in their change of direction to adjust. They'll get one shot off at us, perhaps, but we'll be through the gate by the time any missiles arrive."

"How did you—You know what? I don't care how," Taryn said as she ran the numbers through the ship. A moment later she grinned. "Ship agrees with your math. You scare the hell out of me sometimes."

"Will this work?" Dref-na asked. "I always envisioned dying on a planet leading a charge into the enemy, not among wreckage in space. Dying in space is not the way I want to go."

"We'll find out soon enough," Taryn murmured. She checked the ship's chronometer. "In about six minutes we'll either be wreckage in space or home free and on our way to…. Bishwanath Station. It's the closest neutral refueling point outside this system I could find."

Gravity increased throughout the ship as the *Velut Luna* accelerated. The ship seemed to hum under Taryn's controls, and the little ship gained slowly on the cruiser battle group.

Sunshine nervously chewed her bottom lip, worried. The numbers and solution had simply appeared in her head and she had no idea *how*. It had been a recurring theme ever since she had been "pinned" back on Earth. Combined with her improved English, she was terrified someone had messed around with her brain.

There were a few possibilities she could think of, none of them good. The best-case scenario was also the worst: someone had implanted some kind of alien supercomputer in her brain during the pinning process. It meant someone had violated her trust, going beyond what she had agreed to in order to do…what? She didn't know. There were certain gaps in her knowledge, mostly social norms and cues she used to know but now couldn't recall. Living on the streets as a small teenaged girl in the middle of Monrovia had taught her how to survive, to watch the body language of others and determine if they were a threat or not. She could still do this, although in a different manner. She had been able to see just how the Jivool would react, though there was no reason for her to be able to do so. They were *aliens*, and the first Jivool she had ever seen in her life. She should have been terrified or, at the very least, awe-struck at seeing real live alien lifeforms.

Zion and Thorpi did something to me when we were in Miami, she thought as Taryn expertly killed the engines exactly at the six-minute-mark.

She shoved her concern aside. She could always dwell on it later. Gravity ceased and Sunshine gripped the back of Dref-na's seat as her feet left the deck. The *Velut Luna* stopped accelerating and maintained a constant speed as all eyes turned to the cruisers in front of them. They looked dangerously close on the Tri-V but outside they were still many kilometers away.

Just as she predicted, the cruiser battle group turned when they were roughly one thousand kilometers from the stargate. Coasting along like a specter in the night, the only way the cruisers would be able to detect the *Velut Luna* before Taryn wanted them to was if they collided with one of the cruisers or satellites.

They were very close, but just as Sunshine predicted, they remained undetected…mostly.

* * *

Clan Kanonko Cruiser *Dark Infinity*, It'iek System

XenSha tech was a curious thing when compared to the rest of the Galactic Union. It performed precisely as the XenSha designed it to. However, *understanding* the quirks of XenSha technology and psychology was oftentimes best left to the species themselves, and not for those who had picked up the cruisers at a cut-rate deal without so much as a series of trial runs. Bad things happened to those who took shortcuts. Space was inherently dangerous, especially for a species as perpetually poor as the Pushtal.

"Curse these XenSha ships!" Commander Drayher of Clan Ka-nonko snarled as he slammed his furry paw down on the arm of his captain's chair. He proceeded to espouse, quite vocally, just *how* and *why* the XenSha should be dragged through the streets by their ears and pelted with rocks or anything else the commander could think of. It was a familiar and frequent rant for his crew, most of whom had been with the ship's CO since they first accepted the contract to protect the mining colony two years before. None paid him any mind, focusing intently on their tasks at hand.

Having a reputation as nothing more than scum and pirates often had an undesired effect on other species when they dealt with the Pushtal. Many assumed the tiger-like aliens would be either stupid or naïve when it came to business deals. While this was true regarding complex contractual agreements, every Pushtal could add and sub-tract fairly well. They clearly understood the concept of money. The Pushtal on these ships were paid, and paid well, for their discretion regarding anything which might happen on Zav'ax.

Perhaps they were a little too focused on ignoring their com-mander, so much so they were not paying full attention to their sta-tions. It was thirty seconds before one of the satellite sensor techs noticed the loss of Sat-3. There was a quick check via diagnostics to see if they had simply lost connection with the satellite again. Sat-3 was notorious for randomly dropping signal before coming back online a few moments later. Once the diagnostic was complete, it quickly became apparent to the technician that something had hap-pened to Sat-3. She opened her mouth to speak but paused, uncer-tain. XenSha technology was very fickle, designed specifically for the XenSha. She believed her kind belonged on a planet's surface in combat, not floating through space in a 3D tactical environment, even *if* her race was fairly competent at it. Despite the commander's rants regarding the readiness of XenSha tech, it was rather easy to tell when something on one of the cruisers was not working. Figuring out *why* it wasn't working, on the other hand, was something else entirely.

"Commander Drayher?" she called out timidly. The glowering visage of her commanding officer turned on her, and she suddenly wished she had not spoken up.

"Yes?"

"Sat-3 just dropped again, Commander," she said and pointed at the Tri-V display before her. The commander punched in a few commands at his own console, swore violently when he brought up the wrong station, and finally pulled up the right station so he was able to see what the technician was talking about.

Stupid XenSha piece of… he thought acidly. "Did you run a diagnostic?"

"Yes, Commander."

"And?"

"Still not there, Commander."

"Try it again," he ordered. Seconds passed before the technician looked up at him. She had a fearful expression on her face. He was not going to like what she had to say next.

"Commander, Sat-3 is simply…*gone*."

* * *

Velut Luna, It'iek System

"I can't *believe* you ran into a satellite!" Sunshine declared looking at the cloud of debris from the destroyed satellite surrounding the bow of the small ship.

"It's not like I planned on it!" Taryn snapped back, her hands flying across the console. "Oh my God, Mister Zorgama is going to *kill* me!"

"Is that a dent in the hull?" Dref-na asked as she pointed toward the ship schematics on another, smaller display. Sunshine peered closely and saw the small divot in the outline of the ship.

"Looks like it to me," Sunshine agreed. "I don't think that'll buff out."

"Big dent," Dref-na added. "At least two meters wide. Oh wow, there goes the paint job. That is not an unnoticeable scratch."

"Shut up! I'm so dead, I'm so dead…"

* * *

Clan Kanonko Cruiser *Dark Infinity*, It'iek System

"Commander, Sat-1 is picking up a scattered signal from the last known location of Sat-3," a different technician called out. Commander Drayher leaned back in his ill-fitting command seat and brought up the console in question. The data flowed to his chair, and he nodded sagely, as though he understood every little morsel of data collected there. He hoped they were under the impression he knew what he was looking at, but much like the rest of the XenSha-built ship, the systems within were not easily discernible for the Pushtal. Not for the first time did he wish they'd simply swapped out the XenSha tech for some sort of hybrid type he could understand.

The Jeha made quality tech, he thought tiredly.

Drayher did not know his crew already knew he had no idea what he was looking at. Two years on contract at this station had allowed them to pick up on his habits and tells. One of the easiest for them to discover was that Drayher became calmer and more studious when he did not know what was going on. An admirable feat to be sure, though when something *did* happen, he became very excitable.

"Give me options, Technician," Commander Drayher said. The technician blinked. The commander pressed. "What could have happened to Sat-3?"

"Uh..."

"Anytime now," Drayher pressed.

Sat-1's satellite technician swallowed nervously. "Sat-3 is...destroyed?" the tech offered. He was fraught with nervous tension.

"That makes sense," Drayher nodded a second time. "Did it hit an asteroid?"

"No commander," Sat-3's technician interjected, letting her voice be heard. "Active sensors would have detected it as it passed by."

"Was it shot down?" Drayher wondered, mostly to himself, before he chuffed at the idea. "No, the sensors would have detected the energy needed to either fire kinetics or a missile."

"Perhaps something rammed into it?"

"Entropy!" Commander Drayher suddenly screamed. Something *had* rammed into Sat-3. More than likely it was the very thing they were hunting. Somehow the spies that had infiltrated the planet and assassinated one of B'Hono Corporation's senior VPs had gotten into close range of the *Dark Infinity* without being detected. If they escaped from him now, he could probably kiss the sweetest contract his clan had goodbye. This would not sit well with his First Claw back home. "Bring us back around! Turn our sensors toward the stargate! Now!"

"We're already turning the wrong way, commander!" the Pushtal on the conn stated. He sounded annoyed. "Reverse the course now, and we'll burn too much fuel. Recommend we continue on our present course and make a complete circle."

"Fine, do it!" Commander Drayher shouted as he looked at his weapons team. "Missiles? Guns? Anything?"

"Can't shoot at something we don't see, Commander."

"Entropy!"

"Commander! Gate activation!" a sensor tech called out from his station. "Still no sign of whatever—There! Engine plume, energy signature identical to the *Velut Luna*! Targeting…No lock, repeat, no lock. Gate's open…and closed. Sir—sir, they got away."

"ENTROPY!"

* * *

Velut Luna, Hyperspace, Enroute to Bishwanath Station

"That was too close," Sunshine grumbled as she tried to figure out how to activate the magnetic boots Taryn had let her borrow in order to move more easily around the ship. She looked at Taryn, who was slumped over the console. Her face was hidden in the crook of her elbow. If Sunshine hadn't known better, she would have assumed Taryn was asleep. "Hey, Taryn? Don't worry. I'll explain to your boss, and I'll clear everything up."

"But the dent…" Taryn's voice trailed off as she moaned piteously.

"I'll pay for it," Sunshine offered.

"It's not that," Taryn mumbled in a bitter voice. "I kinda borrowed the *Velut Luna* without, you know…asking first."

"Oh."

"I mean, he's never said no before…and he did say I should meet with you."

"I see." She didn't but there was no way Sunshine was about to tell the distraught woman this.

"He's gonna kill me!" Taryn wailed. "I scratched his *baby*!"

"I doubt it…" Sunshine said, though she was not entirely convinced herself. She had never met the guy, after all, and men were weird about odd and unusual things. She shifted the conversation to something less aggravating for the distraught woman. "I won't let him. I'll have Dref-na eat him."

"No, tiny fierceness," Dref-na replied from behind her. "I am not foolish enough to cross Zorgama. I've heard the stories. I've seen him in action, once. She's on her own with him."

"Oh, you're not being very helpful!"

"I'm so dead…" Taryn moaned as she picked her head up from the console. She looked horrible. "I don't drink, but I could really get wasted right now."

"It won't make the problem go away." Sunshine frowned. She hated mind-altering substances like drugs and alcohol, though not for the usual reasons. Her own ghosts threatened to raise their ugly heads, but she squashed those memories down, hard. This was not the time for remembering. "You'll feel worse after. Trust me."

"I'm going to go throw up," Taryn said as she activated her magnetic boots before standing up. Swaying slightly as she adjusted to the footing, she made her way to her berthing space, leaving Sunshine alone with Dref-na.

"I'm going to take a nap," the Besquith announced. "Bishwanath Station is seven days away, and I will want to be rested before we arrive. Plus the nanite spray is making me sleepy."

"How's the Jeha?" she asked. Dref-na's wide maw split open into a terrifying imitation of a Human smile.

"Go and see," Dref-na answered. "The sedation will keep her asleep for days, but will accelerate the healing process. She should be awake by the time we get to Bishwanath Station."

"So basically, I have time to kill and nobody to talk to," Sunshine grumbled.

"You have sims, tiny fierceness." Dref-na shrugged apologetically. "Space travel is about occupying yourself in the downtime. It is the life of a merc. Personally? I'm going to get some sleep." The Besquith walked toward her private berthing area, leaving Sunshine alone with her thoughts.

After a quick glance around the cockpit and not seeing anything interesting, Sunshine strapped herself into the copilot's chair and linked up with the ship's database. She wanted to learn everything she could about Bishwanath Station, as well as try to figure out just what was back on the mining world which would make the B'Hono Corporation try to kill them.

She wasn't sure if she would find anything, but it wouldn't be from a lack of effort.

* * *

Docking Ring E, Bishwanath Station, Ampheon System

Vah Gorna walked the corridors of Bishwanath Station in a daze, her mind scattered. The crew of the shuttle had been rather kind to her, beyond what they had been paid by the Information Guild to do on her behalf. It was a racial thing, she knew. It was hard for any race to look at the diminutive CozSha and not feel any empathy. In Human terms, the CozSha were simply *adorable*.

It was both a blessing and a curse at times. It was hard for the majority of aliens who worked with the CozSha to remain angry at them for long. Besides their looks, the CozSha were just too efficient and good at their jobs to get rid of. While many races were cogs in the great machine of the galaxy, the CozSha were often viewed as the grease which made everything run smoothly.

All this went through the back of her mind as she blindly navigated the run-down corridors of the station. It was clear it had seen better days. Perhaps dozens of years before it had been a shiny new station, but now Bishwanath was little more than a cosmic joke.

Vah Gorna's mental haze continued to cloud her sense of direction and purpose. Aimless walking made one a target, especially in the crime-ridden Bishwanath Station. More than one criminal element sized up the young CozSha before dismissing her. *Berthing,* she told herself as she became somewhat aware of her surroundings. *I need to find berthing somewhere. How though? Oh, right.* She accessed her pinplants for information and found there were berthing units with short-term rental agreements at the end of a long corridor on her current level. She could stay there, gather herself, and wait for further orders. *The Administrator will find use for me,* she thought as her mind drifted once again. *I am efficient at my job. He needs me still, doesn't he? Of course, he does. I am very efficient.*

Someone bumped into her, nearly knocking her over. Vah, lost in a swirl of thoughts, mumbled an apology of sorts before continuing down the long corridor. She was unaware of the trio of Zuparti watching her go, comparing her face to the image on their slate.

* * *

Xeno Guild Outpost, North American District, Earth, Sol System

I t was time for him to leave the outpost and head for his next waypoint.

The Humans had finally decided to tighten their hold over the system and had politely asked most non-combatants and neutral parties to leave while they conducted operations around their home world. The Merchant Guild threw a fit, which was to be expected. Humans imported quite a bit of GalTech into their system, and any sort of tariff system was going to ruffle more than a few feathers. While they claimed it wasn't anything of the sort, he knew from long experience the Humans were not to be trusted.

"Humanity is a poison which must be purged from the galaxy," he said before shutting down the outpost and taking his personal shuttle into orbit. There he joined with the Xeno Guild ship, *Kara Berkat*, before going through the stargate. His next destination was planned long in advance since it was almost impossible to gather all five Senior Commissioners of the Xeno Guild together without months of preparation. It was time for their yearly face-to-face, which he detested. Not because the others would see him, but because it was a waste of time. The Administrator wouldn't be there, as usual, but would remote in.

Somehow.

It was infuriating that the Administrator seemed to defy the rules of interstellar communication and the restrictions of physics. It didn't matter where in the galaxy they held their yearly meeting, the Administrator, as head of the Xeno Guild, always seemed to be able to have instantaneous communication to whatever station they were at. It was vexing for the Senior Commissioner, and he was not one who enjoyed not having all the information available.

At least this year it would be held at the Xeno Guild headquarters, which was hidden from the other guilds and not actually on Capital Planet. Only the pilots had the coordinates, and they weren't talking. He would know. He once tried to bribe one of the Pendal pilots to sell him the coordinates and was flatly denied. They took their jobs very seriously.

The guild would look at the many problems at hand. He offered just one solution. Unfortunately, it was not something he could accomplish at this moment. The time frame for his plan to come to fruition was still months away, perhaps longer. He'd been patient this long; he could last a little bit longer. Until then, he would keep his head down, not espouse any opinions regarding Humans, and hope like hell whatever was going on at his facility at Zav'ax was cleared up before anyone noticed anything odd about the B'Hono Corporation.

He didn't need any other distractions right now. His endgame was still far away, though the first steps of the final leg were at hand. If all went according to plan, he would be the new Guild Master of the Xeno Guild within one year.

If he failed, the galaxy would burn upon *their* arrival. It was the one thing he and Peepo agreed upon.

* * *

Valyn Starport, Valyn, Entilles System

For six days, DexKarr sat at the starport inside his ship. Waiting for something, anything, which could lead him to his target's destination. All his usual contacts had suddenly gone silent, and he didn't know why. It was as though the galaxy was holding its breath for something. He found it disconcerting.

DexKarr managed to build up a decent psychological profile of all three of the Kakata Korps' officers during the down time, using the information he found on Humans from their region on Earth as well as scraps of information passed along to the Mercenary Guild by their leader before his execution. The problem was that he did not like what he had found.

Official reports stated all three command officers were dead after the Battle of Monrovia. The city had then suffered some sort of catastrophic disaster, resulting in the deaths of almost three million Humans. The Mercenary Guild blamed the local politicians as well as the Kakata Korps, though nobody could say for certain what had happened. Everything from a containment failure of a reactor to a massive ship crashing into the city had been proposed and rejected. It was one of those official mysteries where the simplest theory was

96 | JASON CORDOVA

the truth, and fear caused everyone to deny it. DexKarr was mildly interested to know what the truth really was.

He also found one additional footnote posted by one Captain Beeko. It seemed the Humans of Earth, once the occupation began, stopped passing their VOWS save for those in the Liberian nation-state. This pleased Peepo for some reason, but the captain had urged caution before celebrating these results. DexKarr frowned as he re-read the passage for a fifth time. *What was so important about the Humans passing their VOWS if Peepo was just going to kill them all?*

Nothing made sense to him. Not Peepo's invasion of Earth, the subsequent rebellion, and, most especially, the destruction of Monrovia. He brought up the official TOE of the Korps on his slate. The three names of the company commanders were all highlighted on-screen. Grumbling, he flipped through and scanned the list of names of every single registered mercenary within the Korps. The highlights continued to catch his eye, though, so he disengaged them. Now every name was the same on his screen, which made it a little easier.

"Who are *you?*" he hissed as something caught his eye. Using his claw, he zoomed in on a name which had escaped his notice previously. It was a single name, much like Thorpi, and he hadn't even noticed it due to it not being in one of the three largest companies of the Korps. How had he missed this before? His jaw dropped as her status, due to the filing of her VOWS and her age, did not have her listed purely as an officer in the mercenary company. She was instead listed as a beneficiary and junior officer cadet of the company commander, Mulbah Luo. DexKarr smiled, triumphant. He now knew who the female with Taryn Lupo was, and who he needed to hunt.

A single chime of his slate caused him to close the Korps' TOE and read the new message. His smile grew wider, and he began to warm up his ship's engines. A Besquith and two Humans had recently kidnapped a Jeha under the employ of the B'Hono Corporation from Zav'ax before disappearing into hyperspace. According to his man, the descriptions of the Humans were "female mercenaries." Unless they were suddenly in a galaxy filled with Human female mercenaries in the company of a lone Besquith, these were the individuals he was looking for. His profile of Taryn Lupo suggested she liked to hide out at seedy places where civilized society did not like to tread. He quickly pulled up a list of destinations no self-respecting Human would normally be seen at, and his eyes immediately drifted to Bishwanath Station.

"*I* wouldn't even want to be seen there," he muttered softly. Something in the back of his mind told him he was probably correct. Bishwanath was exactly the sort of place she would run to after pulling a job.

A harsh pounding on his loading bay door distracted him. He scowled at the interruption. Setting the slate down, he looked at the security cam feed via his Tri-V display to see who it was. His frown deepened. Three rather large individuals filled most of his screen, along with a short, squat Veetanho—*no*, he mentally corrected, *that's an Aposo*—in the front of the group. Two Lumar were immediately behind the Aposo, and behind them loomed one of the galaxy's most dangerous creatures—a deep purple Oogar roughly the size of a house.

DexKarr sighed and killed the Tri-V. Leaving the engines on idle, he quickly shrugged on his vest armor and double-checked the mounted railgun. Satisfied, he grabbed his slate before moving aft to the loading bay.

"Can I help you?" DexKarr asked over the intercom.

"Docking fees are due," a rough-sounding voice replied. DexKarr rolled his eyes. He'd paid the starport docking authority for a month in advance when he'd first arrived, since he wasn't certain how long he would be on the planet. Plus, he was fairly certain the docking master was a Sidar who rarely left her office. Which meant these upstanding individuals of Valynian society were the local criminal element he had been warned about by the docking master upon his initial arrival.

"Already paid it," DexKarr replied irritably.

"It went up," the Aposo told him, a smug look on his rodent-like face. "Open the doors and pay up."

"Or what?" DexKarr asked, amused. "Your Oogar is a big boy, but he's not strong enough to open up this door."

"No, he's not," the Aposo laughed. "The quad laser anti-aircraft gun I have 'appropriated' and pointed at your engines should be, though."

DexKarr scowled. This was unfortunate, though not entirely unforeseen. He knew Valyn was a rough place, and to think someone wouldn't try to shake him down was absurd. He just hadn't expected heavy weaponry to be involved. Perhaps this criminal element was a little smarter than most? More than likely, they were just better funded. This little tidbit of information would normally be something worth investigating, but now he had other, more pressing matters to attend to.

"Let me unseal the door and then we can negotiate your terms," DexKarr informed them.

"Sure, let's negotiate." The Aposo was evidently amused by all this.

The door hissed and slowly opened, allowing the late afternoon's fading sunlight to flood into the darkened storage bay. DexKarr waited for the door to fully open before stepping out onto the landing platform. His sensors immediately found the anti-aircraft gun, and he made a mental note of its location. There were three Sidar squatting next to the large weapon. While his sensors marked all potential hostiles in the area, his eyes remained locked on the short, squat Aposo in the front of the group. He wanted to make certain the Aposo knew precisely what it had unleashed upon itself.

The Lumar stepped back, surprise evident upon their faces. They might not be known as the brightest in the galaxy, but even they knew that when a Torokar was involved, all cards were on the table. The Aposo seemed alarmed by his appearance as well. Only the Oogar seemed unimpressed by the five-meter long reptilian alien's appearance. If anything, DexKarr guessed the Oogar was actually hoping for a fight. It was what they were best at, after all.

For a brief moment, DexKarr considered negotiating with the criminals, before tossing the idea aside. It wouldn't do any good, and he was certain it would lead to some sort of gunfight which could potentially damage his ship. No, it was best to catch them unawares. They did outnumber him, after all. The last thing he wanted was to give them a fair fight.

His mounted railgun swiveled and targeted the three individuals working the bulky anti-aircraft gun. Without warning the railgun opened fire. The Sidar died before they realized they were under attack. For good measure DexKarr put four additional rounds into the large gun. He didn't want any survivors, if there happened to be any, to take a parting shot at him as he left.

Swiveling his hips slightly, his tail lashed out and caught the furthest Lumar with the tip. With a loud *crack!* the Lumar dropped to the landing pad as four hundred pounds of pressure impacted on a four-millimeter wide spot just above its temple. It was either dead or permanently brain damaged. DexKarr wasn't sure. He'd missed his intended spot by three centimeters, which would have killed the Lumar instantly and without doubt.

You're out of practice, old one.

DexKarr lunged forward and grabbed the second Lumar's face with his teeth. For an instant, he felt the scream of the surprised

Lumar tickle his tongue before he bit the alien's head in half. Crunching on bone as he chewed, he used his right leg to kick the dead Lumar away before spitting out its ruined face. There would be no doubts about this one.

The Oogar roared and swung a meaty right paw at his face. DexKarr, knowing his balance was off-center, took the brunt of the blow on his muscular neck and staggered back, stunned. If he had been caught unawares the blow would have been disabling. However, DexKarr understood how to take a punch. Years of training instilled automatic muscular and psychological responses. The worst thing was to panic if he suddenly became disoriented, as he currently was.

Instead of wildly defending himself, DexKarr stepped back and used his tail to distract the Oogar. The large purple alien had already seen the amount of damage his tail could do and wisely avoided it, but he failed to recognize the feint until DexKarr pivoted and punted the Aposo directly into the Oogar's chest. The short, burly alien squealed in pain from the blow, and the Oogar, not knowing what else to do, caught the Aposo in mid-flight.

Giving himself a quick shake, DexKarr moved to the Oogar's left and closed the distance. The Oogar was clearly caught off guard by this maneuver. After all, everyone knew the best way to fight an Oogar was to not fight one at all; if that failed, keep a safe distance and use heavy weaponry. The Oogar hurriedly dropped his Aposo buddy and brought his large, powerful claws up and tried to remove DexKarr's head with a second punch.

Instead of dodging the blow, DexKarr simply *ate* the Oogar's furry paw.

The Oogar's face shifted from enraged to surprised pain and finally terror as DexKarr bit through the mass of fur and sinew. Now it was the Oogar's turn to panic, and he frantically tried to jerk his claw out of the Torokar's mouth. This was the worst possible thing he could have done, since the only thing holding the Oogar's hand to his wrist was a thin strip of ligament and some skin. The Oogar's own strength worked against him, and he suddenly staggered back, free from DexKarr, but missing his large paw.

Rage combined with shock made the Oogar stumble back another step as he stared dumbly at his bloody stump. DexKarr spit out the purple paw and looked at the Oogar, who was clearly done with the fight. However, a message needed to be sent. A lone bounty hunter was not an individual to be trifled with, no matter what race they might be.

Stepping on the fallen Aposo and crushing his larynx, DexKarr lashed out with his own claws. The sharp, diamond-hard claws ripped into the massive belly of the Oogar, who roared angrily. Staggering, the giant purple alien dropped to a knee as his good arm struggled to protect his bloodied stomach. Instead of delivering the killing blow, DexKarr moved back to the Aposo, who was clearly having breathing issues. He picked the small rodent up off the landing pad and shook him slightly.

"I think we're done here," DexKarr growled. "Unless you have anything to add?"

The unconscious Aposo didn't respond, unsurprisingly. DexKarr grunted and tossed him to the ground before looking at the Oogar. The severely wounded alien shook his head and wheezed. "No, we're good."

"Better move before I lift off," DexKarr warned as he boarded his ship.

Once everything was secured, he checked his security cams from the pilot's seat. The Oogar had dragged the Aposo out of the blast area of his engines. Neither of the Lumar had moved, and DexKarr doubted the Oogar would rush to haul their carcasses out of the way.

Powering up his engines, DexKarr lifted off and headed off world. His next destination? The It'iek System and the planet Zav'ax.

He dictated a brief summation for his employer and fired off the message as he exited Valyn's atmosphere. It was prudent for him to keep the individual updated of his progress just in case he ultimately failed and someone else was hired to complete the job. There was always the risk of oversharing, and the employer giving the clues and leads DexKarr had discovered to someone else with a lower asking price, but experience told him this would not be the case for the current job. This particular individual preferred both anonymity and secrecy. Hiring multiple assassins would risk them fighting one another for the prize, which could cause the trail to grow cold.

He shook off the thought and focused on his prey. Common sense suggested they would have moved on by this point, probably to Bishwanath, but going to Zav'ax was far better than sticking around Valyn and waiting for something else to happen. Anywhere else was preferable to Valyn. Besides, the B'Hono Corporation might be a little more welcoming than the criminal elements on Valyn. And they could have some vital information for him.

The corporate types were usually far more hospitable than common criminals.

* * * * *

Chapter Four

Velut Luna, Hyperspace, en route to Bishwanath Station

Sunshine rubbed her eyes tiredly. They had been in hyperspace for almost a week, and she had studied almost the entire time, delving into every iota of information the _Velut Luna_ had in her databanks. Information on all the mercenary races was at her fingertips, though there seemed to be conflicting accounts of precisely who was a mercenary race. Officially there were 37, but the list was either incomplete or purposely mislabeled for some reason. No amount of finessing the data changed this, either, which she found extremely frustrating.

There were a few races she was very interested in seeing, though not necessarily on the field of battle. She'd seen enough Tortantulas in fights to last her a lifetime. Zuul and Besquith, while ferocious, would not haunt her dreams in quite the same way. Even though she had only seen relays of the battle at the Lion's Gate, watching Antonious and the Jackals get slaughtered while barely putting a dent in the massive Tortantula unit was far more terrifying than anything she had ever experienced.

The other merc races were interesting as well and, while dangerous in their own right, seemed to pale when compared with the Besquith or Tortantulas. Her focused study of the various merc races in the Galactic Union caused her to almost forget about eating. If not for Dref-na's constant complaining about the lack of fresh and bloody meat, Sunshine might have forgotten completely.

Fortunately, food was plentiful on the ship. Taryn's boss kept it fully stocked, something she really hadn't explored when they had departed Valyn originally. Now, with the Jeha recovering, her studies about other races nearly complete, and time to actually relax a little, Sunshine had decided to see what cooking meals in zero gravity was like.

Messy, she decided as she struggled to cook eggs. Cooking in the convection system was actually pretty easy at a theoretical level. One simply needed to crack open the egg and put it into the sealed, magnetic convection system. In seconds, she would have a nicely poached egg. An easy system, designed for ease of use and someone who really didn't like spending a lot of time cooking elaborate meals. A very busy person, in other words, like the enigmatic Mister Z.

The problem came with guiding the egg through zero gravity into the sealed magnetic container in the first place. Only after trying to move the egg yolk floating in midair with her hands did it occur to her to use the container to scoop them up. However, since she had already turned on the source of energy for the convection system, picking up the magnetized container was nigh impossible.

"First time?" a voice asked from behind as she growled in frustration.

"Yes," Sunshine grunted as the yellow yolk slipped through her fingers a fourth time. "Ugh!"

"Mister Z usually only cooks when there's thrust and gravity," Taryn explained as she reached into one of the secured drawers and pulled out a small cup. With a deft motion, she expertly snagged both eggs Sunshine had been struggling with. She used the cup's momentum and skillfully tossed the eggs directly into the convection container. The eggs landed inside, and she quickly sealed the lid and set the timer. Satisfied with her handiwork, she motioned toward Sunshine's magnetized boots. "Sometimes if you're wearing the boots for too long, you forget gravity doesn't exist."

"Yeah." Sunshine nodded, mildly embarrassed. Other than when she slept, she never went anywhere without the magnetic boots firmly upon her feet. Truth be told, she *had* forgotten about gravity. At least, until she had tried to cook. "I thought…I don't know, eggs would be easy?"

"Raw fruits," Taryn said as she opened another drawer. Inside were a variety of fresh fruits. Sunshine's eyes widened in shock.

"Why aren't they bad?"

"Good preservatives." Taryn chuckled. "Keeps them fresh for up to six months; handy trick. Mister Zorgama has them on all of his ships."

"Speaking of…" Sunshine motioned around her. "Are you still freaking out about the damage?"

"A little," Taryn admitted as a random strand of bright pink hair drifted in front of her face. She pushed it out of the way. "I *think* he'll understand and probably won't kill me. I don't think he'll let me take the *Velut Luna* out again anytime soon, though. At least, not unsupervised."

"I can pay for the damages," Sunshine repeated her offer from before. Taryn smiled.

"That right there might be the reason I live."

"I have a question," Sunshine began, twisting uncomfortably to turn and look at Taryn. "My speech patterns are getting better, aren't they?"

"I wasn't going to say anything," Taryn admitted after a moment of contemplation. "Your accent is disappearing. I thought you went heavy on the accent so people would underestimate you, but the more I listen, the more it sounds like you're adjusting naturally."

"What's weird is I'm starting to understand some of Dref-na's Besquith words without the translator," Sunshine said in a quiet tone. Taryn's eyes widened slightly at this.

"Perhaps you're just one of those people who really gets languages?"

"I don't know." Sunshine shook her head. "I never understood any other languages before. Okay, I knew a few Nigerian words besides English. Oh, and I spoke Kolokwa, but everyone did. But alien languages and proper grammar? That's something taught, even with the translators."

"Your egg's done," Taryn said as the cooking system turned off. She popped the lid off and waited as the heating element pushed the egg out of the cooking container and into the air. "Careful, it's probably hot."

"Okay." Sunshine nodded. She turned slightly. "Are we almost there?"

"Four hours until we exit hyperspace," Taryn replied. "Then another two until we dock at Boogadishu."

"Why do you call it that?" Sunshine asked, genuinely curious. There were many quirks about Taryn which intrigued her, beginning with her odd fascination with changing the names of everything.

"Why do you call Kl'nk'nnk 'Klinks?'" Taryn countered.

"It's easier," Sunshine admitted. "But if I understand you correctly, you mean your nickname of Bishwanath Station in a negative way. I don't mean to offend Kl'nk'nnk, and if she doesn't like it, I'll call her by her real name."

"Makes sense. Well, Boogadishu...it's an old joke I picked up from my boss," Taryn stated with a grin. "He's a huge history nerd and he calls certain space stations by derogatory nicknames."

"But Boogadishu?"

"You ever heard of the Battle of Mogadishu?"

"No," Sunshine said, her pinplants immediately searching. There were a lot of references to the city and many battles regarding it but nothing in the ship's database which gave her a clue as to which one Taryn was talking about. Apparently, the city was a hotbed for war and almost as bad as the fabled fertile crescent in the Middle East. At least, before the MinSha were done with it. "Wasn't it the capital of New Somaliland until it got destroyed?"

"Yeah." Taryn nodded. "Well, about eighty years before it was destroyed, there was a huge battle there between the Americans and some Somali warlord and his men. It didn't go well for the Americans. Because of this, a lot of people started calling bad places variations of the name. So, my boss started calling Bishwanath Station Boogadishu because, like I said before, he's a history nerd, and it has a bit of a reputation as the headquarters for scummy villains. We all just started using it, and it stuck."

"Oh." Sunshine thought about it for a moment before smiling. "Okay, I get it now."

"I wonder what the Besquith call it." Taryn said. "It's not like they enjoy the place, either."

Sunshine, not very familiar with eating a floating object in zero gravity, decided to let it sit in the middle of the air for a few moments so it could cool down. She gingerly moved the poached egg to her and took a small bite.

"Ooh, hot," she winced but took another bite. "Ah, still hot!"

"It's only been a few seconds," Taryn laughed. "It'll need more time to cool off."

Sunshine resisted the urge to eat the scalding hot egg immediately. It was one of the many things which came hard to her. Starving as a child and oftentimes fighting with others so she could eat the food given, her time with the Korps had not quite kicked this habit of eating everything she could in a hurry. She understood at an intellectual level that nobody was going to steal her food now, but the problem ran deeper. One couldn't get rid of years of pathological behavior and psychological trauma with a wave of a wand.

Once the egg was cool enough to eat, she wasted little time. Taryn grabbed a tangerine and tossed it through the air to Sunshine, who caught it easily with one hand.

"Eat this," she told the younger girl. "You can take pills for vitamin C, but it's usually best straight from the source."

"Thanks," Sunshine mumbled, her mouth full of egg. She began to peel the tangerine while she finished her egg. "I'm hungrier than I thought I was."

"Yeah, you really haven't eaten anything but protein pouches since we left Valyn," Taryn reminded her as she began to pluck small pieces of tangerine peels from the air. "They taste horrible, even though they'll keep you alive."

"Better than MREs," Sunshine commented after finishing the last piece of tangerine. "Had those once. I'll eat them, but my stomach doesn't like them. Then again, anything is better than starving. Tried that once, too. I don't recommend it."

"Taryn Lupo," Dref-na's voice came over the comms. "The Jeha is awake and coherent. She wants to talk to whoever is in charge."

"You're up," Taryn said as she opened the sealed trash bin and threw the peels away.

"Me?" Sunshine asked, surprised. "This is your ship."

"Well, technically I'm working for you right now, since you're covering the repairs to Mister Z's ship," Taryn corrected. "You also hired Dref-na, and it's your responsibility to pay Kl'nk'nnk for repairing your CASPer and finding this message you're searching for. Everyone here is working for you in some capacity, which means…"

"I'm in charge." Sunshine nodded in understanding. She took a few steps toward the door before pausing. "You coming with me?"

"I'll be there in a few minutes," Taryn said. "I'll clean up in here."

"Oh!" Sunshine exclaimed, embarrassed. "I'm sorry. I can clean it up."

"No, it's my galley, my problem." Taryn shrugged. "Besides, it'll give you some time alone to tell Kl'nk'nnk what you need without me interrupting."

"Okay," Sunshine agreed, though she still felt bad about leaving the mess for Taryn. She moved toward the rear of the ship and the medical bay, where she found Dref-na standing near the coiled form of Kl'nk'nnk. The Jeha had moved herself out of bed and, using her clawed feet, was sticking to the floor somehow.

Sunshine nodded to the Jeha. "Hello again." The alien closely resembled an Earth millipede, only on a nightmarish scale. She was over four feet in length and had more mass than Sunshine had expected. However, everything she had read about Jeha suggested they were considered harmless by most of the other races in the Galactic Union. Sunshine was no fool, though. Any species could be dangerous in its own right. "You're looking better."

"Yes," the Jeha acknowledged. "You are Captain Sunshine Luo, yes?"

"Luo?" Sunshine asked, confused. She looked over at Dref-na.

"Your clan," Dref-na said. "Sunshine Kakata sounded strange, and Korps was even worse. I gave your clan name as your old boss, Mulbah Luo. Does this bother you, tiny fierceness?"

"No, I don't think it does," Sunshine said after giving it some thought. "I guess it makes sense. He was the one who officially hired me into the Korps and made me an officer, after all."

"Honor the memory of your clan," Dref-na told her. Sunshine grunted. *Sunshine Luo.* She tested the name silently in her head. For reasons she couldn't explain, it worked for her, though a tiny part wished she could remember what her parents had named her, before she ended up with Major General Sparkles. She mentally pushed this aside. There was a time for a journey down the memory rabbit hole, and this was not it.

"May I call you Klinks?" Sunshine asked the Jeha.

"Klinks…" the Jeha seemed to mull the idea over before responding. "This is acceptable. I greet you, Captain."

"And I you, Klinks." Sunshine smiled. "I'm sorry I got you shot."

"They were planning on killing me," Klinks replied emotionlessly. "In a way, being shot saved me from dying."

"Why were they going to kill you?" Sunshine asked.

"Why were you at Zav'ax?" Klinks queried instead of answering. "Surely I have not angered a mercenary company? My work is in the engineering of life support systems only, although I do dabble in the occasional electrical and mechanical side of things. This is more of a hobby."

Blinking, Sunshine realized suddenly she had never really told Klinks the truth of the matter between the time they had sprung her from the police station until their frantic escape into hyperspace.

"Oh, I'm sorry. You don't have a warrant issued by anyone from Earth," Sunshine acknowledged. "That lie was for the security forces of B'Hono Corp. Nobody on Earth wants you in jail. I think, *menh*. No, I need your help. I want to hire you."

Sunshine quickly explained what had happened on Earth, from the time Peepo had turned on the Korps until her eventual departure from her home planet. The entire time Klinks listened without interrupting, and soon she finished with their arrival to Zav'ax and their successful rescue attempt.

"Your subterfuge was clever," Klinks acknowledged as soon as Sunshine finished her tale. "And necessary. The B'Hono Corps security forces are good, but they don't know Humans very well. Bringing the Besquith along was proper. Why do you want to hire me? I'm an engineer, not a mercenary."

"My old *bass* put a message inside my CASPer," Sunshine explained. "Before the Fall of Liberia. Like I said, he sent me away. I'm supposed to deliver this message to the Peacemaker Guild, but it's hidden somewhere in my CASPer, *ken*? A Fae named Splunk looked at it back on Earth but couldn't find the message."

"Fae?" Klinks asked, confused.

"They're better known as the Dusman," Sunshine explained.

The Jeha drew in a hissing breath. "*Murderers.* Wicked defilers. *World eaters.* They are not to be trusted, the Dusman."

"What? Why not?" Sunshine asked, taken aback. As far as she could tell, the Fae/Dusman seemed to be on the side of humanity. Jim Cartwright seemed especially taken with Splunk, and after hearing of their battles in the Raknar she had let herself believe the Fae/Dusman would help humanity free itself from Peepo and the Mercenary Guild. They were fairly friendly as well, though a bit reclusive. They were helping humanity. Was this not the case?

"It matters not my reasons," Klinks replied after giving it some thought. "Ancient grudges. Old rivalries, past wars. Long forgotten by most. They are…skilled engineers. Better than the Jeha. If they say there is no message, they are either correct or lying."

"Oh," Sunshine said, her tone miserable as she looked down at her borrowed magnetic boots. It was crushing. She had risked so much to get to this point. Would nothing ever go her way?

"I will look at it, however," the Jeha said. Sunshine looked up, surprised. The Jeha almost seemed apologetic to Sunshine. "As I said, it could be lying. I understand the CASPer systems quite well. Zorgama did hire me to redesign his, after all. There are many upgrades on his, and Human technology has gotten better since. I could even upgrade yours."

"That…would be nice," Sunshine said, a hitch in her voice. Trying to sound thankful, she pushed on. "I can pay you for your time."

"Consider it a trade," the Jeha replied.

"A trade?"

"You saved my life," Klinks reminded her. "Dref-na says we are going to Bishwanath Station to refuel, but there are no plans afterwards."

"Yeah," Sunshine nodded. "I thought about it, and, if you're right and there's no message in the suit, I might as well go home. I could always hire more mercs for the Korps. That is, unless they revoke our charter after what happened during Peepo's occupation."

"Return to Earth?" Klinks asked, surprised. "Why?"

"Why not?" Sunshine looked at her. "Where else would I go?"

"Back to Zav'ax," Klinks answered immediately.

"Why?" Sunshine asked. "If we go back and somehow make it past the ships, they'll probably try to kill us for murdering a bunch of their guys. Oh, and we also started a massive forest fire, not to mention the fact we broke a Jeha out of prison on false pretenses. With all of that, I can't see any reason for us to want to go back to the planet in the next hundred years."

"This is all true."

"I'm glad we agree," Sunshine exhaled.

The Jeha appeared unfazed by all this. "There is the matter of the TriRusk being held on Zav'ax, however."

"The what?"

* * *

"The shuttle arrived a few months ago," Klinks began as soon as Taryn had joined Sunshine and Dref-na in the med bay. "I did not notice it at first. It was not my job. My job was to design a series of machines which could accelerate tissue growth. I believed at the time I was hired to help the B'Hono Corporation create a bio-farm for artificial tissue growth to assist with healing abilities when combined with nanites. I understood it had been done in the past but not on the scale proposed when they offered me the contract.

"I did not even recognize the TriRusk at first. Nobody had seen one in hundreds of years, and you Humans have a very curious saying which suits what happened to them: out of sight, out of mind. It was only after I was finishing the calibrations on the final machine when I realized who they were. I was informed by the overseer that they had been hired to be miners on the colony world. This made sense at first, especially if B'Hono was bringing them in slowly, as more were hired. As it was, I suspect this was probably all a lie for my benefit.

"Karvan di Mobiar is the chief of operations at the site and the Jivool who hired me. I asked him about the TriRusk later, and he was insistent they were hired to be miners. The more I thought about it, the less sense it made. TriRusk were known for many things, but mining was not one of them. There were races much better suited for mining who were always hired by the various corporations. The GenSha come to mind. I asked, and Karvan reassured me that what he said was the truth."

"When did you realize things were really off?" Taryn asked. The Jeha's head swiveled to look at her.

"When the TriRusk disappeared."

"They disappeared?" Sunshine looked at her, surprised. The Jeha dipped her head in a very Human-like movement.

"The males did," Klinks clarified.

"How many were there?" Taryn pressed.

"Five males and one female," Klinks responded. "I am not sure of their social dynamic, but from the brief time I saw them all together it appeared they deferred to her. The males disappeared one day, and the female became distraught. I would have consoled her, but soon afterward my work area was quarantined due to a biological outbreak of a virulent disease and I was moved to a different location. I tried to go back and collect my tools but—"

"Was that why they arrested you?" Sunshine asked, curious. "They said it was for spying."

"Corporate espionage," Taryn corrected before frowning. "Eh, spying. You're right. Never mind."

"I believe so," the Jeha agreed after a momentary pause. "I tried to gather my tools but was denied. I asked too many questions and pressed the matter, including asking what disease, could possibly affect a Jeha on this world. I should have known better, but my curiosity got the better of me. I am inquisitive by nature. A flaw in my character. I am told it is genetic."

"So, you found out they had some TriRusk, they quarantined your lab because of a viral outbreak, and then they arrested you for wanting your work tools?" Sunshine cocked her head. "I don't know much about viruses or anything, but it seems like they overreacted, *ken?*"

"She's right," Taryn confirmed. "If it had been a biological outbreak or disease of some sort, they should have quarantined the entire planet. Though...there's no law saying you can't have an alien species on any given planet, and if they had hired the TriRusk then there'd be no need for your arrest, even if they did disappear. If you were trying to harm them, sure, but to arrest you and charge you with corporate espionage?"

"Which is why I suggested returning to Zav'ax," Klinks stated. "The machines I built do not coincide with their stated purpose of mineral mining on the world, and I am no longer convinced they are for their proclaimed pharmaceutical research either. The planet has nothing of value outside of a few metals which are commonplace throughout the galaxy."

"What machines were you designing, anyway?" Taryn asked her. "More specifically, the design, make and model?"

"I signed a non-disclosure agreement," Klinks responded, shaking her insectoid head. "I've already told you all I can. I am sorry."

"Well, we need to refuel at Boog—er, Bishwanath Station before we head back," Taryn stated as she wiped her hands on her utility cargo pants. "Sunshine, you and I will look for some other, ah, supplies while we're at the station. Dref-na, you're our muscle. Kl'nk'nnk, if you're feeling up to it, can you stay and monitor the refueling process?"

"Yes," the Jeha agreed readily. "I promised the captain I would reassemble her suit as well as upgrade it. Staying behind would enable me to do so."

"Thank you," Sunshine said before looking at Dref-na. "Gear up. We're going to Boogadishu."

"I'll never fully understand why Humans must give everything a humorous nickname, tiny fierceness," the Besquith admitted as the ship continued to barrel through hyperspace toward their destination.

"Oh, and Dref-na?" Taryn looked at her friend. "Where'd you put the paracord?"

"The what?"

"The thin rope?"

"Oh, I put it in my pouch," the Besquith said giving her an odd look. "Why?"

"I have a strange feeling we're going to need it."

* * * * *

Chapter Five

Docking Ring E, Bishwanath Station, Ampheon System

"Ugh, you were right," Sunshine muttered as soon as they were off the *Velut Luna* and into the station proper. She inhaled the stale, recycled air within the ancient space station and grimaced. There was trash everywhere, and even the metal grates on the walls appeared to be stained with something very unhygienic. Throw in alien graffiti splashed everywhere, and it almost reminded Sunshine of home. "This is almost as bad as the slums in Chocolate City."

"*Almost* as bad?" Dref-na turned to stare at Sunshine, partly in awe but mostly in disgust. "I thought Earth was advanced?"

"You've obviously never been to Africa," Sunshine responded as her eyes drank in everything.

The station was clearly old, though she had no way to know precisely how old. She had assumed everything alien was always shiny and new, that it was Earth which was backward and poor. Now she realized Earth, in spite of its many faults, was fairly clean when compared to the majority of aliens in the Galactic Union. It was a very odd thing to realize.

It pays to be a merc, she decided as they walked down the docking ring corridor.

The station did not have artificial gravity. Sunshine didn't think it existed, in spite of Klinks' reassurances it was theoretically possible. Using centrifugal force instead, the station's different rings rotated at different speeds, depending on their distance from the center, keeping gravity at changeable rates for the various species which inhabited and used the space station on each ring. Docking Ring E was almost identical to Earth and thus, one of the more populated rings. Many aliens had similar gravity on their worlds, and Sunshine briefly wondered if it was an evolutionary thing.

She gave herself a mental shake. Her mind kept going to odd places these days. Ever since she had been pinned back on Earth, it felt as though her brain was constantly figuring out problems and equations she didn't even know existed. It was beginning to drive her a little crazy, the constant bombardment of questions and ideas. The only time it seemed to shut off was when she was asleep. She hated sleeping, though. Sleep was when the dead returned to haunt her dreams, as well as the nightmares she could never remember afterward.

A few aliens she had never seen before passed, and she tried not to stare. It was hard. On an intellectual level she knew there were thousands of aliens in the galaxy. Seeing them, on the other hand, was an entirely different matter altogether. Still, she was able to keep her face straight and not openly gawk. There were a few, though, which earned a second, and even third, glance. Aliens were just *weird*.

"Keep an eye on your yacks," Taryn suddenly warned them as a group of lithe, furry aliens rounded the corner. Behind her Sunshine heard Dref-na snort in disgust.

"Zuparti," the Besquith grumbled. "I hate Zuparti."

"Taste bad?" Sunshine asked sarcastically.

"No," Dref-na replied, evidently missing the irony in the question. Or more than likely, ignoring it outright. "They taste fine, actually. I dislike them for other reasons, tiny fierceness. They're thieves, and not even good ones. They are usually located where you would find a criminal underworld, either in charge or close to it."

"They sound like they'd fit right in back home," Taryn interjected as she made a subtle motion with her hand. "Look, they're following someone."

"What is *that*?" Sunshine whispered as she stared at the alien which held the Zuparti's attention. "It looks like a baby goat with a snazzy jacket."

"A CozSha," Taryn hissed. "I've never seen one up close before. Aww, look at it. It's adorable!"

It actually was, Sunshine realized upon further inspection. It was short, barely one meter tall, and walked on two legs like a Human, albeit legs which ended in hooves of a sort. While it didn't appear to be wearing pants, it wore a very nice coat with a shirt of some type beneath it. The CozSha had Human-like arms with fingers, all of which was covered with grey fur. Goat-like facial features included small, nubby horns and large, floppy ears. It even had a tiny little beard.

"I wonder what it's doing here?" Taryn said as she watched the CozSha wander aimlessly through the corridor. She saw Sunshine's confused expression and explained. "This isn't their type of environment. They're usually administrators and stick to, well, *cleaner* stations. Paper pushers. Good workers and not very outspoken. Very passive, too. They get overlooked by a lot of races because they won't fight, not even to defend themselves. Boogadishu isn't the sort of station you'd find them on. They're all about order. This? This is pure chaos."

"And nobody's enslaved them yet?" Sunshine asked, surprised.

"Why enslave a race when they'll work for almost nothing, and they love doing it?" Taryn asked. She shook her head. "A CozSha enjoys its menial job, from what I heard. It's strange."

"So why are those Zuparti following the CozSha?" Sunshine frowned as the weasel-looking aliens changed course in the middle of the corridor and closed the distance between themselves and the CozSha.

"Hey, I think they're going to—yep," Taryn said as all three watched the Zuparti grab the small CozSha and throw a bag over its head. They looked around to see if anyone was going to stop them before hustling the goat-like alien down one of the smaller corridors which led away from Docking Ring E. "That was a pretty professional snatch."

"They kidnapped it!" Sunshine's jaw dropped in surprise. She shook her head, amazed. "In the open, and nobody even cared! It's like I'm back home again."

"Why would Zuparti want to abduct a CozSha, Taryn Lupo?" Dref-na rumbled softly. Other than their group, it appeared nobody else in the busy corridor had seen the abduction occur. Or more pointedly, nobody had paid it any attention. Everything appeared to be business as usual on Bishwanath Station.

"Not our problem," Taryn decided before looking at Sunshine questioningly. "Unless we're making it our problem?"

"No," Sunshine stated after a brief moment of reflection. They had their own issues to deal with. "We're here to refuel. Focus on the mission."

That's what the bass *would say, wouldn't it?* Sunshine wasn't sure. While her old *bass* had been a stickler for completing the mission, he had a clearer grasp of his own moral code. Sunshine didn't know what hers was yet. The only absolute certainty in her life was to complete the last assignment given to her by Mulbah. Everything else took a back seat.

Why should everything else come second, though? It was a question she was afraid to answer. Not because of the answer itself, but because it would lead to more questions, uncertainty she could ill-afford to deal with at the moment. While she had Dref-na and Taryn with her, Sunshine still felt more alone than ever in this vast galaxy. It was terrifying to think of life without a mission, a goal. Staying focused on the task was the easiest way for her to deal with the potential emotional storm which could break forth at any moment.

"We can check it out later if you want," Sunshine added, thinking not only of Mulbah but Zion, as well. He wouldn't have been okay with a kidnapping. She was certain of that.

"We should gather some weapons while we're here," Dref-na suggested as they moved onward through the corridor. It was strange for Sunshine, watching the various aliens conduct their business within the corridors. If not for the constant differing appearances of each species, it was almost like being within the souks of downtown Monrovia during early autumn. "If we're going back to Zav'ax, I mean."

"Taryn has some guns on her ship," Sunshine reminded her.

"I do, yeah, but they're nothing I'd want to take into a pitched battle," Taryn pointed out as they turned down another corridor. Here the aliens selling their wares appeared to be closing up shop, chasing away the few vagrants who were trying to beg or steal. A few sized up the Humans before catching sight of the Besquith accompanying them and, deciding it was better to be found somewhere else, disappeared down smaller access halls in a flash.

"Heavy weapons then," Sunshine suggested as they turned another corner. Not paying attention to Taryn, she nearly stumbled over the woman when Taryn suddenly stopped. "Hey, what—"

"Ssh!" Taryn hissed and pushed Sunshine back. Dref-na, a bemused expression upon her craggy face, watched as Taryn peeked around the corner once more. She began to bounce happily on the balls of her feet. "Look! Look!"

"What?" Sunshine asked as she tried to push past Taryn to see what the woman was talking about. After some minor jostling and a few swears, she could see what had Taryn so excited. Her own eyes widened in recognition, as well as the six aliens that were standing around it.

"Are those…weapons crates?" Taryn asked, a hopeful lilt in her voice.

"I think they are," Sunshine replied as she looked at the metal crates stacked five high and the same across. They were similar to the ones used back on Earth to ship rifles and carbines around the world. She would know. During the lead up to the final stand of the Korps, similar crates had been assigned and issued by the Korps as they desperately tried to arm the Liberian National Army before the Mercenary Guild attacked in full. It had been a good, albeit futile, effort.

"Those are *all* the guns we'd need," Taryn breathed, her eyes wide. Sunshine tapped her shoulder gently, but the woman seemed lost in a strange trance. Taryn began to babble softly under her breath. "I'll take all the pretties. Just walk away with them. Nobody would know. If they cared, they'd have had more guards, right? Of course, they would. Makes sense to me. Doesn't it make sense to you, Sunshine?"

"There are six well-armed Zuparti standing next to the crates," Sunshine pointed out as she looked at the weapons each Zuparti held in their hand. The guns looked like they could do a lot of damage with a single shot. "I'd call those guards."

"Like I said, if they really cared they would have more," Taryn countered breezily. "For that amount of pretties they should have twenty. Or more."

"Six is plenty!"

"Look, they're not even paying any attention."

"Dref-na, help me out here, *ken?*"

"I'm sorry, tiny fierceness, but I am with Taryn Lupo on this. We need weapons."

"Seriously?"

"Ha! All the pretties will be mine!"

The Besquith chuckled softly. "Zuparti taste good. Let's eat them and take their guns."

"Are you on drugs?" Sunshine asked, exasperated. "We can't eat everyone!"

"I can."

"She's a Besquith," Taryn added helpfully. "It's kinda their shtick."

"So, you eat everyone, and then we steal the guns?" Sunshine threw her hands into the air dramatically before rolling her eyes. "This is just wrong. I could just buy them! This is just one of those things you're doing to annoy the crap out of me!"

"I would never do such a thing." Taryn looked almost offended by Sunshine's accusation. "That hurt my feelings. I can't believe you would ever accuse me of deliberately tormenting you just because your forehead has a small vein that pops out when you get angry and frustrated, like it is right now."

"For the love of…" Sunshine's voice trailed off. She sighed, defeated. "Fine. Steal all the guns if you have to, and then we return to Zav'ax to do…something. This is so stupid. We're all going to die…"

"This is Boogadishu," Taryn stated. "If you aren't stealing, you aren't trying."

"Interesting," Dref-na commented. "Those are important words to live by on this station."

"Kl'nk'nnk just pinged me." Taryn changed the subject slightly. "Ship's almost finished refueling. Let's steal the weapons and get out of here."

"This is going to end badly…" Sunshine predicted.

Ten minutes later they were transporting five of the weapon crates toward the *Velut Luna*. Nobody even looked at them as they passed. The "borrowed" hand cart made the transport easy and quick. Taryn's smile was similar to a cat who had caught the canary. Sunshine wasn't sure if she should feel miserable at being proven wrong or upset at Taryn's obvious gloating.

"See? Nobody died," Taryn said proudly.

No, Sunshine decided. It is the gloating that's making me mad.

"Except the Zuparti," she muttered under her breath. Even though it was quiet, Taryn heard her. The smile on the other woman's face grew even wider, if possible.

"They don't count. Besides, it's not like we have anything like that on the ship for Dref-na to eat."

"Nothing fresh," the Besquith amended as she spit out a partially chewed bone. It clattered onto the station's floor and joined the other pieces of litter. "Bah. Their fibulas always stick in the back of my rear incisors. Bothersome."

"You have no idea how annoyed I am by all this," Sunshine said with a growl. Taryn giggled quietly and poked Dref-na in the side, who grinned at Sunshine's expense.

"I have some inkling, tiny fierceness," Dref-na stated as they approached the final stretch of corridor before reaching the docking berth of the *Velut Luna*. The foot traffic, which had filled the area earlier, had ceased, leaving them practically alone in the corridor. "It is still very funny."

"I don't think—uh oh," Sunshine's protests stopped as a well-armed group of Zuparti stood before them. One, decked out in chromed body armor and multiple piercings in his ears, was larger than the rest and appeared to be their leader. Sunshine recalled one of the Korps' missions before she had joined them; she had read the after-action report. Mulbah and the Korps had dealt with underworld Zuparti before and there had been a note in the file about their casual resemblance to third-rate African warlords. "Well, now I know why the corridor's empty."

"A Besquith." The lead Zuparti grunted. Gold flashed in his mouth. "Now I know where my guards went. Give me back my weapons, and you can walk away from this unharmed."

"This is all your fault," Sunshine said as she gave Taryn a sideways glance.

"My fault?" Taryn asked.

"Yes." Sunshine nodded. Taryn thought about it for a moment.

"Okay, you're right. Totally my fault."

"And now we're going to have to paint the walls of this corridor with Zuparti blood in order to get away," Sunshine continued in a loud voice, ignoring the criminals barring their path. She motioned at Dref-na. "She's already devoured six of them. I don't think she can eat another twenty."

"Ten, perhaps," Dref-na conceded as she rubbed her stomach. "I'm a little full at the moment."

The crowd of Zuparti behind the leader stirred nervously. It was clear they were used to being the baddest group around, and the arrival of Dref-na threw every bit of certainty they had straight out the airlock. It was almost amusing, except the armed group was disciplined enough to keep the barrels of their weapons pointed in their direction.

Sunshine looked around. Evidently every other individual on the docking ring had found somewhere else to be. Not even a lone drunken straggler could be seen. The Zuparti, it seemed, controlled the majority of the criminal element at the station. Apparently, the everyday denizens knew better than to hang around when this group was on the prowl. She couldn't blame them. Dealing with criminals like these was sometimes best left to the professionals, or other criminals.

Fortunately, she had a lot of experience dealing with both.

"Give me back my weapons," the leader repeated.

"No," Sunshine said, her tone flat and bored.

The Zuparti seemed taken aback. "I'm warning you—"

"We stole them, and we're keeping them," she replied, unfazed by his threat. She motioned with her left hand toward the armed group behind him, letting her right drift down to her borrowed thigh holster. "You're using large caliber subcarbines, but those would punch holes in the space station if they were fully powered charges, so you're using some sort of low power round in them, I bet. It would punch a big hole in us, and I bet the only thing stopping you from firing is you don't want to accidentally hit the crates, *ken*? So, there's ammunition in these crates too. You don't know which ones we took, which means...Were you guys smuggling *explosives* through here as well?"

"Uh...no?" The leader of the Zuparti was now off balance. He glanced back at the others with him, obviously confused.

"Ha!" Sunshine crowed as she smoothly drew the laser pistol and pointed it directly at his chest. "I didn't even want to steal all this stuff, but now I'm glad we did. Who knows what you idiots would have done with the crap in these? Now, are you going to move or are we going to have to kill you while using the crates as cover?"

"Hey," Taryn whispered under her breath. "I recognize those three thugs on the far right. They're the ones who grabbed the CozSha."

Sunshine squinted to the right side of the group, uncertain. She couldn't be sure about it, but Sunshine also knew her limits. Her abilities were on the field of battle, not distinguishing between the fur patterns of alien life forms. Although it was something she should learn if she were ever going to command a mercenary company properly.

"Hey, before we get to the killing part, why'd you kidnap the CozSha?" Taryn called out to the Zuparti. "They're harmless!"

"Why do you care about a CozSha?" the leader asked. He let out a long, slow breath. An ear rotated back for a moment before turning forward again. *I didn't know they could do that,* Sunshine thought. "The CozSha has nothing to do with what's going on between us."

"Tiny fierceness," Dref-na muttered in a quiet tone. "I think the Zuparti is stalling for time. I suspect there is a second group moving around behind to flank us."

"I'm thinking the same thing," Sunshine replied. "They're not going to shoot at us, not yet. At least, not until they're in the right position. Would you mind?"

"Perhaps I can eat more than ten after all," Dref-na purred before slipping behind the crates and moving back down the corridor. The giant Besquith could move quickly and silently when she wanted, and Sunshine lost sight of her in moments. There was a fifteen-second window of silence before the screams began. They were not the cries of a wounded Besquith.

It was clear the Zuparti leader's hearing worked just fine. As the sound of his reinforcements being slaughtered reached his ears, he began to twitch anxiously. Nervous looks were shared between all of the weasel-like aliens, and Sunshine couldn't help but feel just the tiniest bit of sympathy for the Zuparti. It was clear they had never experienced anything like this before. Truth be told, neither had she.

"I don't think your reinforcements will be joining us," Sunshine called out. In a whisper, she said to Taryn, "I don't know about you, but this is getting old, quick."

"They got peeved about the CozSha," Taryn replied with a nod. "Maybe if we stalled some more? Once they realize Dref-na is close, we can be a little more demanding about getting by."

"I should ask more about the CozSha then?"

"Why not?" Taryn asked with a slight shrug. "It's not like we're going anywhere at the moment. Not until Dref-na circles around, at least."

"True," Sunshine allowed. She raised her voice again. "Why did you kidnap the CozSha?"

"What does everyone want with that stupid little CozSha?" The Zuparti's mouth snapped shut. It was clear the weasel-looking alien was peeved. "She's a *CozSha*. Not mercs, not spies, and so passive we didn't even have to tie her up. They're practically worthless yet everyone seems to want this one!"

"Who else wants her?" Sunshine was genuinely curious now. Behind her, the sounds of dying Zuparti ended with one final, abrupt cry of pain. No shots had been fired the entire time, which meant Dref-na had caught them completely unaware and mowed through them like a chainsaw. It was disturbing just how little the massacre bothered her. The analytical side of her brain simply chalked it up to it being aliens, but a tiny part of her soul wondered if being out in the galaxy was beginning to cost her more than she bargained for.

"Who cares?"

"I do," Sunshine suddenly decided. "Give me the CozSha, and you can all live through this."

"Give me my guns back!"

"Come and take them!"

"Fine!"

"Fine!"

There was a pause as the Zuparti crime lord looked at his underlings, quietly discussing something. Sunshine glanced over at Taryn, who shrugged.

"I have no idea what they're doing," Taryn muttered. "They can't be stalling for time since they have to suspect Dref-na is moving around to flank them by now."

"I think they're not used to anyone telling them no," Sunshine replied in a low tone as the three Zuparti that had taken the CozSha earlier stepped out of the line of fire. A small access corridor cloaked in shadows lay just to the left of the Zuparti. She hadn't seen it before, because of its apparently steep angle. A few tense minutes later they returned with the tiny CozSha in their midst.

"Here's the creature," the Zuparti leader called out. "Now give me back my guns!"

"This is unreal," Sunshine said. She turned and looked back at Taryn. "Are aliens always like this?"

"Not in my experience," the other woman admitted. "I deal with Zuparti all the time. These are…not normal." Claws scraping across the metal floor drew both of their attention back toward the stolen crates.

"Dref-na?" Sunshine was surprised to see the Besquith reappear from the corridor behind them. Her fur was matted with blood and gore, but none of it appeared to be hers. Dref-na was shaking her head and muttering under her breath. "I thought you were going around to hit them from the side?"

"They're using small tunnels between the corridors to move about," Dref-na complained. "Smaller than I can fit through. I came back when I saw there was no cheese at the end of the maze, only pain."

"Oh joy," Taryn complained. "I thought we were going to get through this without a gunfight."

"You just had to steal the guns, didn't you?"

"Hey!" A loud voice interrupted their argument. The trio turned and looked at the Zuparti, who was waiting impatiently. He grabbed the CozSha by the scruff of its neck and shook the little alien. "You want to do this or not?"

"Entropy," Taryn hissed. "There's no way we're making it back to the ship with the guns if we have to fight through them."

"Let's just grab the CozSha, give them back the guns, and *buy* them elsewhere," Sunshine suggested while giving Taryn a rather pointed look.

"But we worked hard to steal these!"

"Dref-na worked hard to steal these, you mean," Sunshine reminded her. Taryn glanced up at the Besquith, who was smiling.

"It wasn't too difficult, tiny fierceness," Dref-na reminded them both. Taryn rolled her eyes but said nothing as Sunshine elbowed her in the ribs.

"Okay!" Sunshine called out to the Zuparti. "We're going to leave these here and the CozSha comes with us, *ken*?"

"Fine!"

"Let her go!"

"You start walking first!"

"Not until she does!"

"On three," the Zuparti called out as he released the CozSha's neck. The little creature appeared dazed from the abuse. Sunshine's heart went out to the innocent looking alien. "One...two...three!"

Sunshine, Taryn, and Dref-na slowly walked forward, leaving the crates behind. Both Human women had their hands on their personal weapons while Dref-na kept her long claws up and ready. The Zuparti kept their own weapons trained on the group but were honoring the agreement and not firing.

"Once the crates aren't behind us anymore they're going to kill us all," Taryn predicted as they drew closer to the Zuparti.

"Grenades?" Sunshine asked. Taryn chuckled and patted the pouch on her left hip.

"Smoke only."

"The minute I grab the CozSha, lob 'em," Sunshine told her. "Then we run like hell."

"Got it."

"How far is the ship?"

"Not far," Taryn responded. "Why?"

"I don't know how heavy the CozSha will be—"

"She doesn't *look* heavy."

"I'm starting to get the feeling we're not very good at talking our way out of situations," Sunshine murmured as they drew closer to the CozSha, which looked at them with wide eyes. "This has got to be the weirdest hostage trade in the history of the galaxy."

"Agreed," Taryn replied. "Oh, Sunshine?"

"Hmm?"

"You should probably get ready to run," Taryn instructed as she reached into her pouch. She flipped the small leather flap up and pulled out two small smoke grenades. Casually pulling the pins, she tossed them in the direction of the Zuparti without missing a step. The weasel-like aliens stared dumbly as the two active grenades bounced toward them, then screeched in horror and dove out of the way from the expected blasts.

Explosions which never happened. Instead, white smoke billowed out of the grenades, flooding the corridor and obscuring everyone's vision. Sunshine scooped up the CozSha, who let out a squeal of surprise, and they ran past the large group of hostile Zuparti. There were more cries of alarm and panic as the Zuparti slowly realized they had been duped. Taryn was hot on her heels before tripping over Dref-na's long legs. Sunshine stopped, uncertain. The CozSha in her arms squirmed slightly but didn't try to resist.

"Go!" Taryn yelled at her from the thick smoke. "We'll catch up!"

Swallowing, Sunshine held the tiny CozSha to her chest and continued on, running the length of the corridor in almost no time at all. The numbers of each berthing space whipped past, counting down until she finally reached Berth 12. She turned the corner and stepped into the small alcove. She quickly punched in the ship's security code, forgetting momentarily it was accessible by pinplants as well as manual entry. The locked changed from red to green, and she ducked inside the secondary door as soon as it opened.

"Who are you?" the CozSha asked, a stunned expression on her goat-like face. Large eyes blinked slowly. It was clear to Sunshine the little alien was in shock.

"Later," Sunshine replied as she ducked inside the secure airlock. Her hand hovered over the "secure" button as she waited for Taryn and Dref-na to catch up. She set the CozSha gently onto the floor. "Stay here."

"Where are you going?"

"To help my friends," Sunshine answered as she brought her gun up. A loud commotion outside signaled their arrival. She leaned out and prepared to shoot, but there weren't any Zuparti to be seen. Taryn came around the corner, her own weapon firing rapidly behind her. Beyond her, Dref-na skid on the metal grating of the floor and slammed into the outer bulkhead before her long claws gained purchase. A small geyser of blood exploded out of her calf as one of the Zuparti managed to wing her. Sunshine ducked out of their way.

Taryn grabbed Dref-na and pulled her out of the direct line of fire. Seeing an opportunity, Sunshine leaned out into the small hallway and aimed her pistol at where she expected the Zuparti to appear. She didn't have to wait long. Within seconds, a small gaggle of the aliens showed up.

Lining up her shot, Sunshine fired and hit the first Zuparti right between the eyes, the laser pistol burning a neat hole in the alien's head. The expression on the Zuparti's face was a mixture of confusion and pain, frozen in place as it slumped to the floor, dead. The six others who started to follow immediately ducked around the corner to avoid being shot.

This momentary lapse in the pursuit allowed Taryn and Dref-na to make it to the secured airlock. Once everyone was inside, Sunshine slammed her hand on the "sealed" button. The airtight doors of the access tunnel closed immediately. A yellow light appeared overhead, warning them of depressurization in thirty seconds. The group quickly boarded the *Velut Luna* and sealed the ship behind them.

Sunshine moved around the CozSha, who was staring fearfully at the towering Besquith. Dref-na was still bleeding. This wound was far worse than the last one, and it was leaking everywhere. Once the ship detached from the station, the blood would go everywhere in zero-G. It could damage electrical components and who knew what else before the thrust from the engines gave them gravity once more.

"Med bay, now," Sunshine ordered the Besquith. Dref-na, clearly in pain, simply nodded and limped down the hall toward the center of the ship. Sunshine looked back at Taryn and the CozSha. "Get…the CozSha situated before we leave."

"Look, I enjoy a gunfight as much as the next girl, but I didn't sign up for this," Taryn complained, ignoring the CozSha at Sunshine's hip. She motioned at the wounded Besquith. "We were just supposed to be refueling the ship!"

"Excuse me?" Sunshine looked at her, shocked. She jabbed a finger angrily at Taryn. "It was *your* stupid idea to steal their guns in the first place!"

"And it was *your* dumb plan to save the CozSha!" Taryn shouted back, red-faced.

"You suggested it!"

"You asked how to stall for time!"

"I wouldn't have had to stall for time if you hadn't stolen the damn guns!"

"If we're going back to Zav'ax we *need* the guns!"

"I could have bought the guns, you moron!"

Taryn stepped away from Sunshine as the ship disconnected from the station. Gravity quickly faded away as they drifted off into space. She glared at Sunshine but said nothing else, her fists clenched at her side. Sunshine glanced at the CozSha, who was watching their interaction with wide eyes. She sighed. It would do nobody any good if she started yelling again. Taking a deep breath, she struggled to rein in her temper.

The engines of the *Velut Luna* powered up, and the ship began to accelerate toward the stargate. Gravity quickly returned, and all three of them drifted back to the ship's deck. Sunshine waited to see if Taryn was going to start yelling again but the older woman was silent.

"Look," Sunshine said as calmly as she could manage given the circumstances. "You said I was in charge, remember? You can't tell me I'm in charge one second and then blame me for you not listening the next. If I'm not in charge, tell me now."

"Argh!" Taryn pulled her ponytail tightly. It was obvious she was frustrated. "You're blaming me?"

"Yes. I'm also blaming myself. I should have stopped you."

"You—I—argh!" Taryn turned and walked toward the cockpit, throwing her hands into the air. She slammed a fist into the bulkhead as she passed the galley. Sunshine let her go without another word and turned her attention onto the CozSha.

"Come with me," she instructed and walked back to the med bay.

"I'm getting tired of being shot, tiny fierceness," Dref-na complained as soon as Sunshine entered the room. The Besquith motioned at the tiny CozSha who was trailing closely behind. "Especially during rescue attempts."

"I'm sorry," Sunshine said as the CozSha moved next to the Besquith and began to inspect the wound on her leg. The diminutive alien looked around and spotted the aerosol nanite spray on the wall.

"Hand me that, please," said the CozSha, speaking for the first time since the rescue. Sunshine dutifully pulled the nanite treatment from the magnetized wall mount and passed it to the CozSha, who immediately applied the treatment to Dref-na's injured leg.

"It is not your fault," Dref-na said as she watched the CozSha work. "Well, it is, but it also isn't. I understand why you did everything, tiny fierceness."

"It still doesn't make me feel better," Sunshine admitted.

"Hard choices are so for a reason."

"Why did the Zuparti grab you?" Sunshine turned and asked the CozSha as soon as the tiny alien was done spraying the hole in Dref-na's leg. The oddly shaped eyes of the small being looked up at her, surprised.

"I don't know," the CozSha answered. "I don't even know where I'm at. I was sent here because I am very good at my job."

"You're at Bishwanath Station," Sunshine informed her. "Ring any bells?"

"I am familiar with it, yes. I boarded the shuttle after following the Administrator's orders at my substation," came a quiet explanation. "Then I ended up here. I don't remember much. I know, it's not very efficient of me, I apologize. The Zuparti grabbed me, then you snatched me afterwards. Now I'm here on your ship."

"Not at all helpful." Sunshine frowned. "And not really my ship. Who's the Administrator?"

"Our guild master," the CozSha stated. Sunshine perked up at this.

"Which guild do you work for?" she asked.

"The Xeno Guild."

"Never heard of it." Sunshine looked up at Dref-na, who was staring at the tiny CozSha with a curious expression. She sighed. "I have a feeling you know who they are."

"I do." Dref-na nodded. "They are very secretive, the Xeno Guild, but I've heard of them. They're a young guild, an offshoot of the Science and Information Guilds. A hybrid of their combined efforts."

"What do they do?" Sunshine asked.

"No idea," Dref-na replied. Both Sunshine and Dref-na looked at the CozSha expectantly.

"Technically, we're officially an offshoot of the *Information* Guild," the CozSha corrected, and she suddenly appeared very nervous and agitated. Her eyes darted back and forth between Sunshine and Dref-na. "We're very efficient. But what you described is technically true. We work on translators. I am very good at my job."

"That's it?" Sunshine asked, dumbfounded. "Translators?"

"You have no idea how stringent the requirements for a proper translator is," the CozSha told them. "Inefficiency is horrible. We are efficient. We all take them for granted but imagine if one did not work properly. Historically speaking, improper translations have led to multiple conflicts breaking out over a misused pronoun, something which could have been fixed easily enough. To waste is to want."

"That's all you do?" Dref-na pressed. The CozSha flinched as the towering form of the Besquith loomed over her. "You do nothing else?"

"Languages are vital! I did my job efficiently!" the CozSha squeaked. Sunshine sighed. There had to be more going on here than the CozSha was telling them. The problem was that Sunshine had no idea how to get it out of her.

"Look, uh…what's your name?" Sunshine asked, trying to determine what, if anything, the CozSha was hiding.

"Vah Gorna. I am a junior administrator within my guild. You only become this by being very efficient at your job."

"Listen, Vah. Those Zuparti were hired to kidnap you," Sunshine told her. Seeing the surprise on the tiny alien's face, she continued, "Who would want that?"

"I don't know," Vah answered in a soft voice. "Maybe one of the senior commissioners? I really don't understand it myself. I did what I was told. I was very efficient at my job."

"Who are they?"

"Who?"

"The senior commissioners," Sunshine clarified, rubbing her temples as a small headache began to form. Dealing with the terrified and slightly neurotic CozSha was beginning to wear on her patience. Leadership was not for the faint of heart, it seemed. "You mentioned them before."

"Oh, them." Vah seemed sad and Sunshine's previous irritation at the alien quickly disappeared. "You would call them upper management in Human terms."

"How do you know Human terms?" Sunshine was surprised.

"I am familiar with all colloquialisms of all alien languages and their various dialects," Vah said with some pride. "I understand almost 65 of your various Human dialects, including slang, *dude*. I am highly efficient at my job."

"So you keep saying…" Sunshine's voice trailed off. She sighed wearily. "We need to get situated before we hit the gate. We didn't get the guns we needed, so we have to search for more options."

"Tiny fierceness?" Dref-na's voice was hesitant, which was unlike what Sunshine had grown used to over the time they had traveled together. "Taryn Lupo has many contacts in the galaxy which can help us."

"I bet she does," Sunshine muttered darkly. She was still irritated at the other woman and wasn't about to try and hide it. Taryn had screwed up and almost gotten them all killed, and Sunshine had no idea how to deal with her yet. She'd never seen Mulbah have to deal with a subordinate yelling at him. *How did he do it?* she silently wondered.

"You really are in charge of all this?" Vah asked, surprise evident upon her features. "But you're so young!"

"Thanks for reminding me," Sunshine grumbled, though the CozSha had a good point. She *was* young for so much responsibility.

"I'm sorry," Vah said, her eyes downcast. "I'm efficient at my work. The best, perhaps. Dealing with other living beings I am…deficient. No, I am bad at it."

Sunshine exhaled. "No, not your fault. Things are *cray cray* right now."

"Your suit is almost finished," Klinks announced as she poked her head into the small medical area. Sensing something was off, she cocked her insectoid head and looked at Dref-na. "Is this one of those 'bad timing' moments I hear so much about?"

"No, it's fine." Sunshine sighed again, wishing things would turn out just a little bit better. "Dref-na, can you get Vah situated? There are a few berthing spaces still open."

"The CozSha doesn't appear to need a lot of space," Dref-na smiled. The CozSha looked terrified. Sunshine scowled.

"Dref-na, quit trying to scare the poor thing," Sunshine ordered. Dref-na continued to smile but nodded in agreement.

"Don't worry, little Vah. I promise to not eat you."

"Ever?" The CozSha's voice was almost a squeak.

"As long as you do not betray the tiny fierceness that is Sunshine," the Besquith vowed. "Now come, Vah. We will find you somewhere to sleep."

Klinks moved to the side of the med bay, allowing Dref-na to guide Vah to one of the smaller side berthing spaces. Sunshine and the Jeha watched them leave before they began to speak.

"You got the suit together?" Sunshine asked.

"Almost," Klinks responded. She did not sound too happy, though. "I am currently working on a few upgrades to help your suit function better in battle."

"Well, that's good, I guess."

"It is," Klinks agreed. "However, I do have some bad news."

"No message?"

"I am very sorry," Klinks stated, confirming what had become a growing suspicion for the teenager. "I went over the coding within the suit's system, checked the hardware redundancies, and ran through the software twice. The cursed wor—ah, Dusman was correct and not lying to you. There is no message hidden within the suit."

Sunshine let out a slow, defeated exhalation. Everything she had done to this point was for a message which didn't seem to exist. She had begun to suspect this not long after departing Earth, but the dream of her exacting revenge upon those who had hurt her family had driven the teen onward. The idea of seeing a Peacemaker dispense justice upon Peepo and her ilk was what had sustained her during her long, lonely journey through the stars.

Now? There would be no justice because nobody cared.

If I can't get my justice, menh, *then I'll just aim for revenge,* she decided suddenly as the idea came to her. The only problem with her plan was that she had no idea where to start.

"You and Taryn must work out your difficulties soon," Klinks abruptly interrupted her silent musings. Sunshine blinked, confused.

"Huh?"

"This issue between you and Taryn must be resolved," Klinks repeated as she formed her arms into an intricate shape before pointing them at her. "My apologies, I was listening in. You and she are the heart of this...group? Yes, that is the correct word. We are not yet *cakōtarikaɬ*. Part of being a leader is knowing when you make a mistake. It is also knowing when to point out to someone they did something wrong. It is the timing of it, not that Taryn was in the wrong. You were right to point out her mistakes, but wrong to do so in front of others. She did not react well because she is embarrassed and knows she messed up."

Sunshine sighed. Klinks was right. While Taryn might have been in the wrong, Sunshine was still learning how to be a leader and could have handled things differently. She recalled Mulbah's explanation why she had been placed in his command squad in the Korps and not as second in command of the Goshawks. Leadership came with experience, and this was one area she was still lacking in. Time in the command squad was supposed to help build it up but, unfortunately, those plans were now nothing more than a smoldering mess buried deeply in the ruins of Monrovia.

"Do I need to apologize to her?" Sunshine asked. The Jeha tilted her head oddly.

"Why should you apologize? It is she who is in the wrong."

"So how do I deal with this?" she asked.

"I don't know," Klinks admitted. "I'm not usually in charge of anything except machines. They do as they're told. Usually."

"Let her come to you, tiny fierceness," Dref-na said, reappearing in the doorway. She nodded toward Klinks. "Since you aren't using the berthing Taryn assigned you, I placed the CozSha in there to rest. She has been through a lot and has suffered some sort of dissociative mental break. She needs time to recover."

"This is acceptable," Klinks agreed.

"Time is a luxury we don't have right now," Sunshine pointed out. Dref-na shrugged as Sunshine continued, "We still don't know where we're going next."

"Once we hit the gate, the timer begins," Dref-na reminded them. "We'll have almost a week to rest. I don't know if that will be enough time for Vah to figure out what is going on in her situation, but it should be plenty of time for Taryn to apologize to you."

"I'm just hoping she doesn't drop us somewhere random and leave," Sunshine said. Dref-na chuckled at her.

"Taryn Lupo is many things," Dref-na stated, "but she will not abandon us. Not until the job is complete. She has a reputation for completing the job, no matter what."

"Why did she yell at me?" Sunshine asked. "If she's at fault, why was she so angry at me?"

"Because I'm angry at myself," an unexpected voice joined in the conversation. Sunshine turned around and saw Taryn standing there, her head hanging in shame. "I'm mad because I got cocky and underestimated the Zuparti, and I got Dref-na hurt."

"Merely a flesh wound," Dref-na reassured her. "Though I do not wish to be shot again. Twice in rapid succession is not good for my health."

"We need to talk," Sunshine said as she eyed Taryn, a little wary. While she was used to being yelled at when others were mad, this was the first real fight she'd had with someone she considered her friend. When she'd been in the Korps, she hadn't even so much as argued. They had been family, and even when they chastised her, she understood why they had done it. This, though? This was something entirely new to her.

"Let's go up front," Taryn said, and they went to the *Velut Luna*'s cockpit. Once situated, Taryn started speaking immediately. "Look, I don't think straight when I get mad. I'm sorry. I shouldn't have yelled."

"I shouldn't have either," Sunshine allowed, thinking about what Klinks had said earlier. "I don't know what to do sometimes. Like I said before, you keep calling me the leader of this group, but nobody seems to listen."

"You're right." Taryn nodded and leaned back in the pilot's seat. Interlacing her fingers together, she put her hands behind her head and sighed. "You're in charge. You hired me to help you find Kl'nk'nnk. I yelled because I know I screwed up, and it's my fault. That's how I respond to things. I either blow it up or yell."

"Thank you for not blowing me up," Sunshine observed drily.

Taryn chuckled. "Dref-na would have murdered me if I did."

"I thought you made illegal drugs?" Sunshine asked, thinking back to the day they first met.

"I used to," Taryn admitted. "Before Mister Z. You could say he refined my skillset a little. Chemistry is good for more than simply cooking illegal drugs, you know."

"Ah."

"Okay, new rules." Taryn shifted back to the more serious topic at hand. Her face changed from the carefree expression Sunshine knew to a serious one. "I'll listen to you and do what you say, since you're in charge, unless it endangers the ship or the others. But unless it's an emergency, I won't do it in front of the others."

"If you have advice, though, I would like to hear it," Sunshine agreed, nodding. "I'm new at this *bass* thing."

"I can help with that," Taryn stated. "I've had to learn a little bit about it myself."

"Good," Sunshine said as she leaned on the copilot's seat. "Not to change the subject, but where are we going next? Do you know of anyone who can sell us some weapons?"

"I do," Taryn replied. "Are you sure this is something we need to do? I mean, I don't want to sound like a selfish jerk, but we don't owe the TriRusk anything. We've never even met them."

"You're right," Sunshine said, dark eyes staring intently at Taryn. "But you're also wrong. The *bass* and his guys didn't know me, didn't owe me anything, and they still saved me. They saved a lot of people they never met. I would like to do the same."

"Without the dying part, though," Taryn added.

"Yes, without dying," Sunshine affirmed. "Let's go to the back and tell them we have a plan. Kind of."

"A weak plan is better than no plan at all," Taryn said before she paused, uncertain. "Well, actually, no plan might be better than some half-cocked plan. No plan usually involves more violence though."

"Can you get everyone in the dining area?" Sunshine asked. "That way we don't have to tell them individually."

"It's called the galley," Taryn laughed and nodded. "Good meeting place. Mister Z liked having his little powwows there as well."

"Any suggestions?" Sunshine asked as they left the cockpit.

"Listen to them if they have ideas," Taryn answered with a shrug. "You already do that, though. Otherwise, just let them know we're off to get weapons before we head back to Zav'ax for a rescue mission."

Sunshine walked toward the center of the ship as Taryn's voice erupted over the general comms, requesting everyone not busy to report to the galley as soon as possible. Glad her little blowup with Taryn was over, Sunshine decided she could dwell more on the problem at hand. More precisely, convincing everyone else the idea of pulling the TriRusk out of the B'Hono Corporation's greedy mitts was a good one. Minus Vah, she felt fairly confident in their desire to follow her lead. Granted, she hadn't mentioned to the CozSha about the TriRusk, but she had a strange gut feeling the Xeno Guild member would be interested in hearing the details.

In the galley, she found Klinks and Dref-na already present, with the latter standing against the wall leading into the cooking area. Klinks was resting on a chair, though Sunshine couldn't be sure if the insect-like alien was sitting or standing on it. Vah hadn't arrived yet, though she knew it was only a matter of time. Curiosity was the mark of a brilliant mind, and she had the CozSha pegged as someone highly intelligent, if a little socially awkward. Taryn arrived and patted Sunshine on the shoulder as she moved past the teen.

"Well, then, you ready to tell them the plan, boss?" Taryn asked as she settled into one of the galley's seats. Sunshine looked around and saw Vah had joined them as well. The tiny CozSha climbed into one of the taller chairs and buckled herself in.

"I didn't want to be alone on this ship," Vah explained. "The interior design is inefficient, and I have been alone for far too long. Strangely, I want to 'hang' with you all."

"Humanisms," Dref-na chuckled darkly. "Even the CozSha are using their phrases now."

"The guild has access to every race's colloquialisms," Vah sniffed. "We don't like to remain ignorant of shifting trends between languages. Languages are guides to the true nature of beings."

"I think the little CozSha called me stupid," Dref-na said as she turned her face and showed the tiny creature her large teeth. "Do it again?"

"As I said, I think the boss here has a plan," Taryn said, ignoring the byplay between the two as she looked at Sunshine. "Okay, the beginnings of a plan, but still."

"Do we have a plan?" Dref-na looked around, amusement evident on her face. Her giant mouth opened wider, and her tongue lolled out. It was clear the Besquith found her new friends to be utterly hilarious. "I thought we would simply blast our way in and kill everyone. You know, as usual?"

"No, we're going to need a plan this time," Sunshine stated as she looked at the gathered group. It was an odd sight to behold. A former slave turned mercenary leading a group on a daring rescue operation. A Besquith, a creature from nightmares and one of the most lethal killers in the galaxy, was joking around with a Human who had once held a gun to her head. A Jeha engineer and a CozSha working together to…what, precisely? Sunshine wasn't sure. In spite of her timid nature, the CozSha appeared to be settling in just fine. It could be she was simply comfortable around the Jeha for some reason. Sunshine wasn't about to try and explain it. "We should figure out what we're going to do when we get back to Zav'ax."

"Find the TriRusk, of course," Klinks proclaimed, looking around at the gathered group. Her feelings were clear on the matter. "Rescue them and take them home. Wherever that is."

"TriRusk?" Vah asked, surprised. "They have finally reappeared?"

"Apparently." Dref-na nodded. "We need still weapons if we're going to go against the entire corporation. Ideas?"

"I know a guy..." Taryn offered cautiously. She looked at Sunshine, who nodded for her to continue. "But it involves dealing with more crooks. Well, these guys are legitimate crooks, but officially still crooks. They're Pushtal, actually."

"Well, it's a start." Sunshine nodded before smiling. "As long as they don't shoot us, I won't have to fire you. You know the way, right? We'll come up with a better plan while in hyperspace. I'm sure we can think of something other than 'steal all the shiny guns' once we arrive."

"Oh my God, I'm never going to hear the end of that," Taryn moaned as she headed toward the cockpit to input their new destination. Everyone laughed, even Vah, though it was clear to Sunshine the CozSha did not understand the context of the joke. It was a good moment to have to ease the tension of their escape from Bishwanath Station and the argument after.

"Oh, and Sunshine? Check your translator matrix before we get there," Klinks informed her. Her insectoid head twisted oddly to look up at the Besquith. It was an unnerving sight. "I've heard a rumor that not everyone's translators understand the various dialects of the Pushtal."

"If Vah truly is from the Xeno Guild, then she should be able to help," Sunshine added with a look at the CozSha, who was nodding.

"I am very efficient," Vah replied. "I know all the Pushtal dialects except for great northern nomadic Haepthaenic clans and their sub-dialects, but those are so rare it is unlikely you will ever come across a speaker in your lifetime. Everyone's translators will be fully functional and at peak efficiency with thirteen of the largest languages of the Pushtal race before we arrive."

We're a very weird little group of randoms, Sunshine thought as the *Velut Luna* slipped through the stargate and into hyperspace.

* * * * *

Chapter Six

Royal House of the Fangmaster, Draxis III, Draxis System

"A re you sure about this?" Sunshine asked for the fifth time in as many minutes. Her eyes darted nervously about the small waiting room, taking in all the collectible antiques that seemed to fill every niche and cubbyhole in the walls. There were dozens of alien artifacts on display and, truth be told, Sunshine wasn't quite sure what to make of it. She had never heard of this species before, though it was clear Taryn knew precisely who they were dealing with. Or rather, what.

"As sure as I can be," Taryn replied and rubbed Sunshine's shoulder in a reassuring manner. "Relax. They're all sorts of things, but one thing they're not is stupid. They'll see the deal for what it is and agree to it. Readily, I might add. They have a bad rep, but if you know how to deal with them, everything'll run smooth."

"If you say so, Taryn Lupo," Dref-na murmured softly. "It's been many years since they were considered to be legitimate businessmen, as it were. Even longer for anyone to label them as manageable."

"Redemption can be a slow process," Taryn reminded her. "Even the Besquith can respect that."

"Truth," Dref-na acknowledged with a slow nod.

"Besides, I sent a message ahead when we first arrived," Taryn continued with a smile. She shot Sunshine a reaffirming look. "So, manageable. I just know they're going to love you!"

"You've got a lot of nerve showing up around here," a voice hissed from the shadows. A short, cloaked figured emerged and stood before them. A cowl was pulled up over the head to conceal the wearer's identity. "The Fangmaster warned you against returning, *Human.*"

"No," Taryn countered, her voice cautious and her words measured in spite of her previous reassurances. "He warned against showing my face again if I wasted his time. I didn't waste his time, and I'm not wasting it now, so here I am, *Pushtal.*"

"Boldly spoken," the cloaked figure said. The cowl was removed, and Sunshine gasped. The alien was almost identical to a tiger in appearance, though there were a few minor differences. There were even similar markings upon its face. As far as Sunshine could tell, it was a Bengal tiger walking on two legs, albeit a short tiger, wearing some form of body armor beneath the billowing cloak. The alien turned its furry face to look closely at Taryn. "How goes the tricks, Taryn?"

"Can't believe you would screw with me like that. You're such a bitch, Jorna." Taryn exhaled sharply before she smiled. The short, slender Pushtal female opened her arms for an embrace. Taryn stepped into it, and they hugged. "How're things in the pirate life?"

"Same as always," Jorna replied, her furred face smiling. She released Taryn and nodded toward the Besquith. "Dref-na? Wow, never thought I'd see the two of you together again. Last time I saw you, Taryn was holding a gun to your head, and you were one wrist flick away from spilling her guts across the floor. I see things haven't changed too much."

"There's no weapon this time, Jorna of Clan Arwoon." Dref-na chuckled darkly. "Speaking of weapons, how is your father?"

"For a Pushtal in his prime, he sure is a grumpy old coot," Jorna admitted, her grin fading a little bit. "He asked me to greet you while he takes care of some clan business. Something bad happened."

"Oh?" Taryn asked. Jorna nodded, her features somber.

"The…clan leader for Roxtador was killed recently, but not by a challenger," Jorna informed them. "Unfortunately, this individual…did not have a family, per se. It's a situation we knew might happen one day, but it still caught us unawares. Father is—struggling is the best way to describe it. The clan leader was one of his closest friends, even though they rarely were able to see one another over the past few years. There was a bond between them which is hard to describe to outsiders. It was the bond of spirit, forged during the last great Moot."

"Wait…was that—" Taryn's hands covered her mouth as realization dawned on her. "Oh. I'm so sorry! I hadn't heard!"

"Not many have yet," Jorna stated. "My sister says this is because Rsach is deliberately keeping it quiet, though he was kind enough to inform my father of his death. So much is occurring right now, and it's only going to get messier. Everyone is going to need allies, and soon."

"What have you heard?" Sunshine asked, concerned. Everything the Pushtal was saying fell in line with what she had surmised since this journey of hers began. There was something dark pulsing beneath the very fabric of Galactic civilization, only nobody seemed to know precisely what it was. The unknown would always be terrifying, but what lurked in the shadows was beyond comprehension.

The Pushtal looked at her, a strange mixture of menace and amusement splashed upon her furred features. "And who might you be?"

"Jorna, this is Captain Sunshine of the Kakata Korps Mercenary Company," Taryn said, introducing them. "Sunshine, this is Jorna, fifth daughter of the Fangmaster and leader of the Pushtal Republic."

"Technically, we're officially a government-in-exile." Jorna shrugged her muscular shoulders. "But yeah, that's me. The MinSha stopped paying attention to us a few decades back after it was ruled the populace of Vorrhurna Prime were still the official representatives of the Pushtal Empire. Even though, you know, it no longer exists because the MinSha conquered it. Legalese states the denizens of Draxis III are members of the Pushtal *Republic*, but apparently getting the personalized letterheads we sent to the Galactic Union to change it is too problematic for them. Plus, only two other Galactic races have recognized us so far, and neither of them have any clout whatsoever. My father believes the Information Guild is wavering in their opinion of us, but I think that's just wishful thinking on his part."

"I'm certain it'll all get straightened out in the end," Taryn reassured her.

"I'd never heard of the Pushtal before this," Sunshine admitted after the introductions were completed. "I dug through the ship's records and there were a lot of redacted names in the races of the Mercenary Guild database, though. Are you one of those?"

"I did mention you shouldn't be digging around the ship's secured databanks without my permission, didn't I?" Taryn asked rhetorically.

"Deliberate obfuscation on the Mercenary Guild's part, I think," Jorna said breezily with a wave of her furry hand. She buffed her claws on the shoulder harness which held one of her many pistols. "Easier to control what nobody knows about. My great-grandfather was atrocious with contract negotiations. The MinSha were able to walk circles around him at the negotiations table somehow, then he tried to make up for the losses by accepting riskier and riskier contracts from the guild. Combine that with a failed push for a leadership position within the Mercenary Guild and it's no wonder we're not listed on the guild rolls any longer."

"So, *are* you mercenaries?" Sunshine asked, confused. It seemed to be a constant state of existence lately.

"Depends on who you ask." Jorna smiled in reply, revealing large incisor fangs. "According to just about everyone running the galaxy, we're nothing more than deplorable pirate scum."

"My kind of scum," Taryn stated. "Deplorable, with untraceable guns for sale."

"This is why I love you." Jorna laughed before turning her attention back to Sunshine. "The message Taryn sent suggested you might be interested in purchasing some decent hardware which couldn't be traced back to the seller, correct?"

"Uh, yes." Sunshine paused to gather her composure. She wasn't ready to negotiate quite yet. "I don't want the seller to get into trouble."

"Well, you've definitely come to the right place." Jorna chuckled. "The details and batch numbers of both the ammunition and firearms we have for sale have been changed and altered so many times *we're* not even sure where they're originally from. Gives us a deniability most species can only dream of."

"If you're pirates, why do you care about deniability?" Sunshine asked.

Jorna's face broke into a huge smile. "There's a huge difference between having a reputation as a pirate versus outright admitting you're a pirate," Jorna clarified. "It seems silly, but it keeps the Peacemakers off our back. Well, it keeps them off the backs of all the *major* clans. The lesser ones do what they want and ignore us. But since they don't dictate policy within the Pushtal as a whole, they can go off and get killed all they want."

"Tribal politics," Sunshine acknowledged and perked up at this revelation. It was a subject she was intimately familiar with, after all. Even while she "worked" for Major General Sparkles, it was clear to her young mind the differences between the various tribal conflicts in Chocolate City alone, much less western Africa as a whole. The tribal differences across species? Trying to keep them straight would drive anyone into the comforting arms of madness.

A bell chimed, and Jorna looked over her shoulder at a plain wooden door behind her. It was unlike the ornately designed doors to Sunshine's right. The young woman recognized it was the servant's entrance.

The Pushtal jerked her head for them to follow. "Let's help you get your guns," Jorna said as she sauntered to the door. She rapped on it three times, then twice. A small buzzer sounded, and a lock within clicked. The door swung open into a dark tunnel. "Follow me."

The foursome trekked through the long and seemingly endless tunnel. Around them the air grew cooler. Darkness hid a lot of small nooks and crannies, and the few Sunshine could see into led away with no apparent end. They passed no other Pushtal along the way. The only sound she could hear were their footsteps upon the old cobblestone floor. It was a long, silent, and increasingly uncomfortable journey.

"Where are we going?" Sunshine finally asked.

"We can't keep the weapons near the House of the Fangmaster," Jorna explained as the lengthy tunnel grew noticeably brighter. "All deniability would go out the door if we did that. We have a separate warehouse where we store them."

"Oh," Sunshine nodded as they arrived at a pair of doors. Above the doors was a single light. "That makes sense."

Jorna waited until they heard a subtle *click!* and she pushed the doors open. Beyond it was a warehouse very much like the one the Korps' had back on Earth, though it wasn't filled with nearly as many crates. In fact, it appeared the warehouse was filled with nothing but foodstuffs, until they arrived at a small open area just off to the side of the main storage area. In the center, next to four crates, was a muscular Pushtal in nice clothing surrounded by armed guards. Sunshine smiled at the sight and wondered who would be stupid enough to try to rip off an arms dealer at their own location.

It's not like we can just outright steal them, she thought as the well-dressed Pushtal stepped forward from the group.

"Greetings," the dealer said. "I hear you're interested in our goods."

"I am, yes." Sunshine nodded.

"I have a variety of goods available," the dealer continued as he shot Jorna an odd look. "Unfortunately, I have nothing for a CASPer except grenades, both smoke and frag, and portable fuel depots which can be dropped into position. We do have a nice array of quality subcarbines, perfectly suitable for both boarding actions in space and combat in gravity. Today we're having a special—buy one crate of subcarbines and three crates of ammunition, and get CASPer grenades for free."

"That sounds about what we need." Sunshine nodded. "What's the price?"

"With the extra fees we have to throw on due to the rush order, one hundred thousand credits," the weapons dealer proclaimed. "Twenty thousand per crate, and twenty for the rush."

"Excuse me?" Sunshine cocked her head in irritation. "Who do you think you're dealing with? I'm not paying any extra fees."

"Consider it a retainer for future business ventures with me," the dealer said breezily. The Pushtal appeared to have a weird air of aloofness about him, as though this were more of a hobby for him than actual business. It threw Sunshine off a little bit and made her even more uncomfortable than she already was. "It's a terrific deal."

"You're trying to cheat me," Sunshine said, getting into the Pushtal's face. Trusting her instincts on how to respond, she invaded his personal space just enough to fully grab his attention. She had never considered herself very tall, but she was able to keep her eyes locked onto his. He clearly was not pleased with her posturing, but she didn't care. Sunshine was tired of everyone trying to push her around just because they believed she was inexperienced. The Pushtal guards grew nervous, with more than one fingering his weapon. "If you keep it up, I'm going to gut you like a pig and feed you your entrails."

The Pushtal blinked. He brought his large paw up and waggled his retractable claws near the side of her face. There was a slight tremor to them, and Sunshine was certain it wasn't from fear but from anger. "You have no idea who you're threatening, child. One hundred thousand for the crates. Keep the sassy attitude and the price goes up."

"I know what you are better than you do," Sunshine growled in a low tone. "You're a swindler. Quit trying to cheat me or we're going to have serious problems."

"Problems? *Problems?*"

"Yes," Sunshine nodded, refusing to back down from the clearly annoyed Pushtal. "I can do math, too, you know. Four crates at twenty thousand each is eighty thousand. I'm not paying any extra fees, and that's final. If you want me to walk, then fine, I walk. But you're losing out on all my future business, too, *ken?* And since I am the owner of a licensed mercenary company, you're going to want my future business, especially when all the contracts completed mean I can spend more money."

The Pushtal weapons dealer leaned back and sniffed. His eyes narrowed as he sized up the determined female before him. Sunshine refused to blink as she met his gaze levelly. He finally grunted and crossed his arms.

"Eighty thousand it is, angry little Human," he declared before turning to look at Jorna, who was doing her best to control herself. Sunshine saw the female Pushtal's shoulders move violently up and down. For the young mercenary commander, it was obviously a sign of just how angry Jorna truly was at the perceived insult Sunshine had shown the arms dealer. For a brief moment, Sunshine wondered if Jorna was going to murder her as soon as the other Pushtal left. The arms dealer frowned at the sight of the female Pushtal's evident rage but said nothing. "I'll still let you have the CASPer grenades though. Consider it a token of goodwill. Jorna will handle everything from here. In fact, I believe she will accompany you off world to ensure you learn how to use these particular weapons properly, as well as observe your mercenary company in action. Call it…research for future joint endeavors."

"What?" Jorna froze, confused. She turned to look at the arms dealer, but he had already turned and walked away. The small retinue of armed Pushtal followed him, leaving a frustrated Jorna alone with Sunshine and Taryn, the latter of which looked entertained for some reason. Sunshine made a mental note to ask her what she found so funny later. Now, she needed to figure out how to handle Jorna before the female Pushtal murdered her for insulting the weapons dealer.

It turned out she didn't need to worry. Jorna, though displeased by the instructions to go with the Humans, was clearly used to conducting the final aspects of business deals with the arms dealer and potential clients. The crates were loaded onto a small transport sled and transported to the *Velut Luna*, with Sunshine, Taryn, and Jorna following closely behind on foot.

"He's not going to betray us, is he?" Sunshine asked, her eyes locked on the transport ahead of them. The sled was open, and the crates easily seen, but Sunshine was taking no chances. According to what Dref-na had told her before their arrival, the Pushtal had a bad reputation for a reason. It would be idiotic of her to underestimate them. "I think I might have made him angry."

"No, he won't," Jorna replied. "It's not his style to betray someone once the agreement has been struck. He might try to screw someone over during the negotiations, but not after."

"You deal with him often?" Sunshine asked. Jorna's smile was wide and her fangs, while not as big as Dref-na's, were very bright indeed.

"On a regular basis. You could say he's been watching over me since I was a young cub."

* * *

"You know something?" Taryn asked Sunshine after Jorna boarded the *Velut Luna* once the crates of guns and ammo had been loaded. The younger woman looked at Taryn questioningly, who offered the young mercenary commander a smile. "You're a natural leader. Everyone seems to follow you without too much issue. It's...impressive."

"I don't know why," Sunshine admitted as the loading bay door was sealed. "I'm not doing anything special. Am I?"

Taryn shrugged. "You're likeable and brave. That's a start. Also, you are confident. The way you handled yourself with Magnus was like an experienced negotiator. Not a lot of people can stand toe to toe with the Fangmaster of the Pushtal Republic and walk away with his respect after threatening to gut him like a pig."

"Wait—that guy was *Magnus*? *That* was the Fangmaster?" Sunshine's dark face paled. "He's their leader? I thought he was just a regular arms dealer!"

"You didn't know?" Taryn asked, surprised. Seeing Sunshine shake her head, she began to laugh. After a moment she regained her composure, though there was a twinkle in her eye which had not been there before. "Dref-na was right. You are utterly fierce."

"Should I, I don't know, apologize to Jorna? Wasn't that her dad? Oh my God, I just realized what she meant by him watching over her. I'm such an idiot!"

"Don't sweat it," Taryn said once she checked the seal on the cargo door. She moved to the containers and tested their tie lines before finishing, "I'm certain she thought it was hilarious."

"How do you know?"

"You didn't see her shaking the entire time?"

"I thought she was angry," Sunshine admitted. "I was ready for her to try to kill me once he left."

"She was trying to not laugh at her dad in front of strangers," Taryn declared after some thought. "Pushtal facial expressions are subtle. You missed it, but his were mixed. He wasn't sure if he should be offended or amused. Magnus? I think he decided on amused."

"How—how can you tell?"

"If he had shot you after the threat, it would have meant he didn't find it funny at all."

"Sunshine?" Klinks' voice came over the ship's comms, interrupting the duo. The Jeha sounded a bit insistent. "I have completed the modifications you requested for your CASPer. Do you have time to calibrate it?"

"Duty calls," Sunshine said and shook her head. It never ceased to amaze her how her luck sometimes went. It was either very good or really bad. There was no middle ground to it. She looked back at Taryn. "How long until we go through the gate?"

"Two hours," Taryn responded after consulting her pinplants. "Ninety minutes until we kill the thrust, though, which means no gravity. Better hurry."

"Got it," Sunshine said. She replied via the comms. "Klinks? I'll be there in a minute. Where are you?"

"What Taryn laughingly calls the machine shop," came the quick reply. Sunshine's brow furrowed in confusion, and she looked to Taryn for help.

"It's a secondary cargo hold below this one," Taryn explained after a weary sigh. It was clear she had heard this complaint many times before from other individuals. "Go forward two sections to the galley, then down that ladder which is roped off, then head aft...toward the back."

"How'd she get my CASPer down there?" Sunshine asked. "That ladder is too narrow for even Dref-na to fit down it!"

"You'll have to ask Klinks," Taryn admitted, concerned. "I have no idea."

"How am I supposed to get it out?"

"I think the hold's original design was for an emergency escape shuttle," Taryn stated. "I'll check the schematics, but it should be easy. I'm pretty sure there's a way to rig it open so we can use your suit. Klinks'll know."

"Hope so," Sunshine said. "Otherwise whatever we do on Zav'ax is going to be the shortest mission ever."

"I'm going to go see how Jorna and Vah are settling in," Taryn said after reaching out and giving Sunshine's arm a squeeze. "I should introduce them so the CozSha doesn't go catatonic seeing another predatory species on this ship. Go and get your suit ready. Next stop on this weird little adventure nobody's ever going to believe if I told them about it? Zav'ax."

After the ship launched and left Draxis III behind, Sunshine followed Taryn's directions to the secondary hold. After one wrong turn at the bottom of the ladder she found herself in the secondary hold. The space was clearly designed to function as a machine shop as well. She was surprised as its size, considering Klinks' complaints. It was larger than expected but lacked the wide-open feel found in the main cargo hold area, primarily because it was filled with the crates she had been shipping her CASPer around in.

Sunshine spotted Klinks near her CASPer. However, it looked nothing like her old suit. The Jeha appeared pleased with herself.

"How'd you get this down here?" Sunshine asked, awed as she walked around the suit. It seemed smaller somehow, yet sleeker. It more resembled a work of art, not a killing machine.

The rough edges of the suit, which had been prevalent on the Mk 7, were gone, smoothed out by Klinks' natural engineering aesthetics. Klinks had also painted the entire CASPer a midnight black color, though instead of reflecting the light the paint seemed to absorb it. There was a silver lion's head cast into the center of the pilot canopy and the only part of the suit not painted black.

The arm blades had been reshaped. Before, they more resembled what a butcher would use in their shop on a chopping block. Now they were slightly curved and followed the natural flow of the arm. On the shoulders, instead of the old grenade launchers used for sieges, Klinks had added a laser system unlike anything she had ever seen before. There were numerous emitters tightly clustered, each with a millimeter-sized barrel aimed at a different angle. They all appeared to be aimed at the chest-height or higher.

That's an anti-missile system if I've ever seen one, she realized. But where are the grenade launchers?

After a few seconds of close inspection, she found them. They were still on the shoulders but had been milled down to appear to be nothing more than a few almost unnoticeable holes in the suit. They were smaller in diameter than before and, if Sunshine guessed correctly, had been retrofitted to handle 20mm grenades instead of the usual 40mm.

"I was able to move your suit down here piece by piece," Klinks said as her long body flowed out from behind a discarded crate. "This is similar to the design I did for Zorgama years ago, though his suit was older. I fabricated some of the materials for your CASPer to make it lighter without losing any structural integrity. I also weaved carbon graphite throughout the armor. It's no longer plated or as thick, but it's tougher and lighter. I also upgraded your electronics to respond better with your pinplants. We need to calibrate it so I can adjust the responses of your suit to your stimuli reflexology. That might take a while."

"How long?" Sunshine asked as she continued to marvel over the CASPer. She had never really thought a machine could be considered sexy before. This, however? This machine was most decidedly sexy.

"Maybe a few days?" Klinks sounded apologetic. "We'll take breaks for food and such, but this suit is smaller and faster than anything you've piloted before. I would say it is even better than the proposed Mk 9s. It's still tall, but not nearly as lumbering as before. The legs actually work like Human legs instead of robotic ones. Also, if you lose your balance, your natural equilibrium will keep you upright, even if you're sliding down a hill. This is why we need to calibrate, so the suit doesn't overcompensate your reactions and throw you off balance in the opposite direction."

"Specs?" Sunshine asked, her heart hammering excitedly in her chest.

"The arms feature a cyclic minigun laser system for close quarters combat," Klinks said as she flowed around to Sunshine's side. The Jeha's odd little pincer legs made a complex motion and pointed out the suit's features as the insectoid alien continued, "On your shoulders is a point defense laser system, good against missiles, or a crowd if you get swarmed and knocked down. Your blades are extremely well honed, so be careful what you hit with those. Scattered within your point defense system are four grenade launchers, two on each side. They have 20-millimeter caseless grenades in them. I used the smaller size because they aren't as heavy when you carry the same number. Weight is a concern with this suit; I didn't want it to be too heavy. Plus, I've seen CASPers use grenade launchers in the past—Humans are far more surgical with their grenades than most species, so I figured the smaller size would work to your advantage. On your back right shoulder blade area is a magnetic accelerator cannon. It is retractable and remains flush against your suit when not in use."

"This isn't a Mk 7, *menh*," Sunshine whispered as her fingertips traced over the silver lion's head. She glanced over to Klinks. "It's beautiful. Does it have a name or anything?"

"Whatever you want to call it," the Jeha replied. "I don't designate machinery; I only craft it. However, I am partial to *C'tnk'sarch'nnink*."

"Wha—"

"It loosely translates to 'Death Strikes from Darkness and Destroys Evil' in the Human English tongue," Klinks supplied. Sunshine mulled the translation over in her head before smiling as the image of a large cat came to mind.

"Let's just call it the Leopard."

"Leopard?"

"It's the callsign of an old friend who died," Sunshine explained, a hint of sadness creeping into her voice as she thought of Zion. "Unofficially, it was the first squad I ever joined. Plus, it's an animal from my planet which is considered to be the best hunter in the world. It should be in the ship's databanks if you want to look them up."

"I will." Klinks nodded as her expression became a little vacant. After a moment, she grunted, apparently pleased. "A large cat indigenous to your home world; a hunter which lives in the shadows…yes. Yes, this will do nicely. Plus, it honors your friend."

The Jeha picked up a small slate from a nearby workbench and began tapping the screen. A moment later, the pilot's cockpit slid open. Inside lay a very comfortably padded interior. Sunshine's eyes widened in surprise. This was a far cry from what she had dealt with the last time she had been in the CASPer. It was cleaner than it had ever been, even before her life-changing trek across the Sahara. Even the rancid stench of unwashed Human was gone.

"I interlinked everything via a closed-circuit connection between your pinplants and the suit," Klinks continued as Sunshine climbed into the CASPer. "The suit is not only effective in the vacuum of space, but the shielding on the armor now acts as a reflective heat shield, so no worries about overheating within the CASPer should you find yourself in direct light while in vacuum. It also has the strength to withstand high water pressure. I have not tested it yet, but estimates suggest a crush depth of almost one thousand meters in open ocean. Then again, it could be twice that. The simulators hadn't experienced anything like your suit before and estimates may vary."

"Whoa," Sunshine exhaled sharply. It was one thing for a CASPer to be rated for water and the vacuum of space. For the suit to be able to go deep in the water and have no fear of being crushed was something else entirely. "I hope I never need to test the crush depth."

"Me, too," Klinks replied. She fiddled with the controls on the outside. "Ready to seal the suit and begin calibration tests. Once the suit is sealed, you will see a series of prompts on your Tri-V display. They're easy to follow, and I'll guide you through them remotely at first. As you become more attuned to the system, your pinplants will automatically begin to assert more and more control over the suit. Once you have full control, we will begin the calibrations."

"Got it," Sunshine said when the first prompt appeared. She followed the instructions and locked the suit onto her biometrics only. This would ensure nobody else could ever pilot the CASPer, lessening her worry about someone trying to hijack the suit should something happen to her. While she trusted Taryn, there was no need to tempt fate with the unknowns she would undoubtedly come across. It also saved her from trying to remember a password during an emergency. Other prompts appeared and were dealt with in rapid succession. Surveying the area with her Tri-V display, she realized the initial command prompts had ceased. She activated the external speakers. "Klinks? The command prompts are done already. Now what?"

"You're done already?" Klinks asked, surprised. "You already figured out the speaker system as well. Odd. I had anticipated these first steps to take the better part of an hour."

"There weren't that many, really," Sunshine answered, almost apologetically. "Maybe I accidentally skipped a step or two?"

"One moment, I will check," Klinks replied. A few seconds passed before Klinks spoke again. "No, everything was done in accordance with the programming. Perhaps I underestimated your reaction time? Zorgama was the only other Human I have ever helped calibrate a suit for, and he was older than you. He was also a male of your species. He could be inferior in this matter. Humans are collectively an odd bunch."

"Well, calibrating the suit might take longer," Sunshine admitted. "I've never fully calibrated a suit before. I mean, I did okay before, but this is something else, *ken?*"

"Indeed," Klinks agreed as she tapped a few instructions onto the slate. They appeared on Sunshine's Tri-V almost immediately. "I just sent you a coded encrypted command. Do you see it?"

"Yes," she said. "My pinplants decrypted it as soon as it arrived."

"Curious," Klinks muttered.

"What?" Sunshine asked her.

"You shouldn't have been able to decrypt the command code sequence yet."

"Why?"

"I have yet to upload the key."

* * *

Once the suit was calibrated to suit Klinks' and her demanding requirements, Sunshine decided to get some sleep. They had been at it for almost three hours, and in zero-G it was more difficult for Sunshine to keep from being overly frustrated at the minute corrections. The Jeha was equally tired, but there were some things she had seen during the calibration process which she needed to talk to someone about. The first and most obvious individual was Taryn Lupo. However, Klinks wasn't certain how to broach the subject with the other Human. Taryn had shown protective tendencies over the younger female and the last thing Klinks wanted to do was to create a rift between anyone in the crew.

She decided discretion was best and calling Taryn to the secondary hold would cause the others to take notice. No, she needed to go to the Human and bring her to a quiet area to discuss the matter. Where on the crowded ship they could find privacy was not obvious to the Jeha, though. After much consideration she decided to risk a general ping through the ship's comms.

"Taryn, it's Kl'nk'nnk," she said over the comms. "Are you in the cockpit?"

"Yeah, what's up?"

"Just wondering," the Jeha said. "I'm coming forward to talk for a minute. Anyone else up there?"

"Just Vah, but she's heading aft for some sleep," Taryn replied.

It was as subtle as she could be without alerting anyone who might be listening. It wasn't for lack of trust but more about uncertainty as to how Sunshine would react knowing she was being discussed without being present. In Jeha society, it was something nobody really worried about, especially among scientists and engineers. What was said in private was expected to reach the receptors of the Jeha in question. It was an easy way to pass compliments or reprimands without directly insulting the individual in question.

Klinks passed Vah as she moved through the ship's galley, the tiny CozSha giving her a strange look before she passed. The CozSha was the one individual on the ship Klinks wasn't too certain about. It wasn't because the tiny creature was untrustworthy, but nobody seemed to know much about her. The Xeno Guild member was not the most forthcoming individual, either, and seemed as secretive as her guild.

Klinks found Taryn in the cockpit of the *Velut Luna* watching an entertainment vid on one of the secondary Tri-V displays mounted on the dash. It was a classic show, Klinks recognized immediately. The colors seemed more muted than expected and involved some sort of archaic vehicle flying around in the middle of a storm. It looked interesting, at least, though the physics of the ship seemed illogical and unworkable.

Taryn paused the vid once she saw Klinks and swiveled in the pilot's seat. She steepled her hands before her and waited.

"It's about Sunshine," Klinks announced without preamble. Taryn nodded slowly.

"I guessed as much," Taryn replied. "Good or bad?"

"Depends on how you look at it," Klinks admitted. "I am confused by my findings."

"Care to expand on that? I rather like her."

"Nothing negative, no," Klinks clarified hastily. "It's more of a physiological question. She *is* Human, yes, though remains a child?"

"Well, biologically she's old enough to have children of her own, though I doubt that's on her plate anytime soon," Taryn said as she pursed her lips thoughtfully. "She's been through a lot, even more than what I went through before Mister Z found me. But she's still very, very young. Maybe not mentally, but physically she is a teenager."

"No, that's not it, then." Klinks shook her head. "Well, perhaps it is…I'm not certain. Do Humans practice cloning on a species-wide scale yet?"

"Cloning?" Taryn asked, surprised. "No, I don't think so. I mean, I've heard rumors of it on colony worlds, but they're just that…rumors."

"Well, if that's accurate, then my only theory remaining is that Sunshine is, for lack of a better term, a genetic freak of nature."

"Care to explain?" Taryn leaned back in her pilot's seat. It was clear even to Klinks the Human was not pleased with the direction of their conversation.

"Her neurological process speed is faster than any Human should have," Klinks admitted after recognizing the look on Taryn's face. "Faster than most alien life I've come across, for that matter."

"So? She's really sharp," Taryn reminded her. "Highly intelligent and adaptive. She's a top-notch merc. She's already proven many times over just how smart she is."

"It's more than that," Klinks countered, struggling to explain. "It's one thing to be highly intelligent and have fast reflexes. It's another to process what you're seeing and form a cohesive mental stimuli response faster than a reflexive action. What's going on in Sunshine's brain, or neurological functions as a whole, shouldn't be possible. You understand how neurons work? How neuron receptors process information and data, stimulating the Human brain? Hers work far *better* than yours. Not just by a little; hers make both yours and Zorgama's comparable to a lower life form, and a particularly young one at that. No offense."

"None taken. You think she has some cybernetic upgrades we didn't know about?" Taryn asked.

The Jeha shook her head. "I would have picked up on that during her suit calibrations," Klinks stated. "No, this is something more. There are other questions about her mental performance which make me wonder about...the evolutionary state of Humans at this current time, but she is an outlier when I line her up with all of the information I have about every other Human out there, including

Zorgama. This is a very peculiar mystery, one which will not be solved easily or anytime soon, I'm afraid."

"Keep it quiet for now," Taryn told her, considering the impact it could have on the young girl's psyche. "She's got a lot going on, and she's finally happy after all this time. She's already dealt with the loss of her company and family. Don't throw anything else on her just yet."

"I won't," Klinks agreed. "But Taryn?"

"Yeah?"

"She's going to wonder about things eventually," Klinks warned. "She'll ask what is different about her and use that brain of hers to investigate. Sunshine already suspects something is wrong with her because of how quickly she breezed through my protocols during the suit's initiation period. She may discover the truth before we do. It might be useful to tell her we suspect something is wrong, just so we can have a head start on figuring it out for all of us."

"It just might." Taryn nodded. "But remember she's very young. She's a tough girl, but young. She deserves to know the truth, but let's wait for a better time. There's a lot going on right now. We can look at it later, okay?"

"Very well."

"One last thing." Klinks raised four of her legs before Taryn could get up.

"Argh!"

"Why did you let the Pushtal come with us?"

"Oh." Taryn shrugged her shoulders. "I don't know. Sunshine went along with the Fangmaster's decision, though. Jorna's working for Sunshine, not me, so in the end it's really not my call."

"Even though this is your ship?"

"Well, this is Zorgama's ship, remember?" Taryn reminded her. "Also, I work for Sunshine right now, which means the ship is hers to use as she wants, to a degree. We all work for her."

"But, Taryn, you're no longer bound to her," Klinks stated. "She hired you to find me. I am here. Job completed. Why do you stick around now?"

"Honestly? I never had a little sister before."

"And?"

"It's…kinda nice."

* * * * *

Chapter Seven

Faces of the dead continued to haunt her dreams. It was why she refused to sleep more than necessary. But in those minutes when exhaustion finally claimed her, she could taste the sea of her homeland and smell the clean air when a breeze came in from the south. She relished those moments because they were quickly replaced by the screams of the men dying beneath the claws of Tortantulas as they struggled to make their last stand at the Lion's Gate.

The hardest thing she had ever had to do in her life was walk away from the fighting when Mulbah had ordered her to. Hearing those she had grown to care about being brutally slaughtered at the hands of Peepo's mercenaries caused a great chasm to open in her soul, a poisoned wound which festered to this day. Time with Tsan had helped to a degree, but it was always beneath the surface, lurking, waiting for sleep to come. It was here, as the memories of her home emerged from her subconscious, when the nightmares truly began.

This time it was different. Instead of shadowy figures snatching CASPers from their fighting positions, it was a simple plaza with scattered café tables. Birds chirped and sang in the trees while a few squirrels ran around in search of crumbs. The sky overhead was clear, and the weather was warm and comfortable. There was not a cloud in sight. It was Liberia, but her idealized version to it. How Mulbah saw it, really, she admitted to herself as she tried to enjoy the moment.

Sunshine knew something was up almost immediately. The scenery was too clean, appearing almost sterile to the teen. It was supposed to resemble her home, but it looked like something that would be better suited elsewhere. Even in its best days, long before Peepo had destroyed it, Monrovia never looked this good. *Would* never look as good, either. The Mercenary Guild had made certain of this.

"Yes, you're dreaming," a voice from her left stated. She turned and saw the most peculiar thing—a penguin. The longer she looked at it the more she realized it wasn't exactly a penguin, but it certainly resembled one. Large yellow tufts rose just above its eyes, giving the alien an impression of being surprised. The alien was short, though not as short as she would have expected. Then again, she was barely over five feet tall herself; who was she to judge what was short?

"I am Durande," the little penguinlike alien said. "Yes, I'm an alien in your head. Your dreams, to be precise. We don't have much time, so I'm going to try and make this brief."

"How are you in my dreams?" Sunshine asked as she squatted down and reached out to touch the alien. Sure enough, the feathers on its white belly were soft and bird-like. She noticed on the ends of the flipperlike wings were fingers instead of the typical rounded edge of Earth penguins.

"I said I was going to make this brief," the alien reminded her before sighing. "Well, technically, you are sleeping, for a long time wouldn't hurt, but your physiological readings suggest you haven't been sleeping well. Is something interrupting your REM cycles?"

"Bad dreams," Sunshine muttered as she looked around. It *felt* like home, but it clearly wasn't. In fact, it looked more like something she would have found in America than anywhere in Liberia. She waved around at their surroundings. "Where are we?"

"I have no idea," the alien replied. "You brought us here. I'm just a memory."

"A memory?" Sunshine asked, surprised. "I've never met a talking penguin in my life and I'm certain I've never seen a place like this."

"A Sphen-Eudy, you mean," it corrected. "And yes, you have. You just don't remember. Otherwise, all this wouldn't exist."

"I think I would remember an alien that looks like a rockhopper penguin and could talk," she pointed out. "Or some Euro plaza trying to be African on a planet with two moons."

The alien's beak open and closed, clearly amused. "I helped Ray when you were pinned," Durande replied. "A Wrogul doesn't usually need any help, but I was around for other reasons. We have a mutual friend: Thorpi."

"Thorpi?" Sunshine blinked. This was a revelation. As far as she knew, the Veetanho didn't have any friends outside of the Korps. "Is he alive?"

"How would I know?" Durande cocked his head to the left. The Sphen-Eudy seemed as confused as she was. "I'm just a memory, remember?"

"Right," Sunshine nodded. "You'd only know what I know, though you'd also know what's in my subconscious because of my fears and hopes. And dreams."

"Well, I'm glad to see *that* took," Durande grunted.

"What took?"

Instead of answering, the Sphen-Eudy's gaze drifted out across the park. A bright light was cresting the horizon, which was odd since it appeared to be the middle of the day. "It's almost time to wake you up, but not yet. It's too soon, even though we're running out of time. Thorpi worked with me. I'm in the Information Guild, but I also work with another organization which is trying to right the wrongs of the past. I can't tell you who yet because it's not the correct moment. But you really, really should believe your gut. Intuition is a very powerful tool."

"Intuition?"

"Yes." Durande nodded. "Listen to yourself."

"I don't understand."

"Neither do I," he admitted. "Though I did think this would be a lot harder. Your mind is very adaptable. Makes me glad we chose you."

"Chose me for what?"

"For what it's worth, the *bass* was on board with the suggestion when he found out about you," the Sphen-Eudy declared as he looked up. The light around them was blindingly bright. "Ah, time to wake up. Perhaps we'll meet again. Trust your intuition, Sunshine."

"Wait!" Sunshine flailed but something held her in place. The Sphen-Eudy hopped across the plaza and disappeared into a crowd of squirrels which were slowly growing in size. Their eyes began to glow red as they morphed into giant armored spiders. On their backs, the squirrels remained, only now they appeared to be armed with pistols and were laughing maniacally. Sunshine's hand dropped to her hip, but she was not armed. Looking around wildly, she saw CASPers standing around, unpowered. It was clear they did not see the Tortantulas approaching.

"Hey! You're under attack!" she shrieked at the top of her lungs, but the suits did not seem to hear. "Fight! Fight them off!"

"Why?" one of the CASPers turned. The cockpit was open, and inside she could see the bloodied face of Zion staring back at her. She recoiled in horror as his tone turned accusatory. "You didn't fight, why should we? We all died while you escaped. Why do you want to fight now?"

More Tortantulas appeared, a never-ending wave of large, deadly spiders washing over everything she could see. Tables were crushed under their weight, cars tossed aside haphazardly. What had been a clean and orderly plaza was now nothing more than a destroyed ruin, an orgy of violence and chaos. One by one, the CASPers were taken down, all without firing a single shot. In the far distance she could hear a keening wail which threatened to shatter her eardrums. There was no end to the carnage and destruction around her. There *could* be no end. It was beyond war, and any other imaginable horror. This was merely the beginning of something else.

The Tortantulas moved through the plaza. Instead of stopping to enjoy the slaughter as they were wont to do, though, they continued onward. They were in a hurry. *No,* she realized with dismay, *they're running from something. But what?*

Their speed increased. The Flatar which rode upon the Tortantulas looked back and even Sunshine, who had never felt anything other than revulsion at the horrid creatures in her short life, pitied them. It was clear they were terrified. The fear they felt was something no creature, no matter how evil, should suffer through. Her eyes followed their gaze and her chest felt tight.

Something large enough to blot out the glaring sunlight emerged from behind a row of skyscrapers in the distance. Its roar shattered the windows of the buildings and caused the Tortantulas to scatter frantically. There was nothing else living in the plaza except for her. Even the bloody face of Zion Jacobs was gone. It was only her, whatever monster which loomed above her, and the terrible wail of desperation and fear echoing throughout the emptiness.

It was she who was wailing. Her throat was raw, and her ears hurt. The destruction continued around her unabated. There was nothing she could do. Everything living fled from such a being. The sky wept blood and fire as the clouds gathered above her. It was unstoppable. This was the inevitable end of the world. Her family's wo—

With a startled scream she tried to bolt upright, but something held her down. Panicking, she kicked out and her exposed toe connected with metal. She shrieked as pain from her toe lanced through her foot. As she struggled, the safety harness holding her down in her bed came undone. Confused and disoriented, she floated off her bed, and her thrashing continued. A closed fist punched the steel barrier above her head, bloodying her knuckles. Her toe throbbing and her fist aching, she struggled to gain control of her breathing as she tried to wake up.

When her eyes were finally open, she realized she was not seated in a plaza in the middle of a warzone, but was, in fact, safe on the *Velut Luna* and in her berthing space. They were still in hyperspace on their way back to Zav'ax. There was no looming darkness ready to wipe out all life. No Tortantulas and no dead faces filled with contempt and recriminations. It was just a dream. *Just a dream.*

Sunshine reached out and grabbed the safety harness. She pulled herself down to the bed and fastened one of the straps to hold her in place. Grabbing the corner of her blanket, she pulled it to her chest and let out a long, shuddering breath. She closed her eyes and struggled to regain her calm.

Breathe in through the nose, hold for three seconds, and exhale. She repeated the mantra over and over again in her head. Shoulders shaking, Sunshine fought for control over her emotions. The maelstrom raging within her did not want to abate, though. There was only one thing which could potentially help. Eyes clenched tightly shut, she let herself cry for the first time in what seemed like forever.

The memories, both of the Sphen-Eudy and the looming darkness beyond, were forgotten as the face of Zion Jacobs filled her mind instead, soon joined by Mulbah, Samson, and even the often-irritating Antonious. Hot, bitter tears collected in her eyes, causing them to sting. She buried her face into the blanket, and the tears were wiped away by the cloth before they could float away and make a further mess. For the first time, she wished she were anywhere but in space.

I miss you all, she silently told them. As usual, the ghosts of her past didn't respond. However, the guilt wasn't as bad this time around.

* * *

Asa Condé Station, Xeno Guild HQ, Crapti Region, Jesc Arm

Boileau hated these stupid meetings with the fiery passion of a thousand stars going supernova simultaneously in the midst of a black hole. The problem? Attendance was absolutely mandatory for all senior commissioners within the Xeno Guild. Bureaucratic history of the guild demanded it, and the current guild master was, at the very least, a traditionalist. They acquiesced to the Administrator's demands for continued bureaucracy and in exchange, the five senior commissioners maintained their hold on their powerful positions. No, this wasn't the worst part. The Administrator never appeared in person, snubbing the meetings and remoting in somehow. This ruffled the Buma's feathers more than anything else.

Boileau had dressed down for the occasion, intent on showing the rest of the senior commissioners his true feelings regarding the required meeting. He was wearing his comfortable cloak and cowl, which was both stylish and utilitarian, if a bit warm for the environment. A fitted harness crossed his chest. Attached to it were many interchangeable pouches, most of which he kept filled with snacks, usually freeze-dried rodents of some sort. On his hip he wore a single laser pistol in a highly polished holster. The pistol was more for show than anything else. Until recently, the Buma hadn't even fired it on a practice range since he'd purchased it years before.

He looked around the gathered group and couldn't help but feel a little disdain for them all. None had any ambition; they were secure in their own sense of power and importance. None wanted to do anything more with their position. It was sad. He was a Buma after all, a race dedicated to exploring the galaxy and encouraging the growth of the Galactic Union simultaneously. Every new species brought a unique element to the union, and it was the Xeno Guild's job to bring these new species into the fold and allow them to communicate with the others. It was in his genetics to strive to learn more, yet there were times he doubted the objective nature of his fellow guildmembers.

The other four were weak, complacent. They had grown lazy in their years at the top of the heap. Boileau knew he was the visionary of the group, the radical new thinker. He'd only been on the Board of Commissioners for 82 years, after all. He was a mere infant when compared to the others in terms of time served on the board. However, he offered one thing none of the others brought to the table—actual experience.

Boileau had started off in the Merchant Guild long ago before abruptly leaving and joining the Xeno Guild. He had seen opportunity for growth in the smaller guild, whereas the Merchant Guild was stagnant and offered him little in terms of a challenge. He had sworn to change the culture and mindset of those within the Xeno Guild, to embrace their power and opportunity to curtail the expanding corruption of the other guilds. He'd been successful, to a degree. Eventually the Administrator, the Guild Master of the Xeno Guild, had seen his effectiveness and brought him onto the Board of Commissioners.

He looked around at the other four, curious. His own motivations aside, he didn't know what drove *them* to do their jobs. The only thing a senior commissioner seemed to do was approve minor changes within the dialectic matrix of the translators across the Galactic Union. Like everything else in the galaxy, time brought change to languages as they drifted. Slang became permanent sayings, and classical uses and phrasings became archaic. It was their guild's job to ensure the changes were both meaningful and effective. This was one of the primary reasons he'd pushed so hard for a position within the senior commissioners.

He had watched as the archaic language of the Pushtal was mistranslated during contract negotiations and couldn't help but wonder why. Pushing for their contracts to be suspended for an investigation, his concerns had been brushed off by his contemporaries for disturbing the natural process of the Galactic Union. Outvoted 4-1, Boileau had been forced to sit by and wait for things to play out. As he had predicted, it had not gone well for the Pushtal. He glanced around at the others, remembering their votes on the matter as disgust welled up from within.

To his immediate right sat Faab, one of the oldest members of the Xeno Guild. The Izlian was unusual because he enjoyed associating with air breathers. Faab practically reveled in these meetings, since he had probably the most unusual friendship in the galaxy with the being seated to Boileau's left. Sphen-Eudys normally got along with no one, but Patoolle and Faab had a friendship dating back decades, if not longer. It was odd to say the least.

It suddenly dawned on Boileau the seating arrangement was segmented into "sides" in spite of the round table they were situated at. Across from him was Roostalopad, the Sumatozou he had clashed with many times in the past over just how the guild should upgrade and adapt to changes. Next to the elephantlike alien was Zzix, the

Hano. Both of them were staunchly opposed to any changes and were extremely vocal about it.

Boileau looked back at Faab and Patoolle. There was a deeper division at the table than he initially thought, and he was the potential tie-breaking vote if anything came about. Unless the Administrator deemed otherwise, of course. Everything boiled down to their guild master in the end.

On the center of the table was a simple, if ancient, speaker box. It was how the Administrator would remote in for their meetings. The simple display of the raw power the Administrator was able to bring frustrated Boileau to no end. Nobody had ever seen the individual who ran the guild in person; they had only heard his voice. Boileau personally believed him to be a Grimm, one of the nightmarish species who were notorious spies and saboteurs. It made sense. Nobody trusted a Grimm and to keep his identity hidden from the others was an ideal way for the mysterious individual to remain guild master for so long.

The Sphen-Eudy, Boileau recalled, had once suggested it was a collective of ancient aliens. He'd scoffed at the absurd idea. Considering how difficult it was to get the Board of Commissioners to agree on anything, he simply couldn't see a collective agreeing on anything for a long period of time. Faab believed the Administrator remained on a ship nearby, afraid of possible violence and cowardly in nature. Perhaps even one of the supposed "extinct" races. This, Boileau conceded, was far more believable than any of the other outlandish theories. Within range of a laser comm and yet safely hidden on a ship, was probably how the Administrator was able to remote into the different locations they held their meetings.

A single bell chimed over the speaker, bringing all of their conversations to a halt. Everyone took their seat—or in the case of Faab, floated in his tank—and the meeting began. As usual, the Administrator spoke first and did not waste any time getting to the point.

"Efficiency in our translation matrix has decreased 2.54% in the past year," the Administrator's disembodied voice came through the speaker. To Boileau he didn't sound overly angry about this, though. The Administrator almost sounded apathetic, as though it was an expected occurrence. Which ran opposite of Boileau's numbers, actually. There was something wrong here, though Boileau wasn't sure what it was. The Buma coughed slightly before speaking, not wanting to sound rude to the guild master.

"With respect, Administrator, my statistics show a slightly different number," Boileau said as he pulled out a slate from one of his pouches and began to scroll through the data he'd compiled. "I believe—"

"If I wanted your opinion, Senior Commissioner Boileau, I would give it to you," the Administrator interrupted harshly. Boileau stopped scrolling and looked at the speaker, surprised. In his decades as a senior member of the guild, he'd never been spoken to in such a manner by the guild master. In fact, Boileau had never heard anyone being treated in such a contemptuous way.

Does he know what I'm doing? The thought came to him suddenly, and he almost panicked. Boileau had been extremely careful in his dealings with both the B'Hono Corporation as well as his acquisition of the TriRusk individuals—swapping out his usual translator for a "clean" one, all the while speaking in a dialect different than the one he used in public settings. There should be no way someone could put it all together until he wanted it to happen. *No,* he decided a few heartbeats later, *this is just my random paranoia. Something else is at play here.*

"The translation matrix has created more conflict over the past six months than we have seen in three decades," the Administrator continued after a momentary pause. "Patoolle has come up with a possible solution, but before we do this, we must investigate the problem."

"It is unerringly the fault of the newest members of the Galactic Union," Roostalopad complained, raising his trunk and jabbing with it for emphasis. "These Humans are a nuisance and must be dealt with."

Boileau couldn't find any fault with this statement. He disliked the mammalian creatures as much as the next person. However, he wasn't stupid enough to let his own hatred be publicly known in such a setting. The Sumatozou, Boileau surmised, had been in his position for far too long, and his distaste for anything reeking of new was a running joke among the other senior commissioners. Roostalopad hated any new alien species discovered, mercenary or otherwise.

"Humans aren't to blame," Patoolle countered, his beak clomping shut emphatically. "Fear-mongering and a constant state of low-level warfare has created inefficiencies within the overall translation matrix. New events and situations force adaptations to any language. The union is expanding and with it the languages."

"If I have to translate 'entropy' into one more ancient language, I'm going to murder a Human," Zzix complained. "This and their constant corruption of tense usage irritates me to no end."

The Hano has a good point, Boileau thought as he leaned back in his chair and ruffled his chest feathers a bit to allow himself time to cool off. He removed his cowl so he could breathe a little better; it was rather stuffy in the room, which was partly Zzix's fault. The Hano's reptilian body needed more heat, and the meeting room was kept warmer than the Buma would have preferred. Chilly breezes were the preference on the Buma home world over the heat wave Zzix needed.

"Options?" the Administrator asked, ignoring Zzix's outburst.

"We fix the matrix by updating all of the translators throughout the Union, starting from scratch," Patoolle stated firmly, which caused Roostalopad to gasp in shock and horror. Zzix also seemed caught off guard by this proposal, Boileau noticed. Only the Izlian seemed unsurprised at the Sphen-Eudy's suggestion, which cemented the idea of who belonged to which alliance within the Board of Commissioners. Boileau now had confirmation he was the only free agent in the room. The Sphen-Eudy continued, "In order to avoid service interruptions, we can update them in stages. Smaller updates instead of one giant patch which could create issues. It'll also allow us to fix bugs as they come up before the next micropatch is released and give us time to stay in front of any issues."

"Stupid tosser would casually discard all of the hard work we and our forebearers accomplished in order to make things 'right?'" Roostalopad snarled as he slammed both fists on the table, leaving two distinct impressions upon the ceramic material. "Unbelievable! There is nothing wrong with the translation matrix! It is the foolishness of new aliens corrupting older, established languages with their damnable slang words and corruptions within their own languages!"

"You support the idiotic proposal, Faab?" Zzix hissed, eyeing the Izlian warily.

"I do," Faab burbled through his translator as he waved a few of his tentacles in the air to emphasize his words. "We've let the status quo dictate our policies for too long a time, and this has led us down a path which we would be unlikely to recover from unless drastic measures are taken. This is, indeed, a drastic measure, but a necessary one."

"You're both fools." Zzix rose to his feet. "I can't believe you would risk everything to fix minor issues that wouldn't even be a problem in any other situation!"

"This isn't like anything we've ever seen before!" Patoolle countered, his temper clearly flaring. Boileau managed not to laugh at the angry display. Sphen-Eudy, while not particularly dangerous to most, could still cause damage when riled up. Certain elements of their species were particularly dangerous unless one was prepared. Patoolle continued, "Minor issues quickly turned into major ones."

"You've been quiet, Boileau," Roostalopad commented as he leaned upon the table. His thick forearms were crossed upon his chest. He jabbed at him with one of his trunks. "Care to weigh in?"

"Being verbally put down by our guild master tends to make one rethink their plan," Boileau replied. There wasn't any heat or anger in his tone, just marked neutrality.

"Ignore the insult for a moment then," Roostalopad murmured as he eyed him from across the table. "You spoke of numbers before. Did you have a plan to propose?"

"Plan?" Boileau chuckled darkly. "I offer many plans, some of which you might actually listen to without fighting about."

"Pick one of the many you speak of, then," the Sumatozou said with a grunt.

Boileau offered what the Buma would consider a very benign smile. "That is *precisely* my plan. Offer varying plans for the translators across the galaxy. Let those who wish to upgrade pay more to the guild for the privilege of having better translations. Those who will not pay will receive substandard, older variations of the dialect. Allow us to charge every time we have to upgrade during the shift in languages and word usage. The best part? We're the ones in charge of determining when the upgrades are necessary. We are still providing a service while ensuring our own needs are met."

"That's robbery!" Faab spat. The Izlian appeared horrified at the prospect.

"Is it?" Boileau asked. "Everyone already pays for translators. Yes, they're cheap, but the value of our mandated updates for the language matrixes are worth so much more."

"He has a point," Zzix stated, his eye slits staring at Boileau suspiciously. "It's a rather bold idea."

"In addition, we continue our work with the Information Guild regarding what the translators catch and upload to us," Boileau continued, pleased some of them were actually listening to his proposal. "We raise the price slightly for the information we sell them, but we limit their access to only a few terabytes at a time. This will generate more revenue for us in the short term while we follow the Sphen-Eudy's proposal to upgrade the translator matrixes across the galaxy."

"Very bold," Faab gurgled.

"I would expect nothing less from the Buma," the Administrator interrupted their discussion. To Boileau's ears the Administrator sounded...hollow, as though the creature at the other end was speaking through a tube. There was just a hint of reproof, however, which drew everyone's attention to the speaker on the table. "Profit is where his six-chambered heart lies. But tell us more, Senior Commissioner Boileau. Please. Tell us more."

Boileau smelled a trap but could not see it. "It's rather simple. Those who can afford the best receive the best. Those who cannot, do not. It's simplistic yet elegant."

"Spoken like a true mercenary," the Administrator stated. Boileau's ears flattened at the perceived insult. The Administrator continued, "I'm not surprised at your suggestion, however. After all, you are the one who is trying to farm TriRusk for personal gain in the midst of their trying times."

Boileau's blood ran cold. There was no possible way for the Administrator to know this, yet he did. His earlier fear had come true.

Somehow the guild master knew what he was planning and what had already occurred. Everything he had done was now in the open, courtesy of the uncaring being on the other end of the speaker. He swiveled his head to look at the others, all of whom were staring at him with undisguised horror and distaste.

"You've done *what?*" Patoolle screamed. He waved his odd flipperlike arms around frantically and began to hop up and down on his seat. "They only recently decided to rejoin the galactic civilization, and now you want to put this at risk for personal gain? Are you insane?"

"Far from it," Boileau said, struggling to sound as nonchalant as he could; it was difficult. "I wish to build order from this chaotic galaxy."

"*Order?*" Faab warbled inside his breathing apparatus, apparently amused. "Moments ago, you were talking about chaos by abusing the trust of the markets, and now you speak of *order?*"

Roostalopad rose to his feet and his large hands gripped the edge of the table. The Sumatozou's face was twisted, contorted by outrage. "You were given your position because you were trusted, Boileau. Trust! Have you no concept of the word? Our mission in this guild is to enable trust! If one cannot trust what is being said, then anarchy reigns supreme, and war will tear this entire galaxy apart!"

"Spoken like someone who wants misunderstandings to continue to cause wars for all time!" Boileau snapped back. He stabbed a feathered hand toward Faab. "They want to fix a broken system, and you scream about chaos! I want to charge everyone to fix it in a more efficient manner, you scream anarchy! You archaic fool! If it were left to you, the galaxy could be in flames, and you would still be screaming against changing anything because you believed anything else would lead to, what? More war? Just to protect your delicate sensibilities? Your kind would just *love* that, wouldn't they?"

"What do you mean, 'your kind?'" Roostalopad recoiled as if physically slapped. "We are builders, like you, Buma!"

"You are nothing like us," Boileau retorted angrily. "You aren't willing to make the hard choices, only the easy ones."

"You know nothing of hard choices!" Roostalopad screamed. Boileau turned and glared at him. His blood boiled, and his heart hammered in his chest. The Buma had never felt anger and fear combined in this manner before.

"Let me show you an easy choice then," he snapped his beak and pulled out his pistol. The Izlian recoiled in horror as it recognized the weapon in Boileau's feathered hand before he pulled the trigger.

In spite of his time spent at the range, his first shot went wide of the Izlian's tank, and his tentacles jerked back in surprise. The others started yelling but Boileau focused, and his next shot burned a hole through the tank and Faab's head. The squid-like alien's body drifted to the bottom of the tank as the caustic, poisonous air spewed from the holes Boileau had punched through it. Faab's lack of movement indicated he was probably dead.

Boileau turned and started shooting at the Sumatozou and Hano. Roostalopad barely had time to react before three quick shots struck him in the chest. He let out a cry of pain and fell backward out of his seat, clutching his wounds. The Hano was not so lucky, as both of Boileau's shots struck the reptilian alien in the face. Zzix fell onto the table, his blood quickly pooling onto its surface.

Blinding pain lanced through Boileau's hip. He barely managed to avoid screaming and looked down to discover a long knife had been stuck through his upper leg. He looked at the Sphen-Eudy, who was pulling out a second knife. Snarling, Boileau turned the barrel of the pistol toward Patoolle.

"You won't get away with this," the Sphen-Eudy swore.

"I already have," Boileau retorted calmly before shooting Patoolle in the head. The knife dropped from his nerveless fingers and fell to the floor. The Sphen-Eudy stared at him with an expression of confusion and pain before dropping to his knees. Boileau blinked as Patoolle tumbled to the ground. Before that moment he hadn't been aware the Sphen-Eudy had knees.

"Do you know what I've always appreciated about you, Boileau?" the disembodied voice of the Administrator asked through the speaker box. "You're predictable, if a little slow. I thought you would pull something like this fifty years ago. What took you so long?"

Boileau tried not to let the voice startle him, but the deep cut of the words still managed to surprise him. The Administrator had *known* he would do this? Boileau ruffled his neck feathers, irritated. *No,* he decided after looking away from the speaker. *There is no way that creature could have known what I would do; what I was planning.* The idea had only come to him the year before. Or was there a deeper meaning to the Administrator's words, something he was missing?

"Hindsight makes one appear smarter than they really are," Boileau countered as calmly as he could manage. The caustic air seeping from the Izlian's tank was beginning to irritate his windpipe and lungs. "It's easy to say you knew I would do this afterwards. Why didn't you stop me if you knew this would occur?"

"All of you senior commissioners were lacking in vision," the Administrator declared, his voice still flat and bored. "You were the only one who dared stir the waters, so to speak. You shook their little secure space up and made them consider new avenues of approach. Yet you fell into the same trap they all did: greed and complacency. Every one of you claimed to be trying to bring about order in the galaxy. Did it never occur to you that chaos creates the environment for information to thrive in?"

"That's—" Boileau's beak snapped shut. Irritated, he turned and kicked over his chair. The wound in his hip flared painfully. *Stupid, insipid Sphen-Eudy,* he silently complained at the dead. The chair landed in the growing puddle of mess where Faab's rebreather apparatus had broken when the Izlian fell to the floor. While he had thought this might happen, and even planned for it, Boileau was still surprised he'd had the wherewithal to actually go through with it.

"What is your plan now?" the disembodied voice asked. If he hadn't known better, he would have sworn the Administrator was mocking him. "There's no escape from this aftermath. There's no escape from *me.* Now that I have confirmed what you're capable of, you think you'll ever come within a thousand light years of me? You overreached, Boileau. I am unsurprised by your decisions, both today and regarding the TriRusk. But tell me, my feathered friend, did you ever stop to ask yourself why I would allow you to do this?"

Boileau coughed once, then he killed the connection with a shot from his pistol. Truth be told, he hadn't quite thought this far ahead. The overall plan wasn't far enough along for him to retire comfortably in a system of his own, surrounded by well-paid mercs to protect him from any repercussions. He still didn't have access to his funds, for starters. Of course, if DexKarr was as good as Boileau remembered him being, then the Torokar would have the individual in question secured before too long.

There would be a reckoning for his actions, he knew, and soon. As long as he stayed within the admittedly long reach of the Xeno Guild, he was vulnerable—nothing more than a target with a timer counting down. It would only be a matter of time before someone found him. The Administrator had not become master of their guild through stupidity and laziness.

Boileau held his breath as he removed the translator from around his neck and set it on the blood-soaked table. The easiest way to track and monitor his movements was now removed. He didn't give a damn about leaving evidence behind. Outside of the station blowing up, there was no way to hide what he'd done without alerting anyone else. It would be plainly obvious to anyone investigating who had done the shooting. The only thing going for him now was that he had a tremendous head start. If he could get into the wilds and find somewhere to hide, he had a shot. Once things calmed down, he could reemerge. Only then would he be able to truly start a new life comfortably away from the long reach of the Administrator.

Unfortunately, this meant he would have to deal with the B'Hono Corporation again as he waited for DexKarr to bring him what he needed.

Gods, I hate Zav'ax and that whiny, petulant Karvan.

He took one last look around at the ruined bodies of his former guild members.

"No plan survives contact with the enemy; it's why they're called the enemy," he quoted as he brought the cowl up to cover his head. "As irritating as they are, Humans sometimes have the best sayings."

* * * * *

Chapter Eight

Velut Luna, Near Lagrange Four Point, It'iek System

The Velut Luna emerged from hyperspace with little fanfare. The emergence zones were over hundreds of thousands of kilometers large and a ship could enter a system from almost anywhere in the zone and from any angle. This made ambushing any potential arrival almost impossible...Unless one was very lucky.

Or unlucky, depending on the side of the credit chit one looked at.

"Sensors up," Taryn said as her hands swept across the controls of the ship's console while the engines accelerated them toward Zav'ax. Her eyes were locked on the Tri-V display before them. Next to her, Sunshine had just finished strapping herself into the copilot's chair. She didn't know why Taryn wanted her up in the cockpit, but figured it was better than sitting in the galley with the others, twiddling her thumbs and waiting for something to happen. "Powering up engines...now. Sunshine, keep an eye on our approach angle."

"That's this little green thing, *ken?*" Sunshine asked with a grin. Taryn looked over at her before heaving a weary sigh.

"You're such a...yes, that little green thing."

One of the sensors on the console suddenly lit up, and an alarm sounded. Taryn groaned and began fiddling with the controls. A moment later, the source of the alarm appeared on the Tri-V. She groaned a second time and shook her head.

"Remember these guys?"

Sunshine recognized the signatures from the new arrivals' engines almost immediately. They were the same XenSha ships they had narrowly avoided on their first go-round. Almost avoided if one wanted to get technical. The damaged nose of the *Velut Luna* would be a long-standing reminder of just how close it had been. Sunshine shot a look over at Taryn, who was busy piloting the ship.

"You think they saw us?" Sunshine asked, though she was pretty sure she already knew the answer.

"There's no way they missed our engines lighting up," Taryn murmured. "They have our signature, too. I don't see any possibility of us sneaking down to the planet now."

"You could do a hard burn until we reach the outer atmosphere of Zav'ax," Sunshine stated, closing her eyes. The math wasn't hard, really. It was just a matter of knowing the design of the ship, as well as the damage it had already taken, which made it slightly difficult. "A forty-five-degree angle at less than one thousand kilometers per second should keep us from breaking up. Anything over that speed is going to cause the ship's structural integrity to fail. Your heat deflectors should be able to withstand an entry at that speed. Mostly."

"I'll be cutting the safety margins close if I start a burn now," Taryn pointed out. Sunshine shrugged.

"Better now than later," Sunshine said as she opened her eyes and pointed at the Tri-V. "Especially since they're probably going to start their own burn soon. Or start shooting."

"I'm beginning to hate when you're right about my impending death," Taryn grumbled and increased power to the engines. She flipped on the intercom. "Dref-na? Get everyone into the crash harnesses back in the galley seats."

"Why? Are we about to die?" the Besquith asked seconds later.

"Probably…maybe?" Taryn said, uncertain.

"Again?" Dref-na sounded irritated. "What have I told you about getting us killed in space?"

"Just get everyone situated, please." Taryn killed the comms and sighed. She looked over at Sunshine. "I'm glad you find this amusing."

"Me, too." Sunshine's smile was particularly toothy. "I'm very amused. Can't you tell?"

Gravity on the ship increased as the engines kicked in. Everything felt weird for a moment as Sunshine's normal weight returned, then grew as more G-forces pushed her back into her seat. The pressure continued to grow before the engines stopped, having achieved the pre-programmed velocity. Sunshine felt a little woozy.

"I hate that part."

"We're going to have to do it again, I think," Taryn stated.

"Ungquba," Sunshine muttered darkly.

"What does that mean?"

"Don't worry about it."

"Velut Luna, this is the Pushtal Cruiser *Dark Infinity*," the voice said over the comms. "You are ordered to heave-to or be destroyed."

"Pushtal, eh?" Taryn looked at her console, a curious expression on her face. "Interesting. Explains why they're using outdated XenSha cruisers. I wonder what clan they are. Maybe we should get Jorna up here just in case?"

"And run the risk of them shooting us because they have a grudge against the Fangmaster or Jorna's clan?" Sunshine asked.

"Good point," Taryn nodded. "Jorna didn't mention these guys even after we told her where we were going. She might not know they're here. Definitely not clans Arwoon or Roxtador."

"Are they here as mercs or something else?" Sunshine wondered aloud. Taryn grunted. Satisfied, Sunshine continued. "If they were hired by the B'Hono Corporation, then they don't need to be mercs. Unless the guild is territorial when it comes to stuff like this?"

"B'Hono must really be trying to save a few credits by hiring them," Taryn acknowledged in a thoughtful voice. "Pushtal aren't a recognized mercenary race anymore. Well, there are a few companies here and there, but the race as a whole? No. Odd they managed to snag some cruisers. Those aren't cheap."

"Well, as long as they don't follow us down to Zav'ax, we should be fine," Sunshine said. "I don't want to be there if they realize who's on board with us."

"We should find out who they are," Taryn pointed out. "In case the Fangmaster wants to deal with them later. Pushtal don't take disobeying the Fangmaster's decrees lightly. Especially when it's someone as respected as Magnus. These guys have a lot to lose here."

"*Velut Luna*, heave-to and prepare to be boarded," the voice from the lead ship demanded again. There was a distinct threat in the speaker's tone. "This is your final warning."

"Piss off, you wanker," Taryn transmitted loudly before killing the comms. She looked over at Sunshine. "Bet you a donut they're Clan Haepthae. They're both stupid and ambitious enough to try something like this. Let them argue about what to do next. What'll happen if I increase speed by a factor of five but make our entry angle shallower?"

"Uh," Sunshine blinked, startled. "Oh! We'll break up in the atmosphere! Don't...don't do that, *ken*?"

"Well that sucks," Taryn growled. "How fast do you think we can go and not break up?"

"If you drop to thirty degrees, I *think* you can pull 1,500 kilometers per second when you hit the exosphere." Sunshine heavily stressed the word "think." She didn't want to be subtle about it. "I don't know the structural integrity of your ship with the damage, or the atmospheric pressure of the upper atmospheres of the planet. I'm basing my estimates off of porous asteroids and Earth's atmospheric pressure. I do know that if we slow down before we hit the stratosphere it increases our odds of survival."

"Ship disagrees," Taryn said as she punched in the calculations.

Sunshine snorted. "Then why ask me?"

"Because I think you're right."

"Oh."

The vibrations of the engines could be felt throughout the entire ship as the *Velut Luna* continued to increase speed. The G-forces went from normal to inconvenient and rapidly became barely tolerable as thrust continued. Sunshine felt her sight begin to tunnel as blackness clouded the edges of her vision. The air began to taste funny as her eyes rolled up, and unconsciousness threatened to take her. Past experience as well as the training sims forced upon her by Mulbah and Zion reminded her how to prevent a total blackout. She began to grunt softly and clenched her core muscles, forcing the blood pooling there to go back to her brain. Doing this rapidly became exhausting, but it was better than the alternative.

Beside her, Sunshine noticed Taryn was doing the same thing. The rhythmic grunting would normally have been hilarious for the duo. However, neither had the time nor inclination to laugh at the absurd noises they were making; this was a matter of life and death. They could laugh later, assuming they survived.

"Killing thrust…now!" Taryn gasped, and the engines of the *Velut Luna* suddenly powered down to almost nothing. Maintaining minimal thrust, the G-forces dissipated but did not disappear entirely. Sunshine breathed a sigh of relief as the blackness faded, and the strange, metallic taste went away. She really needed to work more on her core muscles if this was going to be a common thing. She hadn't really exercised since before she'd fled Liberia.

"That was exciting." Sunshine tried for humor, but it fell flat.

"We're not out of the woods just yet," Taryn muttered. She jerked her head at the Tri-V. "Look."

The leading Pushtal cruiser was accelerating toward them, its powerful engines creating a massive heat signature on the screen. The other three were hanging back, obviously aware of how the *Velut Luna* escaped the last time, determined to prevent such a thing from happening again. It was clear the Pushtal were moving into a more advantageous firing position and would achieve it about the same time they reached the atmosphere of Zav'ax.

"This is gonna suck," Taryn predicted.

"It's going to be close," Sunshine acknowledged, her eyes locked on the Tri-V.

The *Velut Luna*'s sensors abruptly screamed in warning as the lead ship targeted them. Taryn deftly maneuvered the smaller ship, trying to create a difficult shot for their pursuer. Sunshine wasn't sure it helped, but it definitely perked Taryn up a bit. The woman seemed to be enjoying this a little too much for Sunshine's liking.

The ship unexpectedly shuddered as something solid struck one of the nubby wings used by the *Velut Luna* for atmospheric flight. Alarms blared as bits of the heat deflector shield fell away from the damaged area on the wing. Sunshine looked at the readout and saw the area affected wasn't completely destroyed, but it would hamper their ability to maneuver once they hit the atmosphere. It would also be another hit to her pocketbook, since she had promised Taryn she'd pay for any damages to the ship.

If she lived through all of this, they would *definitely* need to revisit their contract.

"Secondary outboard aileron on the starboard side is destroyed," Taryn reported as she surveyed the damage coming in over the sensors. "That's going to make landing difficult. Damage to the spar as well. Yuck. I think that entire wing is gone. Glad we have three others on that side."

"Can we, I don't know, launch some chaff or something?" Sunshine asked as she looked at the controls on the console. "This thing is supposed to have mag strips to use as decoys."

"What, deploying the chaff strips right when we hit the exosphere to simulate breaking up upon entry?" Taryn asked, incredulous. "Kill the power to the engines and float away undetected while switching out to a rogue transponder they don't recognize? Yeah, that'll fool them…not. Crap like that only works in the movies!"

"Can we shoot back?" Sunshine asked before catching herself. "No, stupid question. Sorry."

"I would *love* to shoot our railguns at them, except they're above us and our railguns are more of an anti-personnel thing," Taryn replied, seething. "If we live through this, remind me to tell my boss to put some goddamn missiles on this thing!"

The ship suddenly tipped heavily, and Sunshine yelped in surprise. She glanced at Taryn, who seemed to be fighting to level out the ship. The shaking grew worse, and Sunshine felt one of the *Velut Luna*'s wings shear off from the laser fire from the pursuing cruiser. More alarms screamed in the cockpit, confirming her suspicion. The added swearing from Taryn was the nail in the coffin of doubt.

Sunshine reached out and manipulated the controls. The volume of the alarms dropped to almost nothing. A sudden silence filled the cockpit, creating a sense of eerie premonition, as if they were one wrong breath from absolute disaster. The tension in the air, already thick, became worse as the two women stared at the display. The numbers continued to tick down as they approached the planet. Neither was aware they were holding their breath as they waited to see if the Pushtal cruiser would be able to finish them off before they hit the atmosphere.

It failed.

The atmospheric sensors chirped and the ride, already bumpy from the maneuverings of Taryn and the damage from being shot to pieces, grew worse.

"We're coming in hot!" Taryn warned as the ship shook violently when they hit the exosphere of Zav'ax. "Our trajectory is off by three degrees. The angle is too sharp but if I make it any shallower those bastards behind us will have an easier target."

"Then stay on course!" Sunshine said through clenched jaws, her mind racing through calculations. "Decrease speed by six kilometers per second!"

The lead ship stayed close as the *Velut Luna* continued its steep dive toward the planet, their forward laser weaponry continuing to fire rapidly at the fleeing vessel. Their targeting was either off or they were simply poor shots, as each burst only came close enough to set off the sensors a few times. The rest burned oxygen molecules as they zipped harmlessly through the upper atmosphere. Harmless, at least, until they blasted into the planet far below.

Light *could* bend if gravity was strong enough. It was primarily why a black hole could be monitored; light bent toward it. Gravity on Zav'ax wasn't as powerful as a black hole, which everyone within a light-year was immensely thankful for, but it was still a gravity well in space. Thus, when the laser shots from the *Dark Infinity* streaked past, their targeting was off because nobody on the ship was accounting for the curvature of the planet's surface, as well as the gravity well present as they grew closer. It was a bit of fortuitous luck for the *Velut Luna*, though only Sunshine was aware of the possible reason why the Pushtal cruiser was such a horrible shot. This did not bode well for those on the ground, however. Anyone not under cover was potentially an inadvertent target.

All of this passed through Sunshine's head in the span of a heartbeat. Something came to her mind, long forgotten, part of a past she could no longer identify with. It was the face of an angel looking down on her, with eyes darker than night yet containing more love than Sunshine felt she deserved. She felt ashamed this figure saw the girl she was and the woman she was to become.

Where's this coming from? she silently screamed at herself. It felt like her mind was being torn in two. One side was determined to finish the mission, to accomplish their goal and free the TriRusk from the clutches of the B'Hono Corp. The other, though, held all the self-doubt and recriminations she hated herself for. The things she had done to hurt others over her short life, or when she had not recognized that Mulbah had lied to her to save her from the horrors of what befell the Korps. Was she willfully ignorant of it or had she suspected it, even then?

Stop it.

The voice was a flash of light in a vast sea of darkness, a clarion bell clear and pure. Her head snapped up and she looked around, almost certain the voice had spoken aloud. Nobody was looking at her, though. Taryn was deftly maneuvering the *Velut Luna* through the atmosphere, still weaving left-to-right to dodge the rapidly diminishing laser fire. Klinks and the rest were in the galley, seated in the crash seats and secured with safety harnesses. Nobody had said a word to her, yet she had heard it. There was no denying the voice. It was achingly familiar, but from where, she would not hazard a guess.

This isn't the time for getting lost in memories that aren't mine, she reprimanded herself. *Focus on the mission.*

"We're landing at the original coordinates," Taryn growled, her teeth clenched tightly in concentration. "You strapped in tight?"

"Yeah, I think so," Sunshine answered after checking her five-point safety harness. She hadn't thought about it when Taryn had asked her to copilot the *Velut Luna* just before they came out of the gate. It wasn't as if she knew much about piloting, after all. Yet Taryn had been oddly insistent. She realized now it was because she was the only other person on the vessel who could fit in the safety restraints as well as come up with entry trajectory solutions on the fly. Plus, she suspected there was another reason as well.

Taryn doesn't want to be alone in case we all die, she thought. *She knew we might run into the cruisers again.* Fighting against the climbing G-forces, she reached out and gently squeezed Taryn's upper arm. "Don't worry. You've got this."

"I better," Taryn grunted. "Otherwise we're going to be a fiery ball crashing down from the sky soon."

"Think positive!"

"Fine. I'm positive if I screw this up, we're all gonna die."

"I guess that's better."

Power to the engines faltered as the *Velut Luna* dipped toward to the surface. Sunshine managed not to scream as her stomach leapt into her throat, but it was a near thing. She looked at Taryn, who was slightly pale after the sudden drop in altitude. The power to the cockpit faded for an instant before it came back fully. Power returned to the engines, and the *Velut Luna* leveled out meters above the treetops of Zav'ax. Taryn let out a slow breath.

"That was closer than I would have liked," she admitted as her eyes went to the Tri-V display. "No sign of the Pushtal ships. I didn't think they would try the atmosphere. They're less agile than we are, and I may have mentioned we're not the most maneuverable?"

"Well, at least they stopped shooting," Sunshine pointed out.

"Only after putting three holes in the ship," Taryn reminded her as she checked the sensors. "Damn. I didn't even notice the third one."

"True. Can you fix it?"

"Kl'nk'nnk probably can," Taryn responded after a moment. "She'll have time. Uh…maybe. We're going to have every single Jivool on this planet gunning for us if we're here too long, though."

"We need to find out where the TriRusk are at in a hurry, *menh*," Sunshine muttered as she stared at the Tri-V display. She touched a command and the larger areas of population appeared on the screen. "There are three larger enclaves…small towns, really. Population centers that are small but consistent in occupants. Hmmm…I don't know about you, but I'd want to keep this as quiet as possible, so away from the usual mining locales. Klinks built the machinery, *ken?* How big was it?"

"Kl'nk'nnk," Taryn called out toward the galley. "We need your help for a minute."

"I'm not leaving this safety harness until I am certain we're not all about to die in a horrible crash, Taryn," came the Jeha's curt reply. Taryn rolled her eyes, but Sunshine couldn't fault her. They *had* almost died, and not for the first time.

"You're not going to die in a crash," Taryn murmured as she glanced over at the comm panel. She sighed and gave Sunshine a look. "I'm so used to flying this thing solo that I forget we have an intercom sometimes."

"Ah." Sunshine didn't know what else to say. She had been looking deliberately at the comms for almost thirty seconds, and Taryn hadn't noticed. Then again, their pilot had a lot on her mind. It would be rude to point it out to her.

"Sorry, forgot," Taryn said after activating the ship's intercom. "You can stay there. The machinery you built for the Jivool down on the surface, was it large?"

"No larger than usual," Klinks responded a moment later. "Two and a half meters. They might have been life support cubes. There were thirteen of them in all."

"No idea what they were being used for, other than life support?" Taryn asked.

"I'm sorry, no," Klinks apologized. "I did sign an agreement to not talk about it. Yes, they did try to kill me after, but I still keep my word. I can say I'm not entirely certain they were life support cubes, however. They were missing certain parts."

"Parts?"

"Well, this is all theoretically speaking, of course, but there was no system in place to use nanite regeneration therapy," Klinks explained. "The transistors they were demanding I use were capable of handling more power than what was required. Of course, logic dictates they could simply be overcompensating, but it was simply odd. Theoretically speaking, of course."

"Of course, this is all theoretical. Those cubes are small enough to be easily transported anywhere," Sunshine grumbled as she mulled it over. "We're going to have to ask someone who might know."

"Ask?" Taryn raised an eyebrow questioningly.

"Interrogate," Sunshine clarified. "With violent force."

"Okay, that's what I thought."

"Sounds like fun," Dref-na added.

"Klinks?" Sunshine looked at the Tri-V display and searched the larger population centers of the mining colony. "We've been to the Korvar and Satuur Districts on Zav'ax. Satuur is out of the question, since we kinda burned it down last time we were here, and I really don't want to go back there. Korvar we've been to already…they might be okay. At least, until the shooting starts. They're the ones who directed us to you in the first place, Klinks, which leaves Garnon, if the map is correct. What do you know about the place?"

"Garnon is an administrative center," the Jeha responded. "That would be a good place to begin the search."

Sunshine killed the comms and looked at Taryn, who was studying the map intently.

"Glad Kl'nk'nnk upgraded the information of the planet for us," Taryn murmured as she looked at the map. "You know what's odd?"

"What?"

"All three cities line up perfectly along the planet's northern tenth parallel line. Interesting."

"Why? There's twenty-seven more minutes of sunlight there than anywhere else on the planet, considering the axial tilt of the planet," Sunshine rattled off instinctively. "For energy conservation purposes, it makes sense. Especially when you take into account the extreme polar regions."

Taryn looked at her oddly. "Oookay," she dragged the word out before shaking her head. "You're scary."

"It's just basic science," Sunshine said, mildly embarrassed. "The ship's databanks know this."

"You did that without using the databanks, though, didn't you?"

Instead of answering, Sunshine busied herself by looking up the information they had on Zav'ax's third population center, helpfully provided by Klinks during their journey from Draxis III. There was nothing too surprising, though the fact the B'Hono Corporation would bother to build an administrative center in such a small enclave on a mining world was interesting. However, to the casual observer it could be explained easily enough.

But Sunshine and her group were far from the casual observer.

The *Velut Luna* rocketed through the atmosphere, blissfully unaware of the chaos their return had caused.

* * *

Clan Kanonko Cruiser *Dark Infinity*, 12 Km Above Zav'ax, It'iek System

"I want every single one of the aliens in the holds to get in one of those entropy-cursed assault pods and drop down to the planet's surface," Commander

Drayher ordered his junior officers. He was angry none of his gunners had been able to finish off the *Velut Luna*. This time, however, he had a cunning plan, one which would surely satisfy the B'Hono Corporation, as well as ensure they would not lose the precious contract his clan's First Claw had managed to snag two years before. "If they can fight, they can go. Have them attack the mercs on that ship with everything they've got. Tell them to tear them to bone and bits. We *need* this contract. Our clan stands to lose *everything* if we don't pull this off. Everyone in our clan needs this to succeed, not just on Draxis III but at Darkhomme as well. Do you understand?"

A few murmured quietly in assent. The rest stared mutely at their commander. Displeased, Drayher raised his voice as loud as he possible could and repeated himself.

"DO. YOU. *UNDERSTAND?*"

"Yes, Commander!" they chorused, shaken. Drayher may have been known for many things among the crew, and privately they called him far worse, but nobody had ever used the term "motivational leader" in the same sentence as his name before. Until today. Traditionally, Clan Kanonko was not known for any sort of leadership. Stepping up and demanding their loyalty was…oddly refreshing.

"Then get them down there and tell them kill everyone on the *Velut Luna*," he told them. "Do you understand me? Every single one."

The officers filed out. None were truly ready to fight on Zav'ax and were thankful he hadn't ordered them down to the surface. The Jivool had their own security forces. The Pushtal were supposed to be protecting the gate and preventing piracy. No ground excursions. Boring work, but it paid well. It was a sweet deal. Or had been, before the *Velut Luna* had come along and ruined everything. Drastic times called for drastic measures. Clan Kanonko would not lose this contract.

Word quickly passed between the four ships. It was time to make a new deal with the small alien life forms the Pushtal had acquired with the cruisers, courtesy of their former KzSha owners. The little aliens were slaves originally, but the Pushtal didn't really like the concept of slavery as a whole and treated these strange little aliens more like servants, including offering them their freedom. The Pushtal had once been in the same position themselves, after all, at the hands of the MinSha. A good chunk of them still were, back on their original home world. However, nobody seemed to know where the aliens were from, or even what species they were. Because of this, and the fact the aliens were more than happy to live on the ships with the Pushtal as servants and neighbors, they had mostly been left alone.

Until now, that is.

One thing Commander Drayher had noticed when they first met was the tiny alien species' teeth. Rather, how large they were. Razor-sharp and capable of rending carbon fiber, they were excellent at scrap disposal, which was a bonus considering all they seemed to eat was metal and non-organics. While they *could* eat organic material, it wasn't good for the little aliens in the long run. Give them nickel and palladium, however, and they were practically euphoric. It made for a very unusual dynamic between them and the Pushtal, where scrap metal became payment for the former slaves in exchange for menial labor. The Pushtal thought they were getting one over on the tiny aliens. They, in turn, believed they were ripping off the Pushtal.

When the various commanders went to the cargo holds the little aliens called home on board the *Dark Infinity*, they were greeted warmly by them. Each Pushtal officer told them what was needed, and after a few communication complications, it was all worked out. The aliens agreed to the bargain. Besides, the possibility of new types of metals to eat on the planet was tempting. In addition, they could eat the vessels which would deliver them to the planet. It was almost too good to be true.

The various Pushtal officers giving the briefings weren't confident about their chances of returning them to the *Dark Infinity* and told them so, but the aliens didn't seem bothered. They were realists, each and every one. Opportunists as well, though this word wasn't in their vocabulary. It didn't matter if they knew the meaning of the word. All could count, Pushtal and little aliens alike.

Return to the ships? The odds of this occurring were horrible, the tiny aliens knew. This didn't trouble them greatly, each insisted when individually questioned. An exciting ride to the planet in a vehicle that could kill them? "Sign me up," was a constant refrain. Plus, surviving long enough to eat the pods as well as the ship that had irritated their Pushtal friends was considered a bonus. In the end, every single one of the tiny aliens volunteered to go to the planet for the potential buffet line. For the tiny little alien eating machines, it was a chance to eat their way to the afterlife with a full belly.

* * *

**Velut Luna, 5 km from Garnon District, Zav'ax,
It'iek System**

"There!" Sunshine pointed as Garnon District appeared on the Tri-V. At the same time, something else appeared on the screen, moving toward the *Velut Luna* at high speed. Sunshine began to swear. "Missiles! Inbound missiles!"

"Not quite," Taryn grunted as she maneuvered the ship to the left with all the grace of a drunken hippopotamus. The damaged wings caused the ship to flutter slightly. A high-pitched whine of tensile metals bending could be heard throughout the ship. The intercom came to life a moment after.

"What was that?" Klinks asked. She was definitely worried. "It sounded like something important fell off."

"Nothing fell off," Taryn said, grimacing. "I'm just—it's okay. Everything's okay."

"It doesn't sound okay," Klinks said.

"Hey, are those drones?" Sunshine asked, eyes widening in recognition as she looked back at the screen.

"Drones?" Dref-na interrupted loudly. "Oh, please let me get on the guns and shoot them this time, Taryn Lupo. Please?"

"Stay in your safety harness!" Taryn yelled as she steered the ship back to the right. "If we go down, you'll at least have a chance at survival back there!"

"You suck, Taryn Lupo!"

"Go eat spoiled meat, Dref-na!"

"Oh my God, are we going to just yell at each other before we all die horribly?" Sunshine asked.

"It's better than doing it in absolute silence." Taryn swore as the *Velut Luna* pirouetted in the air, one shining moment of grace and elegance in the lifetime of sluggish atmospheric maneuverings. The drones, caught off guard by the move, slammed into the engine mount on the port side. The engine coughed, sputtered, and failed as a piece of shrapnel created by a destroyed drone nicked a coolant line. Instead of overheating as most engines would, the automatic sensors of the engine killed it immediately, before the heat could build up to a high enough temperature to cause irreparable damage.

In space, this wouldn't have been a big deal. In atmospheric conditions, it was almost catastrophic, but Taryn almost managed to save it and perform a perfect landing upon the platform. "Almost perfect" as in they did not crash...much.

"This is gonna suck!" Taryn shouted as the *Velut Luna* landed hard on the platform. The struts absorbed most of the impact—but not all—and the nose scraped against the tarmac. They were jarred by the impact and multiple cries of alarm were heard from the galley. Sunshine grunted as the distinct sound of metal crumpling beneath the weight of the ship was heard through the hull. It sounded expensive. Taryn's eyes widened, but she didn't panic. Yet. Her gaze met Sunshine's. "If I don't make it, you tell Zorgama this was not my fault!"

"You tell him yourself!" Sunshine shouted back as she unbuckled herself from the crash harness. "We're not going to die!"

"Tell that to the Pushtal ships who *just shot us down!*"

"Let me get my suit on and I will," Sunshine growled as she slid out of the copilot's chair and hurried through the ship. As she passed the galley, she noticed everyone had survived the hard landing in relative good health, though Vah appeared to be in shock again. She wasn't too surprised by this, though; the CozSha seemed to exist in a state of perpetual dismay.

"Tiny fierceness?" Dref-na stopped her just before she descended to the lower cargo hold. The Besquith seemed concerned. "Is the ship badly damaged?"

"Nothing Klinks can't fix," Sunshine replied as she looked over at the Jeha. "Minor damage to the nose. Landing strut is shot from the sounds of Taryn's cursing. How do I get my suit out of the cargo hold down below?"

"Uh." Klinks paused, uncertain. "I think I can fix the strut, as long as I'm not being shot at. I'll see what other damage I can repair as well. The wings might need some work. The best way to get the suit out of the hold is through the secondary loading door."

"How do I open it?"

"Large blue button on the bulkhead. You can't miss it."

"Right." Sunshine nodded. "Dref-na, you and Taryn track down someone in the upper levels of B'Hono management and get the information about the TriRusk from them. I don't care how you do it, okay?"

Dref-na's smile was a terrifying sight to behold. "Perfect."

"Vah? You stay and help Klinks with whatever she needs," Sunshine continued, looking at the diminutive CozSha. "When the time comes, I'll need you to use weapons to keep her safe. If you use the ship's railguns, it is very efficient to shoot all the Jivool you see, okay? Efficiency is life, right?"

"Right?" Vah mumbled questioningly.

"Are you efficient at your job?" Sunshine pressed.

"I am very efficient."

"Then be efficient and work those railguns when the time comes," Sunshine ordered. "Any Jivool who step foot on the landing pad are reducing efficiency of this…crap, I don't know, rescue op? Yes! That's it—a rescue op. Jivool on the tarmac of the landing pad decreases efficiency during our rescue operation. Removing the inefficient beings from the equation with the railguns is immensely resourceful and increases efficiency by a large quota. Do you understand me? You have to be efficient."

"I...I can be efficient." Vah nodded slowly, her mouth working as she struggled to digest the information and psychological manipulations. While difficult for her, after many deep, calming breaths, the CozSha seemed to process it all. "I am very efficient!"

"Good." Sunshine nodded before looking at Jorna. "You're with me on site security. The priority is Klinks and then the ship, okay? If the landing strut isn't fixed before we take off, it probably won't be any good for vacuum, *ken?*"

"Got it."

"Let's get to it," Sunshine ordered and scrambled down the ladder and to the secondary hold. She activated her pinplants and pinged Taryn. "You hear all that?"

"It's a good plan," Taryn replied after a moment. "Just one problem—how do you expect us to find the one Jivool who'll know where they are?"

"Klinks knows who their upper management is," Sunshine reminded her. "Have her give you a list. From there it should be a simple snatch-and-grab."

"Oh boy, a kidnapping!" Taryn replied sarcastically. "Like we haven't seen one of those before. Remind me again what happened the last time?"

"It's the best plan I have," Sunshine retorted as she activated her suit via her pinplants. The CASPer came online quickly, and the cockpit opened so she could climb inside. She found a bench next to the suit and clambered up. It took her a minute to get situated; slower than she would have liked but faster than she'd ever managed to do it before. Once settled, however, the suit felt as comfortable as a pair of fuzzy pajamas. She made a mental note to come up with an excuse not to give Taryn back her borrowed PJs. "Oh wow…Klinks did a fantastic job with this."

"All right, I just finished showing Vah how to work the railguns," Taryn called down to the cargo hold. She sounded doubtful. "You sure about her?"

"No," Sunshine admitted. "But I need her to back up me and Jorna. Otherwise, she'll just be dead weight."

"That's usually describing a CozSha in combat anyway!"

"Quit being a bitch about it and let's do this!"

"Fine!"

"Fine!"

"Hey, Sunshine?" Taryn's tone changed subtly. Sunshine looked out across the small area and saw Taryn's face dangling upside down near the ladder. Her dyed streak of hair hung loosely in front of her eyes. "Be careful, okay?"

"You, too."

Taryn disappeared from view. Sunshine took a deep breath as the last of her systems came online and synced with her pinplants. Everything blurred for a moment before snapping back into place, crystal clear and perfect. Her mind was fairly buzzing from the sensory feedback she received from the suit. Marveling at the upgrades Klinks had made, she reached out with the CASPer's hand and touched the aforementioned large blue button. A loud *clang!* reverberated throughout the hold.

The outer locks disengaged, a doorway opened, and a ramp crashed solidly upon the landing pad. The opening was just large enough for her CASPer. If not for Klinks' upgrades, there would have been no way for the suit to fit through the opening without seriously damaging the structure of the ship. The Jeha had thought of everything, it appeared. Sunshine couldn't have been happier with the suit.

As she exited the ship into the harsh light of It'iek's red dwarf star, she changed her mind. The CASPer practically floated as she walked. It was almost magical being inside something so advanced, especially when compared to the clunky old Mk 7 she was used to. The hardware upgrades Klinks used to increase the processor speeds made the response time to reactions dwindle to milliseconds at worst. In addition, the new shock absorbers the Jeha had somehow managed to manufacture while they were in hyperspace made each step feel almost as if she were walking on pillows. The controls were extremely responsive, and she forgot for a moment how hard piloting a CASPer was supposed to be.

I need to give Klinks a huge bonus, Sunshine told herself as she turned and scanned the area. Her Jeha friend had done a magnificent job restructuring the suit.

The sensors finished sweeping the area. To the naked eye there wasn't anything to see, but the scanner detected stray hits from laser comms being used in the vicinity of the landing pad, roughly half a kilometer away and closing. The Jivool knew where they were, and they were coming in hot. Sunshine was certain they would hit them with everything they had in the region, if not the entire planet.

"Taryn? Are you picking up what I'm seeing?" Sunshine asked, her eyes flitting between the in-screen readouts on the Tri-V. Her pinplants made processing all the information easy.

"Your CASPer is relaying everything perfectly," Taryn replied. "Vah is set up and about as ready as she can be. I still don't know about this plan of yours, but it's better than anything I can come up with. Well, except sticking Jorna on the guns, but then we lose a second gun, so…eh. I'm about to head out with Dref-na. Klinks identified a few of the potential Jivool we need to find. If everything's still up to date, they're in this enclave."

"How many people know? In case you need to kill him to set an example?"

"Klinks suggests there are upwards of two dozen in the administration center who could possibly know," Taryn replied after a brief pause. It was clear she was relaying questions to the Jeha instead of tying her into their comms. "Though Dref-na's pretty certain she can convince the first target to talk. Something about eating him slowly…"

"That's a lot of people for a big secret," Sunshine pointed out.

"The best secrets are often hidden right out in the open," Taryn replied. Sunshine frowned but said nothing. It was accurate, all things considered. It was just the most backward way of looking at things. Taryn continued, "The HQ probably has some sort of information blackout anyway."

"Okay, so what *are* they doing with the Tri-Rusk?" Sunshine asked. "That's the one thing we never figured out."

"Let me go find out," Taryn answered. There was an edge in her voice which hadn't been there before. "Oh, by the way, we're all on the same frequency now. Encryption should keep us safe, but Vah says any encryption is potentially breakable. Considering who she works for…Well, we're off. Good luck."

"Luck," Sunshine acknowledged. The CozSha might not be the most aware individual, but she did know her stuff when it came to anything relating to her guild's work. "Jorna? Vah? Comms check."

"Loud and clear, boss lady," the Pushtal replied instantly. "I'm up and ready for a perimeter sweep."

"Hold that," Sunshine ordered as she spotted Dref-na and Taryn dashing off into the thick undergrowth of the jungle. They had their job; she had hers. "I've got Dref-na and Taryn on my scanners. Relaying everything now. Vah? It would not be efficient if you shot these two when they returned, okay?"

"I am efficient," the CozSha responded flatly. It seemed to Sunshine the tiny goat-like alien was still in shock, but she would have to make do. "I will not fail in my task."

"Good, good," Sunshine murmured. "Oh, and don't shoot us, either."

"Only Jivool will be removed from the platform for being wasteful," Vah promised. Her response was tenuous but it was the best they could hope for.

"Okay, Jorna, we should have company soon," Sunshine warned the Pushtal. "Let's make them hate the experience."

She swallowed, her mouth dry. Her palms felt sweaty and there was an irritating itch growing between the pinky and ring fingers on her left hand. It was the first time she would be in sustained combat since Monrovia. Her stomach flipped before settling down. She had trained for this. The itch disappeared as her mind became dangerously focused. The edge which had seemingly disappeared during her escape from Monrovia was back, and it felt good.

She was the most dangerous predator on the planet, and nothing could stop her now.

* * *

Lagrange Four Point, It'iek System

As his ship emerged from hyperspace, something very curious caught DexKarr's eye. Another ship had emerged minutes before he had and was coasting slowly toward the planet of Zav'ax. It was clearly a late-model ship with all the bells and whistles one would expect from some sort of high-ranking official. It was interesting, but since it wasn't Taryn Lupo in the *Velut Luna*, he dismissed it almost immediately.

Until the ship contacted him. Curious, and with time to kill, he activated the comms.

"DexKarr," the voice greeted him.

He jerked his head back, surprised. As far as he knew, only one other person in the galaxy knew he was coming to the It'iek System. The voice chuckled and continued, "Surprised?"

"Yes," DexKarr admitted as he ran a second security sweep of his comms. The voice on the other end had to be the individual who had hired him. He'd always requested anonymity in the past, and DexKarr was professional enough to respect his wishes. Plus, he paid well enough for DexKarr to not be too interested in his identity. This breach of protocol was unlike his employer. "You could say that."

"Your target is on the planet below," the voice continued. "I need her alive for questioning. Once I am through with her, you may kill her."

"She's here?" DexKarr asked, surprised. *What a delicious turn of events.* "I thought she'd left."

"She has returned," the voice replied. "I'm sending you her coordinates now. The local Jivool security forces are converging on her location to arrest her for me, but I'm concerned with the Pushtal mercenaries in orbit. They aren't responding to my hails and were shooting at the planet for some reason."

Did you offer them credits? But DexKarr didn't ask. It would have been rude, and his employer had never shown a sense of humor before. Instead, he merely grunted. "Protect the girl from the Pushtal on the surface, then snatch her when I have a chance?"

"Something like that," the voice purred. The sinister tone caused a shiver to run down his spine. Whoever the individual was, a calm and measured tone was clearly not a favored response. "I don't care what you do with the rest of them. Kill, torture, eat—doesn't matter. But the girl you told me about in your update? Sunshine? She must live long enough to spill her secrets to me and nobody else. Do that, and you will be richly rewarded."

The communication ended, and DexKarr stared numbly at the console for a moment.

"The things I do for my bank account," he muttered as his engines powered up. If he was going to keep the girl alive long enough for questioning, he needed to get to the planet before the Pushtal dropped. Otherwise, there wouldn't be anything left for *anyone* to question. Pushtal had a reputation for savagery only matched by a few merc races. Pirate scum, one and all. He hated Pushtal almost as much as he hated Zuparti. A message needed to be sent to these pirates—respond when hailed or face dire consequences.

He grinned in anticipation. Sometimes the enemy simply needed their faces eaten. It was the best way to send a message, after all.

* * * * *

Chapter Nine

Garnon District Building 31, Zav'ax, It'iek System

Taryn and Dref-na moved rapidly into the central area of the small enclave, trying to get to their objective before any security forces realized where they were. It was the main reason it was just the two of them. A larger group, especially with the Besquith involved, could create a full-on emergency response, which meant more guns pointed their way. Besides, Taryn and Dref-na had experience working together in the past. True, it had ended in a stand-off, but at least the initial part of the plan had gone off without a hitch.

Staying off the main streets, they managed to find their way to the central hub of the B'Hono Corporation's administrative building without too much trouble. Kl'nk'nnk had done an excellent job mapping the best route for them to take, as well as which building they needed to target first. The only problem was that neither of the duo knew exactly what any of their potential Jivool targets looked like.

Leaning against the side of the main administrative building, Taryn reached into her pocket and pulled out a small slate. She scrolled through the list of names and open source information on the building. After fruitless searching she found one possible target who wasn't located on an upper floor. She handed the slate over to Dref-na and pointed at the name.

"What do you think?" she asked.

The Besquith eyed the name and location of the target before grunting. "Looks good to me," Dref-na replied. She peeked around the corner and scanned the building's entrance. Armed guards stood inside the building's glass doors and large windows. She pulled back before any looked their way. "I count seven guards just inside the door."

"How do they look?" Taryn asked as she looked around. The small street was vacant, but they knew this would change if anyone spotted them.

"Armed and scared. More than likely they will shoot first and ask questions later, Taryn Lupo."

"About what I figured," Taryn muttered and looked up. Her eyes narrowed as she looked at the building across from their position. "Hmm…I wonder what's in there."

"According to Klinks, it's an older building that's being refurbished," Dref-na answered after consulting the slate. "Vacant except for the construction crews."

"Interesting," Taryn murmured as she traced the building's rooftop. There was some sort of lift attached to one side. Nearby were building materials which appeared to be for refurbishing an interior office space. The lift appeared operational and went all the way to the rooftop. Running alongside the lift was a disposal tube for refuse disposal, which ended in a large receptacle on the street. Taryn's eyes drifted back to the pavement and the narrow road separating the two buildings. "How wide do you think this street is?"

"Oh, perhaps twelve meters, why?"

"I have a really stupid idea," Taryn said and looked up. Dref-na's eyes followed Taryn's and she frowned almost immediately.

"You won't make it," Dref-na pointed out.

"No, but you can."

"What are you suggesting?" It was clear from the Besquith's tone she did not like where this was going.

"Jump across, get inside on the upper level, slaughter some Jivool, draw their security forces deeper into the building and away from the front door," Taryn answered. "Then I can walk in and find the guy we're looking for while they chase you. I'll drag him out here and you ghost out of the place."

Dref-na sniffed. "I don't 'ghost' very well, Taryn Lupo. Not the best plan of attack for someone with my abilities."

"Well, if we charge in there, we'll be lucky if they don't kill us before we reach the door," Taryn observed. "Besides, I only need you to escape as noisily as possible back out the top."

"I see." There was a sarcastic edge to her voice. "I leap across the street from a building to a lower building, tear my way through anyone I feel like, draw every single armed security guard in the building to my position, lead them around on a merry old chase through the building, maybe kill more Jivool, get shot at, maybe wounded, possibly killed, and then escape cleanly somehow while they're still pursuing me. Meanwhile, you get to simply walk in the front door, walk up one flight of stairs, hold a gun to Cranston Vi Karvok's head, and walk out with him through the front without so much as a second glance or any raised alarm?"

"Well, when you put it that way...yes, that's *precisely* what's going to happen."

"I hate you, Taryn Lupo."

"Don't be like that, Dref-na. Think about the drinking story this will be!"

"My hatred has not diminished, and our drinking stories always begin with 'so, Taryn had this stupid idea…'"

"Give it time," Taryn replied. She checked the slate one final time before putting it away. "You got this."

"Much hate…" Dref-na muttered as she skulked away. In the distance, multiple sharp *cracks* of thunder rolled across the sky. Taryn looked up and frowned. There wasn't a cloud to be seen and the sky remained an eerie deep red color, courtesy of the It'iek system's M-class red dwarf star. There was no storm brewing anywhere on the horizon.

Odd, she thought and turned back to the task at hand.

* * *

Landing Pad 4, Garnon District, Zav'ax, It'iek System

Inside her upgraded CASPer, Sunshine was tied into everyone's comms as well as the *Velut Luna*'s sensor systems. While her CASPer was top-of-the-line, the sensor suite on Taryn's ship surpassed anything she had ever seen in her life. The technical upgrades on the ship told her quite a bit about the amount of influence and power the mysterious "Mister Z" brought to the table. She really wanted to meet Taryn's enigmatic boss one day.

Her suit pinged a warning, and her scanners immediately started to search the skies above. It wasn't from the direction of attack she was expecting, but it made sense. Outside the three cleared areas for the enclaves, the only other places they had seen while they were inbound were the icy regions to the north and south of the narrow green equatorial strip and the mining exclusion zones. Using short-range air transports to haul security forces around was the easiest solution she could think of. Earth had a long history of doing such, and she was positive the concept of an airborne assault was not limited to Human ingenuity. At least, she didn't think it was.

"I'm picking up twenty-four objects moving at high speed through the atmosphere, Sunshine," Jorna said from near the *Velut Luna*. "They look like assault drop pods, similar to what you Humans use for your CASPers."

"Assault pods?" Sunshine looked over the readings pouring forth from the sensory suite of the *Velut Luna*. The more she delved into the information, the odder it became. "I've read about them, but never seen them in a battle."

"You've never battled the Pushtal before, have you?" Jorna asked.

"I only met them for the first time last week."

"We have little care for casualties in combat at first glance," Jorna explained. "A lot of clans use old, discarded equipment and materials. Depending on the clan, you'll see a variety of tactics. I hope it's not one of the more savage clans. It could get ugly. I will admit, I'm surprised to see them using those old *Kona* ships of the XenSha. They're pricey, and even my clan can't afford them."

The 24 assault pods appeared on her Tri-V, interposed over a topographical map of the planet's surface. Speed, angle, and altitude were accounted for before the suit determined the potential landing areas of the pods. The closest would fall less than a kilometer away, the furthest would be almost eight klicks from the Garnon District. If she timed it correctly, she could kill all the Pushtal mercenaries before they coalesced into a single, unified mass.

She didn't know a lot about the Pushtal. What she did was courtesy of Taryn's databanks on the ship and what she had gleaned from talking with Jorna. Information regarding size, strength, or appearance was strangely lacking. If not for Jorna, and her own personal experiences, she would never have guessed the aliens resembled short, muscular tigers. Whatever the Mercenary Guild thought of the Pushtal, they clearly weren't a popular race.

"Targeting the pods," Sunshine said as her magnetic accelerator cannon began to track the sky. High above and still unseen, the pods continued their descent. Their signatures were bright against the cooler atmosphere, and the targeting system of the CASPer, synced with the *Velut Luna*, had little trouble spotting them. They were within range of her MAC as well, though the missile system didn't quite have the range just yet. She wasn't certain whether the MAC rounds would be able to penetrate the thick bottom armor of the assault pods, let alone hit the high-speed objects. Still, she had to try.

The assault pods were 75 kilometers above the surface of the planet before she had a full firing solution ready. Her brain rapidly spun calculations based on their trajectory angles and speed and figured she had roughly eleven seconds before she needed to move to the first pod as it crashed to the ground. Raising her left arm, she let the automated targeting system track the target before firing.

The sound of the MAC firing four-round bursts was music to her ears. It had been far too long since she had been in her natural element. The MAC rounds, fired at over 1,700 meters per second, reached their dedicated area in the blink of an eye. They were perfect shots, and she *should* have seen what happens when a cluster of MAC rounds punched into a rapidly descending assault drop pod.

Unfortunately, every round from the first batch missed as the pod's heat shields' ventral surface opened and slowed their descent. This caused the MAC rounds to miss by a large margin—almost one-half meter each.

Twenty seconds. Sunshine opened fire again, focusing another burst on the closest drop pod. This time she hit, but the damage was negligible as the substantial heat shields absorbed the impacts. Cursing in two languages, she had the suit shift the target area slightly higher to avoid the extra protection the heat shield provided.

Fifteen seconds. Another burst, and this time she saw the rounds had some effect. The lead drop pod wobbled as the hypersonic rounds punched through the armor. No longer stable in flight, the heat shield flew off in large chunks as the drop pod tore itself apart. Sunshine watched in morbid fascination as the assault pod disintegrated and millions of pieces of debris spread out across the sky. She wasn't certain, but she thought she saw body parts mixed in with the shattered pieces of the pod.

Ten seconds. She cursed herself for not paying attention to everything else around her. She knew precisely how many MAC rounds she had left in the suit and realized if she wasted all her ammunition trying to take down the drop pods they would be stuck relying on the *Velut Luna* for their ranged defense. And her lasers, but those used more power than anything else on the suit and could render her inoperable. Which, she suspected, would lead to their death.

Five seconds. She decided to try to take out three more pods, which would leave her twenty to deal with on the ground. It wasn't great, but it was far better than letting all of the pods land and chew them to pieces. At the speed which they were approaching the ground, however, she began to wonder if anyone would survive. The G-forces inside would be so immense there might be nothing but paste inside after it was all said and done. Then again, she did not know the G-force tolerance of the Pushtal. Better safe than sorry.

Three seconds. She fired again. This time, the MAC rounds ripped through the unarmored upper halves of all three drop pods. The force of the rounds, combined with the thickened atmosphere of the planet, blew all three apart. Remnants of the three drops pods fell from the sky, showering the neighboring jungle with shards of metal and fire.

At two seconds, the cold gas thrusters atop the lead assault pod fired, leveling it out. At the same time, the thrusters on the bottom of the pod lit up, slowing the descent to a manageable speed. The amount of force generated by the engines was almost forty times Zav'ax's normal gravity. The shockwave of the engines blew a large cluster of trees over, creating a landing area of sorts. Fifteen meters from the ground four landing struts dropped from the sides. The engine flared one final time before the pod landed heavily on the ruined jungle floor with a gentle bump.

"Jorna?" Sunshine called out. More blasts could be heard as the remaining pods fired their landing rockets. The Pushtal was out in the open and unprotected from the inevitable gusts of wind which would be arriving in short order. "Find cover!"

"Already done," Jorna responded from the interior of the *Velut Luna.* "I'm not some idiot running around in a CASPer, you know."

"Watch for any Jivool," Sunshine ordered as she tracked the landings of the assault pods and mapped a route to each of them. "I'm going after the pods before they can all join up and rush us."

"Good plan," the Pushtal said. "Although Pushtal don't really charge blindly into a gunfight. I'll just stay here and wait for them to come at us, I suppose."

With all its systems humming beautifully, the black-painted CAS-Per melted into the jungle. It was time for Sunshine to show just why Mulbah and Zion had put so much faith in her and her abilities.

* * *

Garnon District Building 29, Zav'ax, It'iek System

"I hate that woman," Dref-na growled as she reached the ledge of the ten-story building. Using her claws to pull herself off the lift—which, despite Taryn's assurances, only worked halfway up the building before jamming—she scraped her knee on the concrete ledge. Muttering frustrated curses, Dref-na was on the roof at last. It had taken her far longer than expected and now she was definitely starving. Burning calories meant she needed to eat a lot of protein soon or dizziness could kick in. She was already grouchy.

Lunch waited for her on the other side of the street. Looking across and down at Building 31, she wondered if her estimate of the distance might have been a little off. It certainly *looked* farther away than she had initially thought. Still, it shouldn't be too much of a challenge. She'd jumped further many times before. Though all of those times she hadn't been exhausted while running on an empty belly, and she'd been much younger, too.

Focus. She gave herself a mental shake. Too much introspection in her advanced years. It was a bad habit she had fallen into lately. Being older than most Besquith mercenaries had made her a bit of an outcast, as had the shift from wanton slaughter in battle to careful, surgical ambushes and assaults. It had led to her being declared outcast and driven out of her previous mercenary company. Fortunately, Taryn Lupo had contacted her about an opportunity before Dref-na had been forced to crawl back to her old mercenary company, begging the alpha for another chance. She would have never been able to hold her head up with pride again.

Dref-na took a deep breath, then another as she backed away from the ledge. She would need a running start to clear the street and land safely on top of Building 31's roof. Her calf bumped the far edge of the roof and she paused, took another readying breath, and sprinted across the rooftop. Her claws dug into the material coating the surface of the roof, and she used this leverage for more speed. Using her powerful legs, Dref-na jumped as hard as she could.

She cleared the street with ease and landed hard on the opposite rooftop. Dropping her shoulder so she rolled and her momentum was absorbed, her left foot snagged on the roofing material, and her left knee buckled slightly. This threw her entire balance off, so instead of a graceful roll ending with her on her feet and safe, she fell flat on her face and wrenched her knee in the process.

"*Damn* you, Taryn Lupo," Dref-na wheezed painfully as she rolled onto her back and grabbed the injured knee. She didn't know how bad the damage was, but it definitely hurt. Picking herself up off the roof, she looked around. There wasn't much to see, and she found the roof's access door without too much difficulty.

"There you are," Dref-na muttered as she limped toward it, each step sending a fresh jolt of pain up her leg. She tested the handle and found it unlocked. She smiled. "Finally, something's going right for a change."

She pulled the door open and stepped inside. Immediately, a fire alarm went off, setting off an ear-splitting siren throughout the entire building. Wincing, Dref-na ripped the offending device off the doorframe. It made one last, pathetic "beep" before dying. She rubbed her ear, which had begun to twitch wildly, still traumatized from the explosively loud noise. She yawned to clear the ringing sound out of her head, but it did not go away. It quickly dawned on her the fire alarm system was ringing throughout the entire hallway and not just in her ear. The door's fire alarm had been connected to others.

"Oh, you have got to be kidding me!"

Her hate for the situation Taryn had put her in was growing with each passing moment. She hurried down the stairs, taking them four at a time and doing her best to ignore the further damage she was doing to her knee, until she arrived at the first landing. There was an access door to the top floor, which was where Klinks expected the high-ranking executives in this particular building to be. Taking a deep breath to work herself into a right and proper rage, she kicked in the door. The heavy metal bent but didn't give. Her knee, however, almost did. It took everything for her not to crumple to the ground. There was no way she could put all her weight on her left knee again, and she knew kicking in the door with it was impossible.

Dref-na rested her powerful claws on the railing of the stairwell to take the weight off her left knee so she could kick with her right. Two more powerful kicks removed the door from its hinges. Panting heavily and still in quite a bit of pain, Dref-na slipped inside just as the fire alarms were silenced.

Instead of the expected plush executive suite, however, rows upon rows of cubicles filled her view. Unprepared for such a sight, she paused. There was a quiet murmur running through the room as voices spoke into comms. Her large eyes blinked slowly as she took everything in. The setting was both eerie and had an overwhelmingly depressed feeling about it. Despite the damage to her ears from the fire alarm she managed to pick out bits and pieces of random ongoing conversations.

"...we have a *great* deal for a property on Vega Prime..."

"...no sir, you don't have to buy anything at all. This one-time packaged deal..."

"...if you act now, we can throw in a special offer on a set of cutlery for your cooking needs..."

"...and when you arrive, you'll be treated to a visit with a platinum star-rated masseuse of any species of your choice..."

"...and we've been trying to reach you regarding your spaceship's extended warranty plan..."

"...so how does this all sound to you? Interested? Too good to be true? Let me assure you that everything we offer is above board..."

Dref-na snarled softly. It was an automated call center recording station, the bane of all communications transmissions for anyone stuck with trying to send a "free" communication. Oftentimes these advertisements played just before or, more typically in the middle of, recorded messages passed throughout the galaxy. There were prerecorded responses for any question the person on the comms might have, as well as many dodgy continuances if they tried to disconnect or avoid the spam. If a hapless individual accidentally consented to the ad when it appeared, then it became a never-ending loop of prerecorded responses to anything which was said. These ad farms were unusually deceitful when it came to the entire concept of free enterprise, some going so far as to pilfer through other past communiques between consenting parties to tailor their ads to suit the target. They were considered filth, lower than even the lowest of pirate scum, and only slightly above lawyers. At least the pirates had scruples. The less Dref-na said about lawyers, the better.

She had initially felt guilty about murdering innocent persons during the distraction phase of their plan. That guilt was gone, replaced by sweet, sweet anticipation. It was intoxicating. Dref-na licked her lips and grinned. She, much like every other individual who had been targeted by one of these scams in the past, had dreamt about what would happen in the unlikely event they found one of these ad farms. Most involved visions of blood-coated walls and delicious screams of terror.

A Jivool's head appeared above a cubicle and turned to look at her. Another followed suit soon after, then a third. Dref-na's smile grew wider. The scene reminded her of a documentary she had seen once about the Earth creature known as a prairie dog, the way the Jivool kept popping their heads up from their cubicles to see who had just arrived. The constant background noise faded as a thick tension filled the room; not even a whisper could be heard. Dozens of heads popped up and out of their cubicle to see what was going on. She had their full attention now, and best of all, it was *she* who was interrupting *them* and ruining *their* day.

"Thank you, Taryn Lupo. I have fantasized about this moment for *many* years," Dref-na hissed happily as the horrified screams began.

* * *

Garnon District Building 31, Zav'ax, It'iek System

Taryn watched as Dref-na vaulted from the building next door to their target building with relative ease. She didn't understand why the Besquith was so irritated by her assignment. All her life Taryn had been told Besquith loved wanton slaughter and carnage while feasting on their enemies. This should have been a dream come true for the Besquith. It was an office full of corporate types who were doing something horrible to an alien race which, up until recently, everyone in the galaxy had believed extinct.

A small, clear light began flashing at the far end of the building. A warning alarm rang from above, near where Dref-na had disappeared. Taryn looked to her left and saw another flashing light, below it was a sign. She wasn't fluent in Jivool, but she could guess what the sign said.

"Is that a fire alarm?" she wondered aloud. It made sense. Of course, it also meant the distraction Dref-na was going to cause included the possible arrival of firefighting personnel, causing more mayhem. It would be pandemonium in there, which was precisely what they needed. She risked a second glance around the corner and smiled. "Good job, Dref-na."

Whatever the Besquith was doing, it had drawn all the guards into the building. Taryn casually walked to the front doors, which were now completely unwatched by anyone. Smiling, she checked her slate and saw the location where their true target should be. Glancing around, she verified there was nobody on the streets. Probably sent home because of the *Velut Luna*'s arrival, she suspected. It was for the best. As much as Taryn put on a rough and carefree attitude when it came to everyone else, she didn't really enjoy the idea of murdering innocents.

Getting through the secured glass doors was expedited by the use of her flechette-loaded antique shotgun. The flechette darts were tailor-made for this type of environment, designed to break into microscopic pieces upon impact. Plus, they were much quieter than regular shotgun shells. It took her only two shots to destroy the door entirely, and she strolled in as if she owned the place.

With no security guards lurking, she walked down the hall and started for the stairs. Pausing, she spotted an elevator near the stairwell. Curious, she approached and summoned the lift. It arrived within seconds, the doors sliding open smoothly. She stepped inside and pushed the button for the second floor. Apparently, all the security for the building had been on the front door, which suited Taryn just fine. The doors closed, and gentle, yet disturbing, Jivool music played.

The elevator came to a stop, and the doors opened. There was still no sign of any Jivool, so Taryn sauntered down the hallway, checking the numbers next to each door as she went. They were in descending order, which irritated her a bit since she was looking for room 201. At the far end of the hall she found what she was looking for. She checked the handle and realized it was unlocked. She brought her shotgun back up, leaned her shoulder against the door, and pushed in. The door swung open easily and she rushed in. Seated behind an ergonomically designed work desk was a solitary Jivool.

Startled, the Jivool looked up at her. His eyes widened as he realized it was not whoever he was expecting. He opened his mouth to scream but Taryn cut him off by pointing the shotgun at his face. His large mouth snapped shut, and he slowly raised his hands. She looked around but could not find any sign of a name plate. Not that it would have helped any. Taryn couldn't read any of the Jivool languages.

"Cranston Vi Karvok?" she asked. Seeing his fearful, hesitant nod, she continued. "Come with me. Now."

"I, uh, oh dear," the Jivool stammered. He frantically looked around his office, clearly searching for a weapon. Taryn had already glanced around the room and knew the only thing he could possibly hurt her with was the heavy metal paperweight near the edge of the table to his left. She waggled the shotgun back and forth as a warning.

"Don't go for the paperweight," she told him. "I'm not here to kill you, but I *can* hurt you and still get what I need. You need to come with me. Obey, and you live. Disobey? Die."

"I-I understand," Cranston responded. He slowly pushed his chair back and, keeping his hands raised in the air, walked toward Taryn.

"Stop," she said, and he complied. "Turn around, and walk backward toward me, keep your hands on your head."

He quickly complied. As he slowly backed out of the room toward her, Taryn grabbed the flexicuffs she had packed in her left hip pocket. She placed the first one just above the Jivool's elbow and maneuvered it behind his back, then did the same for the right. Now, if the alien tried to use his retractable claws, he would only puncture himself.

Satisfied, Taryn steered him toward the elevator. He did not resist at all. She smiled inwardly to herself. The soft Jivool music inside the elevator continue to play its pleasantly odd jingles. She pinged Dref-na's slate over her pinplant twice to let her know she'd found their guy and was exfiltrating now.

Easiest kidnapping ever, she thought. Dref-na had worried about everything going wrong for no reason at all.

* * *

Garnon District Building 31, Zav'ax, It'iek System

Def-na heard the security guards pounding heavily up the stairwell long before they arrived. She looked around the cubicle farm for a secondary escape but couldn't see one. The fact that the walls, windows, and every other square inch of the room was covered in Jivool blood and guts had nothing to do with it, either.

Time for more slaughter, I guess, she thought as she flicked a bit of blood from her long claws. The carnage she had wrought upon the ad farm had sated not only her appetite but a long-buried rage toward scammers in general. Her knee still hurt from her earlier tumble, but at least her hunger wasn't a raging inferno directing her to kill everything around her anymore. Which was a shame; she would probably need that rage when the armed and vengeful security forces breached the door.

"Hmm…" she looked back at the ruined door thoughtfully. She didn't need to kill them all, simply delay them until Taryn signaled the kidnapping was complete. There were plenty of ruined cubicle walls and desks she could pile in front of the door, all of which would work to impede their progress. More importantly, she needed to figure out a way to escape.

She checked the windows but realized she was too far from the ground to survive the fall. While a young Besquith could probably limp away from it, someone her age would be hard-pressed to even think coherently afterward, especially given her current knee injury. It was just another not-so-subtle reminder she was past her prime.

Taryn needed more time, and Dref-na was going to give it to her. Sighing, she picked up the blood-soaked cubicle walls and began stacking them in front of the door. Next came the desks. These were heavier and would provide better cover against any enterprising guard who decided to stick his firearm through a gap in the cubicle walls to shoot at her. They would also take longer to remove, especially since everything was covered with slowly drying blood of the employees they had been assigned to protect. Either the Jivool would be ready to murder her in retaliation or be so put off by the sights and smells they would not want to breach the doorway anytime soon.

Satisfied with her barrier, Dref-na stepped back and moved to the windows. She could see the building she had leapt from previously across the street. There was no way back to the rooftop, unfortunately. She doubted she could have made it back, though. Her knee was swollen and already throbbing painfully with each step she took. What she wouldn't give for some of the aerosol nanite spray back on the *Velut Luna*...

She looked back out the window, curious. The construction lift was still jammed halfway up the side of the building, lower than her current position. It was possible, though she wasn't sure her knee would be able to make the jump. Could she break through the window though? Pushing against it, she seriously doubted it. There was absolutely zero give to the large sheet of glass. However, this didn't necessarily mean it couldn't be broken; she just needed something heavy with an edge of some sort to swing through it.

Her eyes drifted back to the three scattered, blood-covered desks she hadn't used for her makeshift barrier. The desks were blunted on all sides with no sharp edges. However, she did notice their feet had solid, three-centimeter-wide bottoms. She limped to the nearest one and pushed it onto its side. On the bottom of the desk leg was a small, circular steel peg roughly one centimeter in diameter. They were supposed to keep the desks from sliding around on the carpeted flooring without creating a large footprint which could damage the relatively cheap material. Dref-na snorted. The cost-cutting bean counters of B'Hono Corporation's accounting department would be the individuals who inadvertently helped make her escape.

The security forces finally arrived outside the ad farm's barricaded doorway. Thanks to the heavy desks and the light-yet-bulky cubicle walls, they were unable to see past the blood-covered barrier. However, the sight alone made them stop and wonder what was going on inside. Dref-na chuckled darkly. They had no idea what they were trying to walk into.

Right on time, her slate pinged twice. She smiled. Taryn had the target and was leaving the building. She'd distracted them long enough for the plan to work. She couldn't believe they'd succeeded. Her knee was banged up, and there was Jivool blood stuck on her fur, which would take quite a while to wash out, but otherwise it had gone fairly well. All the negative feelings she had toward Taryn during her initial break-in of the building had disappeared the moment she realized they had inadvertently stumbled upon the ad farm. Not only did it satisfy her, it was a boon for the entirety of the Galactic Union. She was doing all civilization, as well as the guilds, a huge favor.

I wonder if I should send them a bill?

Dref-na picked up the desk and dragged it to the window. She took a deep breath, then exhaled. With a grunt, she twisted her body and swung the desk with all her strength. The solid steel peg at the bottom of the desk leg impacted solidly upon the glass. A crack formed in the window, but it didn't shatter like she was hoping. Frowning, Dref-na pushed the desk away from the window a bit and lined it up for a second shot.

Swinging with all her might, this time the desk went through the window in an explosion of safety glass and broken desk. Now off balance, Dref-na had to let go of the desk to avoid falling out the window. It spun lazily and fell to the ground far below. She sighed and looked at her hands. They were undamaged, which was fortunate.

There was a startled scream from the street. She leaned out the window and looked down. A familiar voice shouted back up at her.

"Dref-na!"

"Oops," the Besquith muttered. Sure enough, there was Taryn with their Jivool captive. Between them was the broken desk, and glass was everywhere. She wasn't certain, but the look on Taryn's face was not an amused one. Dref-na waved at her and tried not to grin. "Sorry!"

No I'm not, she thought as she took a few steps back from the opening and looked at the jammed lift across the way. It was eight meters below and fifteen away. About the same distance as when she had leapt to this building. However, there wasn't a large landing area this time. She could ill-afford any mistakes this time.

The Jivool on the other side of her makeshift barrier began pulling it apart. There were angry snarls as small gaps began to appear. The barrel of a rifle poked through one of the openings, but the angle was wrong. The Jivool began to swear, and Dref-na could hear them frantically trying to get at her.

She was running out of time. It was now or never. She sprinted across the room as best as she could with her injured knee and jumped.

* * *

Garnon District Building 31, Zav'ax, It'iek System

Taryn guided the partially bound Jivool out the ruined front doors and they turned right. There was no sign of any other security forces inbound, which was a surprise, though a welcome one. Taryn had known when she first came up with this horrid plan that they would need all the luck they could get to pull it off. She was not disappointed thus far by their good fortune. Everything was going perfectly.

She pushed her captive down the side street and paused. There had been no reply from Dref-na after the two pings, which told her nothing. Either the Besquith was busy slaughtering or was on the run and would join them eventually. There was little she could do to help her old friend.

A sharp *crack!* drew her gaze upward. Other than the two buildings they were standing between there was nothing to be seen. *More of that strange thunder, maybe?* she wondered. Taryn looked at the Jivool, who was staring at the ground and mumbling something under his breath. Giving his shoulder a hard shake, she pushed him further down the street. She heard glass shatter, and she looked back up in surprise. Falling directly at them was a cloud of glass and a very large object.

Taryn screamed and pushed the Jivool aside before diving out of the way. Her captive landed hard on the pavement but was otherwise safe. Glass showered Taryn's back, and some got into her hair, but whatever had come crashing out of the window landed on the pavement far enough away from them to only give her a minor heart attack. Scrambling to her feet, she looked up and saw a furry and familiar face staring back down at her.

"Dref-na!" she shouted up at her. Dref-na waved at her.

"Sorry!"

"No you're not," Taryn muttered quietly as she waited. There was no way Dref-na could make the leap across to the other rooftop, and she couldn't see any other way the Besquith could get down. *Unless she's crazy enough to just try and jump straight to the ground. Can she do that?*

Dref-na flew out the window, clearing the street, but she was clearly not high enough to land on the opposite roof. However, it quickly became apparent to Taryn what the Besquith's plan was. With her claws fully extended, Dref-na managed to grab one of the stabilizing bars of the lift opposite her. Her momentum swung her upward, and her legs absorbed the impact against the side of Building 29. Pushing off, Dref-na twisted and grabbed the guide cable running alongside the construction lift. The Besquith managed to climb down the cable without any difficulties.

Taryn was jealous. Sometimes what Dref-na was capable of simply wasn't fair.

"Nice jump," Taryn greeted her as Dref-na landed lightly on the ground.

"Thank you," Dref-na replied, grinning. She sounded genuinely pleased as she limped over to them. "Is that our Jivool?"

"Yep." Taryn nodded and hoisted the heavy alien to his feet. He looked around, stunned. It was clear he did not understand what was going on; shock did weird things. "Let's get him somewhere a little quieter before we start asking the important questions."

Dref-na scooped the dazed Jivool up and slung him over her shoulder. "Ooph. He needs to lose a little weight. You were right about one thing; this is going to make an *amazing* drinking story. Remind me to tell you about the *wonderful* time I just had on the top floor…"

* * *

2 Km From Landing Pad 4, Garnon District, Zav'ax, It'iek System

Sunshine moved through the overgrown jungle with ease, her upgraded Leopard CASPer allowing her to avoid the usual difficulties the Mk 7 CASPer had when dealing with this sort of overgrown vegetation. While the floor of the jungle was remarkably clear of most vegetation, there was a prevalent moss covering the shaded areas which would have made the footing treacherous in her old suit. The Leopard, though, traversed it with ease.

As she closed on the site of the first assault drop pod that landed safely, her sensors picked up strange noises and a language she couldn't identify. This was surprising, since Vah had updated all their translators to include every language they might possibly need. Jorna had been particular about making certain they had all of the Pushtal dialects as well. Whoever—or whatever—was talking was not a Pushtal. Curious, she crept forward and kept her sensors dialed up to eleven.

She found a cluster of thin trees which had been knocked over. In the middle of the small, newly created clearing was a large, octagon-shaped drop pod. It was lacking any visible weaponry she could see. Atop the pod was a small radar dish, probably for communicating with the Pushtal ships above. Her eyes drifted around the clearing and her suit identified potential lifeforms gathered near one of the pod's hatches.

The aliens were tiny and blue skinned, with big, bat-like ears. These creatures were definitely *not* Pushtal. They had large mouths, and their eyes were equally big. They were skinny, save for rotund little bellies. They reminded Sunshine of the street children who were common throughout Monrovia before it had been destroyed. The little blue aliens were about as tall, too; just under one meter in height.

"You are kind of cute," she whispered as the suit failed to give her any other information on the aliens. She watched them as they gnawed on the metallic doors of the pod. They were clearly making good progress on it. She blinked. *Were they eating the metal doors?* "What the…?"

She stepped on a dead tree and it snapped in two. All the alien ears twitched and turned in her direction. Heads were raised, and large yellow eyes focused on her. There was something disconcerting in their looks. Their mouths opened and she saw large, sharp teeth. They appeared particularly shiny, almost unnatural. Realization crashed down on her. Her earlier guess had been correct; these aliens had been eating the drop pod, treating it like a snack.

They eat metal, she thought and began to grow a little nervous as she looked down at her CASPer. *I'm a walking tootsie pop to them. Oh boy…*

"*Mog!*" one of the short aliens said. It quickly became a chant, each alien stomping a foot on the ground while saying "*Mog*" in unison. They were staring directly at her and chanting. More precisely, her modified CASPer. Sunshine had no idea what the word meant, and she had the distinct feeling she didn't want to find out, either.

Sunshine brought up her arm and activated the point defense laser system. She had wanted to try out the cyclic laser miniguns since Klinks had told her about them. They were capable of firing over 3,000 laser bolts per minute, and only used a fraction of the power the older version used. She could fire them continuously for upwards of two hours before her suit reached a critical low energy point. Judging by the massive group of the aliens who were gathered around this single drop pod, she was going to need every single bit of that energy.

"*Mog!*" a larger one, presumably their leader, suddenly screamed at the top of his lungs as he pointed at her. In a rush, a tiny blue wave of aliens charged her, their smaller bodies easily navigating around the wreckage of the partially eaten pod. A few still had pieces of metal in their mouths, chewing as they sprinted toward her. Sunshine stepped back, surprised at the sheer ferocity of their attack. Both arms came up as the cyclic laser miniguns began to hum.

The first few reached her and started chewing on her legs. A few managed to sink their teeth into the Leopard, pissing the young teen off.

"No, *menh*, don't you go and scratch my new suit!" she shouted and fired the lasers into them. The narrow bright white beams cut through them, a seemingly continuous beam instead of the tiny individual shots they truly were. The tiny aliens howled as appendages were sliced neatly off and cauterized by the lasers. Seeing an opportunity, Sunshine kicked the few who had bit her suit and they flew away, crashing through some of the larger trees of the jungle. This only stunned the vicious little aliens, however. Sunshine shot them before they could get back to their feet. It wasn't very sporting of her, but then they had tried to eat her suit. Not even Tortantulas would eat a CASPer. Some lines shouldn't be crossed, and these cute but deadly aliens had done just that.

After what seemed like an eternity—but was probably only a few seconds—the horde quit attacking. Panting, Sunshine surveyed the damage. All the little aliens were either injured or dead. The cyclic lasers slowed, then stopped spinning as she powered them down. Checking her levels, she was shocked to see the weapon had drained almost three percent of her power reserves. She had to be more careful when using them.

Her sensors checked the area and reported there were no more threats in the immediate vicinity. She linked back up with the *Velut Luna*, found the other nineteen landing sites, and marked them on the topographical map. While it was fairly flat and level, it was still an overgrown jungle. The going would be tough, even with the Leopard operating at peak efficiency.

It was time to get moving. A CASPer not moving and out in the open was a dead one.

* * *

8 Km Above Garnon District, Zav'ax, It'iek System

DexKarr banked his spaceship over the small Jivool enclave and waited as his system hacked into the air traffic control system. It was slow going, which was a bit of a surprise. He had known many mercenary companies with weaker encryption in their battle comms than the corporation below. While he didn't have any experience dealing with the B'Hono Corporation, they were supposed to be a typical mining company run by the Jivool. He was mildly surprised, therefore, at the distinct lack of evidence of any mining being performed.

Perhaps they only recently set up shop and haven't gotten going yet, he reasoned as he drew up a new flight plan. His indicator finally changed from yellow to green, informing DexKarr the sync with local air traffic control was good. He was finally able to get a good look at the flight paths of the drop pods sent down by the Pushtal, and he saw that four had already been destroyed by ground fire.

Odd. Does the B'Hono Corp have anti-aircraft weapons I didn't see?

It was possible, though unlikely. Nothing in the databanks of the air traffic control system suggested there were no-fly zones anywhere on the planet. These were oftentimes the best indicator when he was looking for anti-aircraft emplacements. Grunting as his ship pulled more Gs as he banked tightly to the right, he pulled up to get a better look at the landing zones of the assault pods.

They had landed within two kilometers of one another, which was helpful. Below, his sensors picked up *something* moving through the jungle. It was a ghost of some sort, popping up on his sensors briefly before disappearing. He blinked and tapped the Tri-V display with his claw. It flickered once but remained steady. The signal, whatever it was, did not. It continued to fade out, then reappear somewhere else a moment later. The only thing he could determine about it was the movement. It was heading in a straight line and coincided with the locations of the drop pods.

Perhaps this was the Besquith?

No, he decided a moment later. His sensors were good, but there was little chance of them picking up a single Besquith beneath the thick vegetation. He wondered if the Jivool had some sort of battle armor running around the jungle before dismissing the idea as absurd. Unless the security forces were using an enhanced ore extractor suit for combat purposes, there was nothing in his records which suggested the Jivool were capable of such.

The only thing he could think of was the Human mercenary, Sunshine. It was entirely possible she had a CASPer down there and was wreaking havoc on the Pushtal in the pods. Except CASPer suits were not usually stealthy, nor were they very good in such a dense environment. Unless she had a Mk 8—and his records showed only a few companies had them, and the Kakata Korps had not been one of them—there was no way she would be able to do what the ghost on his sensors was doing.

And whenever the ghost came up to one of the assault pods, there was a brief flash of energy discharge before the shadow moved on. *Something* down there was murdering and causing carnage in a very efficient manner. Normally it would be a joy to watch, but reason and common sense reminded DexKarr that he was supposed to go down there, defeat the CASPer, and take the girl into custody, alive. This cold truth was a harsh slap in his snout.

"Does she have a Mk 8?" DexKarr idly wondered as he spotted seven of the Pushtal's assault drop pods gathered in a small clearing together. There was a mass of blue amidst the trees. Curious, he banked away and gave his digital cameras a better chance to identify what he was seeing. The blue mass of lifeforms appeared on his Tri-V a moment later, and he frowned. Whatever they were, they were definitely *not* Pushtal. They weren't any of the known mercenary races, either. He snorted and rubbed his leathery snout with a claw, bemused.

This is the weirdest job I've ever taken, he thought as he steered his ship around for another pass. He activated his cluster munitions in the belly of his ship and prepared to even the odds some. *Pushtal using a feral alien race to kill a Human girl I need to keep alive so I can kidnap her to be tortured and killed later? Yes, weird fits.*

The life of a contract killer was never dull.

* * *

5 Km from Landing Pad 4, Garnon District, Zav'ax, It'iek System

The *Velut Luna*'s sensors picked up a high-speed ship approaching her position. Triangulating its trajectory, Sunshine quickly determined it would miss her position by almost one hundred yards. If she didn't know better, she would have sworn the pilot was flying just above the final seven assault drop pod's last known positions.

It had grown ridiculously simple. She would approach the position of the downed assault pod, keep the terrifyingly cute but deadly aliens at range, and launch grenades into their position. She would finish off any survivors with her lasers. Lather, rinse, and repeat. It had become almost dull and routine. She really began to wonder just where the little aliens had come from, and why they were working for the Pushtal.

Sunshine looked up as the mysterious spaceship came in low over the jungle. It was agile; far more so than the *Velut Luna*. It was clearly a ship used to entering and exiting the atmosphere. Her sensors detected cluster munitions falling onto the final seven assault pods. No other warning sounded, though, as the suit marked their trajectory and deemed she was an acceptable distance away. A series of sharp reports ripped throughout the dense jungle as the small munitions rained death upon the last of the tiny, half-naked aliens. It was no longer a battle but an outright massacre, making her sense of guilt ease just a bit. She would not be the one responsible for their deaths. She almost thanked her mysterious benefactor over the open comms but something Mulbah once said came to mind and stopped her.

The enemy of my enemy is my enemy's enemy. Nothing more.

Sunshine wasn't sure where he had heard the saying, but it was sound advice. Glancing at her Tri-V, the *Velut Luna* no longer detected anything near her resembling the vicious little aliens. In fact, so far as she could tell there weren't any left within a five-kilometer radius of her position.

Were they all dead already? Sunshine couldn't be certain, but it appeared to be the case. She nodded and turned the CASPer back toward the *Velut Luna*. The Jivool security forces would either be arriving soon or already in position, and she still wasn't absolutely certain how Vah would react to real combat. She was fairly sure Jorna would be fine, but Vah? If her usual luck held, it would end poorly for them all.

Maybe I should have stuck Jorna on the railguns?

Hindsight had perfect clarity.

* * *

1 Km from Landing Pad 4, Garnon District, Zav'ax, It'iek System

Once Taryn was absolutely certain they had eluded any possible pursuers, she told Dref-na to stop. The Besquith, her limp growing worse the further they went, unceremoniously dumped their captured Jivool onto the ground. He whimpered in fear and pain but said nothing. He watched them carefully and twitched every time Dref-na made any sudden moves.

"How do we start this?" Dref-na asked and winced. She reached down and rubbed her knee.

"You want to eat a foot or something first, let him know we're serious?" Taryn questioned loudly as she prodded the fallen Jivool.

"I'd rather start with a hand," Dref-na answered, shrugging. "Feet aren't my thing."

"You don't have to eat me," the Jivool whined. "I'll talk. Just don't eat me."

"I don't know," Taryn said as she knelt down on the ground next to Cranston. She prodded his shoulder. "She seems pretty hungry. Dref-na, you hungry?"

"Famished."

"I'll talk! Please! Ask me anything!"

"Anything, eh?" Taryn looked over at Dref-na, who appeared bemused. "Where are the TriRusk?"

"The what?"

"There is a facility here on this planet where you're hiding Tri-Rusk," Taryn clarified as she motioned to Dref-na. The Besquith reached over and hoisted the heavy Jivool to his feet. "I want to know where it is."

"I…" his voice trailed off weakly. He closed his eyes. Dref-na pulled back, frowning.

"He's showing more resilience than I expected," she observed as she began testing her damaged knee. It was swollen but not entirely immobile. "He's the administrative type, so eating a hand would probably ruin his career…"

"Where is it?" Taryn asked, grabbing the surviving Jivool by his shoulders. She used all her strength and managed to push the off-balance Jivool into a tree. She leaned in close and grinned ferociously. The rank stench of a terrified Jivool filled her nostrils. It was almost as bad as Boogadishu Station, only without the stale air. Almost, however, meant tolerable to the hardened young woman. The tip of her nose brushed against the Jivool's. She was perfectly aware of just how much of an impact the tiny gesture had on the lumbering mammalian. It was taboo for a Jivool to brush their nose against another's outside of the hearth. Her voice dropped three octaves lower. "Where. Is. It?"

"I...I don't know what...you're talking about," the Jivool replied, his teeth chattering in fear. Taryn's face was one of an enraged goddess about to smite a disbeliever. If the engineer didn't believe in a deity beforehand, he definitely did now.

"Is that so?" she asked, hissing the question. She didn't even blink as she stared into the fearful eyes of the Jivool. Her features were twisted in a mask of pure rage and fury and made her more menacing. "Dref-Na, tear his arms off, then eat them in front of him. Make those disgusting smacking noises while you're at it."

The Besquith growled and licked her lips noisily. The Jivool wet himself. Besquith teeth were *very* large and appeared even sharper when they were mere centimeters away.

"Oh, uh, you meant *that* research facility."

"Yes, *that* facility. What and where is it?"

"It's...a research facility. I don't know where it is!"

"Is that so? A research facility? Dref-na, I changed my mind about his arms. Start with his hand and go from there. Make sure you eat him nice and slow. And make sure you chew..."

"It's true! It's a research facility! Okay, I know where it is but nothing else!" the Jivool protested, his eyes darting frantically between the towering Besquith and the smaller Human. "I swear upon my mother I don't know anything more!"

"Why?" Taryn asked.

"*Why what?*" he squeaked.

"Why are you researching the TriRusk?"

"I don't know! I swear!"

"Fine, let's say I believe you for the moment." Taryn leaned in close to his exposed ear. "What are the coordinates for the facility?"

"On a slate, I can show you where it is," the Jivool replied, his voice still shaky. Taryn shook her head and motioned at Dref-na. The Besquith approached and handed the Jivool a clean slate. The Jivool blinked slowly as a map of all of the planet's continents appeared on the screen. Taryn backed away to give the Jivool more space to work the slate.

"Type them in," Taryn ordered. The Jivool obeyed, and the picture zoomed in immediately. She looked down at the screen. Oddly enough, the coordinates pinpointed a location in the middle of the jungle not far from her ship's landing site. However, she remembered the terrain very well and didn't remember seeing any sign of a building. With the growth of the area, though, it was very possible they had missed it. There was one lingering, nagging question which tugged at the edges of her mind.

What in the hell were they doing with the TriRusk?

She didn't want to ask the Jivool because odds were, he didn't know. While he was one of the B'Hono Corporation stooges Kl'nk'nnk had tagged as highly likely to know about the TriRusk and where they were being held, she wasn't certain about his specific role.

As far as she could tell, he was one of the junior assistants to the site director, a glorified go-fer, but a competent one, who reported directly to the operations manager of the mining colony itself. Kl'nk'nnk hadn't really liked him. Taryn recalled the Jeha saying he seemed slimy.

"Is this the only location they're being kept at?" Taryn asked.

"I…I don't know."

"Dref-na?"

"I think I'll start at his legs, so he'll live longer…"

"I don't know!" the Jivool screamed with tears in his eyes as the Besquith hoisted him into the air. A foul odor filled their nostrils as the terror overwhelmed the Jivool. "I don't know, I don't know! I really don't know! Please don't eat me!"

"Fine," Taryn growled. She doubted they would get anything else out of the Jivool. "Let him go."

Dref-na, clearly disappointed, tossed the heavy Jivool to the ground. He lay in a heap, shaking as he watched them with fearful eyes.

"Run, morsel," Dref-na whispered in a dangerous tone. "Before you learn why it is a fate worse than death to be exhausted when one is eaten alive by a Besquith."

The Jivool scrambled to his feet and ran away as quickly as his powerful legs could carry him. They lost sight of him moments later, his natural fur coloration and drab clothing blending well with the oddly tinted leaves of the jungle around them. Taryn turned and looked at Dref-na, her eyes sparkling in amusement.

"Think we should tell him he's going the wrong way?"

Dref-na paused and considered for a moment before shaking her head. "No. Let him find his own way back."

"Sounds fair to me," Taryn confirmed. "Let's get back to the *Velut Luna*."

* * *

Garnon District Building 11, Zav'ax, It'iek System

Karvan di Mobiar walked into his office, infuriated. Not only had someone managed to sneak in undetected at a secured building not too far from his office and slaughter one of his under-the-table and completely off-book revenue generators, they had somehow managed to kidnap a junior aide without anybody noticing. In fact, the only reason they knew he was missing was because security, while sweeping the building for any other infiltrators, had spotted his open office door. A cursory investigation lasting mere minutes showed his timecard had been punched in earlier that morning, and he should have been in his office at the time of the attack. His pinplant tracker showed he had walked out of the building and out of range of the sensors while it was supposed to be on lockdown. He immediately discounted a spy in their midst because the individual's profile suggested Cranston Vi Karvok was not an original thinker, which left only one option: kidnapping.

There was just one problem with the kidnapping theory. As far as he knew, Cranston Vi Karvok knew literally nothing of importance. Sure, he was a valuable junior aide to Karvan's secondary site supervisor, but nothing more. He had low clearance and no access to anything Karvan was doing on the side, either. As far as Karvan knew, the only thing Cranston was remotely aware of which would be classified was the construction of the underground research facility nearby, which no kidnapper could possibly know about.

Karvan paused when he spotted a large shadowy figure sitting in his expensive chair. Glancing around, he saw nobody else in the room. Cautiously he approached, his hand drifting to his slate to call for security.

"No need for security, Karvan," a terrifyingly familiar voice hissed. Karvan's hand froze centimeters from his pocket. "Let's keep this meeting between two old friends, shall we?"

"You," Karvan growled as he looked across his desk at his so-called benefactor. Ever since the Buma had come into his life, everything had gone to pot. Not for the first time did he regret his past decisions. "What do you want?"

"We need to close down the shop," the Buma said as he easily slid out of the chair and walked across the room. "The secret is out, so to speak."

"Who knows?" Karvan asked, nervous. "We won't survive a second visit from the Peacemakers."

"Not the Peacemakers, that's for certain," the Benefactor said calmly. "What's expendable in the facility?"

"Everything and everyone," Karvan answered immediately, his mind racing. "Most of it is automated anyways."

The Buma nodded. "Good. Destroy it and everything involved. Did you make all the extractions yet?"

"Of the males, yes. They're disposed of. The female needed more time and is still in the facility."

"She is inconsequential," he stated. "Your last report said you've got enough material for at least two dozen with under-developed cerebral cortexes, but you isolated the albinism genomes one and two. We don't need sentience, only their reproductive capabilities. Gather the materials you've extracted and move it all to my ship.

Once this is handled, dispose of the female. Ditch your translator while you're at it and use one of the ones I gave you. Do this by the end of the day, understand?"

"I understand," Karvan responded, even though he really didn't. To his eyes, the Buma seemed spooked by something. Events which he couldn't see were going on in the background. Seeing his benefactor nervous caused Karvan's own paranoia to grow. "You mentioned someone else knows?"

"By the time your pathetic red sun sets, Karvan di Mobiar, I want my aspect of this little side hustle scrubbed," the Benefactor stated, ignoring the Jivool's question. "Keep your mining operation up and running, though, in case someone comes along asking questions later."

"The...m-mining operation?" Karvan stammered slightly. He tried to swallow as his throat suddenly constricted. He'd been collecting checks from the B'Hono Corporation to pay his "laborers." He'd even managed to get bonus hazard pay for the fictional employees while running multiple phishing and ad farms on the side, pocketing millions of credits in the process. If someone investigated before he staged the industrial "accident" and abandoned the project, he would be doomed. A Peacemaker arriving on-planet would be the absolute best-case scenario given the bloodthirsty reputation his forebears in the Iron Sky Mining Company had earned over the years.

The Buma looked at him curiously. "You *do* have a mining operation, don't you?"

"Ah, yes," Karvan nodded before changing his mind. He shook his head. "But no."

"Oh, you ambitious, greedy little Jivool," the Buma chuckled, standing from the comfortable chair. It was clear to Karvan the Buma understood him perfectly. "You have as much, if not more, riding on this then I do. I have deniability at least. You? Well…you had best hurry."

"What are you going to do?" Karvan asked as his Benefactor pushed past him and made his way to the door.

"I have other matters to attend to. This *maskrivoka*? This is no longer necessary. My ship is already at the facility. Load the genetic materials and have your security forces converge on the ship carrying the Humans."

"The ship?" Karvan looked at him in confusion. "Why the Human ship? I don't understand…"

Sighing, the Buma walked out of the office, leaving a very confused and terrified Jivool behind.

* * * * *

Chapter Ten

Outside the Garnon District, Zav'ax, It'iek System

The duo had walked around in the jungle for almost thirty minutes before Taryn finally threw her hands into the air in exasperation.

"Face it," she growled and looked back at Dref-na, who was limping behind slowly. "We're lost."

"If you would just use your slate I'm certain you—" Dref-na began but paused when she saw the furious expression on Taryn's face.

"Oh sure, and admit to Sunshine that I couldn't even find our way back without a slate?"

"She doesn't have to know," Dref-na pointed out.

"Trust me. She'll know. I don't know how, but she will." Taryn shook her head and pointed deep into the alien jungle. "It shouldn't be this damn difficult. That way's west. That's where the *Velut Luna* is. Why aren't we finding it?"

"I see your issue, Taryn Lupo," Dref-na said. She raised a claw and pointed in a different direction entirely. "*That* way is west. You were pointing north. If memory serves correctly, we're now closer to Landing Pad 6 than we are to the *Velut Luna*."

"*Seriously?*" Taryn yelled and kicked at a clump of brightly colored lichen on the ground. "We've been heading north for half an hour? I can't *believe* you didn't say anything!"

"I did try," Dref-na reminded her. "Every five minutes, I warned you I felt we were not headed in the right direction, Taryn Lupo. I believe it was after the third time when you told me to, and I quote, shut my cakehole."

"I never said—okay, fine," Taryn spat, irritated more at herself than the smug expression on Dref-na's face. She dropped her voice to an almost-imperceptible whisper. "And it wasn't shut your cakehole. I said shut your *piehole*." Dref-na grinned some more so Taryn, instead of continuing the argument, turned the proper direction, and struck out toward the correct landing pad.

They passed a clearing, which both quickly identified as the aforementioned Landing Pad 6 and continued on to the *Velut Luna*. The further they went, however, the slower their progress became. It wasn't the terrain, though, but Dref-na's ability to move at a rapid pace was gone thanks to her damaged knee. Until it received proper therapy, she was limited in what she could do.

"How bad is the pain?" Taryn asked as they stopped for a brief rest. Ahead, both could hear the faint sounds of random gunfire. If there was still shooting, then there was hope the others were still alive. Taryn glanced down at Dref-na's injured knee.

"Bad enough to make me want to stop for a longer period of time," the Besquith admitted through clenched teeth. She bent over at the waist and rubbed the offending joint. "Getting old is painful, Taryn Lupo."

"Old?" Taryn looked at her oddly before the growing scream of atmospheric engines interrupted her. They looked up expectantly but the large, oddly shaped trees of Zav'ax prevented them from immediately spotting the source of the noise. The trees swayed when something large passed overhead toward Landing Pad 6. There was a brief flash of a ship before the trees drifted back into their original positions, blocking their view. Taryn grunted, recognizing the ship instantly. "Was that a…?"

"If you were going to ask if that was a Skipjumper, I would say yes, it was," Dref-na confirmed. Taryn's lips curled up into a smile and she looked at her Besquith friend. Dref-na recognized the look and immediately shook her head. "No. No, Taryn Lupo, we cannot steal the ship."

"But *why?*"

"Remember what happened on Boogadishu Station?" Dref-na reminded her. "With the guns? I told you I was not going to get shot again for you. Plus, I'm almost certain Sunshine will kill you this time."

"But—the shiny—"

"No."

"Damn it," Taryn grumbled and kicked at the moss. Dref-na took a few hesitant steps and stopped behind Taryn. Grunting, the Besquith pressed her razor-sharp claws gently into Taryn's shoulder, a not-so-subtle reminder of who was the more dangerous predator at the moment.

"As I said, I will not get shot for you again," Dref-na growled. While not necessarily threatening, and with some humor in it, there was a very distinct undertone which not even Taryn could miss. "I won't eat you, but you *will* listen to me this time. We need to get back to the *Velut Luna*."

"But what if I give the ship to Sunshine as a gift?" Taryn looked up at the looming Besquith. She tried to inject as much innocence into her voice as she could possibly manage and poured on the sweetness. "A ship for Sunshine? Think of how happy this could make her!"

"Hmm…" Dref-na released her grip on Taryn's shoulder and looked thoughtfully toward the landing pad. The sounds of the mysterious ship's engines had faded to almost nothing. The Besquith finally shook her head, bemused. "Perhaps after we rescue the Tri-Rusk we can steal the ship and gift it to the tiny fierceness."

Taryn beamed. "Yay!"

* * *

Landing Pad 6, Garnon District, Zav'ax, It'iek System

DexKarr stepped out of his ship and looked around. The landing pad he had chosen was a mere kilometer away from where the *Velut Luna* was berthed and was in a fairly isolated position compared to the other seven pads. The chances of some random Jivool stumbling upon his ship were low, though not entirely impossible. To ensure nobody messed with his ship while he was hunting, DexKarr sealed the hold door and activated the security net. Now, if anyone came within three meters of his ship, he would get an alert via his pinplant. It might be old-fashioned, but it was definitely effective.

Looking around, he noticed the jungle surrounding the landing pad was odd. Instead of thick undergrowth and bushes, most of the ground was covered with a rich lichen almost orange in color. He could hear animals further away, creating an almost idyllic atmosphere. He glanced up. Topping the tall trees of the jungle were enormous lily pad-like leaves, allowing for the absorption of water and the maximum amount of UV light from the red dwarf star the planet orbited. It was alien and beautiful.

In the distance, a rapid burst of what was clearly gunfire shattered the mood. Distinct screams of wounded and dying Jivool assaulted his ears. He could smell the sweet tang of blood in the air. The heavy musk of burned ozone from heavy laser usage blended uncomfortably with the sweet scent of the planet's heavy, dark soil. He shook his head and listened for the creatures of the forest. They were silent now, their songs drowned out by the sounds of battle.

He sniffed the air. There was a scent in the air he hadn't expected to catch the moment he left his ship, yet there it was—the familiar, tangy aroma of a Besquith. He clicked his tongue and growled low in his throat. The sheer unexpectedness of the scent threw him for a loop. Had the Besquith come for him? It wasn't entirely out of the realm of possibilities. His ship had clearly been seen by the CASPer when he'd made his earlier strafing run.

Nature's idyllic moment ruined, DexKarr sighed heavily and adjusted the mount of the railgun. Time was running short. He gave his equipment a final once-over before setting off into the jungle.

Moving past the beautifully alien trees without a second glance, the predator became one with his surroundings. He had a date with a Human girl and her allies, and his employer did not want him to be late.

* * *

Landing Pad 4, Garnon District, Zav'ax, It'iek System

The Jivool arrived in force just as Taryn returned to the *Velut Luna*. Dref-na was still in the jungle but insisted the Human go ahead to help defend the ship from the Jivool. Taryn, reluctantly, agreed. Upon arrival, Taryn assessed the situation and immediately moved to assist Jorna, who was taking cover near a large cluster of reinforced crates. She was about to ask where the Pushtal had dug them up before recognizing the ammunition crates given to them by Magnus on Draxis III.

"Please tell me you emptied these," Taryn asked as she slid onto the ground next to Jorna. Jorna gave her an odd look as she finished loading a magazine into her small carbine.

"Oh, hi. You're still alive. Good. This isn't my first gunfight, Taryn," Jorna retorted and waved her free hand around at the crates. "I emptied the ones my dad gave us. The others were empty and in your secondary hold. I think they're what Sunshine had her CASPer stored in. Hope she doesn't mind me appropriating these."

"Can they stop a round?"

"I don't know, I—" a single shot bounced off a crate and ricocheted into the jungle. Jorna flinched, then smiled. "Yeah, apparently they can. Awesome."

"Where's Sunshine?" Taryn asked, looking around. There was no sign of the CASPer anywhere.

"Went off to deal with some drop pods," Jorna answered. "Haven't heard from her since."

"Oh." A second shot bounced off the crate, making a loud noise as it glanced harmlessly away. Taryn twitched, surprised. "These clowns aren't playing around, are they?"

"That was a warning shot, criminals," one of the Jivool shouted from nearby. Taryn risked a peek over the crate and saw the security forces spreading out, forming a half-circle around the far end of the landing pad. It was a change from the last time she'd faced B'Hono's security forces. Apparently, they'd learned from their previous encounter. Taryn spotted the speaker, a particularly robust looking Jivool in heavy body armor. He was armed and handled his weapon with passing familiarity. He continued to bellow at them from a safe distance, carefully positioned behind a low barrier surrounding the edge of the landing pad. "We don't want to kill you but will if we have to."

"You know, the last time we were here, they talked a lot then as well," Taryn pointed out to Jorna as she grabbed one of the carbines the Pushtal had already loaded and leaned against a crate. "Must be a Jivool thing."

"Perhaps you bring out the best in people?" Jorna suggested. "I remember the discussion which led to Dref-na almost gutting you not too long ago. Good times. Are we shooting to kill here?"

Taryn gave her an incredulous look. "Of course. What the hell, Jorna?"

The Pushtal offered a wan smile. "Just checking. Humans are weird sometimes."

"You've met, what, four Humans your entire life?"

"And every one of you was weird, even by Pushtal standards."

"Point," Taryn grunted and took aim at one of the Jivool. She didn't fire, though. Instead, she yelled at the approaching enemy forces. "I could have shot you. Just back off, and I won't kill you all." She paused and turned to give Jorna a funny look. "I just had the weirdest sense of *déjà vu.*"

A small projectile smashed hard into one of the crates. The tough material of the crate held, though. Taryn spotted a small bag roughly the size of her hand on the ground. It was brightly colored and reminded her of flattened baseball. She reached out and snagged it. Ducking behind the protective barrier, Taryn inspected it further.

It was a tough material made of some sort of synthetic cloth unlike anything she'd ever seen. Inside the bag were small, hard objects. She rolled it around on her palm for a moment, then realized precisely what it was: a stun bag, used by security forces to deal with protestors and rioters without killing them. Painful, but survivable.

"They're using non-lethals," Taryn proclaimed as she tossed the small bag to Jorna. The Pushtal easily snagged it with a paw and inspected it briefly before tossing it aside. "They're not trying to kill us. Weird."

"Stun bags?" Jorna scoffed. "They must really want to bring us in alive."

"Considering the damage we did the last time we were here, I'm a little surprised," Taryn admitted. She risked a second glance around the crate and saw the Jivool had stopped trying to surround them, content with remaining behind the containment wall of the landing pad. "I'm amazed they don't have gas. I'd be lobbing teargas, or whatever the Jivool use."

"Maybe they don't have experience dealing with angry miners?" Jorna quipped. Taryn gave her an odd look. Jorna smirked. "I bet that first round that deflected off the crate was a rubber one."

"Not taking any bets."

"They probably suck at dealing with angry miners," Jorna observed.

"You do realize these guys used to be the Iron Sky Mining Company, right?"

"Oh," Jorna blinked. Every Pushtal knew about the ISMC and, more importantly, how they had been dealt with. It was legendary, the sort of fable that was told around a bonfire in the middle of the night after drinking and carousing. Clan Arwoon's favorite part of the story was when the Enforcer killed *everyone* in ISMC who shot at him. "No, I didn't know."

"Actually, they probably don't know what sort of gas is good on Humans or Pushtal," Taryn offered. "VX gas is lethal to us, but apparently only gives other races indigestion."

"Taryn?" Klinks looked out from the safety of the *Velut Luna*. The Jeha waved her forearms before pointing toward the front of the ship. "I need a protective barrier around the forward strut if I am to repair it."

"Wait, you haven't fixed it yet?" Taryn asked, her tone incredulous. "What were you doing while we were doing the kidnapping thing?"

"Repairing the engine which had overheated and shorted out the electrical components," the Jeha answered calmly. "I deemed the engines to be more important than the landing strut."

"Okay, that's fair," Taryn allowed. She looked around but the only barrier she could see was the one keeping her from view of the Jivool. She gave a heavy sigh. "Jorna? You're not going to like what we have to do next."

"If you tell me we have to move these crates to cover Klinks, then you're absolutely right, I don't like it," Jorna said as she leaned around a crate to glance at the Jivool. She waved a furry paw around them. "Do you know how long it took me to move these here?"

"Five minutes?"

"Try eight," Jorna replied. "We won't have that long."

"Plan C it is then," Taryn murmured. She activated her comms. "Vah?"

"I'm here," the CozSha answered immediately.

"Why haven't you fired on the Jivool with the ship's guns yet?" Taryn asked the diminutive junior administrator.

"They aren't on the landing pad yet, Taryn," Vah stated. "It's not efficient to fire upon them when they are not fully in range. I might miss and waste ammunition."

Taryn rolled her eyes. Jorna barely managed to stifle a very Human-like giggle.

"You don't need to wait for them to mass up, Vah," Taryn informed the CozSha. "Shoot them now. Individually, single shots."

"It wouldn't be very efficient, though," Vah complained, just a hint of panic at the edge of her tone. "I am very efficient."

"Efficiency would be helping us stay alive out here, Vah," Taryn reminded her. She muted the comms for a second and gave Jorna a sideways look. "Sunshine is much better at this."

"What, leadership?" Jorna teased her as she grabbed one of the crates and began dragging it across the tarmac, keeping it between her and the Jivool.

"Oh, you're absolutely hilarious right now," Taryn growled as she followed suit. "You got jokes. I got jokes, too."

"I hope so," Jorna replied as she angled the makeshift barricade to protect the front half of the ship better. "It's your only redeeming quality."

"Vah?" Taryn said, unmuting her comms and pointedly ignoring Jorna. "It's efficient if we leave the planet alive and in one piece, yes?"

"Yes?" The CozSha sounded uncertain.

Taryn pressed on. "In order to leave the planet in one piece, we all need to be on a working ship, yes?" Taryn continued. "This is most efficient, correct?"

"Yes," Vah continued, surer of herself now.

"If they capture the ship we won't be able to leave, and that is inefficient!" Taryn nearly shouted. *"Now get those guns firing!"*

"Okay," Vah answered, her voice quiet. Three of the four hatches popped open and the defensive railguns appeared. The barrels swung outward to point at the Jivool hiding behind the retaining wall. After a brief pause, the fourth appeared.

"Good job, Vah," Taryn beamed. She looked over at Jorna. "Let's hurry and get these crates moved."

* * *

Near Landing Pad 4, Garnon District, Zav'ax, It'iek System

Dref-na limped carefully through the jungle, pausing every few steps to stop and sniff the air. There was something out there, unlike anything she had encountered in decades. Whatever it was tugged at the very edges of her memory, reminded her of…something. She shook her head and growled softly in frustration. The downside of having a long life was that too many experiences were crammed into a mind and the memories began to blur over time.

She'd had no problem sending Taryn ahead. Wounded as she was, Dref-na wouldn't be able to move quickly enough to be much help during the fighting when she did eventually arrive. She'd never really gotten the hang of firearms, preferring close quarter combat over the ranged thing Humans loved so well. While it definitely shortened the life expectancy of the average Besquith, it was immensely satisfying to hear the enemy screaming while being devoured. Sighing, she reached down and rubbed her injured knee again. The swelling was still bad, but the pain was lessening somewhat. This was good. Now she wouldn't have to pierce her own skin in order to drain the fluid out.

A slight breeze brought the scent back to her. Dref-na was absolutely certain she had smelled whatever was out there before. It remained tantalizingly out of reach, however.

"I hate being old," Dref-na muttered and paused as a nearby branch snapped. Her head swiveled slowly around to look in the direction of the noise. She couldn't see anything, but something dangerous was out there. *What are you,* she wondered. Pausing, she tilted her shaggy head ever so slightly to try to hear better, hoping to pick up something that would clue her in on the tantalizingly familiar smell. Listening told her little except that whatever was out there knew how to move. She knelt and decided to wait for it was to make an appearance.

Besides, it would give her some time to figure out if her knee was going to fail or not.

* * *

The crates were solid but with Vah providing cover, Jorna and Taryn were able to rearrange them to form a barrier between the security forces and the nose of the ship. Once the position was deemed safe by Taryn, the Jeha scuttled down the cargo hold ramp with a large box of tools in one of her delicate pincer hands. She set the box down next to the damaged strut and immediately went to work.

The front portside railgun suddenly belched fire, and two Jivool who had tried sneak over the barrier were disintegrated. Taryn and Jorna dropped to their knees and slapped their hands over their ears, crying out. Both had ringing in their ears from the shot, though it was clear Jorna was suffering far more than Taryn. Shaking her head, she could hear Vah over her comms. The CozSha was saying something.

"Come again, Vah? I couldn't hear you."

"I said that was most efficient," Vah repeated. She sounded pleased and yet detached. It was odd.

"From now on, don't use the front portside railgun," Taryn instructed as she moved to a nearby pylon on the tarmac. It was a landing light, used to guide pilots during night landings. It was also a good marker for the daytime, though the red light atop it wasn't on at the moment. It was as good a place as any to shoot at the Jivool while staying covered and away from Kl'nk'nnk. Repairing the strut would be difficult enough for the Jeha. Doing so while under fire from the security forces would be nearly impossible.

"It is the most efficient railgun on this ship," Vah countered. "It is reading at 93.7% accuracy rating within a radius of forty-two centimeters at fifteen kilometers!"

"I brought this on myself," Taryn muttered to herself before she paused. "No, I can blame Sunshine for this mess. Hey, this time it really isn't my fault!"

"My ears hurt," Jorna said in a loud voice as she rubbed a spot behind her left ear. "I think I ruptured something."

"How's your balance?" Taryn asked, then stopped. She felt stupid. Most felinoid races had excellent balance, Pushtal included. It was what made them so good in zero gravity. Jorna looked at her incredulously. Taryn rubbed her face. "Yeah, dumb question. Sorry."

Jorna suddenly dropped to the ground as a stun bag from one of the security officers smashed into the back of her head. Taryn cried out in alarm as more stun bags smashed into the pylon, and she instinctively flinched back. Determined, she managed to grab Jorna by the arm and dragged the Pushtal behind cover. Taryn checked her pulse and saw she was alive, just unconscious. She raised her carbine and managed to fire off a full burst one-handed to keep the security forces at bay. Jorna's arm fell limply to the tarmac as Taryn released it and she grabbed a spare magazine from the Pushtal's battle harness.

"Sunshine? We need some help here," Taryn said over the linked comms as she reloaded the fresh magazine into her carbine. "Jorna's down."

"How badly is she hurt?"

"Unconscious," Taryn answered as she shot at a Jivool who had stuck its head out for a better look. He yelped and disappeared, uninjured save for his pride. "They're using non-lethal weapons; I think they want to capture us alive."

"Last time we were here, they tried to kill us," Sunshine reminded her. Taryn caught a brief glimpse of the black-painted CASPer moving through the jungle nearby, then heard screams as Sunshine rushed a particularly large group of Jivool hiding behind one of the service fuel tanks just off the edge of the landing pad. "I wonder what changed. One second."

Jivool scattered as Sunshine crashed through them, her suit making short work of the ill-equipped security force. Taryn had expected a little more lethality when it came to the B'Hono Corporation, given the results of their last encounter. However, something *must* have changed, because even in the face of superior firepower from their little group of misfits, the Jivool were sticking with non-lethal weaponry. Granted, non-lethal did not mean painless, but it was something for the woman to consider.

"Taryn?" Dref-na's voice sounded pained over the comms. "There's something else in this jungle besides the Jivool."

"Predators?" Taryn asked, tensing up. The last thing they needed was a super predator of some sort smelling all the blood and deciding they would be a delicious entrée.

"Yes, but not the kind you think," Dref-na explained poorly. "It's something larger than me, but it's not of this world. I have a scent but—I'm following it."

"That sounded rather ominous," Taryn said as she raised her carbine and snapped off another shot. A Jivool howled in pain. Taryn smiled, pleased with herself. She preferred making bombs over shootouts, but there was no reason she couldn't take pride in being a good shot with a carbine.

"Give me a moment, and I will discover what creature stalks us," Dref-na promised. The comms went quiet for a few moments before the Besquith came back on. She sounded worried. "Taryn Lupo, I know what the creature is now. You must remain close to the ship. I will hunt the hunter."

Taryn paused for a moment, considering, before she contacted Sunshine. "You hear all that?"

"Yes," Sunshine answered. "I'm going to swing around the perimeter to see what she's talking about."

"Be careful," Taryn told her. "Dref-na isn't usually so cautious."

"Don't worry," Sunshine assured Taryn. A flash of black appeared and two Jivool heads flew off into the jungle. There was some more screaming, then silence as the distinctive sound of a MAC chattered through the area. "I doubt there's anything on this planet not named Dref-na that could kill me right now."

* * *

Near Landing Pad 4, Garnon District, Zav'ax, It'iek System

DexKarr watched the strangely painted CASPer ruin the day of a collection of Jivool, using its impressive arm blades to slice through them all. There was only enough time for a ragged scream of pain before the first two members of the group were beheaded by the tiny avenging angel inside. He smiled and watched the MAC shred the survivors to bits. There was nothing like going fang-to-fang with a deadly weapon such as a CASPer, especially when the pilot was a magician with a suit. Dex-Karr doubted any of the Jivool would be able to stop the CASPer from killing them all. Not without heavier weaponry, at least. Of which the security forces seemed to be severely lacking.

He figured the pilot was his target, Sunshine. She was the sole, licensed Human mercenary among the group, and therefore the only one who had the skillset to be a quality CASPer pilot.

There were multiple ways to take down a CASPer without killing the pilot inside. First and foremost was to knock it off its feet. Nine times out of ten a pilot would not have the reflexes needed to get back up before he could close on it. However, the longer he watched the black CASPer in action, the more uncertain he became of this plan. The pilot was an absolute wizard inside the armored suit, and DexKarr reassessed the risk versus reward of taking on the CASPer head-on. More importantly, the odds of a successful capture versus losing his own life.

He trilled musically in his throat as he looked around. This hunt was going about as poorly as he could have hoped, with the Jivool security forces in his way. Their arrival also ruined the element of surprise, though DexKarr was forced to admit he wasn't certain there would have been much chance to surprise them on the landing pad. His best shot would have been to pick them off one by one as they moved through the dense jungle, only Sunshine and the rest of her group were well aware of how dangerous it would be to wander around alone in a hostile environment.

DexKarr sniffed the air, but once more the thick stench of blood and burned ozone fouled any chance he had of sensing anything worthwhile. His scanners were going crazy, though, picking up everything within the vicinity. In fact, the longer he read, the more dissatisfied he became with it; the sensors gave him too much information. A slight headache began to form as he struggled to understand just what feedback was important and what was simply background noise.

He raised his railgun and targeted the CASPer, but the tracking software continued to struggle with the jungle trees around him. Growling in frustration, he looked around for any kind of elevated position. He spotted a large boulder but quickly dismissed it. The position was too exposed and if they spotted him, the ship's railguns would make short work of him. While it was true he had a decent shot at the Human known as Taryn Lupo, if he fired now they would be aware of his presence. There was no scenario he could see where it ended with him walking away without being shot at in return by the mercenary in the CASPer. Especially since he needed the other Human female alive.

"Torokar!" a voice roared from the undergrowth. DexKarr's head whipped around as he recognized the snarling sound of an enraged Besquith.

It had found him! But how?

"Come for me and be hunted!"

DexKarr paused, torn. His employer had been very specific when giving him instructions regarding his target, the Human identified as

Sunshine. He was to keep her alive, which was far easier when she was close to him. He had a visual on the young woman now. She was very unlike the others whose images he had procured.

Weighing the pros against the cons, he wrestled with indecision. On one claw, it would be a quick and brutal stalk. Sure, she was inside a CASPer, but he had yet to find a suit of armor that could withstand a direct hit from a railgun. The party was bigger than he had anticipated. The other Human was nearby with the Jeha, both huddled near the ship, pinned down by the Jivool security forces. The Pushtal was out of action for the time being, though when it would rejoin the fight was anybody's guess. He wasn't sure if there was anybody still on the ship. However, it was clear none of them were going anywhere for a while. He could simply hit them from a distance, eliminate any who might still be aboard the ship, grab the girl, and disappear before the Jivool security forces overwhelmed the position. It was too easy.

On the other claw...it was the opportunity to hunt a Besquith in the overgrown forest surrounding the landing pad. A *Besquith*. The ultimate prey, more predator than anything else he had ever hunted. It was a trial of immense difficulty, something which had been eluding him since before he'd won the Gotiro Challenge years before. It would be hard, almost impossible, to track the dangerous creature. It would be an even tougher kill. Was he up to the task?

Stupid question, DexKarr thought. He snapped his teeth and grinned. It was too perfect.

The Humans and their weak allies could wait. He was more than up to the task. It was time to *hunt*.

* * *

Dref-na snarled as she slipped through the shadows created by the trees looming above, her steps taking her rapidly away from the *Velut Luna* and deeper into the forest. Her knee was throbbing now, and she didn't know how much longer it would keep until she would be forced to give up. She didn't want the Torokar to go after the others, even though it was clear to her Sunshine would be the assassin's primary target. While in her CASPer, Sunshine was a terror which needed to be dealt with. The others, though, would be at the mercy of the bloodthirsty Jivool security forces. Sunshine was the only thing keeping the Jivool at bay. The Torokar would take her out first, which made tactical sense, then hunt the others. With no other options at hand, she had challenged the hunter.

She knew all about Torokar. They were honorable to a fault, but this came with caveats and little details often missed in a Besquith's desire to kill one of the most dangerous hunters in the galaxy. If they were on a contract job, all bets were off. The will to succeed in the mission was what drove the large predators, and their honor dictated any method was allowed and acceptable when it came to completing the mission. They excelled at the hunt. They were also skilled mercenaries, though she wasn't certain they were one of the registered races.

Torokar almost never operated alone, preferring their pack mentality. None, typically, wanted to hunt solo. This one was something different and unexpected. Truth be told, it was also unwelcome. It was a surprise, and Dref-na hated surprises.

A rapid burst of gunfire erupted behind her and she ducked behind a massive tree trunk. Overhead a few large branches exploded as the Torokar's railgun decimated them. She doubted he could see her already, but then again, she wasn't certain just what the capabilities of his pinplants were. He could have an infrared targeting array built into his optic nerve to track her down, using them to search the jungle for her higher-than-average body heat. She'd need to be smart about this.

"I will find you, Besquith," the Torokar called out from the southeast. It confirmed who had fired at her. "Your head will make a fine addition to my collection."

He was closer than expected, Dref-na realized as she gingerly knelt down and tested the moisture of the ground. It was soft with sparse cover, though the lichen here was not as heavy as it was closer to the landing pad. Light reached through the trees to the ground, and it showed with the lack of smaller growth on the ground. Larger bushes—parasites really—grew around the bases of the towering trees. Numerous shorter trees grew beyond these, prohibiting anything other than a few of the now-familiar mossy patches to grow in the moist dirt. There would be no hiding her tracks here.

Overhead she saw a small, arboreal mammal watching her progress. There appeared to be a large group up there. She snarled quietly at them and they scattered higher into the trees. A moment later two exploded as railgun rounds passed through them. Tiny chunks of the animals showered the ground nearby. The Torokar was definitely nearby and using thermal imaging to track heat signatures.

I know how to play this game, little hunter, she thought as she pulled out a small butane torch from one of her chest pouches. Dref-na glanced around and saw a small bundle of dried sticks. A few still had green growth on them. She smiled. *Perfect.*

"Hunt like the old ways, Torokar!" she shouted into the jungle. "Hunt me like your ancestors would! Kill by the claw and devour my heart!"

She lit the small bundle on fire and left it near a tree with a lot of brown on it. The dried, sickly bark caught almost instantly, and within moments the tree was engulfed in roaring flames. Dref-na backed away, impressed. She heard a popping noise above and saw the green, healthy trees brushing against the dead one caused a shower of sparks to fall with each successive *pop!*

The tree sap is flammable. Dref-na realized now how they had set such a huge fire during the previous escape from the world. These idiots have been sitting on a fuel source and hadn't even realized it. Or perhaps they had. It wasn't exactly efficient, as it burned too hot, too quick. But burn it did...interesting.

The flames continued to spread rapidly. A true conflagration had begun, and each flame that reached out and touched another of the towering trees caused a small explosion. Dref-na's smile turned feral as more tree sap detonated. *Hunt me now, toothless little lizard.*

* * *

DexKarr heard the challenge and almost dismissed it immediately. He had nothing left to prove. After many years as a mercenary, a bounty hunter, and, more recently, as a contract killer, he had fought and defeated every manner of alien one could think of, and quite a few he hadn't even known existed. It was the Besquith who had to prove it was worthy of being hunted by him.

A large, thick cloud of smoke began to rise nearby, obviously created by the Besquith. He grinned at the creature's cunning. The

Besquith had already figured out how he was tracking it and had adjusted accordingly. This hunt would be one of legend, spoken about for many generations to come. Assuming he survived it, of course.

This little quibble of doubt surprised him. He was DexKarr, the mightiest of his kin, the hunter emulated by all the younglings. His achievements were already the stuff of lore among his kind. There could be no doubt in his supremacy. He was the hunter. The Besquith was the prey.

It was at this moment, he knew, he accepted the Besquith's challenge. He was DexKarr, a Torokar. It was a lowly Besquith. He shrugged off his armor and set the mounted railgun aside. Using the weapon was not as big of an advantage as he would have hoped, anyway. It was time to level the playing field and accept the challenge the prey had set forth. A worthy hunter was able to adapt and overcome. He would use nothing but his wits and his tracking skills to hunt down and kill the Besquith. There could be no doubt as to who was the superior hunter here.

"I am coming for you, prey," he called out. Lashing his tail side to side, he continued through the underbrush, his delicate sense of smell and taste guiding him.

* * *

Dref-na knew the Torokar was behind her somewhere, but she had no idea as to his exact position. The terrifying alien was just as skilled in the forest as she was, and he was better armed to boot. Why she hadn't grabbed a laser rifle or something while she had the chance was beyond her.

Perhaps her desire to protect her newly adopted family overrode all common sense?

It didn't matter. There would be no protecting them if she couldn't do something here and now about the Torokar. The flames were spreading rapidly through the trees, creating a massive forest fire, the second one they were responsible for on this godforsaken planet. Searing heat poured down from above, but other than the occasional sparks landing on her and singeing her fur, it wasn't too bad. More trees caught on fire with a few sap-filled branches letting off random detonations at odd times. The smoke was well above her, the lower level almost devoid of it. The forest was growing darker because of this, giving her another advantage. The heat above was intense, though it lessened nearer to the ground. The thick, roiling smoke turned the already-red sky a deep purple color. She would have found it stunning had she not been running for her life. Well, limping.

Dref-na paused and looked around. The arboreal mammals were coming out of their trees, each howling a strange mournful cry at the loss of their homes. She briefly wondered if they were even sentient before an idea struck her. She quickly went through her pouch and found the paracord she had borrowed from Taryn back on the *Velut Luna*. Dref-na would never have believed the Human-made line would be worth anything more than a time distraction and securing small items, yet here she was, about to use it to save her life.

The strange little mammalian creatures watched her. She slowly knelt and beckoned with one claw. Her bad knee popped, and she hissed in pain. *Whatever that was, it hurt,* she thought.

"Come here," she whispered as gently as a Besquith could. Three of the tiny mammals crept closer, their curiosity overriding their fear.

It was clear to Dref-na they had no natural predators in this part of the forest. As they drew closer, she realized they weren't so small after all. They had slightly more mass than she had originally guessed. Her smile widened. "I'm not going to hurt you..."

* * *

DexKerr growled softly as the heat from above interfered with his sensitive infrared vision. He briefly considered turning it off before dismissing the idea. It was his only enhanced hunting tool left at his disposal, and he wasn't ready to lose it yet.

He chided himself for allowing the Besquith to goad him into ditching his railgun and armor. In the heat of the moment he had made a tactical blunder, and it was too late now to go back and get it. The desire to prove himself superior was sometimes a powerful narcotic. This time, however, it had enabled his prey to cause him to make a mistake.

Flipping between the various thermal settings, he finally found one which would allow him to filter out the fire. He scanned the ground and found a cluster of Besquith-sized footprints slowly cooling in the dirt. Frowning, he pushed aside a small pile of leaves and found more footprints. These were much smaller, with three toes and lacking any claws whatsoever. Their infrared signature was almost identical to the Besquith's.

Odd, he thought. What on this world would be stupid enough to hang around a Besquith?

Other than those back at the *Velut Luna*, he couldn't even imagine. He looked around and noticed the Besquith's tracks leading further away. They were cooling...and alone. DexKarr grunted in recognition. The Besquith, possibly wounded or injured, had stopped for a brief snack of...something. It made sense the more he considered it. A Besquith normally burned calories at a far faster rate than any other alien species out there. Combined with their size and strength, this gave them their immense appetite, as well as an ability to eat almost anything. They were powerful warriors who could do things most creatures only dreamt of. It was an unfair evolution of sorts.

Know thy prey. It was the mantra his mentor had drilled into his head from the time he hatched from his egg. The code of the hunter. He had studied every alien species he could while growing up, and it had paid off as he matured into adulthood and took to the stars. It was why he was still alive and why many of his clutchmates were dead and gone, forgotten by everyone. Failed hunters, they had become prey. The cycle continued after their deaths, with only the best hunters passing their genes on to the future.

He lifted his head and sniffed the air. The smoke from the fire the Besquith had started clouded his sense of smell. All he could taste was oily smoke and a stray bit of animal. Was it the Besquith? He couldn't be sure. The smoke distorted everything. Trusting his senses was no longer an option, and instinct was screaming at him to run, flee. He growled in frustration and switched back to his thermals. He would not run now. The prey was close.

The Besquith's footprints were almost faded now. He was mere minutes behind the creature. The depth of the footprints from right to left changed as he moved along, suggesting it was injured and favoring a leg. Had one of his rounds splintered off and hurt it? The odds were small, since he had been firing into the air primarily to startle it. He didn't smell any blood, either. He probably hadn't shot the beast. More than likely it had been injured before the hunt began, possibly during the *Velut Luna*'s emergency landing. Had it been like this the entire time? Thinking back to when he first started to hunt the creature, he was unable to recall whether or not the footprints showed the injury. He cursed. So enraptured was he with the hunt, he couldn't remember the distinctive nature of the original tracks.

DexKarr increased his pace before the footprints could cool completely, and he lost sight of them. There were a few places where he had to stop and investigate since the dirt was hard-packed and there were no obvious footprints. However, the heat signatures remained constant, betraying the path of the Besquith and allowing him to continue the hunt.

Something caught his eye. A brief flash, but it was larger than anything else he had seen since the hunt began. He slowed, cautious, his eyes locked on the prize. His diamond-hard claws extended and retracted in excitement. This hunt, while not the longest he'd ever had, was definitely turning into the most intense. The ensuing fight would be talked about for generations. He was going to kill a Besquith with nothing more than wit and claws. It would be *glorious*.

The creature moved behind a thick tree trunk. The brief flash of fur was high enough off the ground to be the Besquith. Nothing else nearby would be as large.

Each step was measured, cautious now. He could make no sound. His breathing was slow and steady. His beating heart was tempered as the final moments of the hunt came to him. Evolution had been kind to the Torokar species and instead of adrenaline coursing through his veins and stimulating his receptors, all he felt was calm. The moment before the kill was one of perfect clarity. Everything seemed to still around him. His heart slowed. He touched the large trunk with his claw. The stench of the Besquith was almost overwhelming. He risked a sharp inhale and tasted the Besquith's scent in the air.

Yes! DexKarr exulted silently. It was time. His muscles burned as he rushed around the tree, claws fully extended, and he struck them into the throat of...

...absolutely nothing. Off balance, he tripped and stumbled. He rolled onto the jungle floor and flipped onto his belly. Using his powerful arms, he pushed himself up as scanned the area. His tail flailed about as he regained his feet, his only outward sign of confusion and frustration. He finally saw what he was smelling and tasting in the air. Tied to the tree, at roughly shoulder-height, were three of the mammalian creatures he had seen earlier. They were attempting to climb up the large tree but were stuck, courtesy of some sort of rope tied around all three and they'd been anchored to the ground by a large, heavy stone. They were able to crawl a few meters up the tree before their progress was halted.

"What the...?"

Cautiously, he approached. The creatures were terrified and jabbering, their loud cries causing his ears to ring. He reached out and sliced the strange rope with a claw. The trio chittered and immediately climbed higher into the tree, ignoring the fires raging to the south. Their tones were accusatory, even though he had freed them.

He crouched and picked up the knotted cord as the small mammals bounded through the treetops and disappeared from view. It was some sort of synthetic material, clearly Human in design. On the ground lay a large clump of Besquith fur and a territorial marking of musky urine, as well as a large smear of blood on the tree trunk. She had lured him to this spot, wanted him to find it all. The scene was unlike anything he had ever laid eyes on.

No, he corrected himself. *I have seen this before. Where though?*

A twig snapped just behind his right shoulder. His entire body stiffened. He'd been so distracted by the heat signature given off by the bound mammals he had not paid any attention to his surroundings. It was a youngling's mistake, something a Torokar fresh out the egg would do. His pulse raced as he tried to think of something, anything to counter what was to come. There was nothing.

Hot, rank breath washed over his neck. A long, rough tongue ran across his bare shoulder. Claws sharper than anything imaginable, pressed against his leathery skin. He swallowed. For the first time in his life he felt fear. It was new, and horrifying. The hunt was over. The ending, however, was not what he had expected.

DexKarr suddenly recalled he *had* seen something very much like this before. Fear disappeared for a brief moment as he chuckled softly, finding the moment just before his death tragically ironic. The ancient Human vid had been entertaining when he had watched it. Though unrealistic, it seemed to characterize all forms of Human entertainment from the time period. Absurd, but appealing in the same breath. The creature in the movie had even looked superficially similar to a Torokar.

The Besquith had turned the tables on him, proving it was the most dangerous creature in the forest, though oftentimes the hunted one.

"Clever girl," he whispered just before the fangs of the Besquith ended his hunt permanently.

* * * * *

Chapter Eleven

Landing Pad 4, Garnon District, Zav'ax, It'iek System

"They're trying to keep us pinned down here," Sunshine called as she killed the last of the Jivool lingering near the *Velut Luna*. She pivoted and tried to scan the area but found the jungle was interfering with her sensors. She boosted power to them and reaffirmed the linkup with the *Velut Luna*. Everything snapped back into place with alarming clarity. "I'm not picking up anything else out there right now."

"They're waiting for backup to arrive," Taryn suggested over the comms. Sunshine bounded around the perimeter she and Jorna had established but found no other living B'Hono Corporation security forces.

"What now?" Sunshine asked as she approached the landing pad.

"This is our chance," Taryn replied as she helped get Jorna inside the *Velut Luna*. The Pushtal, while shorter than Taryn, was almost two hundred pounds of solid muscle and not the easiest to move. Fortunately, she was no longer unconscious, merely dazed and able to help out a little. "The coordinates for the research facility I got from the target? It's less than two kilometers away."

"Well, that's handy," Sunshine commented in a dry tone. "How come we didn't see it coming in?"

"Besides the fact we were trying to not get shot down? It's partially buried," Taryn explained as Sunshine approached the landing pad. "They've got some sort of camouflage over it, I guess."

"Stupid," Sunshine commented.

"Who, them?" Taryn asked.

289

"No, us," Sunshine clarified. "We could have just looked for underground power sources with our sensors and followed the line to the site."

"Unless it has a localized power source," Taryn pointed out.

"Oh, yeah."

"That's what I would do," Taryn added. Sunshine blushed, feeling rather stupid.

"I found what was stalking us," Dref-na's pained voice came over the comms, interrupting the two. Sunshine turned and looked around for any sign of the Besquith but couldn't see her through the jungle just yet. "It was a Torokar."

"What's that?" Sunshine asked as her suit picked up a faint heat signature approaching them. Her MAC began to track it, but she powered it down once she recognized Dref-na's distinct shape.

"Dead," Dref-na said as she limped into view. Her furred features were coated with fresh blood mixed with soot. It was clear her leg was bothering her more. Her chest harness was just as dirty, and her claws were completely covered in filth. "The paracord you let me borrow came in handy, Taryn Lupo."

"I lent you paracord?" the young woman asked. "I forgot."

Dref-na ignored the question as she looked around the area. It was clear there had been a huge firefight while she was gone. "Where did all the Jivool go?"

"They ran off after Sunshine charged into them," Taryn said. "Or they're dead."

"They didn't like me running them over in my suit," Sunshine added. "Can you believe it?"

"Unfathomable," Dref-na said in a grave tone. "Let me use the nanite spray before we set off. It won't heal my knee fully, but it will allow me to continue."

* * *

Vah was surprisingly okay with the idea of them continuing on, leaving her and Klinks alone on the ship to watch over Jorna. Looking back on the conversation, Sunshine couldn't really find anything normal about it.

"I've made a few notes for Kl'nk'nnk regarding calibrating the railguns for peak efficiency," Vah told them as soon as Dref-na had applied the nanite spray to her damaged knee. The topical spray was usually best for open wounds, like stabbings or gunshots, but made a decent enough treatment for sprains and internal injuries. The Besquith would need a shot of nanites in order to fully heal the damaged knee.

"Oh," Taryn had said. "Good?"

Sunshine sighed. Vah was definitely a work in progress, as the *bass* would have said. Still, the tiny junior administrator had a lot of promise. She was respectable at following orders, even though her primary goal was to be efficient. It was good, if a little limiting. Creativity was not the CozSha's strong suit.

Following the directions Taryn and Dref-na had gotten from their kidnapping victim, she eventually found a small road leading away from the Garnon District that headed in the direction of their destination. Looking up, Sunshine realized the large, lily pad-like treetops of the jungle had hidden the road from above. She wondered just how many times something in history had been missed via orbital satellite because of simple, old-fashioned, natural camouflage.

Probably a lot, she guessed as she thought back to the final hours during the Battle of Monrovia. The Korps had parked anti-air missiles throughout the outskirts of downtown Monrovia and had used inflatable buildings to mask their presence until they were fired. The assault shuttles employed by the Mercenary Guild had taken a beating when the missiles finally launched, though the sites were subsequently taken out by some sort of atmospheric fighter jets—which were shot down in turn by the rest of the Korps. Sunshine had taken down at least one of the jets, possibly two. She couldn't recall precisely; much had happened since then, most of it frustrating.

After thirty minutes, the trio came upon a half-buried building. Growing atop it were a few large bushes and more of the same lichen found throughout the rest of the jungle. It was cleverly hidden from above, but easily seen from the road. Sunshine marveled at the simple ingenuity for a moment before she set her suit to scan for any signs of security. Surprisingly, she couldn't find any. *Just how good is the security here?* she wondered.

It was a long building, rectangular in shape and made from some sort of concrete she'd never seen before. It wasn't constructed like the other buildings she remembered seeing during their first visit to the planet. The material was dark gray and reminded her of older Earth buildings, though the design was far different. She stood upright in the CASPer, as tall as she could, to see over the building. She was unable to, so she looked at the ramp leading down to what appeared to be the main door.

Dref-na carefully navigated the ramp, her limp nearly gone now thanks to the nanite spray. The Besquith lifted her head slightly and pressed it against the strange concrete wall. She grunted as she pressed her body against the structure.

"What do you hear?" Sunshine asked, intrigued. She had no idea Besquith hearing was sensitive enough for them to hear through walls.

"Uh, nothing," Dref-na replied and gave her a strange look. She pushed herself away from the structure. "My neck is stiff, and I was just stretching it out a bit."

"Oh." Feeling foolish, she approached the door and spotted a small handle attached to the otherwise plain door. Sunshine paused and tested it. It was locked but she doubted the suit would have any trouble with it; it didn't appear to be fortified. The site itself suggested secrecy was the number one security priority. However, she also didn't want to sound the alarm unnecessarily, so she backed away.

"Taryn, can you short out the lock or something without triggering an alarm?" she asked.

"Yeah, hold on," Taryn said as she rummaged through her bag. Eventually she found what she was looking for and pulled out a device. "Courtesy of Jorna."

"What kind of slate is that?" Sunshine looked at it and isolated three different power sources within the casing. It was the most unusual slate she had ever seen.

"Pushtal," Taryn explained. "They use them for remote hacking and security bypasses. Handy and highly illegal. The Merchant Guild has been trying to lock these down for *years*. You could say they haven't had much luck."

"I guess." Sunshine frowned but decided to let Taryn have her fun. The woman approached the door and inspected the frame. After a few moments, she stepped back and looked at Sunshine.

"Go ahead and kick it down," she told her. "There's no alarm."

"How do you know?" Sunshine looked at the door and tried to see if there was anything suggesting just how Taryn knew this, but there must have been some sort of baffler or scan blocker in place because the young teen couldn't see a thing.

"There's no gene lock or hand scanner," Taryn said. "It's just a simple old-fashioned tumbler lock. They're relying on stealth over high-tech security."

"Oh." Sunshine shook her head. The obvious answer was sometimes the simplest one. She'd been overthinking it, again. Taryn must have heard something in her tone, though.

"Hey, sometimes being really smart is a curse," Taryn stated, guessing what was on Sunshine's mind. "You tend to forget a lot of others are pretty stupid and you start to overanalyze things. It happens."

Moving toward the door with a tiny burst of speed, Sunshine kicked the solid-looking door. She struck solid metal, and sparks flew. Frowning, Sunshine delivered another kick. The steel door bent but did not give. She took two more steps back, took a deep breath to calm her nerves, and charged the door. Lowering her shoulder, she drove through the door and crashed into the interior of the hidden facility.

Rolling as she landed, Sunshine was able to lessen the impact falling normally would have had on a CASPer pilot. It still hurt, but not nearly as much as it could have. One of the warning lights inside her suit flickered from green to yellow for a moment before it changed back to the green. She frowned and made a mental note to keep an eye on it.

Pushing herself off the ground, she scanned the darkened entryway. It was large, but it was immediately obvious she would not be able to move much farther into the interior of the facility wearing the CASPer. Not unless she wanted to remove her shoulder mounts, which would require Klinks and about four hours of work. The ceiling was lower than she had expected after seeing how tall the building was outside.

"I'm not picking up any electronic signals in this area," Sunshine announced to the others. "In fact, I'm not getting anything at all. These walls are shielded or something."

"They would have to be in order to hide it from above," Dref-na pointed out.

"That makes sense," Sunshine allowed.

"Try scanning everything again," Taryn suggested as she pulled out her slate and powered it up. Sunshine nodded inside her suit and ran her scans a second time. Just like before, there was nothing out of the ordinary that she could see. The slate was there, but nothing else. They needed a better idea of what they were about to face, but how?

Thinking it over, she instructed her suit to construct a virtual three-dimensional map of the facility as the other two moved around inside it. She pinged Taryn's pinplants and isolated the response, then tied it to her newly created map. Next, she searched for Dref-na's slate. Though on standby, she was able to find it and tie it in to her little experiment.

Taryn shot her a look. "What are you doing?"

"Tracking your pinplant so I can create a map of this place while you two explore it," Sunshine admitted. Taryn's face turned ghostly pale.

"You can't do that."

"I'm sorry," Sunshine apologized and quickly removed Taryn from the link. "I didn't mean to invade your privacy. I just thought it would be easier and faster to create a map of the place."

"Not what I meant." Taryn paused and continued to look at her. "I—damn. Klinks was right about you. *Damn it.* You know what? Never mind. Go ahead and do it if you can. Remind me later that we need to talk about…something else, okay?"

"Oookay," Sunshine said as she reengaged Taryn's pinplants before turning to Dref-na. "My suit isn't small enough to fit. You have any ideas?"

"Yep," Taryn responded. Dref-na, however, was staring at her with an odd expression.

"What's wrong?" Sunshine asked, concerned. The Besquith shook her head.

"Nothing, tiny fierceness," Dref-na said as she motioned down toward her leg. "I will warn you that I am still mildly injured and probably won't be very good in a fight if we get swarmed."

"Let's all be safe and find the TriRusk as quickly as possible, then," Sunshine stated. "We've been pretty lucky so far."

Taryn snorted in amusement, and even Dref-na cracked a smile at this.

"Crap," Taryn said as Sunshine rounded a corner. The young teen paused.

"What's wrong?" Sunshine asked.

"You probably can't tell from your CASPer, but there aren't any lights down here," Taryn explained. She leaned against the wall as Dref-na joined them. Her limp was already beginning to return.

"Does your suit have any sort of topical ointment for pain, tiny fierceness?" Dref-na asked as she bent down and rubbed her knee. Even Sunshine, no expert on xenobiology, could see the extent of the damage Dref-na's knee had taken. The swelling was immense and looked dangerously disproportionate to the other.

"No, sorry," she answered.

"Entropy," Dref-na cursed. "I shall carry on then."

"Any ideas what to do next?" Taryn asked them.

"I'm open to suggestions," Sunshine said after completing her scan. She didn't comment further on Dref-na's knee, though. It wasn't her place to question the Besquith's desire to continue on. "My suit isn't small enough, and we don't know what's down here. Just because we haven't seen any guards yet doesn't mean they're not down here."

"Pretty sure they're all dead back at the landing pad," Taryn observed.

"Probably," Sunshine agreed. "But I don't want to risk it. Taryn?"

"We can go on," the woman answered, though she looked questioningly at Dref-na.

"What? You want me to head back to the ship and find a safe space?" Dref-na asked, wheezing. She shook her shaggy head. "That's not going to happen, Taryn Lupo. I will not leave either of you behind."

"I think you should." Sunshine shook her head. "But I won't make you head back. I can stay here and hold off anyone trying to come in. Taryn, I need you to find the TriRusk. If you're up for it, go with her and keep her safe, Dref-na. Be careful, though. If there are too many guards, come back up, and we'll find another way."

"Yeah, sure, okay." Taryn smiled at her. "Pretty sure we can do that. Then what? Rush back here to save the unstoppable killing machine in the CASPer when the security forces realize where we've gone, and they try to overwhelm you here?"

"I'm serious." Sunshine smiled, though no one else could see it. "I don't want you to die in there."

"Nobody's going to die," Dref-na interjected. Her tone was contemplative. "Well, not me at least. I'm very resilient."

"Just…just keep her safe in there, okay?" Sunshine said, struggling not to laugh at the Besquith. While Dref-na understood most of their jokes, there were some which went over her head. It was more of a cultural thing than anything else, Sunshine guessed as she watched the duo cautiously enter the building. She had thought gallows humor was a universal thing.

Be careful, you two, she silently bade them as she went back outside to await the expected armed response.

* * *

Taryn looked around the dimly lit hallway and grimaced. They were metallic in appearance and had rivets throughout, marking junction points. Whoever had constructed the facility had done it in a hurry.

Clearly this entire venture wasn't planned around a mining colony, she thought.

Struggling to see beyond five meters, she wished Sunshine fit. Her sensors on the Leopard were equipped with low-light cameras which could then be translated onto her Tri-V, allowing the young mercenary to see everything with perfect clarity. Plus, the CASPer had armor and immense firepower. Taryn didn't even have the luxury of night vision goggles and was carrying a simple, cheap knock-off Pushtal carbine. Sometimes life wasn't fair.

"Which way?" Dref-na asked her.

Taryn shrugged. "I'm no soldier," she reminded the Besquith. "How do your kind clear a facility?"

"Violently."

"Okay, let's only do that if they start shooting at us," Taryn clarified. "I don't hear anything except for the ventilation ducts."

"This facility appears to be abandoned already, Taryn Lupo," Dref-na said. She raised a long claw and jabbed in three directions. "There is a hallway leading straight, and one to the right and another on the left. Which one do you prefer to search first?"

"Right," Taryn said. "Do we split up?"

"And risk you accidentally shooting me?" Dref-na chuckled as she gave Taryn's carbine a rather pointed look. "No, we stay together. That way if you shoot me, I can eat you and not be forced to chase you down."

"What is with everyone thinking they're funny today?" Taryn muttered as they turned and went down the wide hallway. "It's like I'm traveling with a troupe of drunken, one-line-spewing comedians."

The hallway was shorter than she had expected, and soon enough they arrived at a T-junction. Taryn sighed and looked both directions. Neither looked promising, but then, she really couldn't see further than a dozen meters down either hall. Glancing left, then right, Taryn sighed again. There was no way she could tell, and without comms the mapping idea Sunshine had was not going to work. She waited expectantly for Dref-na to suggest a route.

Only the Besquith didn't suggest anything. She turned her shaggy head to look down at Taryn.

"Your choice," she said.

"No, it's your turn," Taryn argued. "You pick."

"Left it is then," Dref-na said, and they turned down the new corridor. After a few steps Dref-na paused and pointed. Taryn, who had been watching the Besquith's back and not where they were going, blinked. There was a door on the left-hand side of the corridor with a tall rectangular glass window in the middle of it. Curious, Taryn stepped forward and peeked through.

On the other side of the window was a lab of some sort, though it had clearly been thoroughly ransacked. Equipment had been pushed aside or removed and there were some scattered vials on a counter running along the far wall. A few Tri-V monitors were mounted on the wall, though these were without power. There were also strange holes roughly four centimeters in diameter scattered throughout the floor. Taryn pushed against the door and it swung open easily. She glanced back at Dref-na, who nodded. Taking a deep breath, Taryn stepped inside.

Despite the ramshackle appearance, the lab felt sterile. Walking deeper into the lab, she was able to get a clearer picture of the room. A chemist at heart, Taryn recognized a few of the workstations that had not been dismantled yet. Elements of chemical science had gone on here but what, precisely, she had no idea.

"What do you think these holes are for?" Dref-na asked, pointing a claw at the holes scattered across the floor.

"I was wondering about those myself," Taryn admitted. She dragged the toe of her boot over one, "They kinda look like bolt holes."

"They do," Dref-na agreed and looked around the room. "I wonder what was bolted to the floor?"

"Hmm..." Taryn inspected the holes and how they were placed. Multiple forms began to take shape in her mind as she traced each one and played connect-the-dots. Finally, she simply walked a path between them before turning toward Dref-na, who had been watching her movements. "What does this look like to you?"

"Insanity," Dref-na replied, grinning. Taryn rolled her eyes.

"Seriously." She traced a shape along the ground. "This appears to be about, what, two meters or so? Shaped like a box?"

"The missing life support boxes Kl'nk'nnk designed for the B'Hono Corp." Dref-na nodded, understanding at last. She approached the holes in the flooring and inspected them. "I count thirteen shapes. How many did Kl'nk'nnk say she built?"

"I don't remember," Taryn admitted. "But this is the correct size and everything."

"It appears they were not used for life support purposes, as the Jeha suspected," Dref-na added.

"How can you tell?" Taryn asked before she smacked her palm against her forehead. "This is a research lab, not a hospital room."

"It's also very disturbing in here," Dref-na added. "Healing wards are supposed to be bright and cheery. This is...not."

"Agreed," Taryn said as she shivered inside her body armor. She pulled out her slate and began taking pictures. She explained before Dref-na could even ask. "Taking pictures as evidence in case we need it later."

"For the courts?" Dref-na asked, surprised.

"No," Taryn shook her head. "For blackmailing."

"Ah, there's the Taryn Lupo I know so well," Dref-na proclaimed with another grin. "Bloodthirsty and calculating."

"I'm not that bloodthirsty," Taryn protested as she finished taking the pictures. Satisfied, she slipped the slate back into her pocket. "Let's keep going."

"Why?" Dref-na asked. "This facility is clearly abandoned. What else could there be?"

"I don't know," Taryn answered. "Maybe we'll find evidence of the TriRusk?"

"Perhaps," Dref-na allowed, temporarily mollified. The Besquith shivered. "I do not like this place."

"I wonder why it's so cold," Taryn murmured as she moved toward the door. Casting one final look around the room, she paused when she spotted something on the wall. It was actual paper and had some sort of cell structure printed on it. Curious, she pulled her slate back out and took a picture of this as well. "Well...that's odd."

"What is it?" Dref-na asked, stopping in the doorway.

"I'm not sure," Taryn admitted. "I'm more of a homegrown chemist. I wish we weren't blocked off from my ship right now. Do you know what a mon-oh-fee-nol mon-ox...crap, I can't say it."

"*Monophenol monooxygenase,*" Dref-na pronounced carefully. "And you call yourself a chemist. No, I don't know what it is either."

"I feel like this entire thing has been one big jigsaw puzzle meant for someone else," Taryn muttered under her breath. She looked up at Dref-na. "C'mon, let's finish clearing this place and get back up to Sunshine. She's probably bored out of her mind."

They exited the lab and moved down the hall, continuing along their original path. A second lab appeared, this one with the door wide open but completely bare of any research equipment. It was obvious this one had been clean for a long time, which made the ramshackle state of the first lab they had found all the more confusing. Why clean out one so well and leave the other in such a state?

There was a final room at the end of the hallway. This one was locked, though there was a small window similar to the others. Taryn leaned against the door and tried to peer inside, but with the darkness inside combined with the sharp angle, there was little for her to see. Looking down at the handle, she figured it was pretty sturdy and wouldn't break from her just kicking it. She thought about asking Dref-na to do it before remembering the Besquith's damaged knee and dismissed the idea.

"Can you see inside?" Taryn asked. Dref-na leaned over and looked inside the window. She shook her head.

"Nothing inside except for a few empty hospital beds," Dref-na declared. "I count six in all."

"Six?" Taryn looked inside again but failed to see them. "Hey, how many TriRusk did Kl'nk'nnk say she saw?"

"Five males," Dref-na replied instantly.

"And the one female," Taryn reminded her. "That's six. Hospital beds, lab equipment…something bad is going on here."

"I agree, Taryn Lupo," Dref-na grunted. "Wicked deeds are afoot. Look, another hallway and a second door."

"Let's go," Taryn said, and they quickly made their way down to the next door. This one was only padlocked from the outside, meaning it was designed to keep someone in. Turning the small lever, Taryn pushed the door open. It was lighter in here than any of the other rooms, but still not well-lit enough for her to make out fine details. She was able to make out a lumpy form lying on the single cot in the room, however. Whatever it was, it wasn't moving. She moved closer and pulled out her slate to take more pictures. She paused, however, as she realized the odd lump had once been a living, breathing being.

They had found the kidnapped TriRusk, and it seemed they were too late.

"Oh my…" Taryn's voice trailed off as Dref-na hissed in shock. While she'd never seen one before, the description of the TriRusk was available back on the *Velut Luna*. They resembled a triceratops from ancient Earth's history. The alien's face was elongated slightly more than a triceratops, though it did feature a very prominent horn at the end of its beak. The TriRusk's skull curved out, fanning out over its neck like a protective shield while its body was thick and muscular. The alien wore nothing save for a thin gown similar to ones Taryn remembered from Earth. The TriRusk's eyes stared blankly into nothing. They were flat, devoid of any signs of life.

"Why did they leave this one behind? Is it because it's dead?" Dref-na asked in a quiet voice as she reached out to touch the Tri-Rusk. Neither was able to tell if it was a male or female.

"Looks dead," Taryn said with a sad sigh. Just once she wanted *something* to go right on this forsaken rescue op.

"Don't," the TriRusk croaked in a low tone. Dref-na jerked her claws away. Taryn gasped, nearly screaming in fright. She hadn't realized the alien was still breathing. She crouched next to the plain cot.

"What happened?" Taryn asked as gently as she could. She didn't reach out to touch the alien or make any sudden moves. Instead she simply waited.

"They took…everything…" the TriRusk moaned in a low, heartbreaking voice. There was a desperate edge to it which made Taryn feel sick. The TriRusk's large, articulated hands covered her midsection. The muscular forearms prevented Taryn and Dref-na from seeing if the TriRusk was injured or simply in shock.

"Please, tell us your name?" Taryn tried instead, looking up at Dref-na. The Besquith nodded and backed away slightly, giving the TriRusk space.

"Caarn," the TriRusk answered. The tone was devoid of all emotion. "Daughter of Staarn."

"Hi, Caarn," Taryn said. "My name is Taryn Lupo. The Besquith is named Dref-na. We're here—well, we're here to rescue you."

"You can't," Caarn whispered. Her eyes bore into Taryn, unblinking. There was no light there, no life. Only darkness. It was abysmal and Taryn suddenly felt like crying for the TriRusk. What really bothered her was she did not know *why* she wanted to shed tears for the listless alien. She had seen many horrible things in her young life already but seeing someone, anyone, so devoid of emotion was terrible to try to comprehend. The level of trauma required to psychologically damage someone to this level was beyond what even Taryn could imagine.

"Actually, we can," Taryn corrected her, trying to keep some levity in her tone. "We got the door open and there's a CASPer outside in case someone comes calling. All you need to do is get up and follow us out. I'm pretty sure the Jivool aren't coming back."

"You can't save me," Caarn said and slowly turned onto her back. Her forearms clutched her midsection tightly and her eyes were staring up at the ceiling still. Taryn wasn't sure if the TriRusk had even blinked since they'd found her. "There's nothing to save. I am empty. I am broken. I can't go back. No one will want me now. They took everything…"

"Uh, how about your life?" Confused, Taryn looked back at Dref-na, who shrugged. This was not how they had imagined the rescue going down.

"My life is no longer my own," Caarn whispered. Out of the corner of her eye a single tear began streaming down her face toward her flattened skull. "They took that from me."

"They took—" Taryn was completely lost now but had a sinking feeling in the depths of her soul that she was not going to like whatever it was the TriRusk was talking about. "*What* did they take?"

"Our future," Caarn sobbed suddenly and lifted her forearms from her midsection.

Taryn gasped.

Horrifying lines crisscrossed the TriRusk's lower abdomenal region, a patchwork of hastily stitched scars, still raw from healing. It was clear whoever had done the multiple operations hadn't cared about the appearance of their handiwork, merely the results.

Caarn looked down, a thumb tracing one of the particularly vicious-looking scars that snaked toward her pelvic region.

"They took...everything...said many females chose not to have...but it's *my* choice, not theirs. Not theirs..." the TriRusk whispered, hiccupping slightly as more tears flowed. "They took...them...they took *all* of them..."

"*Fuck,*" Taryn hissed as horrifying realization dawned on her. The scientists—and she used the term as loosely as possible—had harvested the TriRusk's internal reproductive organs and left nothing but a signature of their work behind. Multiple lacerations had been poorly stitched up, leaving thick, ugly scars. Even a merc sewing up a battlefield injury would have taken better care than this. She couldn't believe someone who was sworn to learning and discovery would treat a living being in such a manner. She understood now the cryptic nature of Caarn's early words. The B'Hono Corporation had indeed taken her life away, and that of her future.

Taryn had never seen true evil before, not until today. She'd seen bad people do bad things, sure. But to look into the face of evil and have it mock life in such a way? Wave after wave of horror slapped her in the face. It was relentless as her mind continued down the dark path of what else they could have done. What they *had* done to the poor TriRusk. She gasped, and her mouth felt dry. The room spun as the weight of Caarn's pain and anguish crashed down on her. Taryn couldn't deal with it. Her throat closed and began to burn. "Oh my God—"

Stomach heaving, Taryn turned suddenly and puked onto the floor. It was too much for her to comprehend. Her blasé attitude toward stealing, combined with her fiery and protective nature, was her mask, one she wore to hide the pain and hurt she'd suffered over the years. What Caarn had to deal with, the pain and anguish, stripped Taryn's mask away. She had never imagined this level of evil existing here and now. Opportunists and individuals taking advantage of other creatures was the daily norm, but it wasn't necessarily evil. The raised, pink scars on Caarn's midsection killed any notion of an enlightened galaxy striving to make it a better place for all. This was the face of evil, and Taryn wanted no part of it.

A gentle pressure rested on her back. Spitting out the horrible taste of bile from her mouth, Taryn looked up and saw the genuine concern on the TriRusk's face.

"Are you okay?" Caarn asked her.

The simple gesture of kindness was the straw which broke the proverbial camel's back. The wall Taryn had carefully constructed over the years to deal with her emotions was ripped away by that singular act. Taryn slumped against the TriRusk's cot and started to bawl her eyes out. She cried for the TriRusk, who still cared for others even though she had had so much taken from her.

In this darkest night, that singular light shone the brightest.

It took her a few minutes to regain control of her emotions. Her breathing was shaky but once the tears were out, she felt a little better. Not great, but manageable. It was better than the sick feeling in her stomach. The sadness was replaced by a slow-burning rage unlike anything she had ever felt before in her life. It was scary just how quickly everything had shifted. There was little else she wanted to do now except to make certain the B'Hono Corporation burned to the ground, from the lowliest clerk to the company's CEO; bones ground into dust, bodies turned to ash. She would make it happen, even if it meant calling in every marker she had and bribing everyone else.

There was one ray of gratitude in all this which caught her off guard when she thought about it. She was grateful Sunshine wasn't there. The young teen had already been through so much. To have this thrown into her face, to come face-to-face with such unadulterated evil, was not something Taryn wanted the girl to experience. Hell, *she* didn't want to experience any of this, yet she was glad it was her and not Sunshine. It was a weird realization.

"They had no *right*," Taryn growled. A large calloused hand grasped hers. Looking up, she saw Caarn staring back at her.

"Why do you care so much?" the TriRusk asked in a small voice. Taryn struggled for a moment to find the words before something she'd once heard came to mind.

"Because it's the right thing to do. It costs one nothing to give yet means everything to someone who receives it."

"Do something for me?" the TriRusk asked her after long moment of silent contemplation.

"Anything."

"Help me up?"

* * *

When they arrived back on the surface, Taryn was surprised to find two hundred dead members of B'Hono's security force, eight smoldering transport vehicles, and a very bored sounding Sunshine interrogating the last remaining Jivool. Said Jivool was on his knees, blubbering in fear and terror as Sunshine waved her CASPer's arm blades mere centimeters from his face.

"Uhh…" Taryn pursed her lips as she gazed wonderingly at the carnage surrounding the half-buried research facility. It wasn't a battlefield but a slaughterhouse. "Hey."

"Hey," Sunshine replied. She nudged the Jivool with her armored hand. "I was a little bored, then they showed up for a fight. They came at me the same old way, I killed them all the same old way. Except this guy. This is Karvan di Mobiar. He runs things here on the planet. Head of site operations, I think he said."

"Oh." Taryn blinked. She looked at the blood covered Jivool. She wasn't certain but it seemed as though the blood wasn't his. "Okay."

"Oh, you can tell them everything you told me," Sunshine prodded him. The Jivool swallowed and nodded his head slightly, fully aware of the blade mere centimeters from his exposed throat. "And don't leave anything out, *ken?*"

"I won't," he replied in a feverish tone. "I promise."

"Start at the beginning," Sunshine ordered.

"A while back I was approached by someone calling himself my benefactor," Karvan began quickly, his eyes drifting away from the dangerous arm blades of the CASPer to look at the newly arrived trio. "We never met face-to-face until recently, and he never gave me his name, so he just became the Benefactor. He offered me a deal: Let him build a research lab and staff it with his people, and he'd pay well for us to ignore it. A few of my project managers aided in the construction, built the lab on top of a lot of mining explosives just in case, and we hired a Jeha to design and build self-contained medical units."

"Then what happened?" Sunshine nudged him with the CASPer's knee. "Tell them."

"He arrived with six TriRusk, which surprised all of us. We hadn't known they had reappeared, not after what the Veetanho did to their home world," Karvan continued. "His scientists took them to the research facility, and we never heard anything else. We just…pretended it didn't exist. Then one day the scientists were excited, and they brought us five TriRusk bodies to dispose of. We didn't understand, but we did as we were told because we wanted to keep the Benefactor happy. Then earlier today he had us load up all the gathered materials from the lab—"

"You *animal!*" Taryn shrieked and strode forward. Her boot lashed out and struck the Jivool square in the chest. The Jivool, not expecting the blow, flailed and landed on his back, his breath wheezing in his chest. Taryn grabbed his bloodied jacket and struggled to pull the heavy Jivool back up. After a moment of this fruitless endeavor she let him go with a frustrated yell and went back to kicking him.

Seven solid kicks to the ribs later, Taryn backed off. Groaning piteously, the Jivool rolled onto his side. Taryn, looking down on Karvan, saw something inside his jacket. Recognizing the device for what it was, she reached down and snatched his slate before he could stop her. He watched her with frightful eyes.

"It is password locked," he said in between painful gasps for air. He reached out with one of his hands. "I can unlock it for you."

"Nope," Taryn replied and pocketed the slate. "We have someone who can do it much better without deleting the information on it while doing so."

"You are in charge here?" Caarn suddenly interrupted, her face twisted into something Taryn did not recognize. "You personally?"

"Of the mining operations? Yes," Karvan admitted while clutching his ribs.

"You gave them the materials from the lab," she murmured and glanced away. "Where did you take them?"

"Take what?" Karvan asked as he began to climb back to his feet. Taryn kicked him hard in the stomach, knocking the wind out of him again.

"Stay down," she ordered. The Jivool meekly complied.

"Your benefactor...you said you helped load materials from the lab," Caarn said, her voice unsteady. Taryn watched her as she leaned gently against a small tree, one barely taller than the TriRusk herself. "What were they?"

"I don't know," Karvan admitted. "I was paid well not to ask those sort of questions."

"Who is your benefactor?" Caarn asked.

"I don't know his name."

"What race?"

"He was a Buma."

Caarn recoiled as if slapped in the face. She hissed a single word under her voice. "Boileau."

"Who?" The Jivool looked up at her, his confusion evident even through the pain.

Instead of answering, the TriRusk let out a single, shuddering breath. Grasping the trunk of the young tree with one hand, Caarn suddenly ripped the entire tree out of the ground, roots and all. Turning and wielding the tree like a bat, she swung it with all her force, bringing the trunk down across the head of the Jivool. He tried to bring his hands up to deflect the blow but there was too much raw power behind the swing. Screaming in pain as both his wrists were broken upon impact, Karvan fell back onto the ground. He raised his limp hands above his head.

"Please! Please don—" he tried but Caarn would have none of it. She swung a second time, and then a third, shouting incomprehensibly at the top of her lungs the entire time. Eventually Karvan's screams stopped and the only sound any of them could hear was the hoarse breathing of the TriRusk and the sickening, wet impact of the trunk connecting with the Jivool's crushed skull.

The jungle was suddenly silent when the TriRusk quit beating the dead Jivool. Blood, crushed bone, and brain matter were everywhere. Even Sunshine, a master of carnage and chaos, was slightly put off by the scene. It was one thing to kill someone in combat. It was another thing entirely to beat them to death with a tree. What they had witnessed was a first for all.

"Are you okay?" Taryn finally asked in a quiet voice as Caarn stared down at the broken shape of the Jivool, her muscular shoulders heaving from the exertion. She dropped the tree with her right hand while her left went to her midsection. Caarn winced and dropped to one knee. Uncertain what to do, Taryn simply put her hand on the TriRusk's shoulder and waited for her to be ready.

If someone had told Taryn she would see a TriRusk rip a small tree out of the ground and beat someone to death with it when she woke up that morning, she would have called that individual a liar. What she had just witnessed shouldn't have been feasible, yet there it was. She would never underestimate the power of an enraged Tri-Rusk. Even Dref-na seemed suitably impressed.

"Do I look okay to you?" the TriRusk asked as she looked up at Taryn, who hastily removed her hand from Caarn.

"Well, all right then." Taryn coughed slightly, unnerved by Caarn's hollow stare. "We should get going."

"What about him?" Dref-na asked, looking at the body. Taryn shrugged.

"I don't know." She looked at Sunshine. "Boss?"

"Leave it for the local animals to eat," the teen responded. The CASPer waved an arm around. "It's not like I haven't soaked the ground already, *ken?*"

"Brutal," Dref-na growled approvingly. "I like it."

"If this place has a bomb like he said, then we need to get out of here in a hurry," Sunshine suggested. "I see no sign of a ship, so whoever this Buma is he's long gone. Caarn, are you coming with us?"

"It's not as if I have anywhere else to go," the TriRusk murmured picking herself up off the ground. She brushed away a bit of bloodied dirt which had landed on her leg. "I just—yes, I want to go with you."

"All right, then," Taryn said. She shot Sunshine a look. "Lead the way, boss."

"I still don't like being in charge." Sunshine grunted as the CASPer turned and headed for the *Velut Luna*.

* * *

4 Km Above Garnon District, Zav'ax, It'iek System

Time was ticking, but with the CASPer—or more importantly, the pilot within—and her allies still too close to the research facility, he was reluctant to blow everything up just yet. He let his finger hover just above the command prompt as his scanners showed him the precise location of the CASPer as well as the three lifeforms close behind it. Further out from Sunshine's position and clearly marked on the Tri-V's screen was a dotted red line showing the boundary of the blast zone. Debris and rubble might reach further but he doubted it. The bomb was designed to implode beneath the planet's surface, not explode outward.

The group wasn't moving nearly as fast as he would have expected them to. Perhaps the TriRusk was slowing them down? Boileau grunted and silently urged them onward. As much as he would love to see every single one of them dead, he didn't have access to the Korps' accounts yet, which meant his fortune was still locked away and out of his feathered grasp. As long as Sunshine remained the only individual with the password, he couldn't kill her just yet.

Even though he really, *really* wanted to.

After what felt like an eternity, the small group on the planet finally crossed the dotted red line. He stared at the screen for a moment longer, just in case the calculations were off, before he pushed the command sequence. It took three seconds for the command to reach the planet's surface and trigger the bomb. It took another two seconds for the bomb to activate.

Zav'ax was a mining colony and had been prepped as such. That meant there had been a lot of explosive materials used to find the precious metals buried in the planet's mantle. Rubberized mining explosive agent katepaphone-3, more commonly known KP3, was shipped in to assist with this. The thin, red, rectangular sheets of explosive material could be cut and formed to the heart's content. Karvan wasn't one to skimp on materials—B'Hono Corporation was footing the bill, after all—and he had ordered enough to mine the entire southern dig site ten times over.

Of course, he reported a shortage of almost four tons of the material, and B'Hono had credited his operational budget accordingly...

All the KP3 explosive material—lovingly called "Big Red" by the local Jivool due to its appearance—had been stored safely away for use at a later date. Or, potentially, for sale to the right buyer. KP3 wasn't highly sought after, since there were far more reactive materials which could be used, but KP3 was a miner's delight. It was designed to dig. When Boileau had approached Karvan about building the research facility, the Jivool had readily agreed. Especially when the Buma had offered him a lot of money.

There was a question, though. What happened if someone caught on? Well, Karvan had four tons of KP3 just sitting there, and the Buma was more than willing to pay extra for it. Everybody wins. Well, almost everyone…

The carefully placed KP3 detonated beneath the partially hidden research facility. Some ejecta flew up and outward but the KP3 explosive had been designed in the manner of a shaped charge. Instead of exploding up and out, the blast went into the earth and deep underground, collapsing the large cavern almost 75 meters beneath the lowest level. This caused the facility to collapse on itself, with the crater expanding outward to almost 400 meters before finally coming to a halt.

Boileau whistled softly. He wasn't an explosions, guts, and violence sort of Buma, but even *he* could appreciate the majesty of a properly sequenced blast. The KP3 did precisely what it was designed to do, and now there was a crater perfectly shaped to suggest this location was going to be a new mining area. The added bonus? It appeared Sunshine and her little ragtag group of companions had survived.

Life will always throw the odd pellet at you, he thought as the energy signature from the blast began dissipating. It's how you plan for the eventual failure and the ensuing steps which dictates your luck. Looking back, he could not see any flaw in his plan. Everything had gone wrong because of happenstance and nobody, not even a Buma, could perfectly anticipate the vagaries of chaos. DexKarr would catch her eventually, of this he was certain. Just in case, however, it never hurt to have a tertiary plan to the backup plan.

Taking his eyes off the display, he activated the comms and queued the four Pushtal cruisers currently in orbit. Using a trick only the Xeno Guild knew about, he forced his way through. His call was answered immediately this time. Unsurprising, really, all things considered. Backward his fellow senior commissioners may have been, but one could never really call them stupid. Short-sighted? Definitely, but never stupid.

"Captain." Boileau dipped his head courteously as the face of a confused and angry Pushtal came onto the screen. Hijacking the ship's Tri-V was decidedly easy, especially since Boileau had all the ship's command/control protocols at his feathered fingertips thanks to the translator box hanging around the Pushtal's neck. *Every species in the galaxy has no idea just how much they let slip to us*, he thought as he offered a quaint Buma smile. "I'm glad you decided to accept my call this time."

"How did you override my comms?" the Pushtal growled. He was oddly colored for a Pushtal, more grey and black than anything else. Boileau had only seen that particular pattern in one clan over the decades and figured he was dealing with someone from Clan Kanonko, or perhaps one of the lesser clans. He hoped it was a lesser clan, truth be told. They had the most to gain from what he was about to offer. Kanonko were all very unpredictable these days.

"I have a job for you, Captain," Boileau continued, ignoring the Pushtal's questions. There was no need to rub salt into the wounded pride of the Pushtal. "I have little doubt the *Velut Luna* will escape from the Jivool and try to leave here. I need you to follow them. Do not engage, simply follow. I will pay one million credits for this as well as a monthly retainer for regular updates as to their whereabouts."

"Are you serious?" The Pushtal's face was comical. Rage, confusion, and intrigue were all wrapped up in one furry, angry body. Boileau could have scripted the Pushtal's response perfectly had he the inclination. The species was not known for their long-term planning or careful study of a contract. "We already have a contract."

"It will be canceled soon, if it hasn't been already," Boileau commented icily. "Besides which, the Mercenary Guild is reviewing all active contracts at the moment. I have it on good authority you will lose this contract."

"I don't—just how serious are you about all this?"

"As a Pushtal warrior in a room filled with unarmed MinSha," Boileau replied. "Only one thing—no harm can come to those on the ship. Especially the Humans. Just...observe and report."

"Four cruisers to watch one little ship?"

"If you would like, take your own ship and follow them, and send the rest of your clan home," Boileau suggested. "Less of the bounty to spread around that way. I will send everything you need, including the contract."

"Fine. Send everything you have on the ship and its occupants," the captain replied and killed the connection.

Utterly predictable, Boileau thought as he fired up his ship's engines and headed for the stargate, the precious materials gathered from his science experiments stored safely in his cargo hold. Two thousand successfully fertilized, genetically sequenced albino TriRusk embryos were in the thirteen custom-built life support cubes, awaiting maturation. Their value was immeasurable, and their future worth ten times that. It wasn't enough to fully realize his plans—that still required him to gain access to his hidden credits in the Kakata Korps' accounts—but it was a terrific start. Besides, time was once again on his side.

He could afford to be a little generous. It was in his nature, after all.

* * *

Near Landing Pad 4, Garnon District, Zav'ax, It'iek System

As soon as the pressure wave passed over them, Sunshine was back on her feet. The oddly shaped trees swayed in the breeze but surprisingly all stayed upright. She glanced back in the direction of the research facility, but she couldn't see anything through the trees. Looking up she saw a large cloud of dust rising into the atmosphere. Her suit didn't pick up any sign of debris in the air, which she found odd. Everything she knew about things that went "BOOM" involved random chunks of material being violently tossed high into the sky.

"What was that?" Taryn asked as she picked herself off the ground.

"One big bomb," Sunshine replied as she boosted the power to the CASPer's sensors. The energy residue of the explosion had dissipated enough for her to see there was no one else left alive near the facility. The four of them had miraculously survived somehow. "I don't know if it was remote detonated or on a timer. Either way, we were really lucky."

"Doesn't matter," Dref-na groaned and rolled onto her back. "I'm done, dead, kaput. Go on without me."

"Get up, you big old drama queen," Taryn said and helped hoist the Besquith to her feet. She glanced down, and her face became serious. "How's the knee?"

"It hurts," Dref-na admitted as she flexed it, gingerly testing the damaged knee out. "But I can make it. Entropy. I think I injured my knee again, tiny fierceness."

"We can go as slow as you need us to," Sunshine added after checking on Caarn. The female TriRusk was a bit dazed by the explosion, but, thanks to Vah, the entire group was becoming very adept at handling someone suffering from shock. Using her CASPer, she carefully helped Caarn to her feet before turning to the others.

"I can go ahead, clear the path," Sunshine offered. "Then you two can help Dref-na."

"Makes me wonder how you won that fight earlier against the Torokar," Taryn commented as she leaned up against the Besquith to support her. "Oof. You got fat."

"No, you just got weak," Dref-na countered and let her tongue brush against Taryn's face. "Oops."

"Eww, gross," Taryn complained and wiped Dref-na's saliva away with her sleeve. She helped Dref-na lean against a nearby tree before turning away from the Besquith. "So nasty."

"Are they always like this?" Caarn asked hesitantly.

Sunshine smiled. "They've been like this ever since I met them, *menh,*" she replied without missing a beat. "I think they get along. Mostly."

"I see," the TriRusk responded, though it was clear to Sunshine she did not.

"I think we're good here," Taryn announced as she moved closer to Sunshine and Caarn. "You lead, we'll keep up as best we can."

"I'll try to go slow for everyone," Sunshine promised Dref-na as the Besquith limped over to them.

"Let's go," Dref-na said and set off, which caught the group a little off guard. After a few steps the Besquith rested against one of the larger jungle trees. She turned and gave Taryn a very pointed look. "Are you going to help me limp out of here, or are you going to just sit back and watch, Taryn Lupo?"

Surprised, Taryn hurried over to help her friend and, with some minor assistance from Caarn, they were able to set off on their trip back to the *Velut Luna.*

Sunshine led the group through the dense jungle, only stopping occasionally to allow Dref-na to catch her breath. There was no news from either Klinks or Vah, which could mean anything. She decided to be proactive instead of waiting for them to tell her bad news. "*Velut Luna*, this is Sunshine," she called over the comms. She was answered almost immediately.

"This is Vah," the CozSha answered back. "Did we win? We lost your signal for a bit, and there was a massive explosion near your last recorded location. Was that you blowing up?"

"Not yet and no, we didn't blow anything up," Sunshine answered. "Someone else did that for us. I'll send them a thank you note later. How is your situation?"

"Jorna is trying to help with the railguns but she isn't making a lot of sense. She was being inefficient," Vah answered in a measured voice. Sunshine could tell the little CozSha was freaked out by everything. Unlike anyone else, the worse the situation became, the calmer Vah sounded. It was unnerving. "Kl'nk'nnk had to tie her up and put her in the secondary hold. The security forces haven't arrived. Jorna said something about them lacking proper air transport and them arriving in waves, but she was exhibiting signs of post-concussive syndrome. I don't know if she is correct or simply babbling. Brain injuries can lead to permanent damage to one's overall efficiency."

"Probably correct about the incoming forces but keep her tied down for now just in case," Sunshine said as she linked back with the *Velut Luna*'s scanners. Sure enough, the Jivool had either been run off completely or fallen back so far that the ship's sensors could no longer detect them. She didn't want to count their blessings yet, but the situation looked good. "How are the repairs coming?"

"Kl'nk'nnk is just about done, but she is concerned about the structural integrity of the starboard wing," Vah relayed. "She says it would require more than what she has on hand to fix it permanently, so in the Human vernacular, she duct-taped it and called it a day."

"You really know your Human slang." Sunshine chuckled as she checked the area. "Dref-na is moving slowly, and the TriRusk is injured. It will be roughly thirty minutes before we're back to the *Velut Luna*. Tell Klinks to have the engines running and ready for takeoff, just in case. I doubt B'Hono is going to give up this easily, *ken?*"

"I understand," Vah said before she gasped. "Oh my. More of those Jivool transports just arrived. Lots of armed guards. I will be as efficient as I can, Sunshine, but I think we're going to be ove—"

The comms ended abruptly. Thunderous blasts ripped through the jungle as the *Velut Luna*'s railguns were fired up.

Sunshine checked her display and pinged the location of the ship. A small red dot appeared on the overlay. It was almost a full kilometer away. The CASPer then changed it to green as red dots appeared around the ship. The Jivool had returned and had done so in force. They were clearly not messing around this time.

She stole a glance at Dref-na, who was being helped by Taryn. Caarn was next to them but not really helping, for which Sunshine could not fault her. Neither Taryn nor Dref-na had told her what they had seen down in the labs, but it was enough to rattle the normally affable Besquith. Taryn's humor and sarcasm felt phony to her ears as well, though she did a good job disguising what was bothering her. Whatever horrors the B'Hono Corporation had done to Caarn in the lab were not the kind of things that would heal overnight, if ever.

She understood the silent pain and terror Caarn was dealing with, though she couldn't tell the TriRusk this. Not yet at least. She barely knew her, and her own past before the Korps found her was a drug-induced haze. There was only an occasional face that filled her memories to remind her of…something else. It was part of the reason her nightmares were so horrid. They weren't images of something imaginary which could have happened to her, but were instead memories of past events she'd had forced upon her.

Sunshine would give her time to recover before asking anything of her, or trying to get details of what had occurred in the labs. Caarn needed time to process what had happened and, while in her shocked state, wouldn't be able to properly process any of it. Time was all Sunshine could offer her. To Sunshine, the idea of an abused Human teenager counseling an older alien female was absurd. She was nothing more than a former slave turned merc.

Instead, Sunshine looked back at Taryn and Dref-na. "I'm going ahead. There's nothing in this part of the jungle but some small creatures. The Jivool are at the *Velut Luna,* and I don't know if Vah and Klinks can hold them off alone."

"You know there's a fire in the jungle near the Garnon District, tiny fierceness?" Dref-na asked her.

"Another one?"

"Just a small one," Dref-na corrected. "It helped distract the Torokar."

"We really should quit trying to set this planet on fire," Sunshine sighed.

"While a crude tactic, it was effective in my battle with the creature."

"Hey, focus," Taryn interrupted them, surprising Sunshine. "Go on, save my ship. Let's just get off this damned rock."

Sunshine smiled thinly. "You heard the captain. It's time to get back to the *Velut Luna* and get out of here. I don't ever want to come back here again, *ken?*"

"I agree," Dref-na stated. "This world can die a fiery death."

"Go ahead," Taryn told her. "We'll be right behind you. Promise."

"Vah, it's Sunshine," she called over the comms as she bounded away from the group. "ETA is three minutes. Can you hold on that long?"

No reply was forthcoming, so Sunshine took the answer to be a resounding "no." She increased her speed; aware it would drain her power faster, but terrified at the prospect of losing Klinks and Vah and Jorna to the Jivool.

She sped through the jungle, avoiding the exposed roots of the bizarre trees which loomed high overhead. Her suit navigated it with ease. Though it might have been easier to travel along the road that led to the Garnon District, she would have had to double back and find the *Velut Luna* while fighting her way through the small city. It was tempting, given her experience in urban combat, but it would be time consuming. As she had pointed out earlier when they left the lab, cutting straight through the jungle was still the fastest route.

The railguns fired again, and more red dots disappeared from the overlay on her suit's Tri-V display. Vah was doing well, unless Klinks had taken over the controls, though if this were the case, then Sunshine couldn't figure out why she wasn't firing faster.

No, she decided after a split-second of internal debate, *it has to be Vah on the guns still.*

Sunshine could see the landing pad at last. The small retaining wall surrounding it was protecting a lot of Jivool from the railguns of the *Velut Luna.* The security forces were evidently under the belief the railguns couldn't shoot through the wall. They were still alive only because Vah was trying to be as efficient as possible. It was a condition Sunshine was about to fix.

The security forces were still arriving and showed no signs of stopping, no matter how bloody their casualties were. They were avoiding an area with growing smoke clouds, however. She wasn't sure what was going on there, but at least it was one less direction of attack she needed to be concerned about.

The steady stream of Jivool arriving was getting to the point where Sunshine worried about her ammunition supply. She knew using the CASPer's laser would eat her power up too quickly. If her suit went down, then none of the others would make it off world. It was on her shoulders.

First, she needed to secure the area. The old "run into them and kill everything" trick was the best way she knew. She took a few long strides to build up speed, and soon she was moving at almost 30 kilometers per hour. The exposed Jivool squad had absolutely zero chance to react as she hit them like a small, vengeful, spite-filled wrecking ball.

Body parts flew everywhere as Sunshine crashed into the lead squad. Panicked cries could be heard before the *crunch* of bones replaced everything. The screams began soon after the Jivool landed upon the lichen-covered jungle floor, the moss not breaking their fall enough to prevent serious harm. Those who weren't sliced to ribbons by the modified CASPer's arm blades had bones shattered while being run over, were knocked unconscious by the impact of the suit, or had the unfortunate experience of still being considered potential threats. Immediate threats which needed to be dealt with swiftly and promptly. These individuals barely had time to recognize they were on the ground and still alive before Sunshine finished them off in the most expedient manner possible.

There was a brief lull in the action as the Jivool pulled back, clearly dazed at Sunshine's sudden arrival. Instead of pressing them, though, she waited as Dref-na, Taryn, and Caarn finally arrived. Dref-na looked worse for the wear, and Caarn appeared ready to pass out, but Taryn seemed ready for a fight. It wasn't great, but it was definitely better than nothing.

"Taryn, link up with the ship and help Vah take out the remaining Jivool," Sunshine ordered as she moved toward another cluster of Jivool near one of the reserve fuel tanks. Not wanting to risk another forest fire, Sunshine fired the MAC at the outlying edges of the squad. They shouted in alarm and moved away from the only thing that was preventing Sunshine from shooting them. Free to fire at last, she eliminated them with cold, calculated aggression. "Have Dref-na get Caarn onto the ship and have her check on Jorna while she's there. I don't want to have to explain to the Fangmaster that I got his daughter killed, *ken?*"

Klinks suddenly cut in over the comms. "Sunshine, I have repaired the strut and the *Velut Luna* is fixed enough to leave. I'm pinned down behind the signal pylon, however. I need help."

"On it," Sunshine said, and moved around to the far side of the landing pad, where the remaining Jivool were forming up to rush the ship. Vah hadn't fired the railguns for a bit and Sunshine guessed the Jivool were weighing their odds of survival if they charged. This squad was more spread out than before, but she recognized they weren't a cohesive unit from the look of things.

She watched as the Jivool suddenly all paused and waited. There was a brief moment where it seemed they were all staring off into space before Sunshine realized they were receiving orders via radio comms. She saw them reload, replacing their stun bags with regular magazines. Somebody higher up must have finally decided to quit playing around with the crew.

Wondering what had changed, she figured it out quickly enough when a small armored transport vehicle came hurtling down the road toward the landing pad and the Jivool on the ground moved to the opposite side. Mounted on top of the vehicle was a turreted automatic railgun similar in design to what was on the *Velut Luna*, only smaller. The turret swiveled in her direction, and Sunshine found herself staring down the barrel of a railgun.

She moved before she was even fully aware of it, her finely honed reflexes taking her away from both the fuel tank and the landing pad proper as the railgun opened fire on her. The needle-sized rounds slammed into the jungle trees, creating a shower of sap-covered wood chips with each impact. The turret turned and followed her movements, not giving her a moment to come up with a counterattack. But there simply wasn't enough hard cover in the area for her to use, and she quickly discovered there was a distinct difference between cover and concealment.

"Vah, keep your eyes open," she said as she vaulted over a downed tree, and four rounds from the turreted railgun slammed into the trunk immediately afterward. The tiny rounds didn't punch through the tree though, so she crouched down behind it and hoped for the best. "They've switched over to lethal rounds now. Watch yourselves."

"I am working at peak efficiency at the moment," Vah responded and one of the railguns of the *Velut Luna* opened fire. Five Jivool exploded into a fine mist as the large caliber rounds went through them. The other Jivool found themselves covered in their comrades' blood. It was clear, even to Sunshine, they were all rethinking their life choices which had led to this moment.

"Uh, good?" Sunshine muttered as she looked at the landing pad. More of the Jivool were moving around just below the line of the retaining wall, staying out of sight of Vah and, more importantly, avoiding the line of fire from the guns of the *Velut Luna*. Pinned down, she couldn't do anything about them. Fortunately, Vah was safely inside the ship with Jorna. Klinks, on the other hand, was out in the open, though behind the pylon. Unless the Jivool wanted to lose their heads, she was relatively safe for the moment. Sunshine turned and pointed her shoulders in the direction of the armored transport targeting her. Activating the grenades, she launched fifteen of the tiny explosives at the vehicle.

They arced gracefully through the air; their trajectory calculated by the onboard computer of the CASPer. The grenades were set to explode upon impact, and though she knew they probably wouldn't penetrate the hull of the armored transport, it would hopefully cause enough of a distraction to allow her to move to a better position. If she could find one.

The grenades exploded with sharp reports, the small anti-personnel devices doing absolutely nothing to the thick armor of the transport except sear off some paint and make a lot of noise, though two, surprisingly, did manage to make small dents in the engine compartment cover. The armor of the vehicle wasn't nearly as good as she had initially thought. But it clearly rattled the occupants on the inside as the fire from the turret stopped. This was her chance.

Sunshine was out and running parallel to the transport before the last explosive had shaken the Jivool within. The turret didn't turn to follow her. Accelerating, she altered her angle to avoid a cluster of smaller trees and lined up her approach, so she had a straight line and relatively flat space. Boosting the small CASPer to its maximum speed, she lowered her shoulder and slammed into the side of the vehicle.

"Oof!" she grunted as the thin armor crumpled from the impact. She fell to the ground, stunned. The impact had been rougher than she had expected. Then again, the idea of running one of humanity's best killing machines into a heavier armored vehicle was probably not something the CASPer's original designers at Binnig had in mind. If not for the upgrades Klinks had made to the modified Mk 7, she was almost certain she would be suffering from more than a bruised shoulder at the moment.

But ramming the vehicle had done exactly what she hoped—the side door was dented in enough to see inside. Panicked Jivool were struggling to figure out how to get their turret pointed down at her. Belatedly, she saw the line of sight for the gun was unable to reach the area next to the doors. It would have been easier to have gotten under the line of sight when it was distracted. Ramming the transport had been entirely unnecessary.

Grasping the exposed edge of the side door, she ripped it off its hinges. The Jivool began to shout as they reached for their personal weapons. She opened fire with the MAC and shredded everything inside the armored transport—seats, electronic instruments, and Jivool alike. Satisfied the vehicle was completely wrecked and no longer able to function, she turned to deal with the Jivool who had been creeping up on Klinks' position.

They were very close to the Jeha now, still below the retaining wall and out of Vah's view. The CozSha was not going to take a shot she deemed "wasteful," Sunshine guessed. Leaving the Xeno Guild member to man the guns had probably not been her wisest decision ever. Unfortunately, from her position, she didn't have a clear shot at them either. Unlike Vah, however, Sunshine was willing to risk being inefficient in order to make the kill. She powered up her MAC and took aim at the four Jivool.

A shot ricocheted off her back armor and she spun around, looking for the offending shooter. She spotted a Jivool setting up what appeared to be a long rifle and launched three grenades his way. The impact-fuse grenades hit the ground and exploded, throwing shrapnel and lichen everywhere. The Jivool dropped to the ground, screaming as his legs were turned into a gooey mess. Sunshine grimaced and turned back to the landing pad. The four Jivool were now prepping something in their hands. She zoomed in for a better look.

Grenades, she realized. The Jivool were going to toss grenades up at Klinks. She readied the MAC, but a yellow warning light appeared on her screen. The MAC was dangerously low on ammunition and she couldn't risk a shot. Sprinting as fast as she could, she almost made it to the Jivool position before they attacked.

"Look out!" Sunshine screamed. It didn't matter, though. Two of the grenades landed right next to the distracted and terrified Jeha. Antennae swiveling, Klinks turned at the sound of Sunshine's shout before realizing what was going on. Glancing down, it was obvious even from where Sunshine was at Klinks recognized the grenades for what they were. Klinks looked up at Sunshine, a terrified expression on her insectoid face. The moment stretched forever as the Jeha's eyes remained fixed on the nearby CASPer. Realization struck Sunshine's soul—there was no way she could save the Jeha.

The two grenades exploded simultaneously. Heavy shrapnel ripped through Klinks' body as the Jeha was tossed aside by the blasts. She crashed into the nearby pylon and went limp, her body broken in half. Her blood was everywhere. Sunshine's systems immediately began to scan the Jeha. After a second, it stopped. There were no signs of life detected. Klinks was gone.

"NO!" Sunshine shouted as she began targeting the surviving Jivool with the MAC. Alarmed, the Jivool tossed their weapons aside and raised their hands. Crying inside the suit, Sunshine tried to look at the aliens through blurry eyes. There would be no quarter given. Blood demanded blood. She looked at every single Jivool remaining on the landing pad and felt nothing but rage.

The young teen, who had already had so much taken from her, responded the only way she knew how. The Jivool security forces barely had time to scream before she was among them, her arm blades slashing. One after another they fell, unable to do anything under the furious onslaught of the enraged teen. It wasn't a fight. It wasn't even a battle.

It was cold-blooded slaughter, and it felt *good*.

* * *

Eventually, Sunshine came out of her killing haze and looked around. She had slaughtered the large group of Jivool back at the now-destroyed research lab, but this? This was something else entirely. What she'd just done was beyond everything she had been taught. Rage and anger had replaced cold rationality. She had ceased being a tactician on the field of battle and had instead taken the mantle of death upon her shoulders. It felt good, but it was also more than a little terrifying for her. Nobody had ever told her killing could be this easy.

No, she said as she calmed her breathing some. Mulbah had said so. He said it was what defined us as Humans that we chose not to make it easy to take another life.

Blinking, the black haze which had filled her vision continued to fade. She had gotten her vengeance, just as Caarn had earlier. It was time to step back and take a breath. She tossed the severed head of a Jivool aside as an overwhelming wave of sadness filled her. She had gone too far. Sunshine had never minded the fighting; it was simply a means to an end. Vengeance was something else entirely.

"Engines primed!" Vah commed from inside the *Velut Luna*, interrupting her private musings. "Firing…powered! Sunshine, scanners detect more security forces incoming. Time to leave, people!"

"You heard the CozSha," Sunshine said in a cold, distant voice as she steered the CASPer around a rather large tree trunk and lashed out with her left arm. The Jivool hiding behind the tree squealed in terror as her arm blade sliced his rifle in half. It turned and fled into the jungle. Sunshine thought about chasing him for a moment but decided against it. She was running low on fuel thanks to the amount of shooting and moving around she'd been forced to do. Besides which, she was exhausted. The young teen was tired of losing friends and family, of fighting, and of just about everything else. She jogged back to the ship. "Everyone on board."

"The new arrivals have armored transports," Vah suddenly announced as Sunshine burst into the clearing at the landing pad. Her voice changed. "Hey, is that a missile launcher?"

"A *what?*" Taryn asked, alarmed. Sunshine spotted the ship's captain near the ramp of the cargo hold. Taryn was in an exposed position and had popped her head up to see what Vah was talking about.

"Get down!" Sunshine screamed at her. The CASPer detected a launch from the newly arrived Jivool. Her anti-missile point defense system activated immediately, quickly determined she was not the target, and powered down just as rapidly. The CASPer found the source of the launch and tracked the flight path of the missile in less than one-tenth of a second.

The target was the *Velut Luna*. More specifically, the hot engines which were now fully primed and ready for liftoff.

The tiny heat-seeking missile impacted the starboard engine of the ship, tearing into the engine casing and detonating. Tiny bits of shrapnel irreparably damaged the engine, as well as the mount which held it to the underside of the wing. The engine did not catch fire, thankfully. Instead, the wing bent as the weakened struts were no longer strong enough to support the engine's weight. Screeching metal assaulted their ears as the wing continued to be pulled down by gravity. The tip of the wing stopped it from detaching completely, but the engine continued its downward trajectory.

"Oh no…" Sunshine moaned, defeated. Their escape plan had just blown up in her face.

* * *

"No…" Taryn whispered in horror as the damaged engine separated completely from the *Velut Luna*'s wing. There was no way to fix it, not without a shipyard and a lot of time. Her boss's favorite ship, his personal yacht, his freaking *baby*, was beyond repair. It would remain stuck on a jungle world in the middle of nowhere until someone came along to claim it. Feeling sick to her stomach, Taryn turned and promptly heaved onto the lichen-covered jungle floor.

Her life was over. Perhaps there was some sort of witness protection program in the Union where she could hide from Zorgama? Unlikely, she thought as she recalled their initial meeting on board the *Fortuna*. There was nowhere for her to hide. She might as well report back to him and face her execution as bravely as she could.

"It'll be okay," Dref-na said. "I'll help you run. My family would love a Human warrior in their midst. Perhaps they'll let me keep you as a pet."

"Kill me now," Taryn moaned as she fell to her knees and buried her face in the moss. "Just get it over with."

"I could do that," Dref-na said as she knelt down next to her. The Besquith's wounded knee made a horrid popping sound, but Dref-na ignored it, as well as the searing pain that accompanied it. Her mouth was inches from Taryn's ear. Her voice dropped down to a barely audible whisper. "Or…we could steal that Skipjumper from Landing Pad 6. I'm pretty sure the former owner won't be needing it anymore. We just need to get there before the fire does. The Jivool won't even know where we went if leave now."

Taryn's head snapped up at the comment, and her face brightened immediately.

"He won't kill me if I give him a new ship like that." Taryn nodded eagerly, her mind racing. The more she focused on the other issues at hand, the less time she had to dwell on what she had seen when they had pulled Caarn out of the research lab. It felt better to have her mask in place than to face the cold harshness of reality sometimes. "He might only ground me for a few weeks, at most. I love flying but being grounded for a few weeks is better than dead, right? I mean, only the Depik have ships as stealthy and advanced as a Skipjumper!"

"See?" Dref-na asked as she heaved herself back up. The pain in her knee was growing worse, but she began to hum anyway. It seemed the proper thing to do at the moment, even in the midst of the carnage wrought by their little group. "Always look on the bright side of life."

"We need to get there first. Those transports aren't going to—" Taryn started, but paused as she watched Sunshine open fire on the last remaining group of Jivool. The transports were shredded by the MAC while the CASPer's laser gun took out any of the security forces stupid enough to not stay behind cover.

The black CASPer bounded toward the burning transports, and the teenager made short work of any survivors, wounded or otherwise. Then she ripped into the transport with her armored hands, clearly set on venting her rage and frustration. Fuel began leaking out of one of the ruined vehicles, but Sunshine kept punching it anyway. Taryn rubbed her face at the sight of the carnage. She couldn't imagine what was going through Sunshine's mind at the moment, and, truth be told, she wasn't too certain she wanted to. *Let the girl work out her anger in her own way,* she decided. "Never mind. Second problem, we need to get inside the Skipjumper without damaging it. We have to leave here before the forest fire cuts us off from the other ship."

"Let Sunshine handle the Skipjumper, I'm pretty sure she can hack it somehow," Dref-na told her as Vah staggered out of the damaged *Velut Luna.* The tiny CozSha looked around the area, confusion etched upon her goat-like face. Jorna was limping along behind her, with Caarn carefully assisting the concussed Pushtal. There were no more living Jivool anywhere to be seen.

"The ship was hit by a missile…" Vah's voice trailed off as she realized she could no longer hear the sounds of battle. Her odd little eyes grew wide as she spotted the number of dead Jivool around the landing pad. The CozSha looked at Taryn, amazement clear on her goat-like face. "Hey, did we win? Most efficient."

* * * * *

Chapter Twelve

The "Borrowed" Skipjumper, 11 Km Above Zav'ax, It'iek System

Their departure from the planet was almost anticlimactic. Hacking into the security protocols of the Skipjumper had been child's play for Sunshine.

Helping Jorna stagger over a kilometer through the jungle while the Pushtal was still suffering the effects of a concussion was irritating but not overly dangerous, especially given how Sunshine's quick ruination of the transports had broken the back of the assault. The routed Jivool had fled back to the Garnon District, and no others came for a rematch. It was a hard lesson, but one which was eventually learned by the surviving Jivool.

No, the most difficult part of all was getting the CASPer properly strapped down and stowed away in the cramped cargo hold of the Skipjumper. It had taken some effort, but they had just managed.

It was also challenging to get everything else situated before they killed thrust and gravity disappeared. Their new TriRusk companion, still suffering the effects of multiple surgeries upon her by the geneticists of the B'Hono Corporation, was disoriented and moved around as if in a daze. Vah recognized the symptoms and had assisted the large alien to a place where she could rest while they made their escape.

Then there was the tiny, fierce child inside the giant killing machine to contend with. It was difficult, considering Sunshine did not want to get out of the suit, but eventually, after gentle coaxing from Taryn and Dref-na, she acquiesced. Klinks' death had hurt her far worse than any of them had initially realized.

Surrounded by the comforting cockpit of the Leopard and protected from the outside world, she had allowed herself to cry. Tears ran freely down her cheeks as she mourned the loss of Klinks. The Jeha had quickly become one of those rare individuals Sunshine had been able to bond with, alien or not. It was only long after the tears had dried that she let Taryn and Dref-na talk her out of the suit.

The Pushtal cruisers followed closely behind the Skipjumper, but they made no aggressive maneuvers. Taryn was grateful for this, since nobody was really certain what the capabilities of their recently acquired ship were. If Taryn hadn't known better, she almost would have suspected they had been ordered to back off. By whom, she couldn't venture a guess. It didn't matter; they were away now, safe and headed slowly toward the stargate.

That was, until the ship decided otherwise.

"Wait, what's happening?" Taryn asked as the engines suddenly flared to life. She looked at Dref-na, who was equally confused. Both drifted to the floor of the ship as thrust pushed everything down. She glanced over at the tiny little alien working on her slate nearby. "Vah? Are you doing something with your slate there?"

"This isn't me, Taryn," the CozSha replied after a moment, glancing up and looking at the trio. "I was looking over the clean slate you pulled off that dead Jivool and linked it to your databanks. It was isolated, though. I'm not letting it near your ship's navigation or the databanks just to be sure. But when I started the remote scan, a third party pushed through your databanks' security firewall and then everything got...weird."

"Sunshine," Taryn said as she looked back over her shoulder at the young teen.

"I didn't do anything!" she protested. "I'm not even linked to the ship!"

"I'm sorry to say, but it's definitely you, Sunshine," Vah confirmed after a moment. "Everyone's pinplants leave a slight trace when they've been somewhere. Yours were just connected with this slate and the ship simultaneously, which shouldn't be possible!"

"I swear I didn't do anything!" Sunshine nearly shouted, fresh tears forming in her eyes. "I promise!"

"I believe you," Taryn said, trying to soothe her young friend. "What happened? What were you do—no, what were you thinking about?"

"What?"

"Like you said, go step-by-step over your path to figure out where things went wrong, then fix it," Taryn prodded her gently.

"Y-you remembered that?" Sunshine asked, stammering a little as her breathing slowly came back under control.

"Of course I do," Taryn smiled. "It was good advice from someone so very young. As first impressions go, yours was a lasting one. So, spill. What were you thinking about?"

"I was thinking about my nightmares," Sunshine admitted in a quiet voice. "They hate me so much in my dreams—the Korps, I mean...the *bass*, Zion, all of them—because I didn't stay and fight. I was told to leave, to pass on a message that didn't exist. They died and sent me away."

"Survivor's guilt is a perfectly natural thing," Taryn reminded her. "You can't blame yourself. You did what you were told to."

"It still hurts," Sunshine murmured softly. She wiped her nose on her sleeve and sniffed. "I could have stayed and fought, *ken?*"

"And died," Taryn pointed out. "Needlessly, I'll add. Then we wouldn't have found out about the TriRusk, and we wouldn't have pulled out Caarn from that facility before they blew it up. Nobody would have ever known. Now we do."

"Klinks wouldn't be dead," Sunshine countered.

Taryn shook her head. "You're wrong. B'Hono Corporation was going to kill her long before we got here."

"What *are* you?" Vah interrupted them as her odd alien eyes bore directly into Sunshine's dark brown ones.

"Human," Sunshine responded, confused. She sniffled a little but the urge to cry was gone now.

Vah shook her head. "No, Humans can't do what you did," the CozSha argued, though there was little heat in her tone. "Didn't you notice what the computers did when I had my programs up and running and your pinplants interfaced with them? You entered a destination through your pinplants. The stargate—and the ship—responded."

"No, I didn't tell the ship anything." Sunshine paused before admitting, "I was thinking about something else."

"What?" Vah pressed.

Sunshine shrugged. "Just remembering a nightmare I've had a bunch of times," she admitted after a moment of thought. "There was something in the distance attacking a city. It's right before the Korps start yelling at me. Something big, like those Raknar Jim Cartwright has. Only…it felt *alive*. Tortantulas were running from it. Everything was dying."

"Something?" Taryn asked, kneeling and checking Sunshine's forehead with the backside of her hand. "Warm but not hot; no fever. Then again, we did just get you out of your Leopard."

"Tell me more about this dream," Vah said, leaning forward. It was clear she found it fascinating, though Sunshine couldn't imagine why. "Everything you can remember."

"Vah…" Dref-na warned.

The CozSha looked up at the Besquith, irritated. "I need to know everything," Vah explained.

"I can't," Sunshine said dropping her chin to her chest. "I only remember bits and pieces. Something larger than a city. Tortantulas running. Fire everywhere. A scream. Then the Korps are there and they're angry because I didn't stay and fight. After that, there's only darkness."

"Can I run a diagnostic on your pinplants?" Vah asked. Sunshine nodded, and the diminutive alien pulled her slate from her work pouch. "Okay, you should see it come up. Access it, then allow for me to—"

"Done," Sunshine interrupted her. She closed her eyes. "My pinplants are working just fine. These dreams are just nightmares I always have."

"Did you know sentient beings don't usually have the same nightmare over and over again?" Vah asked as her eyes tracked the data on her screen. "It's only a sense of *déjà vu* when it does occur, caused by a dream that's similar to something which has happened in real life. It's why when you wake up you believe you've had the dream before."

"I swear I have the same nightmare every single time," Sunshine vowed. "It's always the same."

"I believe you," Vah acknowledged. "Which leads me to believe something else might be going on."

"Something?" Taryn asked, confused.

"When you told me about the missing message in your CASPer, I got to thinking about something I've heard about, but I didn't think it was possible; there was too much that could go wrong. The Xeno Guild experimented with something similar in the past, but it was discarded. It was deemed too insecure. The CASPer was not the courier of the message," Vah said as she transferred the data to the Tri-V situated nearby on the bulkhead. The Skipjumper was better equipped than the *Velut Luna* was, and roomier to boot. She then flicked off the slate and slid it back into her pouch. "Sunshine is."

"What?" Sunshine stared at the CozSha. "How?"

"Someone hid a message within your memories, which caused you to have a recurring nightmare," Vah said. "They probably stored it on your pinplants. My guess? It's a warning meant for someone else. Who, though, I have no idea. I'm sorry."

"But what about the computers?" Taryn pressed as she pushed her pink hair out of her face. "Where are we going? Where's it taking us?"

"Could it be part of the message too?" Dref-na asked.

Vah shrugged. "Maybe? My best guess is that data in the pinplants activated the computers and navigation when Sunshine got close," Vah suggested in a neutral tone. "Some sort of perfect storm scenario which only occurred now. Perhaps it was her remembering the dream? Or perhaps her pinplants are enhanced somehow? Or…it could have hacked into the slate of the Xeno Guild which triggered some internal alarm? I don't have enough information to know for certain. I'm sorry."

"They're just normal pinplants though," Taryn said as she gave Sunshine an apologetic look. "I checked."

"That they are," Vah agreed. "My scans say something else is going on...within Sunshine herself, that has little to do with the pinplants. I am having a hard time believing it, though. I wish...I wish Kl'nk'nnk was here. She could help decipher this data better."

"What?" Sunshine asked. She pleaded with the CozSha. "Tell me?"

"I am only guessing here, but if I may?" Sunshine nodded for her to go on, so the Xeno Guild member began to theorize. "Your brain activity is far more energetic than anything I've seen before for a Human. Part of our job in the Xeno Guild is studying every aspect of speech morphology within sentient beings, including their brain patterns. Everything I have on Humans suggests they have roughly 86 billion neurons on average in their brain. You have about seventy-five percent more, which should be impossible without making some adjustments to your glial cells. Quite honestly, you should be dead, yet here you are, very much alive. The Schwann cells in your peripheral nervous system, according to your pinplants, are also found in your central nervous system, repairing damage from your neuron overload. This should not be the case. You also have five percent more mass to your frontal lobe when compared to the rest of your brain matter. There is no sign of disease there, however. No tumor or anything like that. This shouldn't be possible without xenological bioengineering. The only thing I can think of is...you've been uplifted."

"She's *what?*" Dref-na asked, startled.

"Uplifted?" Sunshine crumpled to the floor, confused and disoriented. It was too much for her to cope with. "Wait, how? No, *when?*

I'm a Human! We don't have the technology on Earth to do this! I don't understand…"

"Sometime in the past, you were definitely uplifted," Vah said as she looked away from the Tri-V. Her odd little eyes bored into Sunshine's. "Within the first ten years of your life, if my guess is correct. Before puberty. It leaves telltale signs on your hypothalamus after you begin puberty. I'm sorry, Sunshine. I can't explain how it happened, but you were uplifted. It is highly illegal to uplift a species. And I don't think anyone has ever uplifted a sentient individual before. Were you, ah, different? I believe the polite term in your society is *slow*."

"No," Sunshine said as she looked at the diminutive CozSha. Even seated on the floor of the *Velut Luna* she was still taller than Vah. "I was beaten and other stuff before I was found by the Korps, but I was smart enough. Major General Sparkles thought so, I guess. But I got my pinplants just before final battle at Monrovia. I don't know anymore."

"What's your earliest memory?" Vah asked her. "Before the Korps and before Major General Sparkles."

"It's a cloudy haze," Sunshine admitted, her voice cautious. "I was drugged a lot before I became a merc. I don't really have any memories before Major General Sparkles found me. I remember a really beautiful face looking down on me…but that's it."

"Why would anyone on Earth uplift another Human?" Dref-na asked quietly. "There are great penalties for doing such. Look at what Peepo was able to accomplish using only the accusation."

"An experiment, perhaps, to see what would happen when you uplift an already advanced species?" Vah offered as Dref-na dropped to the floor to sit next to Sunshine. The young girl leaned against the furry body of the Besquith, taking comfort in her closeness and warmth.

"A tool in a war which ended before you could be used," Caarn added from across the hold, surprising them all with her sudden appearance. Though probably not an expert on the subject and still not certain about her rescuers, it was clear she was being careful as she chose her next words. "There are many uplifted species out there, and numerous devices leftover from the Great War. Tools for creating and for killing."

"That sounds about right for me. Nothing but a tool," Sunshine sniffled as she started to cry. She closed her eyes as old memories boiled unbidden to the surface of her mind. Her shoulders shuddered as random faces appeared. Faces of men who had hurt her. She tried to force them out of her mind but like a poison, the insidious evil continued to tear down her emotional defenses. She sobbed. "Just like in Monrovia when Major General Sparkles owned me. Used and thrown away when they were done with me. Every time."

"Oh no, tiny fierceness," Dref-na whispered, gently cupping Sunshine's face with her large claws. There was almost a motherly feel in the gesture. Sunshine would never have believed a Besquith could be so caring, even from one who worked for her. Large golden eyes looked deeply into Sunshine's. Dref-na tutted quietly and tried to comfort Sunshine, recognizing her distress though not the reasoning behind it. "You are not just a tool to be used."

"Then what am I?" Sunshine whispered as tears dripped from her chin and splashed on her utility coveralls. Bass, *what did you do to me?* Her soul cried out for answers, but none were immediately forthcoming. The dead refused to speak and could not provide her the answers she so desperately needed. She and her friends, the survivors from Zav'ax and the crew of the *Velut Luna*, were truly on their own in this vast galaxy.

"You are something amazing," Dref-na said. "Something dangerous as well, perhaps a weapon against an unseen foe. Or perhaps someone who would save your world?"

"A weapon? Why would they do this to me?"

"I'm not certain, tiny fierceness," the Besquith replied gently. She stroked Sunshine's short hair, offering the young girl what comfort she could. "But I will help you find out."

Taryn joined them. She knelt and gingerly touched Sunshine's shoulder. Sunshine's tears dried as calm slowly washed over her.

The young teen had lost everything in her life, yet every time she seemed to gain something in return. One family, gone. A new family dynamic had emerged, sisters by battle and choice, thicker than blood, their bond stronger than any other. They were daughters of war, goddesses in their own right upon the field of battle. There was unconditional love and respect among them, bonding through the fire and flames. It was something for her to think about as the stolen Skipjumper continued its journey through hyperspace and, eventually, their next destination. Wherever it may be.

The loss of Klinks hurt, and Sunshine blamed nobody but herself. Her decisions had led them here, and the group, in spite of the wounds and losses, still followed her. It was something she did not understand. Something she *couldn't* grasp at the most basic level. How could they believe in her so much when she didn't even believe in herself?

Her pinplants chimed. She blinked, disoriented. An automated reminder had popped up. After a moment of confusion, she remembered when she had set it, and why. More tears fell. They were not for what had been done to her, but for the loss of the only family she had really cared about until now. Her brothers of the Kakata Korps, long dead and forgotten by most of humanity, only remembered as the Humans who had worked for Peepo, and not as valiant defenders of the people of Africa. Their people, their tribe. It was really they who had set the reminder, mostly as a joke, but it would have been her first time.

Halfway across the galaxy it was 0600 local time in Monrovia, Liberia. There had been a party planned for the event.

Today she turned 17.

# # # # #

ABOUT THE AUTHOR

A 2015 John W. Campbell Award finalist, Jason Cordova has traveled extensively throughout the U.S. and the world. He has multiple novels and short stories currently in print. He also coaches high school varsity basketball and loves the outdoors.

He currently resides in Virginia.

Catch up with Jason at https://jasoncordova.com/.

* * * * *

The following is an
Excerpt from Book One of the Salvage Title Trilogy:

Salvage Title

Kevin Steverson

Available Now from Theogony Books

eBook, Paperback, and Audio Book

Excerpt from "Salvage Title:"

The first thing Clip did was get power to the door and the access panel. Two of his power cells did the trick once he had them wired to the container. He then pulled out his slate and connected it. It lit up, and his fingers flew across it. It took him a few minutes to establish a link, then he programmed it to search for the combination to the access panel.

"Is it from a human ship?" Harmon asked, curious.

"I don't think so, but it doesn't matter; ones and zeros are still ones and zeros when it comes to computers. It's universal. I mean, there are some things you have to know to get other races' computers to run right, but it's not that hard," Clip said.

Harmon shook his head. *Riiigghht,* he thought. He knew better. Clip's intelligence test results were completely off the charts. Clip opted to go to work at Rinto's right after secondary school because there was nothing for him to learn at the colleges and universities on either Tretra or Joth. He could have received academic scholarships for advanced degrees on a number of nearby systems. He could have even gone all the way to Earth and attended the University of Georgia if he wanted. The problem was getting there. The schools would have provided free tuition if he could just have paid to get there.

Secondary school had been rough on Clip. He was a small guy that made excellent grades without trying. It would have been worse if Harmon hadn't let everyone know that Clip was his brother. They lived in the same foster center, so it was mostly true. The first day of school, Harmon had laid down the law—if you messed with Clip, you messed up.

At the age of fourteen, he beat three seniors senseless for attempting to put Clip in a trash container. One of them was a Yalteen, a member of a race of large humanoids from two systems over. It wasn't a fair fight—they should have brought more people with them. Harmon hated bullies.

351

After the suspension ended, the school's Warball coach came to see him. He started that season as a freshman and worked on using it to earn a scholarship to the academy. By the time he graduated, he was six feet two inches with two hundred and twenty pounds of muscle. He got the scholarship and a shot at going into space. It was the longest time he'd ever spent away from his foster brother, but he couldn't turn it down.

Clip stayed on Joth and went to work for Rinto. He figured it was a job that would get him access to all kinds of technical stuff, servos, motors, and maybe even some alien computers. The first week he was there, he tweaked the equipment and increased the plant's recycled steel production by 12 percent. Rinto was eternally grateful, as it put him solidly into the profit column instead of toeing the line between profit and loss. When Harmon came back to the planet after the academy, Rinto hired him on the spot on Clip's recommendation. After he saw Harmon operate the grappler and got to know him, he was glad he did.

A steady beeping brought Harmon back to the present. Clip's program had succeeded in unlocking the container. "Right on!" Clip exclaimed. He was always using expressions hundreds or more years out of style. "Let's see what we have; I hope this one isn't empty, too." Last month they'd come across a smaller vault, but it had been empty.

Harmon stepped up and wedged his hands into the small opening the door had made when it disengaged the locks. There wasn't enough power in the small cells Clip used to open it any further. He put his weight into it, and the door opened enough for them to get inside. Before they went in, Harmon placed a piece of pipe in the doorway so it couldn't close and lock on them, baking them alive before anyone realized they were missing.

Daylight shone in through the doorway, and they both froze in place; the weapons vault was full.

* * * * *

Get "Salvage Title" now at:
https://www.amazon.com/dp/B07H8Q3HBV.

Find out more about Kevin Steverson and "Salvage Title" at:
http://chriskennedypublishing.com/.

* * * * *

The following is an

Excerpt from Book One of the Mako Saga:

Mako

Ian J. Malone

Now Available from Theogony Books

eBook, Paperback, and Audio

Excerpt from "Mako:"

The trio darted for the lift and dove inside as a staccato of sparks and ricochets peppered the space around them. Once the doors had closed, they got to their feet and checked their weapons.

"I bet it was that little punk-ass tech giving us the stink eye," Danny growled, ejecting his magazine for inspection.

"Agreed," Hamish said.

Lee leapt to his comm. "Mac, you got a copy?"

"I leave you alone for five minutes, and this is what happens?" Mac answered.

"Yeah, yeah." Lee rolled his eyes. "Fire up that shuttle and be ready. We're comin' in hot."

"Belay that!" Link shouted. "Hey, asshat, you got time to listen to me now?"

Lee sneered as the lift indicator ticked past three, moving toward the hangar deck on ten. "Damn it, Link, we've been made. That means it's only a matter of time before the grays find that little package Hamish just left into their energy core. We've gotta go—now. What's so damned important that it can't wait for later?"

"If you'll shut your piehole for a sec, I'll show you."

Lee listened as Link piped in a radio exchange over the comm.

"*Velzer*, this is Morrius Station Tower." A male voice crackled through the static. "You are cleared for fuel service at Bravo Station on platform three. Be advised, we are presently dealing with a security breach near Main Engineering, and thus you are ordered to keep all hatches secured until that's resolved. Please acknowledge."

"Acknowledged, Morrius Tower," another voice said. "All hatches secure. Proceeding to Bravo Three for service. Out."

357

Lee wrinkled his nose. "So what? Another ship is stoppin' for gas. What's the problem?"

"It's a prisoner transport in transit to a POW camp in the Ganlyn System."

Prisoner transport?

"And boss?" Link paused. "Their reported head count is two hundred seventy-six, plus flight crew."

Lee cringed. Never in a million years could he have missed that number's significance.

"Yeah, that struck me, too," Link said.

"Does mean what I think it does?" Danny asked.

Lee hung his head. "The Sygarious 3 colonists are aboard that ship."

"Oh no," Mac murmured. "Guys, if that's true, there are whole families over there."

"I know," Lee snapped, "and they're all about to dock on Platform Three, just in time to die with everyone else on this godforsaken facility."

* * * * *

Get "Mako" now at: https://www.amazon.com/dp/B088X5W3SP

Find out more about Ian J. Malone and "Mako" at: https://chriskennedypublishing.com/imprints-authors/ian-j-malone/

* * * * *

The following is an

Excerpt from Book One of the Singularity War:

Warrior: Integration

David Hallquist

Available from Theogony Books

eBook, Paperback, and (Soon) Audio

Excerpt from "Warrior: Integration:"

I leap into the pit. As I fall in the low gravity, I run my hands and feet along the rock walls, pushing from one side to another, slowing my descent. I hit the pool below and go under.

I swim up through the greenish chemicals and breach the surface. I can see a human head silhouetted against the circle of light above. Time to go. I slide out of the pool quickly. The pool explodes behind me. Grenade, most likely. The tall geyser of steam and spray collapses as I glide into the darkness of the caves ahead.

They are shooting to kill now.

I glide deeper into the rough tunnels. Light grows dimmer. Soon, I can barely see the rock walls around me. I look back. I can see the light from the tunnel reflected upon the pool. They have not come down yet. They're cautious; they won't just rush in. I turn around a bend in the tunnel, and light is lost to absolute darkness.

The darkness means little to me anymore. I can hear them talking as their voices echo off the rock. They are going to send remotes down first. They have also decided to kill me rather than capture me. They figure the docs can study whatever they scrape off the rock walls. That makes my choices simple. I figured I'd have to take out this team anyway.

The remotes are on the way. I can hear the faint whine of micro-turbines. They will be using the sensors on the remotes and their armor, counting on the darkness blinding me. Their sensors against my monster. I wonder which will win.

Everything becomes a kind of gray, blurry haze as my eyes adapt to the deep darkness. I can see the tunnel from sound echoes as I glide down the dark paths. I'm also aware of the remotes spreading out in a search pattern in the tunnel complex.

I'll never outrun them. I need to hide, but I glow in infra-red. One of the remotes is closing, fast.

I back up against a rock wall, and force the monster to hide me. It's hard; it wants to fight, but I need to hide first. I feel the numbing cold return as my temperature drops, hiding my heat. I feel the monster come alive, feel it spread through my body and erupt out of my skin. Fibers spread over my skin, covering me completely in fibrous camouflage. They harden, fusing me to the wall, leaving me unable to move. I can't see, and I can barely breathe. If the remotes find me here, I'm dead.

The remote screams by. I can't see through the fibers, but it sounds like an LB-24, basically a silver cigar equipped with a small laser.

I can hear the remote hover nearby. Can it see me? It pauses and then circles the area. Somehow, the fibers hide me. It can't see me, but it knows something is wrong. It drops on the floor to deposit a sensor package and continues on. Likely it signaled the men upstairs about an anomaly. They'll come and check it out.

The instant I move, the camera will see me. So I wait. I listen to the sounds of the drones moving and water running in the caves. These caves are not as lifeless as I thought; a spider crawls across my face. I'm as still as stone.

Soon, the drones have completed their search pattern and dropped sensors all over the place. I can hear them through the rock, so now I have a mental map of the caves stretching out down here. I wait.

They send the recall, and the drones whine past on the way up. They lower ropes and rappel down the shaft. They pause by the pool, scanning the tunnels and blasting sensor pulses of sound, and likely radar and other scans as well. I wait.

They move carefully down the tunnels. I can feel their every movement through the rock, hear their every word. These men know what they are doing: staying in pairs, staying in constant communication, and checking corners carefully. I wait.

One pair comes up next to me. They pause. One of them has bad breath. I can feel the tension; they know something is wrong. They could shoot me any instant. I wait.

"Let's make sure." I hear a deep voice and a switch clicks.

Heat and fire fill the tunnel. I can see red light through the fibers. Roaring fire sucks all the air away, and the fibers seal my nose before I inhale flame. The fibers protect me from the liquid flame that covers everything. I can feel the heat slowly begin to burn through.

It's time.

* * * * *

Get "Warrior: Integration" now at:
https://www.amazon.com/dp/B0875SPH86

Find out more about David Hallquist and "Warrior: Integration" at:
https://chriskennedypublishing.com/

* * * * *